The Worthy Apprentice

Book Three of

The Apprentice Series

James Cardona

The Worthy Apprentice

Book Three Of
The Apprentice Series

ISBN-13: 978-1-94-369602-4

Edited by Cindy Pedder

Cover Design by Elartwyne

This book is dedicated
to the people who have spoken words
of light into my life.

Praise for
Under The Shadow Of Darkness
Book 1 of The Apprentice Series

Finalist 2014 Wishing Shelf Book Awards, Teenager Category

Laced with signature Cardona humor … hard choices to be made… and a few handy life's lessons … at the sharp end of the bloodthirsty undead hordes's teeth, which certainly keeps his motivation and the overall pace of the book at a rollicking clip. …A most worthwhile read.
—**Marc Secchia,** author of *Shapeshifter Dragons*

A thoroughly entertaining read sure to please middle graders!
—**Kirsten Jany,** author of *Enter To Win*

Fun, interesting, and I enjoyed the characters.
—**Meghan,** The Gal In The Blue Mask Book blog

Light vs dark, Good vs Evil, greed, a quest, adventures, walking dead! This wonderful adventure novel will appeal to all ages.
—**Laura,** Dogsmom Visits Book blog

Praise for
The Dragon's Castle
Book 2 of The Apprentice Series

The Dragon's Castle was fantastic. His unique settings and the way he works with the Wizard archetype make him a must read in this genre. 5 Stars!

—**A.N. Meade,** Author of *Marked*

Exciting, a well-paced and always surprising journey through a complex and concrete world. A unique and memorable spin on the path of the wizard. Vividly imagined.

—**Stephanie R. Sorensen**, Author of *Toru: Wayfarer Returns*

Also by James Cardona

Fantasy

Under the Shadow of Darkness

The Dragon's Castle

The Worthy Apprentice

Coming Soon: Into Darkness

Science Fiction

Community 17

Gabriella and Dr. Duggan's Secret
Dimensional Transport Machine

Gabriella and The Curse of The Black Spot

Coming Soon: Rebirth

Short Fiction

Dragon Hunters

The Night Wolf

Coming Soon: Darkness Dreamer

Children's

Santa Claus vs. The Aliens

Table Of Contents

Table Of Contents

Characters — Sorted By Magical Type

Forest - Female

Meetta	Archmage and adviser to the king of the Greenlands
Shireen	Apprentice of Meetta
Petula	Apprentice

Forest - Male

Nes'egrinon	Archmage from the south western Greenlands
Bel	Apprentice of Nes'egrinon
Drake	Apprentice and friend of Bel
Gedd	Archmage and adviser to King Seol (deceased)

Stone - Female

Sperlith	Archmage from the western stonecutters
Lithia	Apprentice of Sperlith and friend of Shireen
Petra	Archmage from the western stonecutters
Onyx	Apprentice of Petra
Ulta	Apprentice and friend of Aquilo (deceased)

Stone - Male

Jergamemnon	Archmage and teacher at Lasaat
Kerlith	Apprentice searching for a master
Burnd	Archmage from the eastern stonecutters
Rylithnon	Archmage and headmaster at Lasaat (deceased)

Tundra - Male

Jessark	Archmage from the frigid north, in Kandool
Aquilo	Worthy apprentice of Jessark, runs trials
Ke'yush	Archmage from the frigid north, in Kandool
Naga	Apprentice of Ke'yush and friend of Bel

Characters — Sorted By Magical Type

Sand - Female

Zizu Archmage from Ragul
Sammra Worthy apprentice of Zizu, runs trials
Samira Archmage from Ragul
Pren Apprentice of Samira and friend of Shireen
Isha Apprentice from Ragul

Sand - Male

Ali'samm Archmage from Ragul

Avian - Female

Jay Clan-mother from Bald Mountain clan
Leonna Fledgling from Bald Mountain clan, daughter of Jay

Avian - Male

Jeneth Clan-father from Bald Mountain clan, teacher at Lasaat
Ayah Fledgling from Bald Mountain clan
Jonah Nestling from Bald Mountain clan, son of Jeneth
Zhen Clan-father defeated during great war (deceased)

Feline - Female

Felicia Feline cub, sister of Felix

Feline - Male

Sturfelis Clan-father and teacher at Lasaat
Felix Feline cub ranked worthy, runs trials
Jinx Feline cub

Trolls

Barth, Barch, Branch, Budzig, Burn

tundric lands

kesh

worthy
trials

nast

western
stonecutters

lasaat

twern

GREENLaNDS

lavaala

Lier

pesca

eardna

uncharted lands
of the creature~kind

map of the

ndool

W ⊕ E
S

goos

pedra

fey

mont

eastern
stonecutters

sha'la

sha'ane

hinterlands

PROTOLITH

sha'ul

be'ershore

south
be'ershore

sanhardin
lands

RAGUL

aldi
utain

KNOWN WORLD

What Has Gone Before

Under The Shadow Of Darkness
Book 1 Of The Apprentice Series

Bel, a recent graduate of the University of Arts and Magic, arrives at the forest-wizard Nes'egrinon's home to present himself for training as an apprentice and is immediately thrust into an epic adventure.

Someone has torn a hole in reality, allowing the dead (ghoul-kind) to stream out of the Underworld. The ghoul-kind taste and experience life for a short time if they drink human blood so they are eager for it. Unfortunately, being bitten by a ghoul is toxic and can kill a person.

Nes'egrinon and Bel travel across the lands along with a stone-wizard named Muolithnon and his apprentice Kerlith. The team gathers forces along the way and faces several difficult trials.

Along the way, several things trouble Bel. Being a wizard is akin to a royal priesthood and celibacy is one of the many requirements. Bel had sacrificed his love for Shireen, a fellow apprentice candidate at University, in order to become Master Nes'egrinon's apprentice and eventually a wizard. Yet Bel is distraught to see Muolithnon and Kerlith openly fraternizing with the opposite sex and to learn Nes'egrinon had an illegitimate son named Fleck.

At the conclusion of the saga, Muolithnon dies, leaving Kerlith without a master. Bel, Kerlith and Nes'egrinon fight off the evil wizard Rylithnon, and close the breach.

The Dragon's Castle
Book 2 Of The Apprentice Series

A year has passed and the wizard Nes'egrinon and his apprentice, Bel, are called by King Thrashel to Sha'mont, the capital of the Greenlands, to help avert a war. When they arrive, the city is under siege by three armies hired by Seol, ruler of a neighboring kingdom, who is bent upon uniting the Greenlands under a single ruler. Bel and Nes'egrinon confer with Meetta, the sorceress of Dragon's Castle, and her apprentice Shireen.

Shireen and Bel soon realize that they still love each other. The two ponder whether they made the correct decision to give up their love to become wizards.

Nes'egrinon finds that a fellow wizard, Master Gedd, has been influencing the invading king Seol to attack Sha'mont. Seol says the attack is to put his son Fayn on the throne. Nes'egrinon discovers Gedd is a pawn of the avians, a group of creature-kind wizards that control birds.

Nes'egrinon also detects a dark magical item in Dragon's Castle hidden by a powerful spell. The avians' purpose in orchestrating the attack is to capture the magical object, the roc's eye.

But Bel and Shireen find the eye first. When Shireen touches the roc's eye, a dragon that was trapped in an enchantment is released and destroys much of the city. The battle shifts from a fight against invading armies to a war of survival against a fire-breathing dragon. Nes'egrinon is severely wounded and Gedd, Seol, and Thrashel are slain before the beast is finally vanquished.

In the final battle with the dragon, Shireen is about to be consumed by dragon fire when Bel sucks a tremendous amount of life-force from the surrounding people, with no concern for whether or not they will die, in order to save Shireen. Later he feels guilty and comes to the realization that he can't have both—Shireen and wizardry—since he does not trust himself to not kill someone to protect her. Their hearts are breaking for they both know they must sacrifice something or someone they love dearly.

Finally, we find out the roc's eye can be used to commune with and perhaps even raise the dead. Nes'egrinon suspects the avians will use it to reincarnate their greatest military leader, the evil Zhen. When he informs the archmage council, they take no action.

Nes'egrinon and Meetta decide to send Shireen and Bel to the Worthy Apprentice Trials to speak with the apprentices of distant lands to confirm their suspicions.

Chapter One
The Road

Shireen wanted to reach out and touch Bel, right then, right there, the man she loved, but she knew that was impossible. Magicians were forbidden. A Royal Priesthood, they called it. If only she could find a way.

She squeezed the thought out of her mind for what felt like the hundredth time as she tapped her saddlebag, checking it to make sure she had everything. She cleared her throat and spoke without raising her eyes from the dusty trail. "How do you suppose we're going to do this?"

Bel paused for a time before he answered. "You've been quiet for some time. Do what? Pass the trials? Is that what you were thinking about?"

She considered telling him what she was really thinking about. "I have no idea how we're going to pass the trials. How could I? We have no idea what they'll be." She switched topics, her voice an even monotone. "I meant the information, what your master wanted us to find out, the avian conspiracy... ahh, I mean, the plot, if there is one."

He nodded, his head held forward. "True. I guess we'll ask people. Ask them if they've seen anything?"

"But they're going to obviously ask what we mean by

anything. What do we say? Do we tell them what your master thinks? Because you know his theory sounds crazy."

Bel brushed his horse's mane. "I thought I was the only one who thought that."

"Seol and Fayn being controlled by Gedd? And Master Meetta? I still have a hard time believing Gedd was able to get into my master's head." She glanced at him, then hated herself for doing it.

"I saw her locked in a trance with my own eyes. I told you."

Shireen exhaled. "I believe you, it's just so… unbelievable."

"How did he get such power? Where did he learn that? It's forbidden."

Shireen nodded. The air grew quiet for a time. He was right there. She felt like she could reach over and touch him. They were all alone on a desolate path. Who would know? She mumbled, "And the avians."

"That I'm less suspicious of," Bel said. "And that's where I disagree with my master, although I would never openly contradict him."

"What do you mean?"

"The avians figured out the roc's eye was in the castle —I don't know how, but fine. They wanted the eye because it's full of magic—that makes sense. So they make an agreement with Seol to pay him a sum of money for the orb—good. All he needs to do is get the eye for them, so he attacks the castle. Where's the mystery?"

Shireen shook her head. She glanced at him again, longer this time, allowing herself to enjoy a little fantasy. She snapped her eyes away when he looked up at her.

"It's not that they wanted the eye, it's what they want it *for*. My master seems to think such a powerful magical object could only be used for something that would lead to more conflict and death. You know you can commune with the dead using it? It's an eye. Magical eyes are also used to discern the future, the past. Who knows what else it could do?" Shireen shuddered. The warm pulsing sensation washed over her again. The eye and Bel, were the two so different? They both made her lose herself. Her hand shook uncontrollably as if her palm was still on the translucent blue eye. She pushed away the memory of the orb and what it had done, how it had changed her, controlled her.

"Perhaps, but again, how are we supposed to uncover anything at the trials?"

Shireen nodded. "There'll be others we know there."

"Our friends from University, I hope some of them attend. Naga and Pren."

"Lithia, I hope she's there. I can't wait to see her." Shireen tried to picture Lithia to push what she had to do about Bel out of her head. "Naga was your friend. I always thought he was a little weird."

"He's Tundric. What do you expect?"

"You've met so many?"

"No, but I assume. Everyone says."

Shireen chuckled for a few moments then her face slackened and she returned her eyes to the dusty ground.

Bel mumbled, "Maybe Kerlith will be there."

"That would be wonderful," she sneered. "Can't wait to see *him*."

"His master died. I feel bad for him."

"He was a jerk to me."

"Because he had a crush on you."

"How do you know that?"

"I just do."

Shireen paused, her face frozen in disbelief. "Fine way for him to show it." Shireen reached back and tapped her horse's saddle bag for the third time since they had left.

"You think your clothing and foodstuff have disappeared since you last checked your bag?" Bel said with a smile. Shireen could feel his eyes on her.

She exhaled long and slow, took a deep breath then looked up at him, letting their eyes lock as their two horses ambled down the wide path. "I've never been this far from Sha'mont."

"I'll protect you," he offered.

"Like I need *you* to save *me?*" She laughed as she stared at him. She didn't want to look away. "Remember what I said."

"What?"

Shireen wagged her finger at Bel and smiled. "I told you I could take you in a fair fight. Your magic might be powerful, but you announce your moves long before you make them. You're predictable. And you don't protect your mind. It's all fireballs and mage-light with you. No subtlety. I would be in your head in a second. You would be dancing around like a chicken who lost her eggs."

"So you say. Of course, mind control is forbidden." The smile faded from his face.

"You wouldn't be able to tell anyone. I'll erase your memories."

"You can do that?"

"Do you want to find out?"

"Definitely not."

"Know your place then, boy."

Bel snorted. He was smiling widely. "We would make

a good team," he mumbled.

Shireen shuddered as she forced herself to tear her eyes from him. "I suppose it's something we should talk about," she said, vacant and monotone, her eyes staring at the trail but not seeing it.

Bel spoke, his voice unnaturally still, "Before we get much closer. Others may be on the path."

She didn't want to begin since speaking of their end only made it feel more imminent. "You go first."

Bel glanced at her. "I've been thinking about this. What we need is a cover story. An excuse. We need to be prepared if anyone asks us any questions."

"What questions?"

"We can't appear as if we are a couple, or in love, or have had any form of illegal relationship, clearly, because we can't, I mean, we don't, but my emotions are still there and I can't help myself." Bel exhaled long and slow. "I know we promised to leave each other for magic, but I'm not made of stone. My heart and the way I feel, the emotions, they're still there... what if I slip? Or you—not saying you will—but if one of us does something... suspicious. If someone catches me staring at you, for example. I need to be able to explain that away."

Better to not stare at all, to ignore each other, she thought. But what Bel said was true. She didn't trust her wandering eyes to not drift over and fondle him. "So what do you propose?"

"We've been through a lot in the last few days. Together. Everyone must have heard the stories. A dragon in Sha'mont and the two wizards and their apprentices who battled the terrible creature that destroyed two cities. They'll recognize we worked together in such a difficult time, that we went through a significant battle together. Most of the others will know my master was injured and much of your city destroyed. No one will be surprised if either of us were to say kind words to each other, you know, as friends would, because, you know, we've been through so much together."

"We have," Shireen choked out. She tried to rub the tension out of her neck. When she placed her hand back in the saddle in front of her it twitched involuntarily and something about that irritated her to no end. "I became a sorceress's apprentice to help people," she mumbled. *I became their death.*

On the wall, just after she had awakened the dragon, she had tried to sacrifice herself to the dragon so that it wouldn't destroy the city. *Stop lying to yourself, Shireen. You tried to kill yourself and that was wrong.*

"Wrong," she said under her breath. Another death wouldn't have helped anything and she was glad Bel had been able to stop her. But nothing could stop her self-loathing.

"What are you doing?" Bel asked.

"What?"

"You're grinding your teeth."

Shireen opened her mouth and rolled her jaw. "Sorry, I didn't realize."

Bel asked, "So what do you think?"

"About what?"

He threw his hands in the air. His horse leaped forward, then he grabbed the reins and softly pulled them. "About what I said. Weren't you paying attention? Our cover story."

"It's a good idea, I suppose. It's going to be difficult, though."

"How so?"

"To act normal," Shireen said, allowing herself to glance at him. "We're supposed to be friends? And no more?"

"Yes."

"If we are only friends, there would be no problem with us talking to each other and discussing openly how much we've been through. But that might be too much for me to handle. My initial thoughts were to ignore you. To act like we barely knew each other. But that's not going to work either. If I ignored you, the others would assume something was wrong between us and they would start asking questions. So we're back where we started. I don't want the questions, but it seems they are unavoidable."

"And our friends from University as well. People we knew, they'll remember we were friends before too. So if we don't act like we used to—"

"I don't know if I can do this," Shireen said as she pushed her fingers through her hair and tugged it. Her neck hurt. Her back hurt. Every joint in her body was sore. This was the second day of their journey, but they hadn't been riding long. She knew her pain wasn't because of the horse.

Bel repeated, "We have a problem." He bounced his lips against one another, making a popping sound. "So what are we going to do?"

Shireen frowned and that little unconscious facial expression on her face made her realize, more than anything else, that she was completely out of control. Gestures and facial expressions were something her master had trained her to suppress. A sorceress of the court was never to openly display emotion. She needed complete control and mastery over every muscle, to make her face a mask. She recognized immediately when her face contorted. Her initial instinct was to stifle her expression, to make her face placid, but she couldn't bring herself to hide how she felt. "I-I can't do this." Shireen yanked her reins, spinning her horse around.

"Hey, where are you—" Before Bel could finish his sentence, she was off, galloping back the way they had come. Bel gave chase and was quickly next to her. "Where are you going?" he yelled above the hoof beats.

Shireen ignored his question, spurring her horse faster.

Bel caught back up and reached for her reins. She pulled them out of his reach and screamed, "Stop it! I need to go." She stood in her stirrups and pressed the animal faster.

Bel leaped on the back of her horse then promptly slid off, falling to the ground below.

When she realized what had happened, Shireen stopped her horse.

Bel yelled, "See what you made me do?" Bel was rubbing his temple, his hand covered in blood.

Shireen hopped down and went to him. "What did you do that for? Are you some kind of fool?"

"Your horse kicked me," he said.

She wiped his oozing forehead with her rag. "Serves you right. What were you thinking?"

"Me?" Outrage was in his throat. "You turn around and gallop off without saying a word?"

Shireen felt like an idiot. All she did was hurt everyone around her. She held the rag to his head and winced. "I just realized our plan is not going to work. It's better if you go alone so I won't distract you. If I'm there,

there's a good chance we'll both fail. Or worse. If our… situation—that's the word—is found out, we'll be excommunicated. If I'm not there, maybe you can pass. I need to get my head right anyway. My thinking, I'm too distracted. I'm no good for the trials now and I would only make it harder for you. Better if I go back."

Shireen moved to leave, but Bel grabbed her hand, stopping her. She slumped down onto the ground next to him and bit her lower lip. "I'm sorry." The apology was all she could muster and still hold herself together. Shireen wanted to say she was sorry for playing with his mind back at University as if he were one of her childhood toys. She wanted to tell him her emotions had gotten out of control, but she couldn't say that. She would be lying anyway. She didn't remember the exact moment when she fell for him, or how, but she could still remember the chronic burning in her chest, the longing, and pain from his absence. She had fallen headlong into a deep bottomless pit of buttery love and liquid passion. She had refused to stop herself. And she still hadn't hit bottom.

She wanted to apologize. She needed to. His predicament was her fault, their love, the dragon, the burning city, all of it. Her. Fault. Because she awakened the dragon, his master fell from the wall. In effect, she put his master on his deathbed. Shireen caused Bel too much pain, and all because she couldn't stop herself from loving him.

Shireen wanted to say more, but couldn't. She wouldn't because she understood what would happen: she would lose control of her emotions, become a blubbering fool, sitting on the dirt path, out in the open, pouring her heart out to him. She couldn't risk that.

"Shireen, don't apologize. The cut's small. It's already stopped bleeding. My fault for jumping on your horse anyway."

A tear formed in her eye so Shireen stood and wiped her face in one motion, doing it so he would not see. "In any case, I'm headed back." She grabbed her horse's reins.

Bel popped up and chased after her. "No, you're not." He grabbed the reins of her horse. "If anyone's going back, it's me."

"What?"

Bel scanned the area briefly. "Okay. If you ever repeat this, I'm going to deny it, and I'm only going to say this once, so open your ears and listen—" He stopped as if the words were stuck in his throat.

"What?"

Bel exhaled. "I think you have a better chance of passing than I do."

Shireen smiled. "What? You're admitting to that?"

Bel responded, sheepish, "You're right, of course. I tip my hand too soon. It's something I've been working on. When I first started learning magic, I would bellow my words and sweep my arms. I thought I was being dramatic. Fun. I didn't realize the downside until my master explained I was announcing my moves. I've been trying to learn to whisper my spells or even perform them without moving my hands or speaking. I've learned that intent is more important than the words. The words just help us to focus our intent. But it's insanely difficult."

"Wait. Let me get this straight. You're saying I'm a better wizard than you are?"

He chuckled. "That's not what I said." Bel grabbed at her elbows. His touch was electric.

Shireen pulled away, teasing. "That's what I heard."

He opened his hands in front of him. "I said I thought you had a better chance of passing the trials, you know, without me—a better chance than I have passing them, you know, without you. That's all."

"Right." Shireen nodded. "I'm a better wizard. And I agree with you. You've finally come to your senses."

He reached for her. "You—"

Shireen ran, giggling.

Bel ran after and softly tackled her, rolling his body on top of hers.

Shireen let Bel dominate her. He had his hands on her wrists, pinning them next to her head. Gazing up into his big eyes, she let herself smile. His eyes had the oddest translucent blue swirls. The same as the roc's eye. They were mesmerizing, she wanted to stare at them forever, but she knew she couldn't. Every moment they stayed like this they put everything they had worked for at risk. "We can't stay like this. Someone might come."

"I don't care about that."

"That's the problem. That's why I was going to return. I don't trust you to not hide your emotions. You're too reckless. You're no good at deception."

"And you are?" Bel went down to his elbows, hovering only inches above her. The weight of his body bore down into her. His warmth radiated into her torso.

"My master is training me to be a professional liar." She wanted him, the sweet taste of his lips. "But I can't lie to you anymore. I want you."

Then she caught. She was barreling down a path and she knew where it led. She needed to stop. "No, Bel," she whispered.

He nibbled on her neck.

She forced herself to claw her eyes away from him, then pushed her hands on his chest. "We… can't."

He climbed off her almost too quickly. "We can't," Bel repeated, his body sagging.

Shireen grabbed her horse's reins so the animal wouldn't wander any farther. After having Bel's weight and his warmth on her, the breeze blowing down the path chilled her.

Bel muttered, "I want you. You want me. But we can't have each other. I hate this. I'm going to quit."

"No, Bel."

"I'm going to quit. You're going to quit. We're going back to my village… or yours."

"Bel, don't say that."

"That's it. I can't take this anymore. All the lies. They're going to find out and you said it yourself. I can't trick them. Let's stop lying and just face facts. We're supposed to be together."

"Maybe. But there are other things to think—"

"Like what?" he sliced her words in the air.

"I just can't make this decision right now. Can't you understand that? After what we've been through. The dragon, my city destroyed, all those people dead, and you want me to think about—" She couldn't say the word. *Love.*

Bel tried to stroke her arm. She pulled it away.

"No, Bel. You can't," Shireen pleaded. "We need to at least go to the trials. Your master, this is what he wanted. If you walk away, you'll be disobeying him. In his condition, no, you can't do that to him. It would be a slap in the face. Can we just get through the trials? Then we can sort things out later, figure out what we're going to do. I need… time."

"Worry about it later." He snorted his disapproval. "Magic means that much to you." He paused. "More than me."

"It's not that." Shireen was shaking now.

"You're right about my master, though. I don't want to do that to him. But you just tried to ride off and quit yourself. You would be doing the same to your master."

"No, it's different with Master Meetta. She would understand. You? You can't quit."

He grabbed her hands, placing them inside of his. "You can't either then. I'll do this for you. For him. This one last thing."

"One last thing… and then?" She almost didn't want to know what he was going to say.

"Then we either leave magic and spend the rest of our lives together…"

"Or?"

"I can't be around you like this. Can you understand that?"

"You know I do." Shireen and Bel stood immobile. At any moment, someone could ride around the bend. "We can't stay here like this."

"I know." He looked away.

Shireen released his hands then got back on her horse. A small hole was developing in her chest as if a creature were there, slowly eating, bite by bite.

The pair rode in silence. Shireen pursed her lips, then said, "You must be the most hard-headed person in all the lands."

"Besides you?" Bel smiled.

"Okay, we'll both go to the trials. Because you're so stubborn. After the trials, we'll make a decision." She exhaled hard. "Together."

Bel nodded. "I hate waiting. But for you, I will wait an eternity."

"So let's focus on the trials then. You need to act normal around me. You need to keep your mouth shut and your eyes forward. Talk to me like, like maybe, like maybe one of the other guys."

"One of the other guys? Are you crazy? Even worse. No one does that."

Shireen didn't respond. Pretending to be only friends was a hard thing to ask, but they had to sell themselves as friends to all who would be there. And that could be anyone. She had no idea how many apprentices would attend or who would be running the trials. Wizards? Archmages? Would any of them be seers? Would they peer into her mind? In any case, a person didn't need to be a seer to recognize Bel wanted her desperately. He wore his emotions out on his sleeve for all to see. Shireen would be his downfall and she couldn't harbor that on her conscience. She had caused enough heartache and death already. She needed to get this one thing right. She needed him to act normal around her.

Shireen calmed herself, her face washed blank and unemotional. She tugged her horse, stopping it.

"What now? Why are you stopping?" Bel asked.

She waved him closer.

He pulled his horse next to hers and she grabbed his hand. "Look at my face, Bel. Tell me what you see."

He leaned into her and smiled. "You're beautiful. Light brown eyes with tiny blue swirls. A cute little nose. Dimples. I love your dimples. You're blessed with sumptuous skin."

Shireen yanked his arm. "No, not that." She forced the emotion off her face once again. "Tell me what you see."

"Ahh, ohh yeah, I see what you're doing. Blank, stoic, no emotion, like when you're in the court. Or Master Meetta, hers too, the face she makes in the court."

"What else?"

"I guess No one can figure out what's on your mind when you hold your face like that. That what you're looking for?"

"Right. You need to learn. I'm going to show you."

Bel pulled back, furrows forming on his brow. She tugged him closer again. "You won't be able to master it. That took me months. But even a little will help you, you're so bad at it. Close your eyes."

"Here? Now?" Bel surveyed the path.

"Yes, now." Shireen reached up and pushed his eyelids down. He let her close them and relaxed.

A peculiar rush flashed in her head as their two minds intertwined, a sensation of commonness and comfort. She was in his head, connected, merged. Bel's breath flowed in her ear, the sweet bouquet of his body around her. The scent was velvety chocolate and alluring.

Playing with fire, she thought. The more time she spent connected to him, especially in such a close union, the harder their eventual separation would be—if it came to that. But this was necessary. She needed him to be able to fool the probing looks and questioning stares. They were wizards in training, for El's sake. Discernment, some would have. They would know. Shireen needed Bel to be able to hide his emotions. She reached out her translucent blue spirit and grabbed hold of Bel's, trying to feed her calm, tranquil shell of an exterior onto him.

He wrapped his life-force around hers, enveloping her in a preternatural embrace. Then he moaned.

"Stop that," Shireen barked. "That's not what this is about." Still their electric union proved hard to resist, her neck hairs were on end. She opened her eyes while still maintaining the connection. His face was twitching. "Bel, wipe that stupid grin off your face. You're not even trying."

Bel straightened in his saddle. "I don't understand what to do."

"Keep your eyes closed. I'm watching you. Just try to calm yourself. Force your face to blank. Feel the shell I place around me. Imitate that."

Shireen squinted as he slowly rolled his neck, his mouth open in a wide grin, his face enraptured. "Are you at *all* trying?" Shireen slapped him.

Bel popped his eyes open. The connection broke. "What?" Bel asked, placing the palm of his hand on his reddening face. "Why did you slap me?"

"*Why?* Because you're supposed to be concentrating, you should be focusing on not showing any emotion on your face, no matter what you're experiencing. I connected with you to show you, to teach you, not to have you fondle my spirit. You're supposed to hide your emotions, not roll your head and moan like a boar diving into slop. Now quit playing around and focus."

Bel chuckled.

Shireen's face went cold.

"What?" The smile leaked off his face.

She breathed out slowly. "Let me show you something." She closed her eyes and touched his chest.

They were connected again, surrounded by an ocean of blue, their two spirits floating.

Shireen grabbed his hand in the blue and tugged. The haze slowly disintegrated as brown and green dots and blobs formed around them. Quickly they were in a small village on the edge of a forest, one of Shireen's memories.

"Where are we?" Bel asked as he followed her into the village. "Oh wait, I recognize this place. This is where you grew up. We entered from a different way the last time you brought me here. There's your hut up ahead." Bel pointed.

The salty scent of the ocean mixed with pine wafted into the village.

Shireen glanced back at Bel but didn't smile. She stopped in front of a shack. "What I'm about to show you, you can't tell anyone. No one knows. Understand?"

"Sure," Bel said.

Shireen opened the door and walked in. A woman who appeared much like Shireen, a decidedly older version of Shireen, was trying to light the wood below a large pot hanging over the hearth while a small girl played with sticks, flipping them in the air. The house was like many Bel had seen in his own village, a single-room hovel of the struggling poor.

"You?" Bel pointed at the little girl. "You were adorable."

Shireen shushed him. "Watch."

The older woman stood back and grumped in frustration. She glanced at her daughter to make sure she wasn't watching then pushed her hands closer to the wood and mumbled a few words. The logs burst into flame.

Bel gaped. "Your mother? She was—"

"I recall many memories such as this one. She performed many spells. She had been trained."

"So you think—"

"I think she was an apprentice, yes. I think she was

either excommunicated or she quit. When I was older, a teenager, she once mentioned she had given something up to be with my father. She was from a different village, so I had assumed it was that, but now—" Shireen stopped speaking, she couldn't finish the sentence.

A choice she didn't judge her mother for, yet she knew how tragically her mother's life ended. She was so young.

Bel tried to touch Shireen's shoulder. She pulled it away.

"Don't," she said. "We're too close as it is. There's one more thing I need to show you."

The home faded into the blue and the two were floating for a few moments. They found themselves hovering near the top of the thick stone wall bordering Sha'mont, the capital city of the Greenlands. The memory was from only a few days ago.

Bel gasped as the dragon swooped down. "Why did you—"

The experience had burned in Shireen's mind so brightly. She had woken the dragon. She had blamed herself and for some stupid reason she had thought if she only sacrificed herself to the beast maybe, just maybe, the creature would go away. At least, that is what she had told herself.

Her skin bristled. Shireen was embarrassed by what she was about to show him, but Bel needed to watch the scene unfold from her perspective. Shireen squeezed his hand and pointed.

Bel and Shireen watched, floating in the air just behind the memory of themselves. Shireen saw herself standing on the edge of the broken wall, her arms outstretched in an act of sacrifice. Bel, glowing with energy, leaped in front of her as the dragon was about to belch hot fire. The apprentice unleashed a tremendous blast of life-force into the dragon's open mouth, causing the beast to fall back choking, saving Shireen's life.

Shireen pulled her hand away from Bel's chest, interrupting the memory, and waited for him to open his eyes.

He smiled. "Powerful, masterful, excellent, I was, wouldn't you say?"

Shireen shook her head at him. "This is not the time for comedy. Did you see?"

Bel shrugged his shoulders. "See what? Your mom was an apprentice. Makes sense. That's why you were chosen, I guess. And me, I stopped the dragon... at least, for a little while. So what? I don't understand how those two things are connected. But you must admit, I did look impressive."

Shireen grunted loudly. "How did I ever fall in... Forget I showed you anything. You're such a dunce." She pushed her horse forward.

Bel rode next to her. "What's wrong?"

Shireen shook her head.

Bel said, "Just tell me. You already showed me. Now tell me what those memories meant to you."

Shireen squinted at him wanting to display outrage but was not able to force her expressions. He was cute in his cluelessness and his half-smile warmed her. She exhaled. "Okay. I'll tell you. Why I showed you my mother? I guess to tell you I understand what I would be giving up if we were excommunicated. I understand what that life is. I know what being poor and living in the village hand to mouth is all about. Poverty was terrible, but I understand why my mother made that choice. She loved my father desperately. I realize what kind of life we would have and… I'm okay with that. As long as I would be with you, I could tolerate anything."

"Fine. Good." Bel smiled wide.

"The other memory was to show you why I'm having such a hard time choosing that life."

Bel flared his nostrils. "Because of the dragon? My master banished the beast."

"Not the dragon, dummy. Didn't you see anything? Didn't you see yourself?"

"Of course. I tossed a ball of energy into the creature's mouth. Didn't do much from what I could tell except make him angry," Bel said.

"That's not what I saw." Shireen grew quiet. The finality of it all froze her.

"Tell me," Bel pressed.

She scowled then wiped her face with her hand, calming her face muscles. Shireen spoke in a forced monotone, "I watched an apprentice absorb, contain and control more energy than should be metaphysically possible. I would wager that never has a wizard, even an archmage, even one of the powerful ones such as Master Nes'egrinon, done such as you did without a thought or concern. You pulled in an amount of life-force that should have torn you apart. You held a tremendous amount of energy in, channeled it, controlled it, raw life-force mind you, then formed it into an attack against a dragon. It should have killed you, blown you apart. You should be dead, understand? But you just shrugged your shoulders and did it again and again. Who does that? No one. That's who."

"I was pretty good then?"

Shireen rolled her eyes. "And you're an apprentice.

Bel, there's no doubt in my mind you could become the most powerful wizard to walk the lands, perhaps even the most powerful wizard of all time."

"Good, I suppose—don't stop the praise and complements—but I still don't understand the connection with your mother starting the fire—"

Shireen threw up her hands. "You *are* dense, aren't you? My mother—that was me. For me, it's no big deal to quit magic. I can anticipate a future where I give up magic to marry. I mean, not just anyone, but a man I was so in love with I would be willing to make that kind of sacrifice, maybe a man like you."

"Maybe?" he said, smiling.

She exhaled, ignoring the question. "But you? It's not that simple. There's something larger at stake here with you—"

Bel cut her off, "Wait, wait, wait. Let me get this straight. Are you buying into Master Meetta's whole sacrifice for the greater good line? Well, guess what? It might be hard to hear this, but she's wrong. She's your master and I'm not trying to insult her, but she's an old woman who's been left alone too long. Meetta stares in the mirror at all her wrinkles and a head full of gray hair and to justify her decision to stay celibate she says her lonely life was all for the *greater good*."

Shireen recoiled, raising her eyebrows in disbelief. "That was harsh."

Bel rolled his jaw, then held up his hand in mock surrender. "That didn't come out the way I meant it. I really do like your master. Even though she tends to be tough on me."

When Shireen didn't respond, Bel said, "So if I was an apprentice of lesser ability you would be more willing to marry me? If I was more of a loser, you would love me more?"

"No, Bel. I couldn't love you more. And if you're thinking about slacking off so I will change my mind, you're wrong. I'm not searching for a loser, as you insinuate."

"I might as well be a loser because I can't win. The fact of the matter—"

"The fact of the matter is you're not going to change my mind. Not now, anyway. Besides, if the decision was only about love, I would have made it already." Her face changed, shocked at what she had just said.

"I know, but—"

Shireen cut him off. "We're going to the trials. We're both going to pretend to be friends and do our best. We're going to do what our masters wanted: try to figure out if there's something larger going on here and what motivated Seol to attack Sha'mont. We're going to find out if anyone knows anything about the roc's eye and why the avians would be so desperate to get it and what they plan to use the eye for."

Bel nodded as the expression slowly leaked off his face. He tugged his horse and spurred it and Shireen followed. The two ambled their horses. They fell back to their thoughts as they rode for a time, in silence.

Then Shireen spoke, not wanting to dig the churned ground, but also not sensing their discussion completely settled. "Bel—"

"We don't need to talk about anything."

"Bel, it's not that. I don't want to be harsh or mean to you. With your master being injured and all that has happened and the way my heart yearns… I want us to be pleasant to each other. I mean, I needed to tell you that, but I feel like I came across too strong and that's not what I wanted to do."

"Fine."

Shireen wanted to reach over and touch him, to, at least, stroke the back of his hand, but she stopped herself. "What I want to do is to comfort you, but... I can't. We're too close. I love you. You know that."

"I love you too." His voice was cold and distant.

"But no one can know. They just can't."

Before she could continue, Bel said, "Woah. What's that?"

Just up ahead they spied a couple of horses, tied to a pole, unattended, at a crook in the road. Bel and Shireen continued slowly and came up to a small stable. A collection of large, bulky creatures, nearly twice the height of a man, carried immense water jugs to fill the troughs.

A man called out, "Here for the trials?" He was dressed in the typical garb of a servant at Lasaat.

Shireen said, "Yes, the two of us."

"You can tie your horses there. We'll tend them until you return. That path leads to the entrance to the trials. Take what supplies you need and go on foot. The entrance is not much farther."

As Bel dismounted, his eyes trained on the enormous goons carrying the water. "Is there anything more you can tell us?" he asked the servant.

"Me?" The man scowled. "I've never been. All I know is what I hear from those who come out to retrieve their horses. Usually, a few weeks for the last to come out. The first groups, the ones that will come back today and tomorrow are usually injured. Sometimes the trolls take them to Lasaat for medical attention." The man motioned towards the large characters carrying supplies. "The ones that come later, they need medical attention too, although they're usually not as badly injured. The ones who come at the end, those are the ones who most likely passed the trials. They need medical attention too, but, at least, they've advanced."

Shireen protested, "Wait a moment. Are you serious?"

The man chuckled. "I was making a joke. Well, not really. Funny, right? It's all in the delivery. The trolls don't like comedy. I spend a lot of time with them and they never laugh."

Bel grabbed Shireen's elbow. "Let's go."

The two started along the path on foot.

"Good luck," the man shouted at their backs. "I'll be here when they carry you out, I mean, when you return." He laughed.

"What do you think it's going to be like?" Shireen asked.

"I have no idea. You?"

"I've heard the trials are dangerous. People are injured. A few years back I think someone died."

"Died?" Bel muttered.

"Portions of the trials are tailor-made for the individual, I've heard. For every apprentice the trials are different. That's why no one speaks about what they've experienced. It's too personal."

"Died?" Bel repeated.

Chapter Two
Peck Your Flesh

Jay paced the long house for what seemed like the tenth time, examining the various bird cages, some empty, some full.

Leonna couldn't take her mother's pacing anymore. She took Tweetnone from his perch on top of her head, put him into the small cage next to her bed, then walked up and grabbed one of her Jay's hands. "Clan-mother, what's bothering you? The trials?"

Jay stared at the exit door at the far end of the long narrow building as if she were expecting it to open at any moment. "The trials? Not hardly. You are capable. I have confidence in you. Whatever the landers can do, you can do, and probably better. You're an avian."

"What troubles you then? Does father's death still claw you?"

"No. He lived a good life. He died proud and fearless, serving the clan-family. I miss him, yes. But that's not..." She stopped herself from speaking, gazing once again at the far door.

Leonna glanced at the door too. "They'll be back soon."

Leonna's mother peered up into her eyes as if she had decided to confess. "I miss your father. I loved him deeply. But that's not what troubles me. He was the only man in my life and he was your father, but it wasn't always so—" She choked the words in her throat as the door banged against the wall. Jeneth and the other clan-fathers strode in. Their hawks and falcons flapped toward the high ceiling and landed on the perches above.

Jay walked towards them. "Has it been decided?" she asked, her voice hoarse.

As her mother walked to the center of the room to meet the other clan-fathers and clan-mothers, Leonna preoccupied herself with her birds. She opened the cages and laid herself on her bed, then called to them. Nine finches flew out of their cages and landed on her bed and her belly. Tweetnone landed on her forehead. Leonna named him so because he never made a sound.

"Decided?" Jeneth repeated. "Yes. It's the best and safest course of action." He was a smallish man with a crooked back, a war injury. Leonna didn't like him. He had beady eyes.

Jay squared her shoulders in front of the men. "Sending the fledglings to the trials—I have no problem with this. But the nestlings? No, I don't agree. And Jonah doesn't want to go—"

Jeneth cut her off. "It's not up to him. The decision is the clan-family's." Jeneth smiled as if her argument surprised him. "Besides, the trials are a ruse. Tell us what pecks your flesh."

She said, "We are superior—no one questions that—but I don't understand why we're ruffling our feathers over the landers. They believe what they believe. What does that have to do with us? We're content here, aren't we?"

"Truth," the crooked man said, grinning.

She continued, "And you. You volunteer to go to their school, to teach them... what? Things they won't accept anyway? I don't—"

"Jay, there's a bigger world out there than you can see from the top of this mountain. The clan-family has already decided."

She glared at the others for support, but they had none for her. She stepped forward, raising her voice, "We already own the eye of the roc. I was against the tactic. Inciting those men to kill each other, it wasn't right, no matter how you weigh the value of their lives. But we possess the eye now. Isn't it enough?"

Jeneth smiled at her slowly as if she was taking too much rope and her arguments could only end in her hanging herself. The others shuffled their feet nervously.

She shook her hands. Her birds began clucking above. "I understand the landers' place in this world and there are things more valuable than mere human life. I've never argued that point." She stopped herself and crinkled her eyes at Jeneth.

He reached up his arm and his falcon fluttered and landed on his forearm, then repositioned itself on his shoulder. The bird was more than half his size. "Are you quite done? We need to prepare the fledglings. Sturfelis's cubs are leaving today. I want to travel with him through the forest. Safer with numbers."

Leonna's mother mumbled, "So we're going ahead with the plan?"

"Your clan-daughter is the key." Jeneth beckoned for Leonna to step forward.

The young avian pretended to not pay attention to their conversation as she played with her little birds. When he called her name, she popped up in the bed and walked to him, her small finches circling her head like a halo. "Yes, clan-father?"

"Walk with me." Jeneth turned and stepped out of the long house. His bird flew from his shoulder and roosted somewhere in the trees. "The plan is set in motion. I'm trusting you to make sure the others serve the clan-family well."

"Yes, clan-father." Leonna had never ventured far from the mountain. The fact she would be traveling outside of her lands and be responsible, in a way, for the other fledglings ruffled her feathers. She had been to the other villages below, of course. Not all the feline-kind were friendly to avians—their cats had a taste for birds—but Jeneth had made creature-truce with Sturfelis's clan-family some years ago and they had taken to visiting them occasionally and even making barter-trade. Venturing out had become one of her favorite things to do, although she would never tell any of the clan-fathers or clan-mothers that. They would have become suspicious and forbidden her.

"You understand how important this is, don't you?" His voice was soft and reassuring like her own father used to speak, but coming from him, his tone irritated her.

She waved her birds off and nodded her head at him.

"And you understand this may be our only chance?"

She nodded again and looked down at him. He was somewhat shorter than she, his back being so crooked. He crinkled his eyes impatiently.

"I do, clan-father," Leonna said.

"Good, good." He rested his body on a large rock that he often perched his frame on. "I'm sorry to put you in such a position. If you're successful—and you will be

—you'll be a hero to all avian-kind. And yet you may be thinking if something goes afoul, something out of your control, that all will consider you a failure." Jeneth ran his fingers across the hilt of a jewel encrusted dagger tied to his waist. He played with the blade so much that the carvings were worn off. He poked his finger into the hole where the center jewel was missing.

"The thought had crossed my mind." She lied. Success or failure was not in Leonna's head. In fact, the idea of failure hadn't entered her thoughts until Jeneth mentioned it just now. No. What pecked her flesh was something deeper, the sensation deep in her gut that something was not right about stealing from the stonecutters. She shook the emotion away, telling herself whatever benefits the clan-family is good and right. *The law of the clan. It always has been and always will be.*

"Remember, I'll not be far away, at Lasaat, barely a quarter-day's journey. If something unexpected happens, the others understand what to do. I'll come. I'll help." The short, crooked-backed man stood and motioned at his bird high in the trees. The falcon began cawing loudly.

After some moments, into the clearing strode Ayah, her clan-brother. He was nearly her age and full of confidence. His eyes immediately rested on her as he walked up, scanning her up and down. He grinned like a wolf.

Ayah was always grinning at her. Leonna hated the stares, the ogling, the rubbernecking and the glares. All the boys Ayah's age looked at her like that, even some of the men did too. Leonna peered up into the trees, ignoring his eyes fondling her body.

An oversized hawk swooped down and dumped

Jonah off its back. The nestling was giggling. Although they were not blood-related, Leonna shared a strong kinship with Jonah, her younger clan-brother, and was none too happy Jeneth was forcing the nestling to go to the trials. He was barely ten years old, almost a hatchling as far as Leonna was concerned, but she had no voice with the clan-fathers. If her mother couldn't persuade them, she knew to keep her beak shut. He would go to the trials and more than anything else, this was what most concerned Leonna.

Ayah stood rigid in front of Jeneth, pushing out his chest. He didn't acknowledge Leonna's presence, but he was struggling to hold his eyes away. He asked, "Clan-father, are we preparing to leave?"

Jeneth nodded as the rest of the clan-family came out of the long house. Leonna, Ayah and, Jonah were in the center of the circle.

Jeneth waited for them to settle, then held up his hands and addressed them all, "So this is a momentous day. I suspect today will be a day remembered among all avian-kind, for this marks the first time ever an avian will attend the tests of the landers, the so-called Worthy Apprentice Trials."

The other clan-fathers chuckled.

"These three were chosen by the clan-family to attend." He pointed his open palm at Leonna, Ayah, and his own son, Jonah.

The others clapped their elbows against their sides.

"We are avians, a proud people, and our fledglings will serve the clan-family well, of this, there is no doubt. They'll make the landers trust them and the job will be done right under their noses. Leonna will grab the vain eyes of their young men for there's none as beautiful as she among all their kind."

Leonna glanced over at Ayah long enough to observe him flare his nostrils.

Jeneth continued, "Ayah, the strongest fledgling in many generations, will shock them with the strength of his magic. And young Jonah will grab their love with his boyish sweetness and innocence." The crooked man rubbed the boy's head.

Jay exhaled hard and went back inside the long house. The others barely noticed.

Leonna's mind drifted. She had only heard stories of the landers, and they all sounded so unbelievable. She had been told by Ayah that he heard their wizards didn't rule their people. They let people who didn't even know magic rule them. She remembered falling on the floor in laughter. *How ridiculous!*

That the landers stayed mostly in one place seemed to make sense to her, since their magic was tied to the land, but she still found the idea dreadfully claustrophobic. To think if she were one of them she couldn't hop up at any moment and soar, flying in the sky and above the treetops, pushing her spirit into the minds of her birds: it was the most caging idea she could imagine.

As Jeneth continued, he massaged the hilt of his dagger, repeatedly poking his finger at a spot where the large jewel was missing. "Some of you wished to send all the fledglings, but, in the end, we all agreed it better to not scare the landers with our numbers. We didn't want to make them defensive. In sending so few, they will be more inclined to embrace and accept them, I suspect."

Leonna had heard other things, from the felines, but each of the cat-kind had different stories, each one more dubious and contradictory than the previous. The landers didn't come to decisions by will of the clan-family—insane—they were ruled by a single person, almost always a male—silly and stupid—women were considered inferior to men—infuriating—and most upsetting of all, they *ate* birds. Leonna ruffled at the thought. *Perhaps the landers were less than human?* If all she was told was true—and she doubted that were possible—they were barbarians at a minimum.

No, Leonna couldn't believe the stories. She wanted to find out for herself. Her curiosity drove her to spend time among the felines and her inquisitiveness pushed her to volunteer for the trials when Jeneth floated the idea.

Leonna returned her attention to Jeneth when he mumbled something about the moonstone and the clan-family clapped their elbows against their sides. She joined them.

Jeneth announced, "Fledglings, gather your things, your birds. We're traveling down the mountain."

The others clapped their sides once more and Leonna entered the long house, walking past the rows of bunks and cages to her bed. She gathered a few changes of clothing and stuffed them in her sack, slinging the pack over her shoulder. She called her birds, figuring she might as well bring them all. Her nine finches circled her head while her hawk landed on her shoulder and the peregrine flapped behind her and tucked itself into the top of her pack.

She gave her mother a hug and peck first, then stepped away from her to peck the cheeks of the other clan-mothers. She paused briefly when she realized her mother wanted to say something to her, but couldn't for the presence of the other clan-mothers.

Leonna stepped out of the house and waited for Jeneth, Ayah, and Jonah.

When they emerged, the four started off down the path that led down the mountain. Just as they were leaving, Jay ran up to Leonna. "Oh Leonna, I think you forgot your gloves. Wait and I'll retrieve them."

Jeneth said, "Leonna, catch up to us when you are sure you have everything."

Leonna was certain she had her gloves so she frowned and followed her mother back up the path and into the long house as the others continued on. She walked to the end of the narrow structure, ignoring the glare of the other clan-mothers. She whispered to Jay, "What?"

Jay grabbed her hand and pulled her over to her bed and opened her wooden chest, pulling out a few items of clothing. "I wanted to finish what I was telling you before." Her voice was low and shallow as her eyes scanned the building.

Leonna waited for her to continue.

"As I was saying before, about your father, and you, and me…"

"Go ahead. Mom, I'm listening."

She sat next to her and brought her face close. "Have you ever wondered why your name is Leonna? A feline name?"

The girl's mouth opened, but she did not respond.

"Before I met your father, there was another, a feline-kind. He was a good man and I fell in love with him."

Leonna gasped.

Jay continued, her voice a whisper, "No one knows this. Least of all your father. It was as forbidden then as it is now. I would be ejected from the nest for even speaking these words."

"Jeneth cannot know," Leonna mouthed, silently.

Jay exhaled. "It was a different time. Things weren't so rigid and tense like they are now. I was able to mingle with those outside the nest. Interact. It just sort of happened."

"Jeneth changed everything," Leonna finished her thought.

Her mother nodded. "But our relationship wasn't meant to be. I couldn't go against the wishes of the clan-family. I couldn't risk losing my clan, my family, my nest. So I stopped going down the mountain and visiting the felines. Time passed. I married another. Your father. And I truly loved him. Don't misunderstand me."

There was an uncomfortable silence. Leonna moved some of her clothing from inside the box to her bed. She waited. Her mother didn't stop her from going down the mountain to tell her this. There had to be more.

"Time passed. We had a few fights, your father and I. I needed to speak to someone, to sort through some things. I couldn't go to the other women. They would just tell me to listen to my husband."

Leonna nodded, for she knew that was exactly what they would say.

Jay said, "I was confused. I went down the mountain a few times to see him. Just to talk, mind you. The old emotions bubbled up. I never intended to—" Jay's voice caught. Her eyes bulged momentarily.

Leonna realized there was much more to the story, words that Jay refused to speak. In fact, she had already said too much.

Jay gained control of herself and continued, "I made a mistake. So I wanted you to understand, to protect your heart. Things are not much different from those days. You must stay within your clan-family—"

Suddenly Leonna realized where her mother was headed. Her mother knew about Jinx. "Wait. Who told you? Ayah? What did he say?"

Jay recoiled slightly.

"Mother, what did he say?" Leonna repeated.

"I read the letter—"

"I already broke off with Jinx. I'll not—" Leonna was flustered. They had read the letter and they had misunderstood what she wrote. Clearly, her mother thought she loved Jinx, that she was actually contemplating marrying outside the clan.

Jay clarified, "You went too close. It's forbidden. Now you're going to be out there among all those young men. You realize how they'll treat you. I could rub bird droppings on your face and you would still be the most beautiful among them."

"You don't know that."

"I know more than you think. I've flown farther than you realize. There's not a good beak among the whole flock of landers."

Leonna shrugged her shoulders and said nothing. She couldn't tell her the truth, for telling her she was only manipulating Jinx's heart, like she did all the other avian boys, would cast a much darker shadow. She couldn't tell her she didn't respect them, any of them, because all they saw when they stared at her was the curve of her hips, the shape of her body and her pretty face. She couldn't tell her mother that she thought they were all fools and she was toying with them.

Her mother touched her shoulder. "Look, love whoever you want. Marry. Hatch children and be happy. Just find someone within the clan. That's all." She paused for a moment. "That Ayah's an attractive one, don't you think?"

Leonna shook her head and stood as she announced, "Clan-mother, I have my gloves. I need to catch the others." She gave her one last peck then ran for the door and straight down the mountain path.

Once she got out of sight of their home, she slowed. She wasn't eager to catch Jeneth and the others. She wanted some time for her thoughts.

The fact Ayah read her letter and showed the note to her mother didn't surprise her. She trusted him like the fool she was, but of course, he didn't believe in personal emotions much less property. To him, all that mattered was what benefited the clan. Jeneth had him thoroughly brainwashed. Of course, he would read the note. It seemed so obvious now. She wondered how many of the other clan-mothers and clan-fathers had read her confession. She flushed red and heat washed across her cheeks. Sensing her discomfort, her hawk cawed loudly.

"Shhhh!"

Tweetnone pecked her forehead.

"I'm fine, Tweetnone," she said and waved him off the top of her head and into the air.

No, she wasn't shocked by Ayah's lack of discretion or even her mother's warning. The shocking revelation was the fact that Jay had taken a liking to a feline so many years ago. But now it all made perfect sense. Her mother always avoided leaving the mountain when all the others went to barter-trade. Now Leonna understood why. She was avoiding someone. And the fact she had to go to those lengths spoke to Leonna. Her mother must still have feelings for the man. Leonna shook her head.

She spied the others up ahead so she slowed her steps

further as she leaped from boulder to boulder, intentionally taking much more caution than she normally would.

Leonna justified her actions when she wrote the letter to Jinx since they were both still young. If they married, how would they raise their children? As avians? As felines? As some kind of awkward, terrible hybrid? No, the concept was unacceptable and that's what she wrote to him. Of course, that was all just an excuse to shake him away. She had no feelings for him. It was all a game.

When the others reached the bottom of the hill and the path to the feline camp widened, she sped up and caught them.

"Took you long enough," Ayah commented, his eyes on her.

"I was extra careful on the big rocks. I didn't want to become injured on such an important day," Leonna said.

Jeneth raised an eyebrow at her. "Good thinking. I had some last instructions for the three of you. Ayah will fill you in. The others, they are with us."

"The others are with us?" Leonna repeated, letting the thought sink in. There was no turning back now, the plan was in motion.

They reached the edge of the tall grass and could see the village of the felines in the distance. The vinegary, acidic reek of cat urine pervaded the space.

They stopped at the edge of the camp and waited to be invited in.

Jeneth's hawk cawed as a sense of panic washed across all the birds and they took to the air. The four stepped back slightly.

Jeneth held out his arm. "Hold."

Dark gray eyes peered at them between the tall leaves

and dry stalks. Two, then three, plain, tawny colored faces emerged. They were adult cats. Jinx had told her the male cougars were much more aggressive so they used them to guard the perimeter. One hissed loudly. Another growled.

Jeneth motioned for the fledglings to stand behind him. The three cougars crouched deeper, a coiled spring as if they were preparing to leap. A bobcat ran into the space and snarled then the cougars relaxed.

The bobcat wasn't a quarter the size of the cougars and Leonna marveled at why the other would listen to him. She giggled at the thought of her hawk listening to something Tweetnone ordered him to do, if he could squawk that is.

The bobcat contemplated Jeneth and tilted his long pointed ears, turned and walked down the path. Jeneth motioned with his hands and the four followed the cat into the village.

At the small row of three-walled huts, there were a handful of trees, mostly barren of leaves and dead-looking, filled with various kinds of cats. Leonna was able to recognize some of the different kinds of cats after spending so much time with Jinx. There were leopards—those were easy—they were covered in spots. Cougars—those were easy too—they were the biggest of all the cats in the feline village. The others, Leonna had a more difficult time picking out. Bobcats and ocelots, both much smaller, she sometimes confused, especially the cubs. Then there were others, smaller; she did not know the names of the breeds.

The bobcat squatted on its rear haunches.

"Don't look at their eyes," Leonna said to Jonah when she caught him staring up into the trees.

He placed his eyes on the ground. "Why not?"

"Cats view eye contact as a threat. Or a challenge, at least. You don't want to challenge those big cats."

Jeneth chuckled and nodded.

Sturfelis emerged from one of the far huts. He had a towel wrapped around his neck and appeared as if someone was grooming him. "She speaks truth. Observant girl. What's your name again?"

"Leonna. Greetings, Master Sturfelis."

The bobcat left them and curled around Sturfelis's leg. "My wife just finished brushing my mane and my beard. The others should be almost ready." The archmage yelled out, "Felix!"

A tall, attractive young man with deep brown skin, barefoot and wearing nothing but a breechcloth, strode in from between two structures. "The avians are here. Just a moment, please." He ducked into a hut then returned with a sack slung over his shoulder. A bobcat and two cougars followed close behind. Two ocelots were dead asleep, one slung around his neck and another hanging out of his pack. "Sorry to keep you waiting, Master Jeneth. The others will be along quickly. Greetings, Leonna." He nodded his head towards her. "Ayah and oh, is that young Jonah? Is he attending the trials also?" He gazed up at Jeneth, puzzled.

"He's capable. Don't worry." Jeneth answered as if he didn't want to discuss the boy's presence.

Leonna stared at Felix's dark tanned chest. He was tall, muscular, and exuded strength. He seemed nothing like an avian with their pale flesh they always kept covered.

"I understand," Felix said unable to wipe the concern from his face.

Soon the others joined them in the small open space in front of the huts. Leonna remembered the other cubs from her many visits to barter-trade. They were surrounded by the felines and their cats and Leonna shuddered to be enveloped by creatures who so enjoyed preying on birds. Felicia and Jinx walked into the center, placing themselves next to Leonna. She forced her eyes forward for she didn't want to meet Jinx's gaze. If she checked his face she was sure she would recognize whether or not he had yet read her note, but she wasn't sure if she could stay calm in front of the others.

"Fine. We're all here. I would like to say a few things before we leave," Sturfelis said. "I am sure Jeneth has already spoken to his clan, so I would like the opportunity to do the same. Felix has been helping out at the Worthy Apprentice Trials for a number of years, yet none of the creature-kind has seen fit to send any of the young ones, whether fledgling or cub. That is, until this day."

"Today is a good day," Jeneth added.

"A good day, yes, but a word of caution." Sturfelis held up both of his hands as if to garner further attention. "All eyes will be on this small group of fledglings and cubs. There are landers who yet hold malice against the creature-kind for past... conflicts, let us say... and they will depict anything you do in tainted light. For this reason, we were reluctant to send our young cubs." He paused and glanced over at Felix. "To be honest, I was still against sending them. A wizard, that is another story, but to send our cubs? I am being honest in saying I disagreed. Not that I lacked confidence in the abilities of our young felines. To the contrary. But the landers are not like us. They are individuals. They do not follow the will of the clan. Some of you may have heard they do not enjoy such a thing as a clan."

Felicia gasped.

"It's true. Each wizard, each apprentice, they are all alone and by themselves."

"How awful," another cried out.

"As such, we need to remember and treat them as individuals. Some of the landers will be good and treat you fairly. Others less so. Yet they will not judge you in the same light. They will not see you as individuals but lump you all together as one threatening, unknown and suspicious group. All of you. In their minds, the creature-kind are one and together. They view us as the same, whether feline or avian."

"Ridiculous," Jonah said. "Do they not have eyes? How can they picture feline and avian as the same?"

Sturfelis smiled. "Not only us but all the creature-kind. They lump us all together. The foul dogs of the west, the canines, too. Can you believe it? They see cat-kind and dog-kind as the same. I lived among the landers for many years and the idea still itches my fur."

Jeneth added, "Their ways make no sense to our hearing, but the point Master Sturfelis is making is you must be careful. Be on your best behavior and be aware of their customs and perceptions of you. If a misunderstanding crops up, do not hesitate to rectify it immediately. You can call Felix, if necessary."

Felix continued, "Yes, please do. Of course, I will be busy running the trials and cannot be judged as being partial to any apprentice, including creature-kind. I will not be able to help you pass the trials or give you any aid above what any other apprentice would receive. However, if any of you come into an uncertain situation or conflict with any of the landers outside of the trials themselves, feel free to call upon me. I will help clarify any misunderstandings."

The group grew silent and after a short time, Sturfelis said, "Let's be off."

The rest of the feline-kind hugged and kissed Jinx, Felicia, and Felix. The three cubs along with Sturfelis and all their gear and their cats ambled along the far path that led to Lasaat. The avians followed.

After they left the village and the path narrowed, most began walking two by two. Jinx took the opportunity to walk next to Leonna but said nothing for a time. Leonna glanced over at him once, then twice, but he didn't turn his eyes to meet hers.

The longer Leonna walked next to him, the deeper the sense of loss penetrated her. She realized she had lost him as a friend, at least for now. His pain was radiating off him. Leonna, through her birds, could sense his anguish. Their relationship hadn't been anything serious, she thought he only had a little crush. She recognized where he wanted it to go and she snipped it off before he pushed further. She had been leading him on, of course. Letting him think she was interested in him so she could fleece him for information about the felines and their ways, feeding her insatiable curiosity. If she could have what she wanted, she would have had only his friendship. But he needed more so she used that need to make him open up.

That's what pecked her flesh, none of the men could see past her legs, her body or her face. They wanted marriage and love. She was a prize to be won and she hated that. Her face slackened and grew cold as if there were no blood in her cheeks. She felt cursed.

Jinx stared at his feet. "I read the letter."

Leonna didn't know what to say. She couldn't open her mouth for she didn't trust herself to stop once it all started pouring out. And she couldn't do that, especially not in front of Ayah and Felicia.

Jinx added, "I understand." His voice was vacant and empty. After a few more moments of walking next to each other in silence, he sped up, stepping away from her and joining Ayah. Soon enough the two were joking and laughing, but Leonna knew Jinx was pretending, hiding his wound.

When they reached the fork in the road that led to Lasaat, the band stopped. Jeneth and Sturfelis separated from the rest and Sturfelis said, "Remember your training, young cubs. You will do well. Remember, what is important here is building a relationship with the landers and letting them become more accustomed to us. This is not about receiving the meaningless title of Worthy Apprentice. We creature-kind do not recognize such individual recognition. What you do in these days will benefit the clan-cubs in years to come."

Felicia and Jinx nodded then each gave him a hug.

Jeneth smiled with half of his face. "Avians, be excellent. Be flawless." His beady eyes fell to Leonna and he squinted as if to say, *I'll be watching.*

Leonna, Jonah, and Ayah each hugged Jeneth briefly.

Felix regarded the two wizards. "I'll watch over them, both the felines and the avians. I don't expect trouble, but if there is, I'll send for you through the trolls."

Leonna's eyes popped wide. "Trolls? What do mean 'trolls'?"

Felix chuckled. "Not to worry."

The band carried on down the path as Sturfelis and

Jeneth watched them leave. Leonna turned her head back as she walked. Jeneth twisted his hand at her the slightest amount, she knew exactly what the signal meant, a gesture the adults used to tell the children to stop playing and go to work. She nodded slightly, almost imperceptibly and Jeneth smiled and turned away.

The remainder of the path from Lasaat to the trials' entrance was short and they were soon there. The ground widened to an open plain. At the edge of the space was another smallish wood, not large enough to be called a forest. The entrance was a gaping hole, dark and imperceptible. On either side was a set of trolls, towering, nearly as tall as a small tree.

All their eyes went wide at the sight of the immense characters, all except Felix who seemed to be enjoying their surprise immensely.

They slowly approached the trolls.

Felix strode up to them. "Budzig, Barth, how are you this fine morning?"

Neither acknowledged him. Barth chewed his gums then belched.

Felix turned to the rest and explained, "A magical barrier surrounds this wood: troll-spell. The trolls guard the entrance. They won't harm you. One at a time, enter the wood. You will find tests that each of you needs to pass to advance. I cannot help you here, I'm afraid to say. If you arrive at the interior, I'll meet you there. If not, the trolls will collect you. Don't fear them; they're here to help. Now go on."

Felicia and her cats went first, followed quickly by Jinx. Each was swallowed by the blackness.

"Wait, they disappeared," Jonah said in disbelief.

Felix said, "Yes, once you're in, you can't leave. You

either pass the trials or the trolls collect you. See you on the other side." Felix walked in with his cats, his backside disappearing into the blackness.

"Well, here goes," Ayah said running in after him. He was instantly gone.

Jonah stared up at Leonna, tears nearly in his eyes. "I'm afraid."

She bent down to his level and stroked the side of his head. "I'm a little too. You'll be fine and I'll watch over you as much as I can."

She stood and took his hand in hers and the two walked in together.

Chapter Three
This Is It

"I guess this is it," Shireen repeated as the two stood staring at the path into the wood.

Bel nodded. He wanted to touch her, to softly caress her cheek. Not to take pleasure from her, enjoying the sensation of touching her flesh, but to communicate with her in a way words could not. He wanted to let her know how hard his chest thumped at even just the thought of her, one last time, before they stepped through. His heart burned to let her know losing her was more difficult than fighting armies of ghouls, wizards gone wrong and fire-breathing dragons. He wanted to let their spirits merge one last time, but the trolls were standing right there watching them.

"Yes, I guess this is it," he said. Her eyes were on him, but he couldn't return her gaze. Pretending to only be friends was going to be hard enough.

"So I'll go in first," Shireen said, staring at the side of his face.

Bel kept his eyes locked on the path into the forest. He nodded. There was no way he could meet her eyes. Not now. Heat blasted up out of his collar. If they locked eyes he would be forced to touch her, to hug her, to kiss her. And he couldn't, he had to be strong. They couldn't risk being excommunicated, they had to pretend, for now. And he didn't want to think about after anyway. If he couldn't convince her, change her mind, they would have to eventually leave each other and forget. But that was impossible.

"Okay. I guess I'm going in," Shireen said without moving.

Bel stood motionless. When he could bear the tension no longer, he turned his head away from her and closed his eyes. He opened them when he heard her feet scuffing against the dry leaves. He watched her back as she stepped past the trolls and into the dark of the forest. She took a few steps in and turned her head back toward him then instantly disappeared.

"Hey! Where did she go?" Bel said.

The two trolls guarding the entrance peered down at him with indifference.

Bel's eyes were directly in front of the troll's enormous gut and he spied a large amount of gray gelatin-like material hanging out of the creature's belly button. "You should clean that," he mumbled, then yelled, "Hey, I'm talking to you. Are you in there? Where did she go?"

A voice answered from behind him, "There's an enchantment on the forest surrounding the trials. I assume you're an apprentice?"

Two young men approached wearing the heavy white and gray clothing of the Tundric people. Bel looked past the tall one in front then yelled out, "Naga?" Bel ran to greet Naga, slapping his hand to his forearm in the Tundric gesture of camaraderie.

Naga said, "My flesh stands before you, Bel. You're attending this test of might and magic?"

"The Worthy Apprentice Trials? Yes, first time."

"My first and noble thrust was last year. A valiant effort on my part, I might humbly add, but alas, I was ejected like putrid fish from a whale's mouth. In my defense, most First-Years never advance. In fact, only a few have ever accomplished such a feat." Naga pointed his eyes up at the tall one.

"You are correct," the tall Tundric man said.

Naga continued, "Just keep your head tied down to your shoulders, lest you want it separated from your husk. That's vital. Protect your backside. There is no loss of honor in not achieving the goal, just don't leave your blood and body on the battlefield."

Naga extended his hand at the tall one in front in a motion of deference and over to Bel. "Aquilo, this is my friend, Bel. We studied together at University. Bel, this is Aquilo. He's a worthy apprentice for… how many passings of the cold season?"

"Eight," Aquilo said.

"Eight years. He runs the tests of might, ahh… the Worthy Apprentice Trials."

"So there's an enchantment?" Bel asked, turning to Aquilo.

"Yes, didn't your master explain?"

"No, he was injured. Only a last minute decision to send me."

Aquilo frowned. "I understand." He gazed at the trolls and the dark void between them. "The trolls do not speak to the likes of us. You'll not find answers with them." He turned to face Bel and Naga. "The enchantment protects the trials. No one in or out without the trolls. Even the wizards cannot breach the barrier surrounding this small patch of forest without the trolls' permission. Once an apprentice steps into the forest, he or she cannot leave. For your protection, of course." He stopped and scrutinized Bel to make sure he was following him.

When Bel nodded, Aquilo continued, "There are trials in the forest. Magical tests. No one can tell you what they are or what to expect because they will come from inside of you. For each apprentice, they are different."

Bel glanced at Naga. His face gave the impression he had eaten something sour. He addressed Aquilo, "Your Tundric is smooth. You could almost pass for someone from the northern forest."

He said, "I assume you meant that as a compliment?"

"Yes, yes."

"I've spent much time in the forest, helping to run the trials, assisting at Lasaat. The time away from Kandool muddles my tongue. In any case, if you can succeed in the trials of the forest, there will be a large building where everyone will be meeting. Go there. Everything will be explained inside. If you don't, the trolls will retrieve you and escort you out. Good luck."

Bel took that as his cue to go. "So I'll talk to you inside," he said to Naga, then turned and pushed light into the end of his staff.

Perhaps the trials had already started, Bel thought. *Maybe Aquilo is judging me right now.* Bel tried to step confidently, but he found himself staring at the ground, not wanting to trip over an unseen root, branch or depression. He didn't want to appear inept in front of someone who might be grading his every word or motion. He needed to come across as confident.

He stepped between the two hulking guards, through

the hole, and into the dark. After several steps in, he stopped and turned. The entrance was gone. The guards were gone. Everything. Just. Gone.

Filtered sunlight illuminated the sparse trees, striking the moss-covered earth. The earthy stench of rotting wood and the damp, wet scent of nearby herbs wafted around him. The forest was serene, calm and beautiful, but odd. Bel crinkled his forehead as the wood was unlike any he had ever seen. The trees were spaced wide, yet they had tall, thin trunks. It made no sense.

Bel thought of the trees of the southern forest, trees with deep roots, oak, hickory, and walnut—even willow —trees that could support huge amounts of weight. Their trunks were massive, their branches reached high and their canopies were expansive. Not much sunlight touched the mossy earth, leaving large spaces dead and barren of vegetation between each tree.

In the north, on the path from Lasaat to Yagoos, the forest of tightly knit fir grows thin and tall with barely a branch or leaf, except at the top, like strands in a massive web of life, all connected, all touching. In some areas, the firs are so close that a horse and rider cannot pass between them. These were the only two types of forest Bel had experienced. Yet here, in this wood, was an odd mixture of tall thin trees with large spaces between them allowing the sunlight to strike the ground, yet the ground was bare of ground cover and vegetation.

"This makes no sense," Bel said as he slowly turned.

Another thing he realized, the forest appeared nearly identical in every direction. After spinning for a few revolutions, Bel had no idea which way would take him deeper into the forest and which way would lead him closer to the entrance. He was lost.

After viewing the path between the trolls, he had assumed the trials would be set up along the way and each apprentice would stop at a station, take the test and move on if accomplished successfully. He was at a total loss as to what he should do. Should he stand and wait? Is someone going to retrieve him and lead him to the first test? Should he try to find his way back to the path? He wondered if Naga or Aquilo might appear if he waited long enough. He pondered pushing forward and trying to catch up to Shireen.

Then a girl screamed.

"Shireen!" Bel said and darted off in the direction of the sound. He sped up to a full gallop, his heart violently pounding against his breastbone as the idea of her being hurt ran through his head. He trained his ears, trying to detect any sound that would point him in the right direction for he could not see anyone or anything besides an endless forest of thin trees. He slowed to a stop to try to quiet his breathing and listen. He didn't want to run past her.

"No! Stop!" she cried out.

Bel pushed his head back and squinted. *Not Shireen's voice. A girl. Young, that much was certain.* He turned to the left and jogged.

He glimpsed a piece of fabric, so he sped towards it and pushed energy into his staff, holding the magewood in front of him.

"Stop squirming!" a gruff voice barked.

Bel spun and came to a stop. Just to the right of him stood two men, their clothing black, soiled and torn. One held a small girl's shoulder tightly and a dagger at her throat.

"What are you doing here, interrupting our business?

51

Be gone with you," the second man snarled through a mouthful of black and damaged teeth.

Bel pushed his staff forward. "You men, release the child." He was unsure of how to proceed. He surely couldn't blast them, not without injuring the young girl.

"Release her? Boy, who do you think you are, giving me orders? She's mine. I've paid for her and I'll do with her what I please. This is none of your concern."

A sharp, rancid funk came from the two men.

Bel took a step closer. "You have a knife to a child's throat so I think what you are doing is my concern. Tell me how much you paid and I'll buy her from you."

The knife man guffawed. "She's not for sale. Now move along, boy."

Terror flitted in the little girl's light brown eyes. She was struggling against the man's grip, but to no avail.

Bel took one step closer. His mind was spinning. Nothing his master had ever taught prepared him for something like this. All his fireballs and mage-light were no good. He felt helpless. He tried to reason with them, "Listen, my friends, I understand. I came here unexpectedly and you've put that knife to the girl's throat, perhaps because I've startled you. Let me assure you, I mean you no ill. Just take the knife from the girl's throat so I understand you mean her no harm and I'll be on my way." He squeezed his staff harder, hoping the man might pull the blade away long enough to repel him.

The two laughed. The knife man said, "Whether we harm her or not is none of your concern. She's property. Understand, boy? If I decide to raise her as my own sweet daughter, it has nothing to do with you. If I decide to kill her and eat her, that's none of your business." His steely eyes squinted down hard as he tightened his grip.

The other barked, "Now move along."

Bel pushed light into his staff, enveloping him in a bluish tint. He thought maybe he could intimidate them. He hoped they wouldn't call his bluff for trickery was all he could think to do. He raised his voice. "You understand I am a magic user, do you not? You realize what we are capable of, don't you?"

"We are familiar with your kind. Bullies. Only interested in using magic to push people around. Now you want to steal what's mine and I won't allow that to happen." The man spit, wiped his mouth with his shirt sleeve, then narrowed his eyes down on Bel. "You try to do something with that staff of yours and I'll slit this pretty one's throat before the words exit your mouth. She's mine, thief."

Bel held up his hands as the light dissipated from his staff. "Fine. Fine. You win. I'll set down my staff. How's that?" Bel placed his stick on the ground and took another step closer. "I'm not here to threaten you or tell you what to do with what's yours. I think a man's property ought to be respected by all men, whether they be wizards or not."

"Now you're talking sense," the other hissed.

As he spoke, Bel tried something he wasn't sure would work, communicating with the trees. He went to a nearby tree and casually placed his hand on the rough bark as he looked at the two men. He slowly moaned a deep low sound as he tapped the trunk. He said to the two. "Now. You understand I mean you no harm—"

"Of course, I do. And it's going to stay that way because I still got this knife at her pretty throat, don't I?"

Bel tried to communicate his predicament to the

forest. He spoke the few words from the trees' odd language of rustling branches, creaking trunks and swishing sounds. He pretended to be clearing his throat as he made the popping, cracking and swishing sounds. He begged the trees to help him save the girl's life, hoping they would understand.

"You have something more to say, boy?" The second man smiled widely.

Tiny, thin roots slowly peeked through the brown, dead leaves on the ground and rose behind the two men.

Bel said, "Yes, the knife is completely unnecessary. Why don't we sit and talk, as one weary traveler to another? We could share stories—"

"Stories? With you?" he snapped. "No thanks. I think we'll be on our way."

Bel raised his hands in a sign of surrender. "Okay. Nice meeting you two. Hope you enjoy your property." Bel turned his back on the two and stepped away. When he stooped over to pick up his staff, he glanced back. The roots were now towering above the two men, poised to strike. Bel closed his eyes, mumbled further to the trees, popping his lips and hissing.

When the man dropped his knife to his side, the roots quickly grabbed his arms and squeezed, forcing him to release the dagger and the girl.

Bel dodged back.

The girl ran as the knife man was pulled into the air, the roots entangling him. The second man quickly retrieved the dagger and hopped away from the roots, alternately pointing the knife at the trees, then Bel and then the girl.

"Calm down, good sir. I mean you no harm, as I have said before." Bel stroked the girl's head. She had wrapped her arms around his leg and was squeezing tight, preventing him from making any sudden moves. If the man with the dagger came closer, he would blast him and he didn't want to do that. He had no intention of injuring anyone. It wasn't the wizardly way. The men were doing wrong to this child, but he wasn't to judge or mete out punishment as he saw fit. That was the duty of a constable. He would escort them to the nearest town and let the law sort this situation out.

The man with the knife stepped closer. "Release my friend. Give me the girl and I won't cut you."

Bel tilted his hand. "Baru." The weight and density of the dagger increased dramatically and the filthy man could no longer hold the blade. He released the knife. It buried deep into the earth.

The man ran past Bel screaming in fright. His stench followed him a few moments later. Bel smiled, turning to follow him with his eyes, but he was gone. When he glanced back, the first man and the girl were gone also.

They all disappeared. The roots and even the dagger and the hole in the earth the blade made: gone. He scratched his head.

"Just a trial? I wonder if I passed," he said to no one. He pondered if he was supposed to capture the two. Should he have done anything differently? Did he take too long to rescue the girl?

He didn't hurt anyone and that was good. At least, he thought it was.

Bel scanned his eyes across the forest, wondering what he should do next when he noticed something. The forest seemed much the same everywhere except far off to his left. There was a large tree there, out of place to Bel's eyes.

The apprentice trudged towards the oak and as he got closer he saw more and more of them. He continued past the first large tree, making his way into more familiar wood. Trees of ash, maple, and oak, much like the ones in the southern forest near his home. His mind drifted to his master. Bel lifted his face, letting the light and shadow dance across his skin. *Warm.* He inhaled a faint minty whiff as he was reminded of his herb patch behind their hovel. A hummingbird darted by, stuffing its beak into a violet trumpet flower.

Bel felt as if he were home. His thoughts were jarred as a man on a horse rode up and slid to a stop in front of him.

"Are you the apprentice of Archmage Nes'egrinon?" the man on the horse asked.

"I am. What's the—"

The horseman cut him off, "The trolls let me pass so I might retrieve you. I'm only a messenger. I've been sent from Lasaat. It's important you come with me." The messenger reached out his hand to pull Bel up on the back of his horse.

"What happened? Is there a problem? Something with my master?" Bel's heart thudded in his chest as though he already knew the answer. His master was dead.

The man stowed his hand in his lap and turned the horse slightly. "There's no time for words and conversation. We must ride. Now. Your call is of an urgent nature. The archmages wouldn't have sent me past the trolls if the need were not pressing. Do you understand what authority is required to send a messenger into a wood under troll-spell?"

The pressure extended into Bel's temples.

The man reached out his hand once more and smiled.

"Please. Make my job easier. Let me take you back to Lasaat. They can give you the news themselves. Ride with me and I will take you out of this place."

"My master? He's dead, isn't he?" Bel understood exactly what that meant. Every fiber of his being was in pain. A realization bit him hard. He loved the old man. His lungs seized and he had to mentally order his body to breathe. Each inhale and exhale was a battle of will. He had experienced this once before, but the sensation had come on him much slower, the day he realized his father had died on the sea and was never coming back.

The horse rider examined Bel, then exhaled long and slow. "The answer I am not to tell you. However, I see you're not going to come with me until I do, so I have no choice."

Bel nodded.

"Yes, Good Apprentice, Master Nes'egrinon is dead. He passed from the world of the living last night. Master Archmage Jergamemnon received word from Master Meetta. She's the sorceress at Sha'mont. Nice woman. I met her once. In any case, she sent word and Master Archmage Jergamemnon dispatched me to retrieve you. Master Nes'egrinon's mantle now falls to you."

Bel squeezed his eyes down hard and pointed his head at the ground as he waited for the pain of the gut punch to pass. He placed his eyes on the rider's glove and extended his hand. As the messenger reached for Bel's hand, he pulled his arm back at the last moment.

His master's last wish was for him to attend the trials, to discover if there truly was something afoul elsewhere in the lands. If he left now, he would be abandoning his master's final request.

"Is there a problem? I've told you everything," the

rider said.

Bel said, "And for that I thank you." He took a few steps away. Forcing himself to speak calmly, hoping his voice wouldn't crack, that he wouldn't fall to the ground and cry, he said, "Me leaving the trials will not bring him back from the dead. Tell the archmages of Lasaat to not take offense, but I will attend to my master's mantle at the conclusion of the trials."

The rider extended his hand farther, barking, "Are you sure?"

Bel began walking away. His heart rent. He couldn't say anything more for his neck was swollen and his heart was pulsing hard and fast. He waved his hand behind his head.

He heard a sound that reminded him of sand pouring. He turned. The horse and its rider were gone.

The apprentice thought perhaps the rider and his message were only another trial. He hoped that's all they were. *But still, it's entirely possible my master is dead.* Bel shuddered and tried to flush the thought from his mind as he walked through the wood.

Just as Bel passed into another clearing he jumped back in shock. A girl was slumped over on the ground, crying.

"Shireen!" He ran to her.

Bel shook her shoulder, "Shireen! Shireen! What happened?"

Shireen slowly wiped her face.

"Are you all right?" he said.

The girl sat up and pushed her back against a tree, "I-I guess."

"What happened? Why are you crying? Why are you lying here?"

Shireen exhaled as she pursed her lips. She was trying hard to stop herself from weeping again.

"The trials?" Bel asked. "What happened?"

"I don't want to say."

Bel sat next to her and tried to come up with something positive to say. "It doesn't matter if you fail. There's always next year."

"I didn't fail. Not yet," Shireen said.

"What happened? Why are you crying? Did someone... do something?"

She glanced at him. "No, not at all."

Bel finally slouched next to her on the soft moss-covered earth.

After some moments, he tried again. "A few moments ago I thought my master was dead. Some kind of false image. A trial. What did they show you? Was it that bad?"

"You first. Tell me about yours."

Bel paused. His heart was still fluttering. "It's hard to say. I saw some things. I reacted. A messenger with terrible news. A couple of killers. Cannibals, maybe. Were they trials? I guess so. Not what I expected."

"Me too. I passed the first four easy enough."

"There's, at least, five? I think I've only seen two of them." Bel wiped a tear from her cheek.

"There was a seer."

Guilt washed over Bel. "What happened?"

Shireen leaned back and grimaced. "I ran. That's what happened. I ran and hid from him. I thought, and after what my master told me, and yours too, I thought—I mean I *knew* we would be read, but that wasn't supposed to be *now*. It was supposed to be years later, after I had time to get ready for it, at the Wizard Trials. Not *now*. It's not fair."

"You ran? So what does that mean? You didn't fail? You can still go back and—"

Shireen slowly stood and waved her hand. "No. What happened was this: I ran. And do you know what happened next? I had a realization." Bel stood in front of her as she continued, "I can't run forever. Sooner or later, someone's going to find out about us. Whether it's a seer, another magician, a king, prince or courtier, and what? Do you realize how easy it would be to blackmail one of us? To get us to perform magic for personal gain, to kept our love a secret?"

Bel's eyes widened. "Shireen, what are you saying?"

She grabbed his two hands. "This. Just this. I'm tired of running from you, my love. You win. You've won my heart. I love you, Bel, and I want to spend the rest of my life with you. I don't care what happens to me or where we go, as long as I'm with you."

Bel gazed into Shireen's eyes, wondering if she were serious. His heart began to race, thumping in his chest. Now, finally, after all the discussions, the begging, and pleading, after all the waiting and dreaming, she was agreeing to what he always wanted: a life together.

His voice shook. "Shireen, are you sure? This is sudden. I mean, you know, it's all I ever wanted. But are you sure you're not going to, you know, change your mind? Are you sure you're not going to regret this?"

She released his one hand, turned and pulled on the other, getting him to follow her. Bel came up beside her as she said, "I've never been surer of anything in my entire life. We could keep wasting time, keep lying to ourselves and be found out tomorrow or three years from now. In either case, sure, we'll be together after they kick us out. But is that fair to our two masters? They've been diligently training us with the expectation we would succeed, become full-fledged wizards. Your master said he's grooming you as his replacement and he doesn't have time to waste finding another. Is that fair to him? He isn't getting any younger."

Bel stopped. The thought his master might yet be dead flashed through his head. "No, you're right," he mumbled. "It's not fair to him."

Shireen tugged his hand again. Just having her hand in his made him feel giddy. Her flesh was so soft. He rubbed his thumb in her palm, caressing it.

"Where are we going?" he asked.

"This way," Shireen said as she pulled, nearly dragging him.

"But where does this lead? How do you know your way? Did you find the path?"

"Yes, the path is over here," Shireen said. "Just past that group of trees. The trolls are there. We'll leave."

Bel pulled back. Something didn't seem right and he couldn't exactly put his finger on what it was.

Shireen stopped and turned toward him. "I was just there, Bel." She smiled and stroked his cheek. "Trust me, my love. We're going to be together. Together forever. Has a lovely ring, doesn't it?"

"Yes," Bel answered as he rubbed his temple. *A life together with Shireen. Almost too perfect. Could this be another trial?* Bel moved closer to Shireen, placing his face only inches from hers.

"Bel, what are you doing? We should be leaving."

He eyed her, scanning every nook and cranny of her face. She was slightly tanned but lighter than him, her skin a luscious, translucent almond. Shireen's eyes caressed, the light blue swirls mesmerizing. Her long auburn hair bordered her perfect, heart-shaped face like a bow around a wonderful present. She wore no red on her lips or color on her eyelids like the city women of Sha'mont. She didn't need it. There was something entirely wholesome about her beauty. "Your skin is so perfect."

Shireen smiled. "Thanks, yours is fine too. What's wrong?"

Grabbing her hands and pulling them up, Bel inspected them. Soft. She kept her nails trimmed just past the tips. She didn't paint them. He sniffed her neck, then touched the ruffles on her shirt. "That's your perfume, sure enough."

"Master Meetta gave the scent-oil to me. I wasn't aware you noticed."

"Are you crazy? I notice everything about you." Bel backed away and gave her another once over.

"Bel, if you don't want to leave, that's fine. We can sit next to that tree for days if you would like. As long as I'm with you, nothing matters to me anymore."

"Truly?"

"Whatever you want. I've already told you. I'm yours." Shireen smiled, grabbed his hands and gave him a peck on the cheek. She giggled and pulled away, then walked over to the tree and sat under the canopy. "Come sit next to me."

Bel walked over and stood in front of her. "I can't help thinking this is another trial. That you're... not real."

Shireen laughed. "Me? Not real? Do you hear what you're saying?"

"It's... this place... and these trees. You look like you

and you smell like you. I bet if I gave you a little nibble, your skin would even taste like you, but still—"

"Well, there's one way to find out. Just come down here and have a bite." Her voice was enticing, seductive.

Bel struggled to not bend his knees and crumble before her, falling into her arms and embracing her soft body. He squirmed in his skin. Bel turned his eyes from her. "I'm going to go now—"

"Go?" Shireen yelled. "What do you mean *go?*"

Bel refused to give her his eyes. "I'm going to continue on with the trials. If I don't advance, we can meet on the outside." Bel took a few steps but stopped when she screamed at him.

"Bel, don't you dare walk away from me after what I just did!"

He stopped, waiting for her to continue. He forced his shoulders to relax, light headed.

"I gave my heart to you. I can't believe this… Bel, you turn and look at me."

Bel slowly turned as Shireen popped to her knees in front of him. "Bel, look at what you're making me do. I'm begging you. I'm pleading with you. Please, stay with me, please. I need you now. I can't do this without you. Please, stay?"

Every fiber of his being told him to stay, to unlock his knees and fall to the earth before her. Bel couldn't handle the fact she was actually on her knees before him. *I'm the one that should be begging her,* he thought. "I can't," he mumbled as he turned and began to step away, his eyes watering, his breath short.

As he walked away, he heard Shireen say, "Bel, I'm not going to yell at you. I'm not going to scream because I want you to know I'm not mad. I'm going to plainly and coherently tell you that if you walk away from me now it's over between us. You'll never get a second chance."

Bel stopped walking, his hands were trembling.

Shireen continued, "Think. Walk away from me now and you walk away forever."

Could he do that? He thought about moving his legs, but they were unexpectedly cemented to the ground. He wanted to stay, he wanted to lay on the soft earth and love her. Her skin was so perfect, her smile so beautiful, her eyes so enticing. She was right there. Her fragrant perfume, her subtle way, her distinct mannerisms, even down to the way she twisted her neck and tilted her hips. *How could they fake that? No, they couldn't. It was her.* His heart was beating through his chest as he forced his legs to move.

"I'm sorry," Bel said as he began walking away.

He stopped when he heard a sound like rushing sand and bit his lip. His stomach muscles were contracting hard and he couldn't stop them. He clenched his gut. He turned back. Shireen was gone.

A light flashed in front of him and a small village appeared not far away. He wiped his face with the palms of his hands, calmed his breathing and started towards the camp.

Chapter Four
The Trials Begin

A bright light flashed in the sky and a village appeared just at the border of the forest. Shireen marveled how the small village could be cloaked. Why hadn't she seen it before?

A collection of huts clustered about here and there and one large round building sat in the center. The light she followed came from a round object suspended above the central building. The sky was dusk yet the light from the object, what she now realized was a glowing stone, illuminated the entire camp as if it were midday. She couldn't take her eyes off the hovering rock. Shireen had seen stone mages cause rocks to glow before—crystals were especially easy for them, but she had never witnessed a stone so small provide so much light.

"It's the moonstone," a voice answered her unspoken question behind her.

Shireen turned. "Lithia!" She hugged the thick woman immediately. "You're here. I hoped I would see you."

Lithia gave her a kiss on the cheek and squeezed her. "You too. This is exciting. Have you found anyone else? I've just arrived."

Shireen gasped at Lithia's strong bear hug. She had

always been wide, strong and man-like. Almost all the stonecutter women from the western mountains were masculine, Lithia was no different. Her bare arms were brawny and thick, her chest the size of an ale barrel and her legs the trunks of trees. And she had grown stronger since Shireen had last received a Lithia-squeeze. "No. Me too," she gasped as Lithia finally released her.

"First time, right? I didn't see you last year."

"Master Meetta didn't send me. So yes, first time."

"Meetta? You're in Sha'mont? With the dragon?"

"You heard about that?"

"I bet everyone has."

A bobcat rubbed against Lithia's leg and she jumped, pulled out her stone and pushed life-force into the glowing green crystal.

"Tsk tsk," Another girl pushed out air between her lips and the bobcat leaped to her side. She squinted hard at Lithia. "Stonecutters always quick to attack. Typical."

Shireen's mouth hung open. The brown-skinned girl walked away with several small cats following her. She wore a rough-cut tan animal-skin blouse that barely extended low enough to cover her bosom and a too-short, torn animal-skin skirt. She was barefoot and covered in soft blond hair.

Hot, moist air breathed on Shireen's back. She spun. A cat twice the size of the other stared at her. "Umm, nice kitty?" Her voice shook as she slowly stepped back.

The cougar ran after the feline-girl.

Shireen tried to stop her heart from racing. "Creature-kind. At the trials," Shireen mumbled in disbelief. Her heart pulsed in her throat as she forced her face to calm. *The murderers are here.*

"One of the felines runs the trials. You'll see. But he

was the only one last year." Lithia pointed at the large central building. "The introduction will start soon. Do you want to go in?"

Shireen shook her head and scanned her eyes across the wide variety of people with different manners of speaking and greeting, wearing odd clothing. There were apprentices representing all the various lands. Some walked around, looking for old friends and surveying the place. Many seemed to know where they were going as if they had been here before.

"I want to walk around for a few. Save me a seat?" Shireen needed time to compose herself before she went in.

"Sure." Lithia gave her another hug. "It's good to see you." The stone apprentice walked into the large central building.

Shireen surveyed the small village, still amazed she actually passed the trials. There were only three and they weren't even that difficult. "Except the last one," she mumbled to herself. She had to be mean to Bel and break his heart and the experience, leaving him, was painful. Stung. She had been so relieved when he had disappeared and she had realized it was only another trial.

Now I'm a worthy apprentice! She smiled to herself. "All that's left is to go in and retrieve my congratulations and acknowledgment. Master Meetta will be so proud and the trials hadn't been that hard." Shireen wondered why she was even so worried.

She looked over each of the young men and women moving about as she walked through the tiny village. Besides Lithia, Shireen didn't recognize anyone else yet. That surprised her. She thought she would have seen others from her class at University, but the apprentices here appeared much older.

As most of the others were now headed toward the circular building sitting under the glowing moonstone, she turned and followed, gazing side to side at the various huts, the trolls, and all the other apprentices.

Shireen stopped her advance when she spied the girl with the cats and another girl wearing a long flowing outfit, draped over her shoulders and hanging down to just below her crotch. She was barefoot and nothing covered her pale, white legs. The odd cape was dappled, mostly white with splotches of gray. Birds circled her head. The two were tucked behind a small hut. Shireen eased up to the edge of one of the huts to listen. She still couldn't believe there were creature-kind here.

"Felicia, I'll take care of my kind. Thank you, but it's none of your concern," the smaller girl wearing mottled gray said.

Felicia's cat growled so she tapped her leg to quiet the cougar and said, "It *is* my concern. I'm part of this, whether you like it or not. We're all creature-kind to them and I won't let you and your kind ruin this for me."

Shireen shuddered. *The other wearing the parka must be an avian.* One small bird sat on top of her head. The arms of the parka were too long, extending past her hands by several inches, yet the bottom was cut short, revealing her long legs. Shireen shook her head at that.

Another girl wearing western stonecutter apparel similar to Lithia's was standing nearby, listening to the creature-kind girls' conversation too. Shireen stepped back so the stonecutter wouldn't catch her watching.

"He won't ruin anything. I'm taking care of this." Birds fluttered around the avian girl's head.

Felicia flared her nostrils. "I don't understand. Don't the birds push their young out of the nest? Why are you coddling him? Jeneth said he was ready. It's his son."

"I'm not coddling him. He entered the trials. Don't ruffle your feathers over him."

"I don't have feathers," she sneered. "And now?"

"And now I'll take care of him." The girl with the bird on top of her head didn't sound so sure.

Felicia turned to her cougar and hissed. "Wait! What's this? A spy?"

A shot of fear ran through Shireen.

Two cougars leaped towards the stonecutter. She stepped out from behind the building, extending her hand in a wave. "Hello, I'm Onyx. Sorry, you caught me watching you. I've never met creature-kind before. I was interested. I couldn't help myself."

Felicia's cats growled as she stared at the apprentice's open hand. "And what did you hear?"

Shireen shrank back further. She held her breath, afraid to make a sound.

"Nothing. I was just watching you two." Onyx shrugged. "I was too far away to hear anything."

Felicia snarled then stomped into the large round building. Her cougar growled, then the cats ran after Felicia.

Onyx, the female stonecutter, quickly followed them in.

Shireen waited for the girl with the birds to go, but she only stood there. The girl with the birds didn't seem as threatening as the one with the cats—Felicia, the feline's name was. At least, this one had her big bird on her shoulder and wasn't sending big cats to sneak behind people and sniff their backsides.

Shireen popped out from behind the building, pretending she had been walking by and not standing there. The avian-girl turned and went into the building when she saw Shireen approaching.

Shireen followed her in. She went through the large double doors, past two trolls in a lobby area and into a room nearly the size of the entire building. Birds flew above. The ceiling had to be at least thirty feet high. The room was round, like the rest of the building, and chairs were arranged in a circle, facing the center of the room.

The room was already mostly full and the shock of finding so many different apprentices wearing so many different styles of clothing grabbed her. *I made it,* Shireen thought in exultation. Tundric apprentices wearing thick white felt and stonecutters from the east and west were present. It was easy for Shireen to distinguish them for she grew up not far from the lands of the western stonecutters and they often visited her village. People from the desert lands wearing long pale, tan robes and the forest people with their green camouflage of branches and leaves were mixed in.

Lithia was along the back and to the left so Shireen made her way over to her. Seated next to her was Pren, wearing the tan robes of the Sanhardin. Shireen smiled wide. *At least, I know two people here.*

She grabbed the seat between them and gave Pren a kiss on both cheeks. Shireen pulled back and wiped her face.

"Sorry," Pren said smiling. "It's the sand. Gets everywhere."

Lithia introduced the girl seated next to her, "Shireen, this is my friend Onyx. She's a stonecutter from my lands. Apprentice to Master Petra. She's been here before."

"Pleasure to meet you," Shireen said, shaking her hand. She peered at her oddly, wanting to discern if Onyx was aware Shireen was spying on the two creature-kind too. Onyx, by her demeanor, had never laid eyes on Shireen before.

"Aye, greetings from the land of the western stonecutters. Your accent, faintly sounds of the west?"

"I grew up in Twern," Shireen said.

"Not far from our mountains."

Shireen wanted to ask Onyx what she thought about the two creature-kind girls arguing, but didn't know how she would take Shireen saying she saw her spying. Stonecutters were always a little edgy about things like that.

"Excuse me a moment," Lithia said as she stood. "I need to give something to someone." She stepped around them with a large brown envelope in her hand.

Leaning closer to Pren, Shireen said, "Live in the desert or near the city? Tell me everything. How is your training? Your master?" She asked and at the same time gaped at all the other apprentices. There had to be, at least, twenty-five, maybe even thirty. The ones around her she didn't recognize. Those on the far side of the room she wasn't sure about, for her view was blocked.

"I'm in the desert, in Ragul. It's the only city we are blessed with. The Bedouin are the only desert people who don't live near the city and the Bedouin boast no magicians. Master Samira is my teacher, mentor, and friend. I'm learning the ways of sand from her," Pren said as her eyes followed Lithia.

Lithia stepped to the center of the room and up to a large man wearing the white felt of the Tundric people, his heavy shirt draped open exposing a thick, bare chest.

"I'm in the Greenlands. Not far from here. In Sha'mont, with Master Meetta Eglin," Shireen said as her eyes watched Lithia.

Pren frowned. "Wait. Sha'mont? With the dragon?"

Lithia mumbled a few words to the thick-chested man and handed him the package. He took the brown envelope and opened it as Lithia walked away.

Shireen said, "Yes, I almost died. Terrifying experience." She moved her head around, then spied someone she recognized, a teenager from University that graduated a year before her, Naga. He was Tundric. Then she caught sight of another she knew, Drake. He was a forest mage, like herself. He graduated University a few years before her. Drake was friendly to Naga and Bel, Shireen remembered.

"After the meeting, you must tell us every single detail. Everything." Pren scooted up so Lithia could pass by and take her seat.

Other apprentices were still filing into the building.

"What was that all about?" Pren asked.

Lithia said, "Master Jergamemnon is from our village. He was returning to Lasaat, so he escorted me to the edge of the forest. He asked me to deliver that package to Aquilo."

"Aquilo?" Shireen repeated. "Who is he? A wizard?"

Pren answered, "No, there are no wizards here. Only apprentices. The wizards at Lasaat are too lazy, ahem, I mean too busy for this." She chuckled.

Onyx added, "Worthys run the trials. Aquilo is one of them. He was here last year too."

Everyone silenced themselves when a tremendous growl shuddered through the room.

Two cougars paced into the space followed by a tall man wearing a spotted cloak and another woman dressed much like Pren in the long robes of the desert people.

There was a decidedly raw, feline quality to the way the man sauntered in, like a lion ready to pounce, his body relaxed, yet coiled, prepared to spring at the slightest sound. His frame was lean and muscular and Shireen couldn't help but notice his brawny chest and chiseled stomach. He wore the cloak of a leopard skin slung over his right shoulder, a small cloth about his waist to cover his private parts and not much more.

He was a stark contrast to the Sanhardin girl, in her long robes of thick fabric. Burlap, Shireen thought. Itchy. She was covered from head to toe.

Shireen leaned to the side in her chair and whispered, "Who's that?"

Pren said, "The one with the cats is Felix. Sammra is the other. She's tough but fair. She's from Ragul."

Felix strode behind his cats to the center of the room. All eyes were on him and those who hadn't yet taken their seats quickly sat down.

"Tss," he hissed and his two cougars growled loudly. The room was instantly silent.

Felix smiled. "I greet you in the hospitality and graciousness of my kind and extend a good welcome from the wizards of Lasaat to you, young apprentices and candidates for the Worthy Apprentice Trials. My name is Felix. I am a worthy apprentice and have aided in running these trials for four seasons now." He opened his palm toward Sammra and Aquilo. "This is Sammra, from Ragul, a worthy apprentice and student of the magic taught in the desert lands of the Sanhardin, apprentice to Master Zizu."

Sammra raised her hand and turned in a circle so all could get a good look at her. Shireen's eyes fell to the jeweled necklace around Sammra's neck, simple yet elegant.

Felix continued, "And Aquilo, from the frigid north, the fierce Tundric lands, apprentice to Master Jessark. You'll find him sweating about here and there, unable to keep himself cool in this blistering heat, as he aids in running these trials."

The crowd chuckled.

"Aquilo has assisted in the worthy trials for several more years than me, but has granted me the honor of being lead this year."

One of Felix's cats yawned wide so he tilted his hand at them. The two laid down on the floor and placed their chins on their paws and closed their eyes.

The rear door opened and three more apprentices entered. Shireen's face lit up. One of them was Bel. She wiped her hand across her mouth, making sure she wasn't smiling too wide. She didn't want to appear excited. Shireen quickly glanced at Onyx, Pren, and Lithia, making sure they hadn't noticed her smile, then thought she was being stupid. Of course, she should be happy he passed. That's what a friend would do. She let herself smile again, but her grin was muted.

Felix waited for the three to find seats.

Bel found one near the back, sitting next to the avian-girl that argued with Felicia outside. He immediately began eyeballing the crowd for friends.

Felix continued, "Fine, good. Glad you made it and welcome, new arrivals. We've just begun so you haven't missed much."

He turned and pointed at the ceiling. "What led you

here was the moonstone. We are excited to hold such a jewel. Those of you who've been here before know each year, to recognize the importance of these trials and give honor to those who pass them, a different, powerful, magical object is suspended above this hallowed hall. This year, the western stonecutters have graciously supplied the moonstone, an object of immense power. Many magicians lost their lives in obtaining the stone, but that is a story for another day." Felix restored his arm at his side. "Let its light be a reminder to you of the gravity and importance of these trials. Your masters and the wizards of Lasaat expect nothing less than excellence."

"Wait. Didn't we already—" Shireen began to whisper when someone in front of her shushed her.

Felix motioned to Sammra. She said, "What happens next? For those of you attending for the first time and thought you had already passed the trials by accomplishing the tasks in the forest and arriving in this building—sorry."

Felix, Aquilo, and Sammra chuckled and were joined by many of the others in the room who were apparently in on the joke.

Heat fired up from Shireen's collar and her cheeks flush red.

Aquilo spoke next, "The tests you went through to get here were merely an entrance test, a verification. We don't have the time or patience to put apprentices through the trials who cannot pass the simplest of tests so we established them to weed out those who couldn't possibly be ready."

"And for safety," Felix added. "Unlike the visions in the forest, the trials which you all will go through in the next days and weeks are real. You may be injured if you are not careful. You'll not have your masters protecting you. Each one of you will be responsible for your own conduct and safety and no one will be there to stop you from getting yourself injured or—"

Sammra tugged Felix's elbow, stopping him.

"Right," Felix said. "So watch yourselves and above all, be safe in what you do."

Aquilo added, "I don't want to have to clean up body parts like last year."

Sammra frowned at Aquilo and stepped forward. "The trials are yet to come in the following days. They are of escalating difficulty. They are dangerous and people can most certainly die or become mentally or physically wounded as my fellow worthy apprentices so aptly warned you. But here and now, we don't want to fill your minds with fear. We're here to give you a general outline of what is to come."

Felix smiled at her and nodded. "The trials are six. Each one designed to test a different attribute, a wizardly quality deemed of value by Lasaat. We cannot tell you what you will face or in what order the trails will come. A wizard often receives no warning when his metal is tested."

"Or hers," Sammra added.

Aquilo continued the introduction, "You will go through tests to check your physical strength, magical power, and decision making—wisdom if you will."

Sammra added, "Your courage and stamina will be tried. In these trials, you will come under extreme physical stresses and be exposed to your worst nightmares. And to those who overcome will be granted one of the highest honors in all the lands, the title of

Worthy Apprentice. You will be one step closer to becoming a wizard."

Shireen's hand trembled under her legs. She had learned how to read people. She could do a few other spells, the common ones everyone learned at Lasaat. Was she ready? She certainly didn't feel ready. Her worst fears? She wondered what they were. Losing Bel? Losing her master like she lost her mother and Mama Engresa? Being alone? Her chest tightened. She didn't want to be here, in this hall, listening to these people tell her about what she was going to face. She had run from her mother's death. She had fled from Mama Engresa's too. She still hadn't decided how she was going to face Bel when the time came to finally leave him. Nausea blanketed her stomach.

"Few pass all the trials." Felix's face was even and stiff. "If the worthy trials were easy, there would be no honor and recognition." He nodded to himself. "For those of you who are new here, when a trial is not passed, you will be collected by the trolls and escorted out of the wood."

Aquilo said, "First-timers, keep your wits about you. If you do not pass, there is always next year."

Sammra spoke next. "The trolls provide the security around the perimeter, but this camp doesn't run itself, so when you are not in the trials, there's work to be done. Each of you will be assigned duties each day, cooking, cleaning and other such things. This, in a way, is part of the trials too and we expect your diligence."

"Excellent," Pren mumbled. "I came here to clean."

Lithia shrugged her shoulders. "What else is new. Apprentice. Servant. Slave. Same thing."

Shireen stared at her fingernails, clean and

manicured. She would need to trim them. She didn't want to appear a princess. She understood what hard work was, she had been raised a farm girl. Yet she hadn't broken a nail in Dragon's Castle because Thrashel, the king, wouldn't allow his advisers to do menial labor. They needed to keep up the appearance of being equal with royalty. Shireen was actually eager to get her hands on a frying pan, dice some vegetables and cook. She loved to cook.

Felix continued, "During the days when no trial is scheduled, there will be a time of sharing, a time to engage in an open and public discussion. This is an important part of these trials and we expect everyone to pay attention and to participate in them. These trials are not only for the purpose of approving who is ready, but also to form and tighten bonds between the wizards of the nine forms. The wizards of Lasaat, when they created these trials so many years ago, deemed that one of the most vital aspects of this gathering would be sharing, groups from distant lands coming together and learning from each other, gaining knowledge and understanding of each kind, fostering tolerance, perhaps even to forming friendships."

Aquilo continued, "During the sharing, apprentices can either ask questions or share stories of their lands and their experiences, publicly, with the others. Everyone is expected to share and participate. I want to point out there are a few here who recently had a run-in with a dragon. Where are they?"

The crowd murmured.

Shireen's throat tightened as she spied Bel.

"I was told by the trolls they had passed through the forest. Master Nes'egrinon and Master Meetta's apprentices? If you are here, please stand."

Bel and Shireen stood slowly, looking at each other, then at Aquilo.

"Welcome. Yes, Bel. We met on the outside. Shireen, welcome first-timer. Some days ago, a dragon attacked Sha'mont and these two had the unlucky opportunity to fight the beast. I, for one, am eager to listen to this story from each of you. No one has seen a dragon in several generations so I am sure the memory will be a fine one to share in."

He nodded at the two and they sat back down. Shireen's throat was still tight, her back cramped. *What did he mean by 'share the memory'?* She hoped he didn't mean they were expected to connect minds. No way was she letting anyone in her head.

Felix added, "Also, as everyone has noticed, this is a unique year as creature-kind are attending the trials of the worthy apprentice for the first time in the history of the trials. The trials were originally designed as a way to bring the nine forms together, however up until now they were only attended by the four northern forms, the so-called landers. I am sure many of you from the north, whether from the forest, desert, the lands of ice and snow or the mountains of stone, may be apprehensive at seeing animals about. Rest assured the avians and felines are here to foster bonds and relationships too, a vital first step to a continued and long-lasting peace between all our kinds. I can only hope in the future the other creature-kind will also join us."

There was a space of silence as the three worthy apprentices scanned the room.

Sammra spoke, "Lastly, we wish to recognize any here who are in their first year of their apprenticeship. Please stand."

Bel slowly stood, expecting others to stand, but he was the only one.

Felix mumbled, "A dragonslayer and a First-Year too?"

Bel nodded, eyes wide as if he had done something wrong. "I'm not a dragonslayer."

Felix encouraged, "A rare thing for a master to send a First-Year. Even rarer for a First-Year to advance through the entrance tests. And even rarer for one to pass the trials."

Aquilo added, "The last to pass the worthy trials as a First-Year was you, Sammra, I believe?"

She nodded.

"Ahh, excuse me? He's not a First-Year," a voice from the other side of the room called out.

Everyone turned towards the one who spoke. Shireen recognized him immediately. *Kerlith.* She squeezed back the bile rushing into her throat.

"I'm just saying," Kerlith added. "He was held back a year at Lasaat. He's supposed to be in his second year. So he's not—"

Felix clipped his words in the air. "What's your name?"

"Kerlith," he said. "Formerly of the Hinterlands, on the edge of the eastern stone lands."

Bel sat down.

Felix's eyes barreled into Kerlith so he leaned back into his chair.

"The day is late and many of you traveled a distance." Felix shook the grimace off his face and smiled. "My cats are exhausted." He pointed at the sleeping cougars. Several of the girls in the front row giggled for Felix was attractive. Shireen rolled her eyes.

"So for tonight, find yourselves a bunk room. Some of you already have. There are four to a room. Males and females separate, obviously. After you're settled in, you can grab a bite to eat at the feed tent. You'll be eating what the trolls prepared tonight. You'll do well to not let the trolls hear any complaining about their cooking and to clean your plates. If the trolls discover you throwing away their food, they'll become agitated and that's not a pretty sight. Turn in early and rest well from your long journey."

The apprentices began to shuffle their feet, gathering their belongs when Aquilo held up his hand and said, "One moment, please." He dodged up the aisle to a troll who was standing in the doorway.

The troll spoke to Aquilo in a language Shireen couldn't come close to understanding.

Aquilo returned to the center and whispered to Felix. Consternation grabbed the feline's face. "I understand," he said.

Aquilo addressed the crowd. "As I've only now been informed, an apprentice is missing. He entered the forest but hasn't yet arrived and the trolls are searching for him."

Felix eyed the avian-girl sitting next to Bel. "He's young, only about this tall." He held his hand to his chest. "He's an avian. His name is Jonah. If any of you know of his whereabouts or caught sight of him, please speak to me immediately."

The room was quiet. Shireen locked her eyes on the girl seated next to Bel. The avian seemed upset.

Shireen wondered if this had anything to do with what the avian and Felicia were discussing before they entered. She listened to them arguing out of curiosity but she couldn't exactly remember everything they said. It was the first time Shireen laid eyes on a feline-kind or an avian outside of Sturfelis and Jeneth at Lasaat.

She scanned the room, quickly finding Felicia. There was a wide space of empty chairs around her. Apparently no one wanted to come close to her big cats. She was stoking a bobcat's neck sitting on her lap. Felicia gave the smallest glance to the avian and squinted at her in disapproval.

Shireen tried to remember what Felicia had said. Something about coddling someone who shouldn't have come? Jeneth's son? *Jeneth's an avian.* Shireen tightened her eyes slightly. *They must have been talking about this missing boy. Something happened to him and they know and are not saying.*

"If no one has any information you are all dismissed to find your huts," Felix said.

Everyone stood and collected their things. The room was quickly filled with conversations of old friends who hadn't seen each other in a long time.

As Lithia, Pren and Shireen followed the others to the exit doors, Aquilo intercepted them.

"What's this?" he said to Lithia, shaking the package at her.

Lithia said, "Master Jergamemnon gave the envelope to me to give to you. Like I said."

"Are you sure?" his voice was tight and hard. "Did you open the package? Is there any chance someone else came into contact with it?"

Her voice shook. "Yes, absolutely certain. He escorted me to the entrance. He gave the envelope to me there. Sealed. The package never left my person. I promise. I hand delivered it to you, like he asked."

Aquilo stepped away, flaring his nostrils.

Pren mumbled, "What's his problem?"

Shireen put her arm around Lithia and tugged her. "Don't let him bother you. He's Tundric. You remember how they are. Too much ice on the brain."

Chapter Five
Girls And Boys

Bel took a deep breath before he reached Shireen and the others. "Lithia, Pren, good to see you."

Pren hugged him and kissed both of his cheeks. "Blessings. Blessings."

"Thanks, Pren. You too."

Lithia smiled as she squeezed him so hard he thought he felt some of his life-force squeeze out. "Hey Bel, how was that extra year at University? Sweet of Kerlith to bring that up."

Bel shrugged, "Doesn't bother me. I don't deny I was held back. Not sure what his problem is, though." He bumped his shoulder into Shireen intentionally throwing her slightly off balance, and smiled wide. "Shireen, glad you got in." He hoped the gesture would be taken by Pren and Lithia as something two friends might do.

"You too," Shireen said.

Lithia introduced her friend Onyx to Bel.

Pren added, "Kerlith's an idiot. That's his problem."

Naga walked up to the group, "Greetings all, my flesh stands before you and is exceedingly glad."

Pren greeted him by kissing his cheeks. Lithia, Onyx, and Shireen hugged him. Bel slapped his hand on his elbow in the traditional Tundric greeting.

Drake walked up next. "Hey all, welcome to the trials."

Bel and Naga slapped hands with the forest apprentice.

"Hey Drake, how goes?" Bel said.

The girls hugged and kissed him.

Another apprentice near the door yelled out, "Hey Drake, come on!"

Drake said to the group, "Third attempt at the trials for me. I'm optimistic this time. Been practicing all year. Anyway, only wanted to say hello and wish you all good luck. See you around." He ran after his friend.

The girls collected their things as Shireen asked, "So what's the story with those three, Felix and... what was his name? Aquilo? And the girl?"

They trudged near the back of the crowd, exiting the building. Pren answered, "Sammra, she's a worthy apprentice of the Sanhardin. She lives in Ragul, our only city. She has extraordinary ability and can form practically anything out of sand." There was awe in her voice.

Lithia complimented, "You're good too. I've seen what you can do."

Pren clarified, "All sand-mages can form things out of sand. Besides seeking water, that's what we do most. Can I? Sure. Small things. But her? I've watched her create enormous objects, things I couldn't begin to describe."

"Sounds like she's powerful," Shireen muttered, staring at her feet.

"She is. Master Zizu has taught her well," Pren agreed.

The group shuffled outside. They followed the crowd towards the small four-person huts. Drake was out in front of one hut with two other apprentices, the three looking for a fourth friend.

Onyx said, "I've already got my bunk and my roommates from last year. See you at meal?"

The group nodded and Onyx walked off. They put their stuff on the ground and scanned their eyes about, studying the hustle and bustle of apprentices looking for old bunkmates and jogging from hut to hut.

Naga said, "Aquilo is of ability also. He's from much farther north than I, but we hear the tales of the work of his hands and I've glimpsed his control of snow and ice. Not long ago, during the times of darkness, when the life-giving sun hid her warming face and the Tundra lands were lost to eternal night, the west wind began to blow. Master K'eyush, my master, was out with a group on expedition and I was the lone magic user in the village. I sensed death in the breath of the wind, so I spoke with the elders and we all gathered in the deepest and warmest of huts. The wind, sleet, and snow blustered and flew, pummeling us like hammers swung by angry frost giants. The buildings shook and as I stand in my flesh, I am not embarrassed to reveal my trepidation. I cowered."

The others stared at him in rapt attention.

"When the door shook, we knew not what to expect. To our amazement, the door opened and there stood Aquilo. When I went to him, his hand was outstretched behind him and an amazing white light streamed from his palm, placing a barrier between us and the savage storm. He saved our village."

"He controlled the weather?" Shireen quizzed in disbelief. When Naga nodded, Shireen said, "I'm doomed. I'll never pass the trials."

Lithia slung her arm around her shoulder. "It's not so bad. Don't worry. Pren, Naga and I were all here last year. Pren and I didn't advance past the first trial. Naga, how far did you go?"

"The second," he said.

Lithia humored, "You'll do fine. No one passes the first time anyway. All these apprentices around us? They've probably been here four, five, six times at least."

"Thanks, girls," Shireen said. "Thanks for trying to make me feel better."

Pren smiled wide and chuckled, "Now let me tell you about Felix. Isn't he adorable?"

"Those girls in the front row seemed to think so," Lithia added.

Pren nodded. "Felix has been an apprentice for, I'm guessing, probably, at least, ten years. He's been running the Worthy Trials for six—anyway, he's the only one here to take the Wizard Trials, but he didn't pass the first time."

Bel asked, "How is one of the creature-kind running the trials? You know, not that I have a problem, but doesn't it seem odd?" A vision of the night Valerius died flashed into Bel's mind. They were surrounded by leopards, pushing their horses hard and fast. A leopard—controlled by someone like Felix—ripped Valerius's neck, killing him instantly. Three men died, all at the hands of feline wizards. He shuddered.

Naga said, "Sturfelis probably lobbied. They're from the same village."

Lithia pointed out, "I was terrified when I first saw him last year. Well, not of him, but his big cats. Cougars, I think? But he's professional. Approachable too."

"You approached him?" Pren jabbed Lithia in her

side. "When? You didn't tell me?"

"I didn't. I wanted to talk to him, but I wasn't here long enough to get the chance."

Bel tried to change the subject away from fawning over the lead apprentice. "Felix said he was interested in improving relations between the creature-kind and landers. I bet he had something to do with them sending their apprentices to the trials."

They all nodded.

Pren scowled. "That's the only thing strange about Sammra. She distrusts the creature-kind, all except Felix. In the lands of the Sanhardin, they cast a wary eye at the creature-kind and I think she is much in agreement. However, she speaks highly of Felix."

Kerlith spoke from behind them. "I don't trust any of the creature-kind. None of them. Felix? He's no better than Jeneth or Sturfelis were at University. What did they ever teach? Nothing. They're there to spy and ferret out our weaknesses. Felix is a spy too. What else could he be?"

Shireen nipped at him, "Thanks for your opinion. You can keep walking now."

Bel caught himself staring at Shireen and forced his eyes to look away. He kept finding himself lost in the blue swirl of her eyes. He hadn't mentioned it to her yet, but they had changed. Ever since she touched the roc's eye, they had developed a slight swirl of translucent blue.

Naga added, "Move along, *Former-Apprentice-Of-The-Eastern-Stonecutters*."

Kerlith pinched his face at him then said to Lithia, "You need to learn to stick with your kind." He spun and walked away.

Lithia rubbed her stone as she said, "Not all

stonecutters hate the creature-kind, but those that do are the loudest. Unfortunate."

Shireen chided, "Naga, can't keep your eyes in your head."

Naga was staring at the avian girl that Bel was forced to sit next to in the introduction. He said, "Ahh, her name is Leonna. I overheard Felix speaking with her earlier."

Leonna walked across the space. To Bel, she was beautiful, of course—no one could deny that. Yet, there was something else that drew his eyes to her, something peculiar. Long raven-black hair bordered her pretty face. Her outfit stopped at the top of her thighs exposing her long, thin legs. Her skin was the palest white. Landers were not accustomed to seeing people who exposed so much skin. Between Leonna and her long bare legs, Felix wearing only a breach cloth and Felicia with her three scraps of animal skin hanging across her breasts and crotch, the creature-kind were practically naked. *No wonder Naga was staring*, Bel thought.

Bel checked himself. He appreciated Leonna's beauty, true, but she carried no allure for him. His heart had already been captured. His love was owned, wholly and completely, by the young girl that stood off to his left, a girl he couldn't acknowledge or even look at for even more than a few moments at a time. His hand twitched so he stepped a little farther away from Shireen, not trusting himself. Still, he too could not stop staring at Leonna. There was something about her, something odd that drew his eyes, a puzzle. He shook his head, hoping Shireen hadn't noticed his eyes lingering on Leonna, then said, "Naga, I didn't notice anyone go into that hut over there. Want to go check?" He glanced over at Shireen and noted a puzzled look on her face before she quickly looked away.

"My flesh walks with you," Naga said as he picked up his bag.

"Catch you at meal, ladies," Bel said as he walked away.

Naga bowed to the three then followed Bel.

The two walked towards their newfound hut.

*****

Sammra came up behind the girls. "Let's move, ladies." She pointed at a hut. "If you want to stay together, that's the last hut with three open bunks. I could split you up, but then one of you goes in with the feline. Do any of you mind sleeping in the same room with the cats?"

"Ahh, we'll take the one with three bunks," Shireen said.

Shireen, Pren, and Lithia walked into the room Sammra had pointed out. When they entered, Leonna was arranging her cages. She glanced at them as they stepped in.

Pren said first. "I guess we're rooming together?" She went to her immediately, grabbed her shoulders and kissed her on each cheek.

Leonna stared back at her wide-eyed. Her tiny finches leaped and flew in circles around the room.

Pren explained, "The greeting of my people." A finch landed on Pren's head.

"Tweetnone, get off her. She doesn't know you like that." The bird flew off, placing himself on Leonna's head and lightly pecked her forehead.

The stone apprentice giggled. "I'm Lithia. I hail from the land of the western stonecutters. Your birds are cute."

Leonna glanced back at her two cloaked cages then waved her hand up at the tiny finches. "These ones are. Not too useful but they're my friends. Had them since I was a hatchling."

"Shireen." Saying her name Shireen stepped forward, extending her hand. "It's a pleasure to meet you."

As Leonna shook her hand, a puzzled look washed across her face. She released Shireen's hand and said, "You don't need to be afraid of me."

Shireen said, "I-I'm not. Just nervous. About the trials and all. It's my first time here."

Leonna pursed her lips and said nothing. Shireen set her pack on the farthest bunk and Pren and Lithia began putting their things away. Everyone was silent and the room grew uncomfortable. Shireen was unsure how to handle the situation. She figured this girl probably wasn't with the other avians at Sha'mont. She hoped she wasn't anyway. Shireen figured she would convince herself Leonna wasn't one of them. She had to. It would be the only way she would get any sleep at night.

"If I make you all nervous, I could find another room." Leonna exhaled.

Pren hopped up and went to her, touching her arm, "No, please don't leave. That wouldn't be right. A shame. A shame. Please stay." She gazed back at Lithia and Shireen, her eyes pleading.

Shireen understood Pren's reaction for she had read much about the Sanhardin people in Master Meetta's books. They didn't have much for possessions so they measured their self-worth in honorable deeds. To them, there was nothing worse than doing something that brought shame to one's name.

Shireen added, "Please Leonna. Don't leave because of me. When you shook my hand, you sensed my discomfort. I had a bad experience with the creature-kind once before. I'm a little apprehensive. I'm sorry. It's not your fault. I want you to stay."

Pren smiled at Shireen then turned to Leonna, her eyes hopeful.

"Okay," Leonna answered, which made Pren tremendously happy. A few of Leonna's birds flew down from the rafters and quickly spun in a circle around her head.

Lithia shrugged her shoulders at Shireen as if she didn't understand what was the big deal. "You, I can handle. The girl with the cougars and bobcats? I'm sorry to say I don't think I could sleep in the same room with felines."

Leonna chuckled as she sat on her bed. "I feel the same way."

"Birds good. Cats bad," Pren said.

"Felicia's not that bad," Leonna said as she stared down at her bed. "She and I never got along, but I understand her. We come from nearby clan-families who are not always friendly."

Shireen interrupted, fascinated, "Clan-families?"

Leonna nodded without explaining.

Lithia explained, "Felix spoke about this last year. In the lands of the creature-kind, groups of wizards live together. It's not like what we do, one wizard with one apprentice. They have a clan."

Leonna nodded. "We don't have *lands*, like you do. We don't think of ourselves that way, but yes, that is how we live."

Pren smiled and stepped closer to Leonna. "I'm from the desert, to the north and the east of where you dwell. In my land, one wizard trains one apprentice, but since we occupy only one city, Ragul, where almost everyone lives, I often meet other wizards and their apprentices. I speak with them when I get the chance. Sometimes we travel together into the desert. I only learn from my master, but the apprentices, we talk. It is only natural. It is good to share."

Shireen began unpacking her meager belongings. "I guess it's different everywhere. For Lithia and me, the lands are vast. There are not many wizards of forest and stone so we spread ourselves thin to cover as many villages as possible, to help the people. My master and I are the only ones in Sha'mont, the largest city in the Greenlands."

Pren popped up. "You were supposed to tell me. The dragon? The war? What happened? You almost died?"

Shireen stopped arranging her things, sat on her bunk and considered the three of them. Telling this story was going to be difficult. She hoped she could keep her emotions under control. "So, as I said before, I live in the capital city of the Greenlands. The king of Yagoos, Seol, sent his armies to lay siege. Men were fighting and dying and it was terrible. The crops were set ablaze and many died. I lost—" Her voice caught. *Mama Engresa.*

"I'm so sorry, Shireen. You lost someone? You don't need to continue," Pren said as she stood and walked to Shireen.

Shireen considered leaving it at that but decided to push through the story quickly. She held up her hands. "No, I'm fine. It's something I need to learn to deal with. I'll give you the short version. For now." She let her breath out. "In Sha'mont, the name of the castle is Dragon's Castle, so named for a battle between a roc and a dragon many, many years ago. When the roc defeated the dragon, everyone believed the dragon had fled. Unfortunately, the dragon didn't leave but was enchanted and taken prisoner by the magic of the roc. No one knew, for the magic was powerful and cloaked the creature. I still can't believe it. A dragon was lying at the center of the castle, for decades, and no one knew it was there. Incredible."

"I see. That's where the dragon came from," Lithia contemplated. "And the beast was somehow set free? And began to destroy?"

"Yes," Shireen said, holding a strained smile on her face.

"How did you rid yourself of the dragon?" Pren asked.

"I didn't. I was only trying to stay alive," She lied. There was no way she was telling them she almost gave herself to the dragon's hot fire. "Master Nes'egrinon, Bel's master, did it. He was severely injured in the battle. Bel's still upset. His master may yet die. He was bedridden when we left, bandaged and bleeding. Magic doesn't seem to help him heal faster for some reason. My master is caring for him."

"So this Nes'egrinon was your king?" Leonna asked.

"No," Shireen said. "He was there to help. He's from the southern forest. Bel traveled with him at the request of King Thrashel."

Leonna shook her head as if she was still confused. "But your king, he is a wizard?"

"Thrashel? No, just a man. A short, little, fat man."

"It is true then what I've heard," Leonna muttered.

"What's that?" Shireen asked, wondering if Leonna was going to mention the avians' presence at Sha'mont.

"You said your master is the only wizard in Sha'mont yet she does not rule. You allow people of no magical ability to lord over you."

Pren said, "It is our way. Wizards are to serve the people, not to rule. We are a royal priesthood. Great power corrupts greatly, so we submit ourselves to servitude of the neediest."

Shireen added, "We advise the kings and courts. But rule? No, in the histories that ended badly last time."

Leonna pressed her lips together and searched the faces of the three, one by one, then looked down.

Shireen wished to move the subject away from her before any more probing questions were asked about the roc, the roc's eye or the avians. She didn't feel comfortable speaking about any of that in front of Leonna for she had no idea what this avian knew. It was possible, probably even, that Leonna was in Sha'mont when the roc's eye was seized. "Pren, what about your last two years?" She tried to pump excitement into her voice.

"What's to tell? I spend almost all my time in the desert, using magic to find sources of water and then channeling it once I've found it. I've gotten extremely good at seeking moisture. Two years of doing not much else and you would get good at it too. Manipulating water, less so. There just isn't much to practice with. Ahh, searching for water, it's almost all Master Samira and I do. To tell you the truth, I doubt I'm going to do well at these trials. They won't be testing my ability to locate sources of water." Pren smiled. "When we're bored, we practice making things out of sand. Sometimes the apprentices gather in Ragul and we have little competitions, for fun. Here, I'll show you." Pren grabbed a satchel at her waist and tossed the contents in the air. Sand sprayed everywhere. She opened her palm in front of her and began twisting her fingers. The particles stopped in the air and rushed towards her hand, hovering above her palm in a small cloud. They swirled then formed a circular structure. Stone walls and other details slowly emerged, towers and minarets, buildings and even tiny people. "This is Ragul."

Lithia came closer. "Can you make anything?"

"Anything? It takes much practice." Pren squeezed her eyes shut for a moment. The sand shifted and swirled then coalesced into a rose.

Tweetnone hovered in front of the flower and stuck his beak in. He pulled it out and shook then returned to his perch on Leonna's head. "Tweetnone, there's no nectar there for you," Leonna said.

The four laughed.

Pren held open her bag and the sand dove in. She sealed her pouch. "Lithia, how about you?"

"Stonecutters are notoriously distrustful of everyone. Master Sperlith and I spend a lot of time discerning the truth in local disputes. Discernment, powerful magic. We travel from village to village and there's usually a line of people waiting, accusing each other of this or that. One is accused of stealing a goat. Another, damaging property. Endless squabbling."

Shireen smiled. "Discernment. I have learned that from my master too. And more than that, reading minds, studying thoughts and emotions."

Pren whispered, leaning forward, "You two learned the same magic?"

Lithia looked at the doorway as if someone might be

listening. "The ban. It's ridiculous, isn't it?"

"I've read the histories..." Shireen choked off her words. The three turned their heads. She felt like they were staring at her. She cleared her throat then continued, "It was not always so. Long ago, in the northern lands, one wizard trained one apprentice, like today, yet there was no ban. There was no rule to prevent a wizard from learning the magic of others."

Pren asked, "But there are different forms. How is that possible?"

Shireen paused for some moments, unsure if she should speak openly about such things, especially in front of an avian. She chose her words carefully. "Distance, I suppose. There just weren't that many people back then. Fewer villages and much further apart. The Tundric magic developed in the Tundric lands because that was the type of magic they needed in a land of ice, snow, and perpetual winter. In the forest, people learned to talk to trees. In the desert, people learned to use magic to search for water. Kind of obvious when you think about it."

"And the ban?" Leonna asked.

Shireen's eyes darted to the door. "I don't know if..."

Lithia said, "It was in the histories. You said it. If it happened and it is truth then what is the harm in speaking it?"

"A history some would like to stay buried. Okay, I guess I will tell you. It was established by the kings. I know when but don't exactly know why. It seemed to coincide with the rise of the city-states, Sha'mont, Ragul, Kandool and others. The kingdoms expanded and—I'm not sure why, nationalism maybe?—but laws were passed restricting the exchange of information between kingdoms—that's how it started anyway. Fear. It seemed the kings mistrusted wizards most so the most restrictive laws were placed on them... on us."

"Idiots," Lithia said.

Pren said, "No, Lithia. Don't say that. It's the law."

Lithia rotated toward Pren. "Wouldn't you want to learn the magic of another land? It could help you to, help you to help your people. What's the harm in that?"

"Yes. No. I don't know. I mean, I would like to learn but I don't know how I would feel about others learning my—"

The three stared at Pren as she adjusted the fabric of her long flowing robes. "It's selfish, I know, but I feel like, I don't know... special, like I'm a part of something. And it's the law, anyway."

The four grew somber. Shireen wondered what Leonna thought of all of this and why she sat there, her face emotionless, her eyes popping from one to the other, observing them like a bird looking for a bug to peck and eat. Then Pren asked, "Still, your two masters know the same magic, Discernment? Whose is it? Is Discernment stone-magic and Shireen's master breaks the law or is it forest-magic—"

Shireen interrupted, "Pren, magic belongs to all of us."

The three sat silent for some moments more, then Shireen made an attempt at changing the subject. "No matter. I won't be here long. Discernment alone is not going to help me pass the trials."

Lithia chuckled. "I spend a lot of time serving my master, cooking, and cleaning." She tilted her head to Pren. "Do you think they'll be testing my ability to scrub pots and pans? If so, I'll make Worthy, no problem."

"At least, your magic will be stronger here," Leonna mumbled, then a look of surprise flashed across her face as if she said something out of place.

"You're right," Lithia confirmed. "The moonstone. It's such a powerful element for us stone mages. Just being near the crystal gives me power. But will that be enough?"

"You'll be fine." Shireen's voice was shallow and unconvincing. She was in the same position as Pren and Lithia, but that made her feel no better. They would all fail.

"And you, Shireen? And Bel?" Pren stood, smiling and walking towards her bunk. "You two were an item at University before you took the vow. Lithia and I noticed. We couldn't speak openly, of course. We had a friendly wager. I thought you two would leave magic."

"I think your eyes were playing tricks. There wasn't anything between us."

"That's not what I saw. And I'm sure we weren't the only ones. You two, always in each other's heads. And his face? Rapt ecstasy."

Shireen's jaw clenched tight. She forced herself to smile and shake her head in disagreement.

Lithia added, "Discernment, Shireen. Remember? Don't lie. You had him in your web, you little spider. So what happened? Must have been difficult when he came to Sha'mont."

"There was nothing between us." Her eyes darted between Pren and Lithia. *Need to throw them off. Admit to something, Shireen.* She fidgeted. "He's cute. Gorgeous, yeah. What woman wouldn't want him? But I'm going to be a wizard. So is he. That's that."

Lithia chuckled. "It was hard then. I could imagine."

Shireen swung her eyes away and her gaze landed on Leonna. She was eying her oddly.

Leonna quizzed, "If you love him, why not just marry him?"

"I-I don't love him. And marriage is not allowed among wizards. Obviously."

Leonna's brow dipped momentarily. "Right. Ban on that too. I had forgotten about that. You landers," she mumbled. "This Bel. He sat next to me at the introduction. I wouldn't know him, but they recognized him as a First-Year and a slayer of dragons."

"That's him. Curly brown locks. Muscles and all," Lithia added.

Leonna continued, "And you don't want him?"

Shireen fidgeted, blushing. She forced a laugh but it was too loud and sounded strained to her own ears.

"Bel interests me." Leonna stood and put her small birds in their cage. "Most men fawn over me. People say I have a good beak, but for me, it's been something of a curse. I try to dress as plain and simple as possible. Yet they still treat me as meat, or worse yet, a prize. It pecks my flesh to no end."

"Wish I had your problems," Lithia admitted.

"It's odd to say, but this Bel ignored me. I find him… puzzling. You say you don't want him?"

Shireen's face was abruptly serious. "No, of course not." She was digging herself into a hole. *What did this avian girl plan to do to her Bel? Seduce him? Is that allowed among her kind?* She wanted to ask her outright, but showing concern would clearly prove she was lying about not wanting him. She tried to force the red out of her cheeks. She wasn't controlling her face well at all.

Pren jumped into the silence. "Leonna, can you tell

us anything about where you're from? What they teach you? If you can't say, we understand."

Shireen was glad her friend was changing the subject.

"To share is part of the reason we are here. To foster peace and understanding." Leonna nodded. "I live on Bald Mountain with my clan. A hatchling learns to glimpse through a bird's eyes at an early age. Once she becomes a nestling, she trains to scout, to influence the birds, to tell them where to go and where to fly, to spy for predators and prey. We keep a constant perimeter around the clan and are especially watchful for cats, other birds not under our control and the like. We also search for things to eat: snakes, rabbits, raccoons, squirrels, gophers—even mice, if we're desperate. A fledgling, like myself, learns to hunt, taking full control of the birds, merging with the creatures' minds in a way. I've led several hunts with my team of birds. One time I caught enough to feed the entire clan. That was a good day."

Pren muttered, "We spend our lives looking for water. You spend yours looking for food. Not the glamorous life I envisioned as a child."

Leonna sighed. "True. But there is much higher magic. More difficult. Only the oldest and wisest know it. I have seen some things that I am sorry to say I cannot tell you about. It's sort of our secret weapon."

"We understand," Shireen said.

"Wait," Lithia said. "You hunt with… those?" She pointed at her cage full of finches.

She laughed. "Not those, these." Leonna uncovered the other two cages containing the peregrine and the hawk. The birds opened their eyes and began cawing.

Shireen was in awe at the regal appearance of the hawk: beautiful and deadly.

Pren swept over to the cages. Lithia followed.

"Don't get too close," Leonna cautioned. "I'm not in their heads right now. They might nip at you."

"The smaller one's adorable," Lithia said.

"Fastest bird on the mountain. Flying him quick and hard and slamming his body into prey can knock them out, even kill them sometimes. It's quite fun."

Shireen joined them. She couldn't keep her eyes off the hawk's deadly claws and sharp beak. "I wish I had some real skills. I can read intent, tell if someone's lying. I can even read minds if they're not shielded. Human minds. I think I could control someone. Maybe. Well, maybe not control, but push in a thought or suggestion. No, not control. But we're not allowed to practice that. It's forbidden. Humans, yes, I think I understand how humans think. But animals? I wouldn't know where to start."

"I'm sorry. I'm not allowed to—"

Shireen said, "No, no. I didn't mean for you to show me. We must keep the forms pure." Her eyes darted back and forth, looking at the faces of the other girls as if she had said too much earlier and wanted to take it all back.

Pren repeated, pondering the words, "Keep the forms pure." They now meant something different.

Leonna closed her eyes for a few moments, opened a cage and pulled out her peregrine. "I can tell you a little. It's not that difficult. My opinion, anyway. Of course, I've been doing it all my life." She smiled as she waved her arm sending the bird in the air. The peregrine flew out the window. "A bird's mind is small. Simple. Its thoughts are mainly centered on its needs: food, shelter, instinctual things like mating or predator avoidance. They are born already comprehending what creatures or things are dangerous. To speak to an animal's mind, you cannot use complex justifications or explain motives beyond the obvious. Much easier to use the language of fear, danger, food and shelter."

Lithia rubbed the stone hanging from around her neck. "And you, Shireen, apprentice of the forest, when will you begin speaking to the trees?"

She rolled her eyes. "I wish someone would teach me. Master Meetta thinks such things are a waste of time. I think Bel may be learning. He mentioned as much during his stay in Sha'mont. He said the trees' minds were peculiar. It's not easy, though. Master Nes'egrinon took years to learn how to communicate with the trees."

Pren said, squeezing her purse of sand. "I could imagine. I'm glad, in a twisted way, my sand does not have thoughts of its own. Not sure if I could handle that."

"At least, you can make things with your sand," Shireen chided. "You can pass the trials. Whatever comes at you, create something out of sand to defeat it. Me? What can I do? I have a tiny dagger and I can read minds. I'm going to fail."

Lithia admonished, "All right. I've heard about enough of your wallowing in self-pity. You know more than that. What are you doing? Playing possum?"

"What does that mean?" Leonna asked.

Pren said, "She's pretending."

"I'm not pretending." Shireen opened her arms in defense then shook her head. "I guess I'm just nervous."

"We all are, I think," Leonna said then looked up at the ceiling and paused. "My peregrine is in the trees. Most of the others are going to the feed tent. There's something of a long line."

"We might as well wait then." Lithia pointed at Pren. "I think the two of us are nervous too, even though we've been here before. Probably more nervous in fact because we failed last year and we recognize how hard the trials are."

"Absolutely," Pren added. "It was so hard."

"What happened?" Shireen asked.

The four girls gathered closer, all sitting on Leonna's bed.

Pren cleared her throat. "The first trial. No one gives you a clue as to what you're going to be up against. They tell you to walk down this path into the woods. Okay, fine. I thought someone would be waiting there to explain to me, but no. That's not what happened at all. I'm walking down the path and the longer I walk the more nervous I become. I put my hand on my pouch when the thought entered my head maybe there wasn't going to be any explanation. Maybe something was going to happen.

"My heart was throbbing. The forest was so quiet. I thought I heard someone behind me, like a twig snapped or something. I turned around and no one was there. I started thinking about being even a little more prepared, actually pouring the sand out into my hand, but I thought I was just being silly. That's when it all happened.

"A tree branch swung down behind me. I turned when I heard the noise, just in time to get swatted. I flew in the air and landed about twenty feet away. Boy did that hurt.

"The air was knocked out of my lungs. I dropped my pouch. I tried to get up, but I was dizzy. I stumbled. I was quickly surrounded by branches alternately swinging down at me. The trees were attacking me!"

Pren stood. "I dodged the first few and ran. I spied my pouch and dove for it. I poured the contents out. Another limb crashed into me, grabbing me, pulling me high into the sky then released me.

"I was falling from such a height. I was going to die. I just knew it. I quickly formed my sand into a giant pillow and caught myself. Then I ran." Pren was hyperventilating.

"You ran?" Leonna asked.

"Yes, I ran out of there. That's how I failed. I guess quitting isn't allowed. But I'm still alive. There's no way I could have advanced last year."

"And now?" Shireen quizzed.

"They change the trials every year. I only hope there's something in the forest I can handle."

"Aye," Lithia said. "Me too."

Shireen's heart was pounding. "Looks like I'm not getting any sleep tonight."

*****

Bel and Naga entered the hut then came to an abrupt halt.

"Sorry, guys. You're stuck with me," Kerlith said, laying on the closest bunk, his hands behind his head. "The other huts are all already full."

Bel shrugged his shoulders and asked Naga which bunk he wanted. Naga took the one farthest from Kerlith, in the far corner of the room, and Bel took the one next to his.

The room was sparse, only containing the four bunks, each having a tiny table with a single drawer. Bel opened his drawer, put his few belongings in and stuffed his sack under his bed.

"Do you all mind if I bunk with you?" another asked from the doorway. Bel only saw his silhouette.

"Sure! Come on in," Kerlith said. "Another victim."

Bel froze when the young man bent over and picked up several cages then stepped in. He was an avian. A large colorful bird sat perched on one shoulder.

"I guess this bunk is mine?" the avian said.

"That's yours. Next to me. You're going to be sorry you didn't come sooner." Kerlith seemed to be enjoying himself. He pulled a stone out of his pocket and began floating it in the air above him.

The avian set his cages down on the bed and eyed each of the others, Kerlith, Naga and Bel, one by one, and nodded. "My name is Ayah. I'm an avian, obviously. These are my birds. I'll keep them in cages when any of you are in the room." One cage contained many small birds while the other contained a large hawk that took up the entire cage. Another was empty. On his shoulder sat a parrot.

Everyone stared at Ayah and Bel sensed Naga becoming uncomfortable. Kerlith was smiling wide. Bel had to get past his distrust of the creature-kind, not that he wanted to trust them, but he couldn't show it. His master wanted him to find out if there was some form of creature-kind plot and what better way than to speak with one directly. He needed to become this avian's friend. He walked up to the young man and extended his hand. "I'm Bel, from here, ahh, the Greenlands. I'm learning forest magic. It's good to meet you." When Ayah stared at his hand, Bel added, "In my lands, people shake hands as a sign of greeting or friendship."

The parrot repeated, "Shake hands. Squawk. Ayah. Shake hands. Squawk. Squawk. Shake hands."

Ayah lowered his eyebrows briefly then grinned and shook Bel's hand.

Naga was next. "Greetings Ayah, my flesh stands before you and is glad. My name is Naga and I hail from the frigid north, the Tundra lands of snow and ice. Our greeting is much like the tree-lovers, but you must shake like this." Naga took Ayah's hand and put it on his elbow and he did the same. "The tree-lovers keep their friends at a distance while the Tundric pull their friends in close." Naga smiled wide at Ayah and he nodded and smiled back.

"A pleasure to meet you both. And you?" Ayah turned to Kerlith who was ignoring them as he floated his stone in the air.

"That's Kerlith," Bel explained. "Don't mind him. He's antisocial."

"Right. I'm here to antagonize you and make you generally miserable. Sorry, kid. Tough break." Kerlith snickered.

"Tough break. Ayah. Squawk. Ayah. Tough break," the parrot repeated.

"Shush," Ayah breathed at the parrot.

"Shush, shush, shush. Ayah, shush," the parrot repeated.

"You're going in the cage if you keep it up," Ayah warned, turning his head to the bird.

"You're going in the cage, Ayah. Keep it up, keep it up. Ayah, You're going in the cage if you keep it up."

"Okay, that's it." Ayah opened up the empty cage and stuffed the parrot in. The parrot began squawking, "Keep it up. Keep it up. Ayah, keep it up. Squawk."

When Ayah tossed a cloth over the cage, the bird silenced itself. "Sorry about that."

"Are you kidding me? That was extraordinary," Bel said. He was glad Ayah was his bunkmate and not one of the felines.

Ayah hung his cages and arranged his belongings.

"So you come from south of the Greenlands?" Bel asked, breaking the brief silence.

"Yes, not far from the edge of the forest. Bald mountain. Do you know of it?"

"I can see Bald mountain in the distance from my home," Bel said. "Creature-kind don't go to University; how do you learn magic?"

Ayah stowed his belongings, a frown on his face.

Bel added, "If you can say. You know, I don't mean to pry."

"Doesn't ruffle my feathers. I was confused by your question. We learn as you learn. You are trained by masters?"

"Yes, I'm apprenticed to Master Nes'egrinon, sworn to his service and training."

Naga said, "I'm sworn to the master of wind and storm, the mage of ice and snow, Master K'eyush."

Ayah sat on his bed, pushing his knee up. "We don't learn from a single master, as I understand you do. We live in long houses. The entire clan lives there and we learn and obey all of them. I listen to many clan-fathers and clan-mothers. They are all masters and equal in my eyes. I learn from them all and serve them as well."

Bel wondered about his own situation and whether or not Master Nes'egrinon yet lived. "If a master dies, the apprentice still trains with the other masters then?"

"Of course," Ayah said, not understanding the thrust

of the question.

Bel pursed his lips. "So you live with other apprentices?"

"Yes," he answered. "My clan-sister, Leonna, she's here at the trials also."

Naga nodded hard, "I most definitely saw her."

Ayah snorted. "She gets that reaction everywhere she goes."

"Fine to look. Too bad we can't touch," Naga exhaled.

"You can't," Ayah agreed. "But I can. I intend to mate with her. If she'll accept me."

"What?" Bel gasped.

"She's beautiful and many men would have her. It's my hope I'll yet win her heart."

Kerlith continued to balance his stone in the air, ignoring them.

Naga stated, "The creature-kind are permitted relationships? To marry?"

Ayah shook his head. "I'm not sure what you mean."

Kerlith popped off his bed. "I'm going to the feed tent." Without waiting for anyone, he walked out the door.

"Relationships. Marriage. It's forbidden," Bel explained. "Are you planning on leaving magic for her? She is lovely, but it's such a sacrifice."

"Sacrifice?" Ayah said.

"You can't marry her and still learn magic. You realize what could happen, don't you?" Bel's face racked with frustration.

"Actually, I don't." Ayah shook his head.

Naga turned toward Bel also as if he was unsure of the answer.

Bel explained, "Wizards cannot marry because we

need to focus on the greater good, the needs of the people. A royal priesthood. If we were to marry we could get… distracted. If we were to fall in love, we might be inclined to do things that helped our mate over other people." Bel paused, closing his eyes, "And of course, there's blackmail. If a wizard were found to possess a secret mate, it would be easy to blackmail him."

Ayah stood, consternation on his face. "This makes no sense. What I do is always for the good of the clan-family. If I marry, my wife will also do the will of the clan-family. It could be no other way. I can't comprehend how I could do something that benefits my wife and doesn't benefit the clan. They're one and the same."

Now it was Bel's turn to be confused. "Wait. So you're telling me all the wizards in your clan-family are married? You all live in one big house, a house full of couples?"

Ayah opened his hands and shrugged. "Not all them. Of course, there are a few who haven't yet married or choose to stay single. But most are."

Bel couldn't believe what he was hearing.

Ayah added, "What sounds ridiculous to me is that you cannot marry. Your reasoning makes no sense."

Bel sat on his bed and mumbled, "I guess it doesn't."

Naga stood. "I need to eat. Do you two plan to go to the feed tent?"

Ayah said, "Not sure if I want to eat troll food, but I am hungry and need to gather some seed for my birds."

Bel hopped up. "I'll go." He wanted to speak with Shireen, to tell her about what Ayah had said.

Ayah stood and began shaking a cage. "I'll catch up. Save me a seat?"

"Sure," Bel said and the two stepped outside and

began walking toward the feed tent.

Bel said, "I hope this isn't a mistake. Felix said they were serving troll food. Do you know what trolls eat?"

Naga said, "I thought they ate people."

"Oh, I forgot something. Be right back." Bel changed his mind about leaving his staff unattended. He ran back toward the hut.

As Bel approached the doorway, he overheard Ayah speaking to someone, so he paused, his hand on the door handle.

"I'm in and everything is going according to plan," Ayah said.

Bel frowned and pushed the door open. Ayah stood next to the window, a small bird cupped in his hands. When Bel walked in the bird flew out of the window.

"I forgot my staff," Bel said and retrieved the magewood stick.

Bel walked towards the door and Ayah joined him. "I'm ready."

The two met Naga outside and started towards the feed tent.

Bel thought, *Ayah was sending someone a message. What did he mean by saying 'everything was going according to plan'? Was that merely an oddity of avian speech?*

As they walked, Naga said, "The one Felix spoke of, an avian named Jonah. Do you know of him?"

"He's my clan-brother," Ayah said. "I'm concerned for him. He's only a nestling."

"Nestling?" Naga said. "He's young?"

"Yes, young and small. I don't understand why they sent him. I didn't think he would advance. Now he's lost."

"There were a few other creature-kind at the meeting, a girl and a boy. They had cats," Bel said.

"Hey, don't lump us all together. The felines have nothing to do with us."

"Sorry," Bel said. "I didn't know."

They stopped at the end of the food line and picked up trays and waited.

"Doesn't peck my flesh. The guy's named Jinx. The girl, Felicia. They're both from Felix's clan-family. We made creature-truce with them. I just didn't want you to think all creature-kind are together. We're not the same."

"The Tundric are nothing like the tree-lovers." Naga pushed Bel's shoulder.

Bel said, "True. Makes sense. So your two clans, the avians and felines, they get along?"

Ayah stepped forward and slid his tray towards a large troll wearing a chef's hat and a white apron. He slopped a pile of brownish mush with red specks on his tray. Bel grimaced then did the same. The rancid odor was overpowering. Bel forced himself to not gag.

After Naga received his helping of slop, the three scanned the space for open seats. Kerlith sat by himself so they joined him.

As they sat, Ayah continued, "Not all creature-kind are alike. Not at all. The avians and the cats don't always get along. The dogs and cats hate each other. No one likes the spiders. The reptiles are off on some island and keep to themselves. No one has ever seen one. We're all different."

Bel's mind was being blown. All his life he thought of the creature-kind as the monster in the closet, waiting for him to go to sleep so they could jump out. Of course, the memory of being attacked by leopards in the northern forest hadn't yet faded. But he was beginning to take on a new perspective. They weren't one monolithic bunch. They were a collection of clans. The group that attacked him and Master Nes'egrinon on the path from Yagoos to Sha'mont was probably operating independently of all the other creature-kind, even the other felines. Those felines may not be related or from the same clan as Felix, Jinx, and Felicia. Bel had no right to hold malice against Ayah or any of the others for what some other feline had done. That would be like punishing Meeta for something Gedd did because they were both forest magicians.

"Bleah!" Naga choked.

"That good?" Bel asked.

Ayah dug in, chewed for a bit then grinned. "Hey, not bad." He continued plowing through the slop.

"You can eat mine." Naga slid his plate towards Ayah.

"Kerlith, you don't seem to mind the flavor," Bel said.

Kerlith slowly chewed the mush. "When you've been where I have, you don't complain about a hot meal, no matter what it tastes like."

Bel decided it was time to beat the bushes and find out what came out. "That reminds me, any of you come across anything odd in your lands in the last year or so?"

The three of them stared at Bel so he smiled uncomfortably.

Kerlith spoke through the gruel in his mouth, "What do you mean by *odd?*"

"You know, something out of the ordinary. Odd, you know. Like something you didn't expect."

Naga frowned. "Give me an example."

Bel inhaled slowly. "In the Greenlands, we were attacked by a dragon. But before the dragon, Seol's army attacked the capital. Dragon was odd, the army attacking probably not, political reasons and all. What was really odd, though, was King Seol being controlled by a wizard, a rogue wizard named Gedd."

Ayah shrugged his shoulders and continued eating. Naga appeared as if he had something to say but remained silent.

Kerlith took another large spoonful of slop and said, "I've wandered all the eastern mountains in the last year. I've seen a lot of strange stuff. In fact, I would say there haven't been many normal things I've come across. I don't understand what you're looking for, but whatever it is, it's out there. Just open your eyes and go for a stroll. Get out from under your master's butt, little egg. It's long about time you've hatched."

Ayah chuckled. "A lander hatching? Funny."

Bel smiled. "Thanks for the word of advice, Kerlith. Here, enjoy the rest of my food." He slid his plate across the table and stood. Just as he was about to leave, Shireen, Leonna, and the other girls entered. Bel waved.

*****

Shireen waved back at Bel so he would save them seats and the girls went to the end of the line and retrieved their trays and watched in disgust as the trolls dumped lumps of slop on their plates.

Onyx was at another table, but there were no empty chairs there. Shireen leaned over to Lithia. "You don't mind if we sit with the boys, do you?"

Lithia shrugged her shoulders.

The last troll gurgled at Shireen, "Nose."

Shireen nearly dropped her plate for in the middle of

the brown, stinky goo was a large, hairy snout.

She stepped away, whispering to Pren, "I think I'm going to throw up." She tried to wrinkle her nose, to block the foul stench from entering, but no matter how she tried the smell invaded her nostrils. She tried breathing through her mouth but the thick, musky odor landed on her tongue, coating it. The smell was awful.

The four girls went to the boys' table as they moved in seats for them.

Leonna took a chair, then before sitting down quickly switched, taking the chair Lithia was going for and positioning herself directly across from Bel.

The girls pushed their plates toward the center of the table for the fetid and rotten funk was unbearable.

"What? Not eating your troll-slop, ladies?" Kerlith grinned.

"You're welcome to it," Lithia said.

"I can't eat that," Shireen added.

They all nodded, all except Leonna, who seemed to not be paying attention to the conversation at the table. She was staring intently at Bel. Shireen wanted to kick her.

"Oh, a nose." Kerlith stabbed his fork into the snout on Shireen's plate and pulled it close to his face.

Shireen's eyes darted from Kerlith to Leonna to Bel. Did Bel notice Leonna's lost-puppy-dog-eyes?

Kerlith said, "I think I could eat this, except for the hairs. Might even be a little too gross for me."

Naga chuckled. "Maybe if I was starving."

Bel said, "So I was asking the guys here if they had come across anything they thought was peculiar in the last year or so. I was mentioning the dragon that Shireen and I came against."

Shireen faltered when Bel's eyes fell on her. She pushed Leonna out of her head. "Either of you? Pren? Lithia?"

Pren said, "No, I don't think so."

Lithia added, "No." She rubbed her stone then reconsidered. "There has been one thing the masters complain about. I've only felt it once. The shadows."

"Shadows?" Bel repeated.

"Yes, out in the cold and at night. Shadows where there were no person or thing. Sometimes they move. I didn't believe the stories at first, but then I saw one."

"What do they think they are?" Shireen asked.

"Started after the darkness came, in the days of the ghoul-kind. Some of the masters think all of the ghoul-kind did not return to the Underworld. That they remained in shadow form, the most powerful ones, wizards of old. Perhaps they are right? Who can say."

"I've never witnessed moving shadows." Kerlith tossed the nose back on Shireen's plate, sending a splash of slop on the table. "I think you're nuts and I was there. I saw the ghoul-kind streaming out of the Underworld. I closed the breach."

"Ahem, Master Nes'egrinon closed the breach," Bel corrected. "You and I only helped."

"Whatever. All I'm saying is the breach was closed. There's no ghoul-kind still floating around. Maybe a branch or a bird or something at night scared you. Maybe a hoot owl."

"I know what I saw," Lithia said harshly.

"Know?" Kerlith sneered as he popped to his feet and walked off. "None of you know anything about what's really going on in the world."

Chapter Six
High In Oak

The following day Bel scanned the schedule, but there wasn't anything exciting to do, just chores on the work lists. He overheard others talking, others who made journeys that took several days, so it seemed only right to give them a little rest before they would be tested.

Many of the apprentices were practicing in the central courtyard. Stones were erupting from the ground. Others were pulling water from the earth and forming the liquid into ice or snow, some pelting each other with the slush balls or spraying water.

Drake was near the tree line, his hand touching the bark of an oak. In deep concentration, he appeared to be trying to speak to the tree.

Bel stopped to watch Onyx, the older stonecutter who was friends with Lithia. She was seated cross-legged on the ground, her eyes closed as stones whizzed by. Bel found the sight a little disturbing, the stones were razor sharp and flitted about her at high speeds. One false move and she would be cut severely. He didn't dare make a sound that might break her concentration.

Bel listened as Felix asked some of the older apprentices to help search for Jonah in the woods. He appeared eager to find the boy, saying maybe he twisted an ankle or fell in a hole, but he couldn't explain why the trolls had yet to find Jonah.

Bel walked around the camp several times, observing the sights and sounds of sixty nervous apprentices practicing for the most intense trials of their lives. The village wasn't that big, especially with all the off limits areas guarded by trolls. He couldn't see what was down the small paths leading into the forest. He figured they were probably trial areas.

Bel ate at the feed tent and performed his daily work assignments, but what he really wanted to do was speak privately with Shireen about what he had found out from Ayah. With all the others around, he thought he would never get the chance. He couldn't wait to tell her that creature-kind could marry.

Walking around, Bel chatted up other apprentices about the earlier events and made introductions. Everyone was eager to meet the First-Year who fought a dragon. He was almost famous.

After the midday meal, Bel went to the edge of the forest and practiced communicating with the trees. He tried to hold a conversation with one, an ash, but the tree wasn't interested in speaking to a human. Another, an oak, told Bel to stop bothering him. Finally, a maple spoke to Bel.

While the maple was describing the terrible gusts of wind that afflicted the forest just the other day, or was it fifty years ago, they were interrupted by a scream. Bel broke the connection and ran back to the courtyard.

Several of the apprentices were gathered in a circle. Bel pushed his way in.

Onyx was lying on the ground in a pool of blood, her neck sliced clear across, a sharp stone next to her. She was dead.

A bitter taste filled Bel's mouth.

Felix and Sammra pushed into the space. Felix's cats growled loudly.

"What's going on here?" Sammra barked.

Lithia ran in after them and fell to her knees. "Onyx, no."

Felix barked, "Budzig, come quickly."

Lithia cried out, "She's dead."

Aquilo arrived a moment later. "What hap—" He stopped mid-word. "Is she?"

Another apprentice volunteered, "I saw her. She had her eyes closed. She was flinging those stones around her head, her neck. Too close, I thought."

Another added, "Yes, the stones, too sharp, too close. Her eyes were closed."

Lithia cried out, "No! I don't believe that! She was too good!" Her voice trailed off. "The best of us."

A troll arrived and Aquilo said, "Budzig, take the apprentice to the clinic."

The troll scooped up Onyx's body and took her away.

Another troll stepped into the space and began scrubbing the bloody ground with a dirt-encrusted rag.

Felix said, "You who were witnesses, come with me. Everyone else, back to what you were doing."

Shireen and Pren were comforting Lithia. Bel didn't know what to say. In shock, he walked away.

After the evening meal, as the group walked back from the feed tent to the huts, Bel said, "Lithia, I'm sorry about your friend."

"Thank you, Bel. I'm still shook up. Obviously. She was my friend. It's going to be hard focusing on the trials."

The group was quiet for some time. Bel tried to awkwardly change the subject. "Hey Shireen, I was thinking I could show you something, you know, to help you out tomorrow."

"Ooh, what are you going to show her?" Kerlith howled.

"Shut up, Kerlith," Bel snapped.

Pren added, "You're so immature, Kerlith. So Bel, what *are* you going to show her?"

"Forest magic. A few new things I've been practicing. You all could watch if you want." Bel stopped walking towards the huts and motioned towards the edge of the forest.

Naga said, "I'm going to bed."

Kerlith followed him.

"Me too," Leonna said as she stepped away. "Have fun."

Ayah's voice sounded excited. "I would like to watch what you can do."

Lithia, Pren, and Ayah followed Bel and Shireen to the tree line.

Bel said, "Master Nes'egrinon spent many years alone in the forest and he is one of the few people who has figured out how to communicate with trees."

"Are you sure about that? My master can speak to trees," Shireen pointed out.

"Many forest mages *speak* to trees, asking them to do things. Sometimes the trees listen, other times they don't. I'm not only talking about speaking to the trees, I'm talking about listening to them and understanding what they say, holding a conversation."

"And you've learned to do that?"

"Beginning to. Not the easiest thing in the world, but

I've found they're much more willing to do what you want if you can actually speak in more of a dialog instead of trying to order them around."

"Makes sense," Lithia added, rubbing the stone hanging from her neck.

Bel held his open hand out to Shireen and said, "So connect with me. I'll show you."

Shireen looked at Lithia and Pren then back at Bel's open hand.

"Go ahead," Pren encouraged.

Shireen placed her hand in Bel's and closed her eyes. Immediately they were connected, their minds intertwining. Bel could hear and feel what she could.

—Is this all you wanted, Bel? To connect with me? We can't keep doing this— Shireen spoke into his mind.

—No, I'm going to teach you this. Don't you trust me? Now listen. Watch what I do—

Bel let out a long, deep, wailing moan as he dug his fingers into the bark of the tree. He called out to the oaks to his left, making a swishing sound after the moan.

Their branches swayed lightly in the breeze. One tree shook a few branches, softly, subtly, at the top of the trunk. If Bel weren't listening for the movement of the branches he would have thought it was caused by a small gust, but no, the tree's motion was intentional. It brushed the air forming a melody pitched too low for human ears, but in his spirit, Bel pieced the trees' communication together.

"Hi... Hello... Did you hear it, Shireen? The tree just said hello."

"No, what? I didn't hear anything." Shireen shook her head, then spoke into his mind. *—Bel, you don't need to put on an act for the others—*

—It's not an act. The trees don't have mouths to speak— He said out loud, "Listen to the wind and how they move their branches. The swishing sound the branches make when they pass through the air. That's how they speak."

Shireen said, her eyes still closed, "Okay, try again. I'll listen."

Bel made a deep humming noise as he placed his hand on the trunk of the nearest tree. "Now listen carefully."

Bel caught the tremor of a group of leaves, followed by a tiny shudder of the trunk singing a base note and a few branches swishing a higher pitched tone. Together they formed a kind of music.

Shireen recoiled and cried out, "I heard it!"

Bel opened his eyes, breaking their connection. Shireen's eyes were moist. He smiled. "It's something I've been practicing for a while. Master Nes'egrinon wasn't aware I was doing it—well, at least, I think he didn't know. But when I would do my chores, cooking and cleaning and the like, I would hold short conversations with the trees. I'm still trying to understand their language. I watch carefully when my master does it, watch the way the branches move, the way they swish the air. I've only learned a handful of words."

"Extraordinary."

"Now we need to ask them to do something for us."

Shireen nodded back.

Just as Bel closed his eyes, he said, "Who wants to go flying?"

Ayah mumbled, "What's he talking about?"

Bel stepped behind Shireen and put his arms around her. Shireen tensed hard.

"Bel, what are you doing?"

Bel hummed a low tone and three higher notes and a branch swooped down at them. He whispered, "Hold on."

Pren and Lithia yelled as they leaped out of the way of the huge limb. The branch reached down and scooped up Bel and Shireen.

She screamed as she opened her eyes wide, clutching for a branch, his arms, anything to brace herself, "Bel, what are you doing?"

The branch flipped them in the air and another swung out, caught them and lifted the two higher. They bounced between two more branches as Shireen clutched Bel. The pair landed at the top of the tree, overlooking the entire camp.

"Bel! Bel! Bel! Why didn't you warn me?"

He laughed. "I told you to hold on."

She slugged his arm.

He whispered, "How else was I going to get you alone?" He leaned over the edge and waved down at the three. "Hurry up. Wave to your friends."

"Why should I? Just put me back down."

"Please?"

Shireen leaned over and waved at Lithia, Pren, and Ayah.

"Now we connect. We talk. But first, I'm serious. I want to teach you this. I need you to pass the trials."

"Bel, I appreciate your concern but I'm fine."

"You're fine? Don't you get it? I'm not trying to get you alone. Well maybe that too, but I really want you to pass. I want you to succeed, to pass these trials. Don't you know that I care about you... even if... maybe... I can't have you."

Shireen exhaled. "Show me."

"Okay, listen. It's all about intent. The trees' language has words, of course—well, sounds anyway. But they hear intent. Picture in your mind what you want to communicate and make the tones. What I did was picture us at the top of the tree and then sung to them. Are you ready to try?"

"So I visualize us down on the ground and moan?"

"No, you visualize those three up here with us."

"What?"

Bel chuckled again as he leaned over and waved at Lithia, Pren, and Ayah below. "Hurry, before they walk off."

Shireen closed her eyes and connected to Bel. He saw the picture she was forming. "Make this sound with me." He hummed a bass note. She repeated it.

"Good." He completed the phrase to the tree with a few swishing sounds. Just as Shireen repeated the notes the two tilted precariously as the branches moved. Bel grabbed hold of the limb with one hand and wrapped his other arm around Shireen's torso.

The tree swung a lower branch down at the three apprentices below. Ayah dove out of the way but Pren and Lithia were snatched up and alternately tossed from branch to branch, finally finding themselves at the top of the tree next to Bel and Shireen.

"Shireen! Bel! What are you doing? I'm afraid of heights! Get me down!" Pren's arms and legs were wrapped tightly around a branch.

"Shireen, that wasn't pleasant at all. That second branch scratched me," Lithia said, checking the back of her arm.

A dust cloud formed between the two trees then

solidified into a mass of tan sand. Sammra appeared standing upon it. "What in the world is going on here? Ladies? And you, Bel. What are you doing with Shireen?" Her eyes were shooting daggers. Bel's arm was still wrapped around Shireen's midsection. He quickly released her.

"Just practicing for tomorrow," Shireen said.

Sammra flared her nostrils. "You know the rules on fraternization." Her eyes popped to Pren and Lithia. "Make it quick. Light is going out soon and I want all of you in your bunks." Sammra floated back down and as she left, Pren said, "No, wait. Take me with you."

Bel chuckled. "I'll set you down, Pren."

"Me too," Lithia added.

Bel spoke to the tree and the limb put the two girls back on the ground. They waited for a few moments and when they realized Shireen wouldn't be joining them, they went to their hut.

Bel asked, "So, did you find out anything? Plots?"

"Not yet. It's only been two days." She added, "Onyx's death, though…"

"What about it?" Bel said, not making the connection. "I saw her myself. The stones were too close. I'm sorry to say but that was reckless."

"Maybe."

"You know something else?"

"I do," Shireen said. "But don't jump to conclusions."

Bel waited. When Shireen didn't continue, he prodded, "Go on."

Shireen nodded slowly. "When I first arrived, I caught Onyx spying on an avian and a feline, Felicia and Leonna actually. They were arguing about something. I was spying too but on the other side of the huts. Felicia noticed Onyx there. I didn't realize how Felicia did it, then I figured her cats picked up her scent. Could have been me, but I guess I was upwind and Onyx was downwind. Felicia marched over and yelled at her. Asked her what she heard as if what they were discussing was a secret."

"And now she's dead." Bel frowned. "You don't think?"

"No, like you said. She was probably not being careful. What with the excitement of the trials and so much going on... But still..."

Bel locked on Shireen's eyes. "How's Lithia taking Onyx's death?"

"She's a stonecutter. Gruff. Rough. She tries to not show her emotions, but I can tell she's upset. She can't hide her emotions from me."

The two were quiet for some time. The light from the moonstone began to dim as if someone was turning out the lights on the world.

Bel said, "We each have an avian in our huts. That's good."

"True," Shireen muttered.

"I'm glad you made it in." In the twilight, Bel peered into the blue of her eyes. She glared at him for staring then turned her back on him.

His heart thudded as the fading moonstone light caressed her fair skin. He wanted to speak to her, to say something besides meaningless small talk but said nothing because words were an impediment. He couldn't communicate with her the way he wanted, for the depth of his feelings were inexpressible with mere language and sound. No, words were lies, a paltry imitation of the truth. He touched her shoulder lightly.

"Bel?" She turned back staring into his eyes, a question in them.

Bel tried to not melt before her. The fading sunlight highlighted part of her face and the vision cemented his desire to give himself to her all the more. He wanted to tell Shireen, to say something, but someone might be listening. Words were no good, anyway.

"We can't," she said, then shrugged as if this were the natural order of things, as if these things had always been impossible and always would be. The Law forbid it.

"The creature-kind marry. They live in clans and they mate, wizard with wizard. They bear wizard children." Bel blushed when he finished and repositioned himself on the branch.

"I've heard rumor of such."

"You knew? And you didn't tell me?"

"No. I mean, I just heard, or overheard, just since we have been here. I didn't think, I mean, we're so different from them. What does it matter? Do you even believe them?"

"Why would they lie?" he mumbled, almost as a statement more than a question. Several birds silhouetted in the fading sun, in the distance, circling the village below. He disregarded them.

Shireen gave him a long uncomprehending stare, then her eyes widened in an expression mingling anger and betrayal so plainly Bel could decipher it even by the light of the fast fading light. "They knew. The masters. They had to, yet they made the rule anyway."

"Perhaps they didn't know."

"They had to have found out sometime. Master Nes'egrinon said he was friends with the avians before the war. Master Gedd too."

"Don't mention his name. He tried to kill me twice, remember?"

She touched his hand. "But still. They would have known about this for many years. That other wizards married. Creature-kind, but still, wizards. Why are they so adamant about this rule?"

Bel shrugged his shoulders. "Tradition?"

"Maybe." It sounded like a question.

"Maybe what?"

Shireen choked momentarily as if she was reconsidering even before the first word of the sentence was out of her mouth. "Someone could be listening."

Bel pointed in the air at the circling birds.

Shireen nodded.

Bel held out his hand. Shireen took it and the two quickly connected as if he were a hand and she a glove.

—*Tell me*—

—*I've been thinking about a lot of things. The creature-kind marrying? I don't see how that helps our situation. We can't join them. Obviously. They tried to kill you. They took the roc's eye. We want peace with them, but still they've been our mortal enemy for so long. I just can't trust them. Maybe they do marry. Maybe they're making all that up to sow division among us*—

—*Maybe we can petition the council. Bring this as evidence. Maybe the creature-kind, you know, Sturfelis or Jeneth, could speak to them, tell them the benefits*—

Shireen broke the connection and peeked over the edge. "We have to go." Sammra was saying something and shaking her arm up at Shireen.

Bel peeked over and quickly pulled back when he saw the scowl on the worthy's face. "Right. Time to go down."

Just then something rustled through the leaves below.

"Someone there?" Bel said.

The two peered over the edge of the branch. A dark shadow below was running through the forest.

Bel lost the apparition so he spun to the other side of the branch and scanned the darkening forest below.

"What was that?" Shireen asked.

"Whoever it was was trying to hide. Or maybe whatever it was."

"Whatever?"

"We're surrounded by trolls, remember? Could have been anything."

Shireen nodded. "The missing boy?"

Bel shrugged his shoulders, leaned back and put his hands behind his head and said, "Okay, forest apprentice, ask the trees to set us down."

As Shireen spoke to the tree, something deep down bothered Bel. An avian was missing. Onyx died after overhearing a conversation between a feline and an avian. Something didn't seem right about all of it. Bel's master sent him here to ferret out what the avians were up to, but he didn't want to jump to conclusions either. He didn't want to be thought of in the same way as the other masters looked at his master, a crackpot making wild accusations. Yet, something was there, lodged in his craw, and he was going to find out what it was.

Chapter Seven
Rock On Pole

Leonna woke slowly. She hadn't slept well at all for her dreams were filled with visions of betrayal and failure. As the light crept under the door she got up and readied herself. Today was the first trial and she needed to pass. She couldn't risk being escorted out by the trolls. There was too much at stake.

She opened her cages and took out her birds then left the room as the others began to stir. Stepping outside, she let them take to the air to freshen their wings.

After a time, the other apprentices gathered in the central courtyard and Felix made another announcement about Jonah. "I want everyone to recognize we're doing everything we can to find him. It's only been a few days that Jonah has been missing so we're confident he's still alive. It's only a matter of time before we locate him." He nodded at their silence.

Sammra, Felix, and Aquilo divided the apprentices into random pairs. Felix clearly wanted to make sure none of the creature-kind were paired with each other. When he came to Leonna, he pointed at Bel and said, "Dragonslayer, you're with Leonna."

Bel walked up and stood next to her without saying a word.

Leonna studied the young man. Everything about the lander's behavior was strange and foreign to the avian apprentice. He didn't stare at her face or ogle her body. He had no wolfish grin. She couldn't understand him. Even the male hatchlings wanted her to pick them up so they could snuggle in her bosom. But here was a young man who was completely ignoring her. She was genuinely annoyed, yet she couldn't understand why. *Wasn't that what I always wanted? For men to treat me like a person and not a hunk of meat to be pecked?*

As others were being paired Leonna scanned the crowd, sensing their tension through her birds. When Leonna's eyes met Shireen's, she was taken aback. A brooding and melancholic visage stared back at her. Leonna thought she must have done something wrong this morning to upset the lander, but then realized she wasn't staring at her at all, but at Bel. *It is true what the others said then. This Shireen is in love with this Bel.*

For some reason, the landers didn't allow marriage. Leonna didn't understand why. *They were both from the same clan, the clan of forest magic, were they not? Preventing two marrying of their own kind? A stupid rule.* It made no sense. *What were the landers thinking?* She could understand separating felines from avians, avians from canines, and the like. They were just too different. How could a magician with a troop of cats live in an avian long house, surrounded by birds? Impossible. And the dogs and cats? They would never tolerate each other. The dogs didn't stay in one place anyway. They roamed across vast stretches of land. *Who would want to put up with that? An avian's place is in her nest.*

And the laws were so different. The avians and felines were closest, following the law of tooth and claw: you only kill what you need to eat and use every single piece. Nothing goes to waste, for this is how to respect the life lost so the clan could survive. The canines and the reptilians had no such law. They hunted for sport, she had heard. Leonna snorted as she thought about how the landers grouped the creature-kind together as one. *Preposterous.*

After the pairings, Aquilo asked for volunteers to go first. Without discussing it with Bel, Leonna stepped forward. "We'll go." She wanted to get the trial over, she couldn't stand the waiting.

The Tundric wizard smiled and motioned his hand towards a path into the forest.

Leonna's birds leaped from the trees and flew down, the hawk and peregrine landing on her shoulders. Bel ran to catch up, pushing light into his staff as they broached the forest.

"I guess this trial requires teamwork, you know, for us to coordinate our magic and, you know, trust each other," Bel said.

Leonna said nothing. Teamwork or no, she was getting past this trial. Her mission was too important to the clan for her to fail out early. Ayah couldn't complete the mission on his own and she didn't trust the others, no matter what Jeneth said.

The path curved and ended in a small clearing. The ground was hard-packed dirt, brushed and combed. In the center was a huge rock impossibly balanced on a tall wooden pole sitting on a carpet.

The two stopped and stared. "What are we supposed to do with this?" Leonna looked to Bel for answers. Creases were etched into his forehead.

She stepped forward and as she did she caught herself

as a voice reverberated in her mind.

—Remove the rock. Place it on the ground. The rock must not touch the carpet—

Leonna turned to Bel. At the same time, they both said, "Did you hear that?"

She was at a loss. The rock was huge. It looked as if it weighed a ton. She had no idea how the pole didn't splinter and crack under the weight. The slightest movement would make the rock crash to the earth. And all she had were her birds. What could they do to move such a weight?

Leonna thought the trial was a farce. She threw her hands in the air. "This is ridiculous. What kind of trial is this? Like an avian is ever going to need to move a big rock impossibly stuck on top of a pole. This is stupid." She had failed before she even had a chance to begin. *Now what will happen to our mission?*

Bel disagreed. "I don't think it's about the task itself. It's about the teamwork." His eyes never left the rock.

Leonna found herself staring at him in amazement. The lander wouldn't even look at her. He was cute. Gorgeous, for a lander. She could understand why Shireen was so enamored with him. He was muscular, but not in a brawny way. His hands were rough. He was clearly accustomed to hard work. Leonna approved. An avian man with soft hands would be thrown off Bald Mountain. Everyone was expected to work for the clan. "Teamwork or no, I can't grasp how—"

Bel turned to Leonna and smiled as if he thought it was obvious. "I'm a forest apprentice and we're in a forest, remember?"

Leonna nearly gasped as their eyes met. *He has bird-sign!* His eyes had small wisps of translucent blue mixed into his browns. She nearly walked over to him and grabbed his head so she could inspect his eyes. *How could a lander possibly boast bird-sign?* She forced herself to look away, shaking, as she responded, "So? It's not a tree. It's a big rock. Maybe if you were a stonecutter."

Bel waved his hand at her, cutting her words in the air. He closed his eyes and held out his staff. Nothing happened for a time, then the sky grew darker.

"Impossible. We haven't been here long. It can't be dusk." She gawked. The tree branches were moving, bending and dipping down overhead. They were interlocking and forming a basket. The branches extended down in front of the rock.

Bel opened his eyes and nodded at her. "Can your birds nudge the rock?"

"Of course, but will the branches hold the weight?"

"One way to find out."

Leonna groaned at his answer, but she had no better ideas. She connected her mind with her peregrine and flew around the space and to the rear of the boulder, pushing with the bird's body. The rock moved slightly. She pushed her mind into her hawk and sent him up to help. As the two birds fluttered behind the boulder, pushing it, the rock started to turn and the pole let out a cracking sound.

The boulder tumbled off the pole and into the branches, falling quickly. The branches splintered and cracked. Leaves and acorns fluttered everywhere. The forest was coming down around Leonna's ears. She clenched her eyes down hard then slowly opened them when the noise stopped. The boulder was cradled mere inches above the carpet.

"Now what?" Leonna asked.

Bel's eyes were still held tight. He rolled his staff and the branches shifted slowly, delicately, sliding the boulder forward and away from the carpet.

One of the branches cracked and Leonna jumped at the sound. Finally, the limbs turned, pouring the boulder to the ground inches from the carpet.

Bel opened his eyes and surveyed the clearing. "We did it."

"No, you did." Without thinking, Leonna threw her arms around Bel and kissed his lips. She released him when she spied something she had never seen before: an uncomfortable twist racked Bel's face. Bel was recoiling from her! Yet she couldn't stop staring into his eyes and their hypnotic blue swirls.

Leonna didn't understand what his glare meant. *Did he not enjoy my kiss?* So many men wanted her, she had grown liberal with her affections. A kiss, a hug, an embrace, even a backward glance or a flip of the hair, she used them all to get what she wanted out of men. It was second nature. If they did what she wanted—and they always did—she would give them another kiss and a smile, but no more. The dangling lure of another such kiss kept them coming back for more, fools they were.

Leonna had never met a man who didn't want a hug or peck on the cheek from her. Avians were an affectionate bunch anyway, much more so than the felines. Perhaps even more so than the landers. Leonna puzzled, *Perhaps they were unaccustomed to such contact?* She tensed as she realized she may have offended the boy with bird-sign in his eyes. "I apologize. I don't understand your ways. Did I do something wrong? Did I offend you?"

Leonna continued to stare at the slowly swirling blue.

His bird-sign was subtle. She couldn't remove her eyes from his for she still couldn't believe it. Somehow this lander was part avian. The fact completely puzzled her. She would need to speak with Ayah.

"No, it's not that," Bel said turning away from her. "Nothing wrong with what you did."

She didn't believe him. "You saved me from the trolls. You did. Your magic got the boulder down. I was thanking you. That's all."

"No, no. You helped. Your birds pushed the rock."

Leonna's heart beat faster. *And he's humble too. Not full of bravado like the avian men, crowing about their most meager of accomplishments. This man is a strange bird indeed.* "You could have swatted the back of the rock with another branch. You wanted me to have a part in this. You're not fooling anyone." She touched his hand. "Thank you. It's a polite gesture."

"Don't tell anyone when, you know, they ask. Just say we completed the task together. I think this was a teamwork trial and I don't want anyone thinking we didn't use teamwork. Maybe they would fail us, you know, if they thought I put the boulder down by myself. You helped."

Leonna stared at the translucent blue of his eyes. "There's something…" Leonna paused, searching for the exact word, but not finding it, she continued, "different. Yes, different. There's something different about you. Curious."

Bel cleared his throat. "Are you ready to go back?"

Leonna didn't want to return just yet, for at that moment her heart was warming, a most peculiar sensation, as if someone had poured milk chocolate on her. There was a sweetness to it. She didn't understand the feeling; she had never experienced something like it before.

Bel stepped closer. "Are you okay?"

His sudden proximity sent her heart into palpitations. She let her breath out. "I-I suppose. Yes. Let's go back."

Leonna and Bel hurried down the path side by side and exited into the central courtyard. Leonna smiled at the group of apprentices with an air of exultation. "We did it!"

Felix checked them off and said, "Okay, who's up next?"

Bel and Leonna stood around and watched the other pairs go in one by one. No one had the nerve to ask the two what they saw. Pair after pair returned with smiles on their faces and Leonna felt relieved when Ayah came back and gave her a thumbs up. He passed.

Not long after Jinx and Kerlith returned. They passed also.

A forest apprentice and his partner walked up to Bel as they exited, victorious. "That was easy."

Hey Drake," Bel said, with an odd twist to his face. "Easy huh?"

"I thought so. You?" Drake said, glancing at Leonna several times.

"We did fine." Bel motioned to Leonna, emphasizing that they accomplished the task together.

"Hello, I'm Drake." He extended his hand to her and smiled wide. "Bel and I went to University together. Although I was two years ahead."

Leonna shook his hand and said her name but quickly looked away. She tried to not give him any ideas by maintaining eye contact. She could tell immediately that he was like the rest of them, a man who couldn't keep his eyes off her long legs.

"If they're all as easy as that one, this year's going to be the one I advance. Anyway, see you around, Bel. Nice meeting you, Leonna." He lingered, waiting to catch her eyes.

She nodded briefly, refusing to look at the leer on his face.

Leonna looked back at the path to the trial as two more apprentices exited, bouncing on their heels. Shireen and Felicia had been paired and were readying themselves to go in, standing near the entrance.

Leonna figured she owed it to Felicia to wait for her too. She was the last of the creature-kind who had yet to enter. She hadn't forgotten about her harsh words towards Jonah, but she would try to forgive and forget. Besides, the joyous atmosphere was becoming infectious. Everyone so far had passed. As each successive pair came out, the crowd cheered louder and louder. Leonna was enjoying it. She was discovering a different side to the landers. They were so much more emotional and easy to excite, not like the avians with their dour-faced seriousness. Leonna was cautious about cheering at first. It didn't feel natural to her. But as each successive wave came out, she clapped and yelled praises more enthusiastically. She laughed as she high-fived the victors.

Another pair started toward the path as Sammra motioned that the trial had been reset. Shireen and Felicia were discussing strategy.

Leonna leaned over to Bel as she eyed the two girls. "How do you think your little girlfriend is going to do? Can she get the trees to move like you?"

"Ahh, she's not my girlfriend," Bel said in a low

murmur. He then cleared his throat several times.

"Are you sure?" Leonna stroked his hand, teasing.

Bel jumped, pulling away. He seemed a puzzle to decipher. His face softened. "We went through some tough times. We were at University, studied together. I consider her a friend. A close friend. When my master went to Sha'mont, Shireen and I worked together. We fought side by side. I trust her with my life. But she's just a friend."

The smile leaked off Leonna's face as an emptiness kicked in the pit of her stomach. Bel and Shireen's friendship was deep, no matter what he said. Her finches could sense his emotion; it dripped out of his pours. Hearing him describe their friendly relationship and sensing his strong emotions for Shireen through her birds made Leonna long for such a companion.

A companion, she thought. A problem she never thought she'd have. Sure, the single men in the clan constantly threw themselves at her—even some of the married ones. She could own any of them, but could even one, in love or marriage, provide the type of bond these two landers had only in friendship? Such a union was unattainable to her for some reason she simply could not fathom. Why? Was her beauty truly a curse? Could not, at least, one of them see past her exterior? Love her for her?

"You sound like you cherish her," Leonna said. When Bel twitched, she added, "As a friend."

"As a friend. I do. I care about her as much as a friend could. I hope she passes."

"Must be nice," she mumbled.

Another pair came out and Leonna and Bel cheered and clapped. Leonna had begun to adopt the landers form of slapping their hands together. Clapping that way was much louder.

After the roar died down, Bel touched Leonna's elbow and pulled her closer. "Why would you say that?"

"Say what?"

"I heard you. Before we cheered. Don't tell me you don't keep friends. Or do the avians not do friendship?"

She fidgeted, unable to answer. It was something she barely understood herself. She didn't think she was antisocial. Certainly the clan-mothers and clan-fathers spoke with her, but it was different with them. Her clan-brothers? To the ones her age, she was a potential mate and a prize to be won. She couldn't be herself around them. Perhaps because she didn't respect them. They were too single-minded and Leonna found twisting and manipulating their minds too easy. At first, using them had been a game. Fun. She had enjoyed toying with their minds. Later the game had morphed into something pathetic that she loathed. Leonna hated them all.

"Our relationships are... different." A twinge of despair grabbed Leonna. Perhaps, it was all her fault. Had she treated them better, as friends, they wouldn't have made her into such an icon to win.

Certainly most of her clan-sisters hated her for the way the men treated her and the way she abhorred the men. The girls ruffled their feathers over always being second egg to Leonna. They secretly hoped for her to come to some tragic end involving her falling off Bald Mountain. Some were a little more compassionate, only wishing for Leonna to receive some dreadful scar on her face.

Jonah was the only one. Leonna wished he would maintain his innocence forever, never grow up, for she understood what he would turn into.

"Friends are wonderful but nearly impossible to find. Good friends, that is. Someone you can trust. I think that's one problem we all share." Bel sounded casual, but Leonna could tell he was trying to soothe her. Leonna was revealing too much of herself to this lander and she needed to stop.

Leonna nodded vaguely as if she was no longer interested in the conversation. Shireen and Felicia walked down the path into the forest. Bel yelled, "Good luck. You can do it." Leonna clapped for Felicia out of obligation.

Trust. Bel's words reverberated in her mind. She had love showered on her, too much, in fact. *Well, not love but lust.* And perhaps the desire to have her as a jewel, a sign they were superior to the rest by having the most desirable mate. As a possession, she would boost their ego. *But trust?* She didn't trust any of the clan-brothers, not in the way Bel described. Perhaps that's what she had been missing all along.

A short while later, Shireen and Felicia exited the forest, Shireen holding two thumbs up. She walked toward Pren and Lithia and gave them hugs. Bel joined the three and Leonna followed.

"Hey, good job," Bel said.

Shireen nodded at him without smiling.

Leonna stood next to Bel. "Congratulations, Shireen. I knew you were ruffling your feathers over nothing."

"So how did you do?" Bel asked.

"Easy task. What do you mean?" Shireen said.

"Easy?"

Shireen shook her head lightly. "I just pushed the rock off the pole."

"But what about the carpet?"

"We rolled the carpet up first to move it out of the way. Obviously. What did you do?" Shireen gaped as if it was a stupid question.

Bel coughed a few times, choking on his saliva, then said, "Something like that. Are we waiting for anyone else?"

Pren said, "I don't think so."

Naga joined them and the group headed away from the crowd and back towards their huts. As they walked, Felicia sneered at Leonna, "Surprised you passed, Avian."

Leonna tried to remain calm. "Good job, Felicia."

"Good thing you got a forest mage with you, Leonna. You couldn't have done anything on your own."

Leonna bristled. "What's your problem anyway?"

Felicia's bobcat growled, stepping forward. The others quickly gave them space. Felicia pushed Leonna on the chest. Leonna stumbled, nearly falling to the ground.

Leonna gained her footing then stepped back and stretched her hands out, extending her fingers. "You don't scare me." Her peregrine and her hawk took to the air, floating in circles above.

The circle of apprentices widened when it appeared one of Felicia's cats might leap. She smiled wide. "You have a big mouth for one of so little ability. You come down off your mountain and visit my clan like you own every man in the place. I'm tired of you twisting heads and thinking you're something. How about I shred that pretty little face of yours?"

Leonna bent her knees and tilted her body forward. "Try it. I'll rip your cat's eyes out."

Felicia smiled as if a thought that just popped into her head amused her. Her face contorted into a sickly grin. "And what you did to Jonah—"

Leonna screamed, "You don't know anything!"

Her peregrine dove down hard and fast, swooping like a bullet at Felicia's head. She leaped out of the way at the last moment.

"That's it. You're dead, Bird Flesh." Felicia's two cats roared and charged Leonna who quickly drew her dagger from its sheath.

Her hawk flew down on the cougar from behind, digging its claws into the cats back. The cougar rolled on the ground trying to smash the bird, but it released the cat and flapped out of its reach. The cougar leaped up at the bird, the hawk flapping and cawing.

The peregrine smashed into the bobcat's side, bowling it over then taking to the air. Leonna brandished her blade in front of her, yelling, "Come over here, Felicia. Let's find out whose face gets clawed."

Felix ran into the clearing, screaming, "Felicia! Leonna! Stop!"

Felicia growled at him, baring her teeth, so Felix grabbed her by the upper arm and yanked. He hissed through clenched teeth, "You are embarrassing me."

Sammra walked into the space and stopped in front of Leonna, placing her hands on her hips and glaring.

As Leonna's birds landed on her shoulders, she stowed her blade and said, "Merely a friendly competition between old friends. A creature-kind thing. Sorry if we disturbed you." She spun on her heel and walked some distance away to a set of benches in the middle of the courtyard and plopped herself down.

Sammra yelled at her back, "This doesn't happen again or you're taken away by the trolls."

Leonna sat, scowling, her arms crossed in front of

her. She looked back, wanting to find out what Felix was going to do to Felicia.

Felix barked, "What do you think you're doing? You're embarrassing the whole clan. What did I tell you?"

"It's not me. It's her." Felicia pointed at Leonna.

"I'm not talking to her. I'm talking to you. You hold an obligation to the felines, your clan, remember? I told Sturfelis I didn't want you coming and this is exactly the reason why."

Felicia shook her arm free. "Are you done lecturing me?"

Felix waved his hand angrily and Felicia stormed off to her hut.

After Felicia was gone, Sammra asked, "Are you going to take that from her?"

Felix said, "What am I supposed to do? She's my little sister." He shook his head and went back to the trial staging area to move the next pairing in.

After the last of the pairs exited the forest, Felix, Aquilo, and Sammra walked into the courtyard and Felix held up his hands, waiting for those who were talking and celebrating to quiet.

"So that was your first trial and I am glad to say everyone passed. For those of you who came to these trials in previous years, you may recall there was no such 'teamwork' trial. This was something new Sammra and Aquilo cooked up."

Sammra explained, "Too many apprentices were failing out on the first trial. We figured the apprentices didn't understand how the trials worked. The idea was to create a practice trial to make sure you understood how the trials were going to function."

Aquilo picked up from there, "You need five more to

pass. The rest of the trials will be harder. Also, for the remainder of the trials, each of you will be on your own."

There was a collective sigh and the celebration and party atmosphere left like air released from a balloon.

Felix added, "For the remainder of the day you have your work assignments to keep you busy. You don't stop working until the job is done. I don't care how late you're up. I would advise you to get on those jobs immediately so you can be well rested for tomorrow's sharing and the following day's trial."

Leonna retrieved some seed at the feed tent and set it out for her birds then went to the hut to read her assignment. She and Shireen were assigned to rake the dirt of the courtyard, pick up debris and attend to trash.

Leonna found the rakes and retrieved two. She didn't wait for Shireen. As she raked and smoothed the dirt, she pushed her mind into her little birds. They fluttered throughout the small village, searching for anything that could be disposed of: small scraps of paper, strings from frayed clothing and the like. Tweetnone brought her a lost earring so she turned it over to Sammra.

Shireen finally arrived and took to her rake. "Sorry, I'm late. I needed to go to the bathroom and I didn't know you were going to start immediately after... what happened."

Leonna ignored her.

"That was intense, by the way," Shireen said. "Does that kind of thing happen often where you come from?"

Leonna stopped raking, her expression shifting to chagrin. "Why is it always *where* with you landers? We're not tied to the land, remember? At any moment, my birds and I could be in the sky. We could go to the other side of the world if we wanted without a second thought.

We don't care about the place we live. We care about the clan. You landers should too. The trees don't sustain you, do they? They don't even care whether or not you're in the forest."

Leonna waited and when Shireen didn't respond, she returned to raking, smashing the tool hard into the ground.

Shireen raked near her. "I guess we have a lot to learn about each other. Master Meetta has many books on the various cultures of the world and I've read much. I'm fairly well versed in the court etiquette of the stonecutters and also on Sanhedrin thoughts about cordial behavior and honor. But we, ahh, landers, know almost nothing about the creature-kind, any of them, feline, avian or the others." Leonna gave her an annoyed look, so Shireen added, "I would like to learn."

"Fine. You want to learn? That minuscule spat I had with Felicia had nothing to do with culture, honor or etiquette. She's a jerk. She's always been a jerk; she probably will always be a jerk. That's reality. You don't need some culture book to realize that. She needed to be taken down a few, so that's where I came in."

"Okay." Shireen was uncomfortable with the volume of Leonna's voice, but Leonna wasn't about to lower it.

Several of the apprentices had stopped their walk through the courtyard to watch. Others came out of their huts.

"You want to understand something else about the avians? We don't lie. Not like you landers."

"Wait a moment. I'm not sure why you—"

"Right. Liars. Did I stutter?" Leonna didn't nurse animosity toward Shireen, but, unfortunately for her, she was in the wrong place at the wrong time. Felicia had put

Leonna in a terrible mood and now, she just decided, she was going to take it out on this lander.

Shireen tried to respond calmly. "Do some people lie? Yes. But you can't accuse us all of being liars because of one person not telling the truth."

Leonna snorted. "Fine. Have it your way. I'll clarify my statement. You're a liar."

"What?" Shireen stepped closer. "Where do you get off saying that? I've never lied to you."

"Oh?" Leonna bellowed.

Nearly half of the apprentices were listening. After the last fight between Leonna and Felicia, everyone was excited to watch round two of the female apprentice throw-down.

Leonna harped, "You told me you had nothing to do with Bel." She pointed across the courtyard to Bel who was standing in front of his hut next to Naga. He flushed red and went inside his room. She continued, "But you do. You love the man."

Shireen let her rake fall to the ground and held up her arms in outrage. "You're making that up!" Shireen screeched. She sounded as if the wind had been knocked out of her.

Many in the crowd murmured.

"More lies? I saw the way you stare at him. You two had something going on at University. You're both together. The others said as much. And then you two were together before the dragon attacked. I can see it now. You two, back there in your city, sneaking off to play tickle toes."

Shireen's hands were balled into tight little fists. She hissed, "We're not allowed. It's forbidden."

"Oh, for you. It's not forbidden for me." Leonna

contemplated Shireen's face, wondering how much farther she should push her, but she didn't care. Bel was so different, not like any man she ever met. And he had bird-sign. Even though he was a lander, the clan would accept him if she pushed hard enough. His eyes were avian-blue. Leonna stepped closer and whispered, "I asked you before if I could catch him. I didn't need to do that. I was only being agreeable. But since you boast no claim on him—not that I would care anyway—I'm taking him. I'm going to make him mine. We'll find out where your heart is."

Shireen kicked her rake and stormed off.

"Hey, aren't you going to finish raking, Lander?" Leonna called out after her.

"You finish it!" she screamed.

Leonna chuckled. "So sensitive. She wouldn't last a day in my clan." As she continued to rake, the others dispersed, clearly disappointed the argument didn't escalate to a fight.

Leonna shouldn't have lashed out at Shireen, but a good yell helped her to release some pent up frustration and she figured the lander would get over being told the truth. *I was helping her anyway. If she loves the boy, she should stop lying to herself.*

Tweetnone landed on Leonna's head and pecked it three times. "I know, Tweetnone. I know."

The bird flew off and Leonna continued raking, thinking about what exactly was going on in her head. She certainly felt a little out of sorts. On the trip up she had to sacrifice something she should have never had to give up: her friendship with Jinx. But he forced her hand for clearly he couldn't be around her without falling in love. Jinx made Leonna feel as though she was leading him on. He couldn't stop bringing up romance and how they could bring avians and felines together with their marriage. Leonna didn't care about any of that. She was only spending so much time with him because she was curious about the felines. Playing with him really, like a toy. Still, Jinx was a path to information and she liked him as a friend. A friend and no more. Too bad he couldn't think of her that way.

But now that Bel told her how he viewed his friendship with Shireen, Leonna realized Jinx wasn't a friend at all. In fact, she never truly had a friend. She never had what they had. She smashed the rake into the ground, clawing the tines across the earth, digging deep furrows. She had what they had and she never would either.

The parallel was uncanny, of course. Bel was treating Leonna as a friend, a new friend anyway, and because of it, Leonna was attracted to him in a way she had never experienced before. Now that she thought of her newly budding emotions for Bel, she realized she had never truly been attracted to any man before, not like this.

That wasn't exactly true, she told herself as she smashed the rake into the ground. There were plenty of men she found cute. Sure, there were attractive avians in the clan. Single ones too. But the way they treated her, worshiping the ground she walked on, even when she mistreated them, she just couldn't respect them. No matter how gorgeous, how muscular and slim, how curly their locks, how curved their nose, how well they controlled their birds, she couldn't find their behavior towards her attractive. She refused to be a prize.

Of course, if things continued the way they were, she would need to pick one of them. Eventually, yes, eventually, she would marry. It was their way to marry inside the clan and with that she agreed. Mates were a necessary thing. It bonded them more tightly to the clan, increased their chances of survival. Birds needed to flock together.

To her, the choice of mate hadn't mattered much. She had seen the avian men in the way they treated her; one had been no different from any other. She hadn't thought much about her options. Until now.

Leonna had thrown the comment about seducing Bel at Shireen's face in a fit of rage, but now that she had considered the thought a little longer, mating Bel wasn't such a bad idea. Bel treated her like a human being. He respected her. Could there be more to his heart than that?

And his avian-blue eyes. That had to mean something. He had bird-sign. Fate or destiny had brought them together. Something about their union felt suddenly so warm, so good and so right. Leonna stood upright, arching her back, squeezing out the stooped-over tightness.

Bel, a lander with bird-sign. An impossibility. A man who was part-avian already, a man who treated her like a human being, a man she could talk to. Her heart warmed at the thought. Leonna couldn't believe herself and the way she felt, almost foolish in fact, but she didn't care. And she had just met him!

Leonna decided she was going to spend more time with this Bel, not to ruffle Shireen's feathers. She couldn't care less about what the female lander thought. No, she wanted to explore this new area of her heart she never knew existed. She wanted to discover if anything came of this slightly warm sensation in the center of her chest when she thought of Bel.

She realized one thing, though, she didn't want to act like the avian men who fawned over her. They always came on too strong. No, she needed to hold herself back and be subtle, but that was going to be impossibly difficult. Stopping herself from throwing her arms around his neck and kissing his lips—hard that. Her mind was racing, thinking about how her heart fluttered when their lips met, but yes, she thought she could be soft, slow and subtle, tease his passion out of him, out into the open.

She collected the racks and returned them to the tool shed then turned and gazed across the courtyard at the hut Bel resided in then rested her eyes on the wide patch of ground she had raked. Deep furrows clawed the smooth, hard-packed ground as if an eagle searching for a lost chick had randomly shredded the base of its nest. It was destroyed. She decided right then what she would do. Softly, slowly, subtly, she would seduce him.

Chapter Eight
Sharing

The odd, sugary perfumes invaded Felix's nostrils as if they were in his own nose and not that of his cats. *Landers stink!* Futilely, he tried to snort the fragrance away. His cats snorted and shook their heads but their noses were far too sensitive. The reek was still there.

After six years of venturing away from the feline-kind to work with the landers, he was still unaccustomed to their scent. Aquilo had described it as perfumed soap, but Felix could not be persuaded that adding the odor to their bodies when they bathed was necessary. Washing? Yes. Bathing? Absolutely. But why cover one's body in such a stench one would be detected from miles away? What predator could do that and not starve?

Felix tried to position his cats upwind, but that was nearly impossible because the wind tended to swirl in the clearing and there were too many landers moving to and fro.

He waited for the apprentices to settle and tried to not think about the reek stuffed into his nostrils. He entered the round building and went to the center. He left his cats outside to patrol and round up the others, moving them quickly towards the meeting hall. Most walked fast, others ran, afraid of his cats. The apprentices inside watched him. They didn't understand why he smiled.

Once they were all inside, his cats joined him and he nodded to the trolls, who quickly closed the doors.

Felix addressed the crowd, "Yesterday's trial exceeded my expectations. You've all advanced through your first trial without so much as a scratch or blemish. Enjoy these moments while you can for most of you will not be so lucky a few days from now." The scent of fear smashed his senses. His cougar's pulse jumped, sensing easy prey nearby. He pressed calm into her then she visibly relaxed.

"I also want you to be aware the trolls have already searched a little more than half of the forest looking for Jonah. They've combed every hole and turned over every rock. If he's lying somewhere wounded, they feel they'll find him today." Felix was beginning to wonder if the boy was hiding. He refused to speak this, but the trolls had actually been over every inch of the forest three times now. *One of them knows. Leonna or Ayah, maybe even Felicia or Jinx, they're just not saying.*

He paused and glanced over at Aquilo and Sammra who both nodded back. "Now we take part in something I think to be an equally important aspect of the trials, the sharing. To share with another wizard or apprentice is one of the highest honors. The wizards of Lasaat decreed only those who pass each successive trial could remain here for this reason: to maintain the sanctity of magical sharing. For as you will soon see, we will be sharing much, much more than mere stories of past experiences. Of course, among the landers there is a ban on sharing the manner and ways of magic and there is a saying—"

"Keep the forms pure," Sammra completed the sentence. "We are sharing experiences, not skills and techniques. You are not to give away your master's teachings or muddle the forms. Only share wisdom you have learned to help others make better decisions in the future, share insights into the nature of people, those things we want—no, need—to share."

Aquilo stepped forward, his thick, white shirt draped open down the center, baring his muscular chest. "For many of you this will be your first such experience so, like all things, there is a right way and a wrong way to do it. The three of us will each be communicating to you an experience. Open yourselves up to our words, allow what we send out to seep into your life-force, to bond with the communication as muscle clings to bone. If you don't, what you will hear will only be a story and perhaps not even a good one at that."

Sammra said, "Speak for yourself." She gave him a toothy grin. She scanned the crowd and asked, "So how do you open yourself?"

Many of the apprentices glanced at each other nervously.

Sammra pointed at Pren. "Tell me, apprentice of sand."

Pren cleared her throat as her eyes dodged between Lithia and Shireen who were seated to her sides. "I-I think… I think… I mean, this was something we were supposed to learn at Lasaat. I tried, I did…" She paused, her mouth open, defeated.

Sammra said, "You will learn. The first step to knowledge is realizing you do not know something. The next step is seeking the answer. My own master often said, 'The integrity to admit ignorance coupled with hard work and sweat yields incalculable wisdom.' Yes, the masters taught us to share at Lasaat but the lesson was brief and from my own experience, many didn't master the connecting and sharing of memories. Additionally, what they tried to teach was to simply connect minds, one apprentice to another. Here one will share with many—much more difficult. Perhaps one of your friends might be able to assist you in explaining how."

Lithia spoke, "Clear your mind of all distractions. Attempt to hold no thought of your own in your head. Sometimes connecting is easier if you close your eyes. Allow the words to penetrate you."

"And how do you do that?"

Lithia seemed at a loss for words.

Shireen added, "These types of things are difficult to describe. I suspect our language does not possess words for such experiences as they are not physical or mental."

Felix leaped up, pointing his arm in the air. "Ahhh, exactly." His cats purred. He was surprised to hear such an insightful answer from someone who was at the trials for her first time. "Please continue."

Shireen's eyes met Felix's. "As I said, there are perhaps not *exact* words to describe, but I can try to approximate the experience. I try to visualize something physical and order my life-force do something similar to what I picture in my mind." Shireen seemed to struggle. "For example, I think of opening my arms wide, to give someone an embrace, open and welcoming, inviting this particular person into my bosom, to come extremely close to me, for our flesh could come no closer."

Entranced, he couldn't comprehend the thought, the emotion or why it popped into his mind but Felix imagined he were the person in her embrace. Shireen's eyes broke from Felix's. He felt he had lost something in that moment.

"This is how I understand the process," Shireen added. "Only a visualization. I tell my spirit to do the same thing. How exactly that happens, I cannot describe. You'll recognize when it happens."

Felix clapped. "Good. And from a first-timer no less."

Aquilo spoke, "This night the three of us will speak. But in future nights, those of you who remain will be called on to share. Remember, this is an honor. The goal is to provide wisdom and knowledge to your fellow apprentices so they might gain insight into the true nature of this world. Sharing now might help in political negotiations at some future time, negotiations that would determine the fate of a people. Something you experience now might later help save a village or even just one person. This knowledge might help you save a life, the most precious thing of all. I would ask everyone to think long and hard about your sharing. I consider it a sacred event and not a time to tell jokes or make light of past experiences."

Sammra added, "When one receives a sharing, the experience will be bonded to your life-force for all time as if it were one of your own memories. Please consider how you want all your fellow apprentices to remember you."

"Shall we begin?" Felix turned to Sammra. "Ladies first?"

Sammra said, "I defer to Aquilo. He is the most senior."

"Fine. Aquilo then."

Felix and Sammra sat down and bowed their heads. The trolls circled the space, turning over-sized knobs on the oil lanterns hanging from the walls. The room darkened.

Aquilo remained standing in the center, his head slung low, his arms outstretched, palms open. He mumbled, "Open, open, open. Open yourselves up to the wisdom of my words. Open, open, open."

Felix stretched out his senses across the crowd. Most of the older, more experienced apprentices had already opened up to the experience. As he suspected, most of the newer ones were having difficulty. Connecting in such a way took practice and almost all the new ones wouldn't understand how to open up themselves to the experience. He noted a few exceptions, Bel, Lithia, and Shireen. Yes, Shireen, she was incredibly open. He smiled. There was something about that girl. Felix couldn't quite put his finger on what he detected in her. He couldn't understand why he kept finding his eyes drawn to her. *Attraction? But how can I find attraction to such a one? She was a lander! Insane.* Yet there Felix found himself, staring at Shireen, fondling the slight curvature of her neckline with his eyes, enjoying the drape of her clothing over her legs and unable to comprehend why. He shook his head, trying to push the irrational desire out of his mind.

Aquilo began. "My first year at the trials, I had been a Tundric apprentice to the master of wind and storm, the mage of ice and snow, Master Jessark, for three years and he had recently taught me the wielding way."

In Felix mind's eye, as his eyes were closed, the blackness of the room was slowly replaced by a blizzard of white, blowing and swirling in a harsh wind. Bitter cold lashed at his skin. In the middle of the white, a glint flashed in the distance. His sight flew upon it, quickly approaching what he immediately recognized as Aquilo and another, older Tundric man, a wizard by appearance.

Aquilo's master, Jessark, no doubt. Aquilo was much younger than he is now, Felix thought. The Tundric apprentice was holding his hands up, alternately pushing them this way and that, directing the wind to push the snow into piles. He was controlled the ice and snow, directing the elements to move where he willed.

"He said I was ready," Aquilo continued. "Even with my recent mastery of this new magic, I was uncertain of myself since in the frigid mountains of the north we seldom see people from other lands. What type of trials would I be subjected to? Certainly not the ones I had grown so accustomed to for the trials were in the forest. For those of you who have connected, I do not need to tell you I was nervous."

The panic washed across Felix strongly as if he were having the sensation himself. Yet he could distinguish between his own emotions and those of Aquilo. Still, after all these years of connecting, he marveled at the experience. In his heart, fostering the sharing was one of the most vital things he could do to help all people to understand each other. He maintained the connection to Aquilo and his story as he opened his eyes and scanned the crowd.

Perhaps ten or more of the apprentices had not connected and were on the edge of giving up trying. He frowned at their lack of control and will. *Sometimes I think I'm wasting my time on these children. Why do their masters send them? Clearly they're not ready. They only comprehend the magic of words. They don't understand the intent behind the words is what give them power. They give up on anything internal immediately because they cannot understand how the magic works and they cannot understand because they cannot describe it. It's as the tree lover said, there are not words to describe. Shireen. An observant one she is.*

Felix smiled to himself realizing there was something else about Shireen he found attractive, something much more than her cute little smile. She had a wisdom and understanding well beyond her years. Felix had not met many landers that perceived things so readily the way she had just done. He decided to keep an eye on her. And that wasn't difficult for he found her uncharacteristically attractive.

Shireen's eyes were closed, her face placid. She appeared a porcelain statue. He found himself studying the line of her chin and how it lightly curved up to her ear. He watched her breathe. She was open, receptive, she was taking in the story, allowing Aquilo's tale to bond with her life-force. He could tell she was receiving more than the others. She was good at connecting and that was something to be admired.

Felix nodded to himself. She had just changed his mind for him about the children. No, he couldn't write them all off for she had just disproved his negative ideas. They weren't all unprepared, some of them were ready. She was.

He only wished they could visualize the big picture as well as he could. Perhaps if they could recognize the importance of understanding and fostering cooperation they wouldn't give up so readily. Was sharing hard? Yes. Nothing could be more difficult than trying to look through the eyes of someone you were raised to hate, but how else could they arrest that hatred?

Were they being immature? Of course. Many hadn't yet grown out of their competitiveness and childish ribbing of each other. Felix snorted, thinking of how they behaved openly in the courtyard in front of all the others. They bore no shame. Yet, Shireen's comment had reminded him there was yet hope. He would press on with this good work. Those ten or so probably wouldn't open up enough to bond. They wouldn't be here in another day or so anyway, but with the rest, he would push to make a difference.

Felix closed his eyes and yielded his attention to Aquilo's words. He saw the Tundric apprentice at the trials, many years ago. He wandered around in rapt amazement. He didn't know where to lay his eyes first. There were so many apprentices there from so many different lands. Piles of sand were being transformed into beautiful objects to his left. To his right, the trees were shifting their branches about, flinging objects and catching them. Glowing stones erupted from the ground all around him, forcing him to hop out of the way. He stopped and scanned for the stonecutter who had done it. A girl giggled. He recognized her immediately and smiled back. Ulta. They had attended University together. It was good to stumble upon her, but he couldn't shake the sensation, inside he was fearful and absolutely unprepared for the trials. There were so many here with such powerful abilities. What could he do?

That evening, before bedtime, Aquilo stayed out on the long benches in the courtyard. The light coming from the glowing magewood branch above the round building had dimmed so everyone could sleep.

He couldn't think of lying down, he was so restless. A light drifted towards him. He figured it was the worthys coming to tell him to go to bed, but was surprised to find Ulta holding a glowing rock.

"Hey, Aquilo."

"Can't sleep."

"Me neither. I'm so excited but at the same time so nervous."

"Tomorrow's going to be a big day."

Ulta slid closer to him. The side of her leg touched his. "I missed you."

Aquilo flushed red as he looked around but no one else was out of their huts. "I missed you too," he whispered as he looked down at his feet. After a time, he gained the courage to turn to her. "Do you think we made the right decision?" Aquilo's heart beat faster.

Ulta stared at him. Her eyes were so big, her lips so full. He wanted to press closer to her. He forced his eyes away from her unbearable beauty.

"We made a decision. It's too late now."

When Aquilo did not reply, she stood. He looked up at her and she motioned her head. He looked in that direction. One of the worthys was walking towards them. "Get some rest, Aquilo. Pass the trial. We'll speak afterward."

Aquilo tried to sleep, but he was haunted by visions of Ulta's smile, her pouty lips, her light-brown doe-eyes.

Someone rustled in the room. His eyes popped open. He realized it was morning.

Felix had heard this story before. Aquilo had shared the memory with him a few years back. He was not a little surprised Aquilo was revealing his emotions with so many. *He must have made peace with his loss,* Felix thought. As he listened to Aquilo's words, revealing his heart toward Ulta, Felix's eyes involuntarily drifted back to Shireen. Aquilo was Tundric and his desire had been strong for a stonecutter. The relationship was impossible on so many levels. Felix wondered if the fact that Shireen was a foreign woman was why he found her so interesting. He shook his head. *No, that's not it.* He had been around landers and avians before and he had never had one turn his head. But there was something about this girl.

Scent? His cats attracted each other during the mating time by giving off a specific odor. Perhaps Shireen was doing that to him.

Felix pushed his bobcat forward, it stepping softly into the crowd of apprentices. The cat walked up to Shireen and sniffed her then returned to its spot in front of Felix. He shook his head for she stunk like the others, like rank, perfumed soap.

Felix closed his eyes, letting the image of Aquilo come back into his mind. He was standing in the courtyard, sweating profusely, surrounded by the other apprentices, as Ulta walked down the path into the forest, looking back briefly, nervously, her eyes caressing Aquilo. She turned and stepped in, disappearing into the brush.

The Tundric apprentice couldn't take the waiting. It was against the rules of course, but he sent his life-force out anyway. He wouldn't help her, he couldn't, but he needed to find out how she was handling the trials. He drifted out of his body and into the trees. He kept off the path and sailed through the thick underbrush until he reached a small clearing. Ulta was standing there, looking at a tremendous rock balanced at the top of a pile of smaller rocks. A test of strength, she had to move the immense weight of the stone from the top without disturbing the gravel below.

Aquilo let out a sigh of relief. Ulta was a stonecutter.

She held up her hands, pointing them at the boulder.

Then something happened that worried Aquilo. Ulta faltered. Her hands shook as if the rock was too heavy for her. She sat the boulder back down and wiped her brow. Aquilo didn't understand what was the problem. He wanted to go to her but knew he couldn't. He wasn't supposed to be in the forest.

Ulta stepped closer to the pile and tried again. Clearly, she was unaccustomed to moving stones that were so far away. She levitated the boulder; it trembled in the air. She stepped closer and tried again.

Aquilo began to twitch in his spirit for Ulta was dangerously close. She was nearly standing under the boulder.

Aquilo relaxed as Ulta gained control of the large stone. She began to lower the boulder, standing under it. She inched herself away and to the left. A twig snapped behind her. Aquilo spun wanting to discover who or what it was, hoping he had not been found out. Something large crashed in the forest.

He turned back. A most terrible sight greeted him, the boulder was on the ground, Ulta, his love, pinned underneath. Aquilo's spirit rushed to her side, he didn't care about the rules anymore. Blood was on her lips. She was dying. She only had moments.

The worthys ran into the space and quickly tried to move the boulder away. Aquilo didn't remove his eyes from Ulta.

As the rock lifted off her, she gasped in pain. Her body was completely broken. A few moments later Ulta's spirit rose out of her body and went to Aquilo, floating there, beside him. She caressed his cheek and mouthed, "I will always love you," then faded away.

Felix realized Aquilo had stopped speaking and his

mind was no longer connected to his story. He scanned the crowd in the room and nodded to the trolls who turned up the light.

The apprentices stared at Aquilo, his face slack, his expression blank.

Felix stood. "Of course, the lesson is one of preparation. Be prepared. Know your abilities. Don't put yourself in an unrecoverable situation. You don't have your master here to stop you from doing something dangerous. Think about your surroundings and the dangers around you."

The feline stopped speaking, lost in his thoughts for a short time, then turned to Aquilo. "Good friend, I thank you for sharing your memories and your life with us."

The crowd repeated, "Thank you for sharing your memories and your life with us."

Sammra stood and stepped forward as Aquilo sat. "I hope all of you embraced that story. If you were able to connect, you experienced much deeper layers than simple words could convey. Aquilo was not sharing with you where the mistakes were made so you would condemn him or Ulta, but so you wouldn't fall in the same way. I hope you all can appreciate that. Sharing is a selfless act and at the core of what a wizard is expected to be."

Felix added, "If you were not able to connect, to open yourselves, please do not give up. Please continue to try. You'll eventually succeed." His voice was soft and soothing. He wanted them to understand. Sharing was so important.

Sammra waved at the trolls who dimmed the torches once again.

Her voice started low, almost at a whisper as if she

was still yet convincing herself that she should share this particular story. "The Sanhardin are a proud people. When you live in the desert and keep little for possessions, you tend to seek other things to weigh the value of a person. For them, they weigh each other in the balances of etiquette and behavior." She smiled. "Things the tree-lovers or stonecutters do without a thought would be the most embarrassing and grievous offense to the people of the desert. I tell you, I am familiar with a man who accidentally farted in public once. He rose from his seat and immediately walked out of the room and hid in his house for three months. That was the level of his shame at his offense. This is how the Sanhardin think."

Some in the crowd chuckled.

"With that understanding of my upbringing and cultural heritage, I will now share a story with you." She paused as if she was lost in her thoughts for some brief moments, then she began, sending out her connection to everyone, "It was my first attempt at passing the trials. I was doing quite well. No one had told me First-Years don't pass. I didn't know I wasn't supposed to do so well. After I advanced through the first few tests, I started to notice a few of the other apprentices mumbling as I passed by. I didn't understand why. I was troubled. Had I violated some unknown cultural etiquette from their lands? I tried to be as polite as I could possibly be, but I realized I wasn't familiar with their ways. I was terrified I had brought shame upon the Sanhardin by my behavior."

Felix's mind was lost in Sammra's story. He floated around the courtyard, watching the scene unfold. The others were jealous of her. Some others were irritated that she was doing so well when they were still struggling.

And her, Sammra, walked among them oblivious, worried she had grieved them with rudeness when they should be the ones apologizing to her for their contempt.

A few of the girls whispered to each other, snickering. They walked past Sammra and nodded. "Hey sand-girl," one said.

"A pleasure," Sammra said as she turned and smiled at them, bowing her head slightly.

She was so much more rigid and formal then, Felix thought. *I guess all these years around the others have burnished her edges.* Felix's mind drifted off to his own clan-family and how his life was so incomprehensibly different that the landers. If the landers can't understand each other, how could they possibly understand a feline's way of living?

Felix was glad two members of his clan-family were here, Felicia and Jinx. Even though Felicia was acting childish and disrespecting him, he was still happy she came. Giving the landers more exposure to the good side of creature-kind would only help understanding in the log run. He had hoped more of the clans would have been willing to send their cubs when he sent out the call. And the avians, the largest group of them all and they only sent three. And of the three, one is missing. The loss of Jonah vexed Felix. He had promised he would watch over the cubs and fledglings, all of them, not only the felines but the avians too. He had met Jeneth's eyes when he had spoken the words. The oath of a feline is a powerful thing and now the boy was missing. It did not escape Felix that Jonah was not only an avian but Jeneth's own son. He needed to find out what happened to the boy. He needed to speak with Jinx and Felicia, Leonna and Ayah, separately and alone. Leonna and Felicia, especially. *Those two know more than they're letting on.* Felix pushed Jonah out of his mind and jumped back into the flow of Sammra's story.

Sammra was laying down to sleep. There were three other girls in the room, all in their beds. After Sammra dozed off, two of them tiptoed over to Sammra's bunk. They were the two girls Sammra had greeted earlier in the courtyard.

"Psst, Sammra. Are you awake?" one whispered.

When Sammra didn't stir, the other opened her sand pouch hanging from the corner of her bed and dropped in a few pebbles.

The two stepped back to their beds, giggling.

"The next morning I awoke and readied myself for the next trial. I found out much later the two girls intended only to play a little joke on me. They thought it innocent and humorous to use their stone magic to control the pebbles, to make my pouch bounce when we were in the morning meeting," Sammra said.

As she continued speaking, Felix saw Sammra go to the gathering. The two girls who had put the stones into her pouch were called away. The two forgot all about the rocks in Sammra's pouch.

Sammra walked down the path towards her next trial. Before she reached the clearing, a boulder fell behind her. She leaped. Then another stone fell and another. The rocks coalesced and rose, forming a man of stone who quickly swung a boulder of a fist.

Sammra grabbed at her pouch, but her sand resisted her. The stone-man laughed as the rocks in her pouch bounced about, preventing her from opening the bag. "Pebbles?" the stone-man grumbled and swung again.

Sammra dove to the ground, throwing her pouch at

the stone-man's face. The bag split open on the warrior's flint nose and the sand fell out.

Sammra stood, backing into the clearing, holding one hand out in front of her and calling the sand.

The particles flew across the space forming a large shield. The stone creature swung, hitting nothing as the sand quickly disintegrated. The force of his swing threw him off balance. Sammra turned her hand, sending the sand around the creature's neck, tightening around his throat in a band. The stone-man grasped at the sand, trying to fling it away, but the particles moved tighter and tighter.

"Do you yield?" she barked.

The creature fell to one knee and nodded.

Sammra stopped speaking and the trolls turned the lights up. She waited until the apprentices looked up. "It would seem no one was seriously injured and I still passed the trial so there was little impact to the story. However, against my wishes the two stonecutters were ejected from the trials. At the time, I thought the punishment too severe. They were only playing a little joke, they said. Perhaps, in their eyes, they were even reaching out to me as a friend would. Friends do such things to each other. Jokes. I understand. Fun."

Felix continued the thought. "My wish is everyone would become friendly, but there is a need for order and discipline. If you think of some funny trick to pull on someone, don't." Felix waited for some moments then nodded to Sammra who sat down.

"I am a feline and although my people do not like the term, to you I am one of the creature-kind." He paused again, gathering his thoughts for a few moments. "Our peoples have been somewhat mistrustful of each other for many years. This distrust and suspicion eventually culminated in a war between several of the nine forms. Now whatever your opinion on who did what to whom first or who started the conflict… I am not here to argue or discuss. We learned where that led. So there is a group of us who want to stop that from ever happening again."

Felix began pacing, "Of course, the war didn't solve anything as the distrust and suspicion yet persists and this is one of the reasons so few avians and felines are in attendance this year and none of the other so-called creature-kind chose to attend. However, having these few attend is still progress and I want to celebrate the fact any is here at all. It is a step."

Aquilo clapped first then the rest followed.

"If our peace is to hold, we need things like this to continue and to strengthen. Are we different people? Yes, of course. Do we think and act differently? Sure. But what we need to do is to take time to speak to each other, learn from each other and to understand," Felix said and shook his head. "To let old prejudices die with the aging masters and rise up a new generation who have an understanding of how this world might be different."

Aquilo added, "Changing the world starts with changing the mind of a single person."

Felix smiled. "I want everyone to take what you learned here back to your masters. Speak with them. Some would say this is sacrilege, but an apprentice can indeed teach a master too."

He motioned at the trolls who dimmed the torches. Felix began his tale. "It was my first year at the trials. The felines do not retain such a hierarchy as apprentice and worthy apprentice and so on. This is a lander thing, but the wizards of Lasaat, Master Jeneth and Sturfelis and others, thought one of the creature-kind of such ability could help out at the trials. I volunteered."

Felix sent the vision of his memory out to the crowd.

Felix and his three cats entered the forest of the trials and wandered through the small village. His cats stayed close, nearly hugging his legs, yet apprentices were running from him and some others were taking aggressive positions as if he were single-handedly intent on invading the Worthy Apprentice Trials.

He was nervous. What should he do if one of them attacked him or wounded one of his cats?

Aquilo ran out to him, holding his hand up to the others. He greeted him in the welcoming fashion of the Tundric, touched the heads of each of his cats in a loving way, put his arm over his shoulder and brought him in.

Felix learned from Aquilo and helped where he could. At first, he only did whatever Aquilo instructed him to do. Felix was amazed at the frightened and off-putting behavior of the landers and found he was learning much more about them than they were about him.

It took quite some time, especially for his cats, but he slowly began to feel comfortable around the landers, even though few would speak to him, especially if his cougars were around.

A few days later, Felix heard a cry near the rear of the camp and ran towards the wood. He found a forest apprentice on the ground near the rear edge of the tree line. Apparently she had been practicing and had fallen from one of the trees. She was unconscious, scratched and cut from the branches during the fall. A few moments later a few other apprentices arrived and one pointed and screamed, "The feline mauled Petula."

"No, that's not what happened," Felix said as he began to stand. A blast of sand slammed him on the chest, pummeling him several feet into the forest. He scrambled behind a tree and screamed, "Wait! I didn't hurt her!" Another force, a ball of ice, pelted the ground near him.

Felix glanced around the tree while rocks, ice, sand, and balls of energy struck the earth, sending up clods of dirt and smashing trees, shredding bark.

What should I do? If I use my cats to attack certainly no one would wait for an explanation. Not until he was dead.

Felix pushed his mind into his bobcat and sent it to get Aquilo.

His cougar ran to Felix's side. He touched his head and said, "Sorry, you play decoy today."

A rock smashed into Felix's ear and blood sprayed on his cat.

He shook with rage. He nearly sent his cougar to rip out the stonecutter's throat. There's no way the apprentice of stone could stop the big cat. It would be easy.

Felix wiped his ear and stood, trying to minimize how much of his body was exposed.

The cougar ran out from behind the tree and began leaping and dodging stones, balls of ice, sand, and swooping branches. He never attacked, only ran, leaped, dodged, and hid as the rocks, tree branches, and energy balls spiraled down, smashing into the trees and earth.

"Stop! Stop! Stop!" Aquilo yelled.

After a few moments, the barrage ceased and Felix came out from behind the tree.

Felix stopped feeding the memory to the apprentices and began speaking. "Sometimes we hold our prejudices deep down. As long as things go well, they do not surface. But when certain situations arise, we tend to allow those hidden and deep-seated views to affect our decisions." His voice was flat. "That day, Aquilo saved a life. Whether the life was mine or someone else's, I cannot say. So my story illustrates a point. Don't let the tale depress you, rather I share to give you hope. Prejudice is a problem of all people but we can change that." Felix paused, looking into the eyes of many of the apprentices.

"That is the end of the sharing. For those who did not connect, please try again at the next gathering." Felix nodded. The trolls opened the doors.

The apprentices slowly rose and walked out, many discussing whether or not they were able to fully connect to their stories.

Aquilo leaned over to Felix as they walked out. "I'm glad you brought your young apprentices."

"As am I. Felicia and Jinx, I only hope they represent us well."

"And that one?" he mumbled as he motioned towards Leonna.

"Leonna? The avian?"

"I'm glad she came."

Felix turned to Aquilo with a sly grin on his face. "Oh? Why's that?"

"I can't do anything, but I like to ogle anyway."

"Why torture yourself?"

Aquilo shrugged. "Too bad we can't marry like you felines."

Felix sighed. "And would you if you could?"

"What?"

"If you had to leave the frozen Tundra for your dream

girl over there, would you?"

Aquilo smiled. "Don't get me wrong. She's lovely, but no. Smelling the flowers doesn't mean I want to pick them."

Felix shook his head as he walked out, then he noticed Felicia near the exit. Felix glanced at his cougar. It popped up and ran in front of Felicia and growled.

"What do *you* want?" she said, trying to step around the cat.

Felix caught up to her as she walked outside. He lightly grabbed Felicia's arm. "Hey sis, we need to talk."

"Uhm, let go of my arm."

Felix waited. She turned to walk away. He tugged her again. "Hey, I said we need to talk."

She shook his hand loose. "We? You mean *you* want to lecture me again. Look around. We're not back at the clan."

"Felicia, give me a break. I'm not going to lecture you. I just have a question."

She stared up at him.

Felix continued, "It's about Jonah. I wanted to know —"

She cut him off with a wave of her hand. "Are you serious? I didn't say anything when you asked the group. What do you think? That I'm hiding something?"

She was lying, of course. It was dripping out of her pores. His cats could sense her deceit from a mile away. He forced his face to remain calm and even.

The question was *why* would she lie. If she knew something about the avian boy, why wouldn't she just tell him? It couldn't be the fact that he was her big brother and she loved torturing him, could it? She had to understand Jonah's safety was more important than that.

So why wouldn't she tell him? Did she make some mistake that caused Jonah to get hurt? "I only thought you might have something you might want to say to me that you didn't want to say in front of everyone else."

She sneered up at him, "Well, I don't. Okay? That all?"

She had always been strong and independent, it was the feline in her, but Felix noted that Felicia was acting especially peculiar. She walked away.

"Yeah, I guess so, sis," he mumbled to himself.

A few moments later, Felix jumped as his cats leaped to attention when a scream wailed through the space. He ran toward the source of the scream with his cougars, through the center courtyard and past the men's huts to the edge of the forest. There, lying on the ground, was Drake, his body arranged in an unnatural angle. Blood was in his open mouth, his vacant eyes staring oddly at the sky. His neck was broken.

"Stand back," Felix barked at the gathering apprentices. He checked Drake's life-force and finding none, announced what everyone already knew, "He's dead."

Kerlith said from behind, "He had been practicing, spending a lot of time back here. I saw him. He was always up in the trees. He must have fallen."

Sammra walked up and added, "Obviously, he fell. Why wasn't anyone with him? Why was he alone?" She scanned their faces then shook her head, frowning, when no one said. "No one noticed that he wasn't at the sharing?"

Bel and Naga ran in and dove to their knees in front of the man, Bel crying, "Drake? Drake? No!"

Chapter Nine
The Iron Warrior

Shireen stood next to Lithia, nervously shuffling her feet. Pren had been gone too long. She had gone down the path to the trial just like all the others, but the others had come back quickly. Shireen was growing more nervous by the moment.

"It's been too long," Lithia muttered. "Shouldn't someone check on her?" She glared at the worthys, Aquilo, Felix, and Sammra. They were chatting as if nothing was wrong.

Shireen began pacing. *Where was Pren?*

Lithia tugged her sleeve. "Shireen, stop. You're making me nervous."

"Making you nervous? Where's Pren?"

A loud moan came from the forest. The sand apprentice stumbled out and promptly fell to the ground. Her head was bloody.

Shireen ran to her. "Pren!" She fell to her knees, lifted Pren's head from the ground and wiped away the blood revealing a deep gash. "Somebody, do something!" she screamed.

Lithia joined Shireen at Pren's side. "Pren! Pren! What happened?"

Sammra and Aquilo pushed through the crowd

circling Pren's crumpled body.

Aquilo asked, "Is she alive?"

Tears blinded Shireen. She nodded.

Sammra barked at the closest troll, "Burn, take her to the clinic. Tend to her wounds."

Shireen stared in shock as the troll pulled Pren's body from her arms and lumbered away. She looked down and discovered her hands were covered in Pren's blood, hot and wet.

Sammra barked at everyone, "All of you know the rules. You're not supposed to cross the line while another apprentice is still in a trial. Shireen, you were the first to cross. Sorry. I would like to give you a moment to get your wits about you, but the rules are clear. You crossed the line. Now you go in next. Everyone back up." She waved at Shireen. "Go ahead."

Shireen stood and cleared her throat.

Lithia stared at her, terrified.

Shireen turned her head, not sure exactly what to do. Above the crowd, a hand waved and someone pushed through. It was Bel. He pressed to the front, stopped at the line and said, "Shireen, look at me." When her eyes met his, he shuddered as if he was unsure what exactly he was going to say, then he started, "You can do this, Shireen. You can. Just…" He paused. "Just watch your back. Remember, you don't want to get… hurt. Be careful. You can do this."

Shireen glanced in the direction the troll had taken Pren. She turned and walked down the path, muttering to herself, "Pren, what did you do? Oh El, please watch over her."

Shireen nervously baby-stepped down the path. The vision Sammra had shared of a rock creature jumping out at her was in the front of her mind. She wanted to be ready for anything. Pren was one of the most careful people she knew and her head had been split open by whatever was out here. She could have died.

Shireen tried to shake the image of thick red fluid spurting from Pren's scalp out of her mind. She wiped her hands on her legs again, but the blood had already dried and caked, like paint. She wanted to stop and scrape it off, but she had no time for that.

Shireen stepped into the clearing. Squatting opposite her was a huge statue of metal, a suit of armor holding an immense sword stabbed into the earth. Slowly, the helmet tilted up at her and the metal warrior stood. The statue was nearly ten feet tall and holding a sword easily taller than Shireen.

She gasped as she held her hand up to her eyes to block the sun glare off the metal man. Shireen realized no one was inside the enchanted armor. The challenge was clearly to fight the metal warrior, but how could she defeat him when there was no one inside?

The warrior ran towards Shireen, its sword held high. At the last moment, she dove out of the way as the sword came crashing down into the dirt where she had stood moments before.

Shireen rolled to her feet and ran to the spot the soldier had recently occupied when she walked into the clearing. She was cornered.

"Wait." She held up her two hands, trying to make the warrior pause.

The soldier spun, flinging its sword at her. She tumbled to the right, the blade grazing the flesh of her calf. She rolled, grabbing her leg and wincing in pain.

As the warrior walked towards the sword and wrested

the blade from the earth, Shireen popped up and dodged to the edge of the tree line. She could go no further for to hide in the trees was to quit and accept defeat.

Shireen pulled out her wand and futilely pointed the twig at the metal warrior. It had no brain. She couldn't control the enchanted warrior, yet she tried. "Stop. I command you."

The metal suit of armor did not pause or laugh or do anything but advance on her position, stepping methodically closer to Shireen and swinging its over-sized blade in an arc aimed at removing her head from her body.

The girl ducked then skipped to the edge of the clearing. She touched the bark on the tree, trying to communicate with the oak as Bel had shown her. She moaned and hummed, attempting to tell the tree to swing its branches at the warrior. In a moment, the soldier was upon her. The tree didn't respond so she ran again, racing to the other side of the clearing.

Shireen was starting to tire, she realized, as she gasped for air. She rested her palm on a maple, waiting for the warrior to come closer before she ran to the other side. In the few moments it took for the metal monster to traverse the space, Shireen hummed to the tree. The tiniest of movements rippled in the trunk and she thought she might have communicated with the tree. *Did the tree understand my cry for help?*

The blade swung and Shireen dove. She landed in the dirt between the warrior's legs. The soldier picked up a foot and tried to stomp her so she rolled and inched forward on her elbows and knees. Once she was clear, she hopped back up to her feet and ran to the other side. The soldier turned.

Shireen caught sight of something floating in the air. She reached out and touched the strands, not initially recognizing what they were. She gagged. Tiny strands of her hair. The warrior's sword had nearly scalped her on its last swing.

Shireen seriously thought about quitting then. It wouldn't be difficult. Just wait for the soldier to come closer and run past him. When she reached the other side, she could continue to run down the path and out of the forest. Just one more little run and her time at the Trials would be all over. The trolls would escort her out and she would go back to Sha'mont and her warm bed.

The warrior raised his sword high and swung the blade, stabbing the tip into the earth as Shireen leaped out of the way. She dodged over to the other side, near the clearing entrance and stared at the path. Her heart was racing for she didn't want to quit, but she couldn't figure out how she could defeat the enchanted armor.

The metal man came towards her, his arms outstretched. He was stepping wide, trying to block her from running around him this time. He had left his sword in the ground on the other side of the clearing.

Shireen decided to give the trees one last try. If she could only connect with the trees, maybe she would have a chance.

She popped high in the air, then ducked down when the metal man swung his two arms at her. She dodged around him and ran past his sword. She calmed herself as she placed her hands between two trees and began humming the few words of tree-language Bel had taught her. The bark reverberated under her hands. She pushed the image of a branch picking up the soldier and holding him high in the air into her mind and hummed again.

Something tingled in her fingertips. A few of the branches moved above. She smiled.

As the soldier approached, Shireen tensed, realizing that if the trees did not move she might not be able to escape.

The metal man reached down for her. A branch swung in from the right, battering the soldier, nearly knocking him to the ground. He tottered and swiped his hand at the air for something to right himself. His hand fell to the hilt of his sword. He tumbled back, falling on his bottom, sword in hand.

A tingly sensation pricked all over Shireen. *It was working!*

The soldier got back up and advanced. Another branch swung, battering the soldier's head. From the left, another limb struck. And then another.

Shireen pushed a vision in her mind of the soldier being pummeled to the ground by branches as she moaned, whistled and sung to the trees.

The oak drew its limbs back, swinging at the soldier. As he spun, swinging his sword in the air, he broke two branches and damaged a third. Branches fell all around Shireen forcing her to leap out of the way. The metal man scooped her up in his hand and squeezed.

She released an ear-piercing scream as she squirmed, trying to free herself, her throat closing in panic.

The warrior had her good and tight. Its fingers wrapped around her abdomen and as the soldier tightened its grip, Shireen realized it would take little effort for this enchanted suit of armor to squeeze just a little harder and kill her.

The warrior pulsed its fingers as if it were milking udders. Shireen began to pass out. She wondered why she didn't run down the path. Clearly she wasn't ready. Clearly. Now she was going to die. Another statistic of the Worthy Apprentice Trials. They told her people got hurt, people died, but even after Onyx and Drake, all that didn't seem real until just now. Shireen was about to die and not for trying to save the lives of her people but in the hands of an empty suit of armor. *Ridiculous.*

The hand drew her a little closer to its head as if the empty shell could perceive her struggle and enjoy her frantic, useless efforts to free herself. A light blue tint surrounded the helmet. *The enchantment,* she thought.

The warrior squeezed again and Shireen's vision darkened. Dizzy, she couldn't get enough air in her lungs.

Without thinking, Shireen pulled out her twig of a wand and stabbed the branch into the crease where the helmet and shoulders met. *At least, I'll hit the warrior with something before I die.*

The creature reeled, yanking her away. With its free hand, it clawed at her wand that was wedged into the suit.

Out of the corner of her eye, she saw the smallest of sparkles emanating from the crease where the wand had stuck.

The warrior pulled her close once more as it began its final squeeze, its fist tightening to a ball. Shireen reached out her hand for the wand but was unable to reach the twig.

In desperation, she pushed all the air out of her lungs as she began to black out, shifting her body, forcing her hand the tiniest bit closer. Finally, the tip of her finger struck the wand and she attempted to push the enchantment away.

The suit crumpled to the ground and Shireen fell

from the air, smashing into the metal suit.

Shireen laid there, staring at the blue sky, wondering if she was alive. After some time, she stood and checked herself to determine where she was injured. She figured at least one of her ribs was probably broken since she was still having a difficult time breathing and where the sword struck her leg was still bleeding.

She gathered her wand and stuffed the twig in her sleeve, then limped down the path.

Chapter Ten
Share More

Shireen checked the tightness of her bandages then joined the others in the round hall, preparing for the day's sharing.

Felix addressed the group, "Before we begin, I want to remind everyone to be careful during your practice sessions. The unfortunate responsibility to contact Lasaat has fallen to me twice now, to report the deaths of Onyx and Drake. Telling an archmage that an apprentice died is not something I like to do. The archmages made the connection a most painful experience and they were right to do so because the deaths of these two apprentices were a completely unnecessary loss of life. I don't want to find any more of you hurt or killed. I guess that's all I need to say."

After a long pause, Sammra stood and began speaking. "Today's sharing will be less formal than the previous and, additionally, we will hold a question and answer session at the end. Are there any volunteers who wish to speak about his or her lands, masters or experiences? Remember, we are not to share techniques, skills or specific knowledge of the nine forms."

The crowd grew quiet and Shireen glanced at her two friends.

Sammra added, "There are those who are dying to hear about the dragon."

Shireen's eyes went wide. The last thing she wanted to do was stand and talk about her life. She couldn't let all these people into her head without one of them discovering her feelings for Bel or how she almost killed herself. She shook her head frantically.

Sammra pursed her lips. "Perhaps another day."

The other apprentices nervously spied each other in silence.

Pren raised her hand and Shireen's mouth dropped open.

Sammra called on her. "Pren. Good. You had trouble connecting the first time. This will be good practice for you."

Pren stood and said, "Thank you, everyone, for allowing me the privilege of telling you about my life and my people. It is an honor. I will do my best to not bore you."

"We'll see about that," Kerlith mumbled.

Lithia kicked him and he yelped.

Pren said, "I live in the desert and train under Master Samira. The most important thing a sand wizard can learn is how to locate the source of water. I've spent nearly every waking hour perfecting this skill. Each day, I place my hands on the sand and try to find moisture. One day I hope to be able to channel the water, to collect it and funnel it by moving the sand and earth. Life depends upon it."

Pren placed her hand on the soft earth in the center of the room and closed her eyes. "Here, water is in abundance." As she slowly stood, water erupted from the ground in a spurt, following the direction of her hand.

She smiled and let the water return to the ground.

"Pren, good story so far, but you're not connecting. Send. Open your mind."

"I'll try. In the desert, wizards travel in packs, it is the only way the desert people can survive. To be alone means death for the conditions are too harsh. So, unlike the tree-lovers or stonecutters, I'm usually among other wizards and apprentices besides my own master. At night, during our private time, the apprentices all practice making things out of sand, which, of course, the non-magical kids love."

She sent her sand swirling around the crowd. The particles formed small balls. The orbs swarmed and bobbled around.

"As far as the culture of the Sanhardin, my people are loving and caring. Survival depends upon sharing our meager supplies with others. When someone is in need, everyone gives to help out for no one knows when they will be in the same situation. There is honor in aiding the less fortunate and everyone is eager to share food, clothing and the like. Of course, with resources so scarce, we do not give to those who waste and my people are generally distrustful of foreigners." A weak, embarrassed smile crossed her lips. "I am happy to be here and to learn your ways. My wish is to learn from you and you from me. I believe in what the worthys said, if we learn from each other, distrust will evaporate."

Pren sat quickly and Shireen rubbed her shoulder. "You did good."

Sammra scowled as Pren didn't connect at all. "Okay, that was quick. But quick is not necessarily a bad thing. Any other takers?"

Most of the apprentices averted their eyes.

"Kerlith, how about you?" Sammra asked. "You were with the group that closed the tear that released the ghoul-kind. You told me the story before yourself. It's a good one."

Kerlith said, "Bel here was the big hero. Let him tell the tale." The stonecutter sounded salty.

Sammra paused, considering Kerlith. "Someone else then." She was about to turn to the others when Kerlith spoke again. "I won't tell that story, but I'll tell you what happened after."

Sammra motioned her arm. "You own the floor."

Kerlith cleared his throat and began. "What Sammra said is true. I was there, at the breach. Not pretty. My master was not the only one who wanted to stop the ghoul-kind. Bel and his master did too. Most of you know my master died. I don't fault anyone there. At least, Bel's master answered the call. It's more than I can say of any of the others. They all hid away, protected in their little holes like frightened rabbits. Only my master decided to stand for what was right and it got him killed."

Kerlith stood and began slowly walking up and down the aisle. Everyone was staring at him. "It might sound like I'm bitter, but I'm not. I've made peace with his sacrifice. Everyone dies sometime and my master died doing something heroic. His death fit him for in life he was a hero. At least, to me anyway."

Kerlith stopped talking for a few moments. He nodded at Bel. "Without a master, an apprentice cannot continue to train. It is our… law. I understand that most who have been in my predicament give up and try to go back to their old lives before magic, but that wasn't for me. I'm not a quitter. I determined to find a master, even if I would be a second." Kerlith closed his eyes as he began sending out the vision of what happened.

In a flash, Shireen saw Kerlith's memory. He traveled alone for days and months, visiting village after village, in search of a master. A disgruntled, jaded resentment washed over her. Kerlith hated the fact he lost his master to save the world and now the world was turning its back on him.

"I roamed aimlessly for a while. I must have visited every village in the entire eastern mountains at least twice trying to find a wizard to take me. I figured with what I had done—helped save the world and all, if you think about it—someone would be persuaded to take me as an apprentice. But that proved to be more difficult than I thought."

His voice took on a harsh edge. "I drifted about, like I said, and after a while, I began to notice things, things I never noticed before. They were always there, of course, but I didn't recognize them. The world was much different from what I thought. There was so much need in the villages—the sick and the poor. Magic was not only about doing things like fighting against the ghoul-kind, but helping people in little ways. I felt helpless. I mean, I wanted to help them, but what could I do? My skills and my training weren't equal to the need. I knew how to light stones and pull them out of the ground and make rocks fly to attack ghouls, but how could I use that to help people who didn't have enough to eat?"

Kerlith tried to help children and the frustration at being ineffectual grabbed Shireen's heart in a cold, iron fist. He wanted to help; he didn't know how. If only his master had taught him more of this type of magic, the magic people truly needed, the magic of healing wounds, of soothing emotional distress, and comforting in the time of the death of a loved one.

Kerlith appeared disturbed as he swung his gaze across the hall. "I realized the world was a different place than I had thought. I guess I began to change. I wanted to redirect my focus and training. I continued traveling, but wherever I went, I tried to aid the poor and destitute. Then my big break came. I found out I might be able to join a group of wizards in the desert."

Sammra asked, "When we met you?"

Another vision replaced the last. Shireen saw Kerlith trudging across a barren wasteland of sand, the eastern desert, a no man's land. He was alone, with only a single flask. She couldn't understand how he survived, yet oddly, he had no fear.

Kerlith nodded, "I had no idea if they would take a stonecutter, but the Sanhardin were cordial and their wizards and apprentices traveled in groups. I thought I wouldn't necessarily need a single master with them. It was the longest journey of my life. I traveled across the entire eastern mountain range, on foot most of the way. I found a caravan headed for Ragul that would let me travel with them in exchange for my labor. The trip took two months. And as Sammra said, when I arrived I met her group and stayed with them for a time."

"He was, shall we say, not good at sand." Sammra chuckled.

"Better than you are at stone magic," Kerlith's voice was teasing.

"That was only for a dare," Sammra clarified.

The vision abruptly ceased then Kerlith said, "So, as luck would have it, my deeds hadn't gone unnoticed. A wizard who learned of my work with the poor sent word.

He gave me direction; he took me on. I won't say his name because he hasn't yet officially granted me the status as his apprentice, however, he's told me if I pass the trials I will be blessed with a new master. And that is what I intend to do."

Kerlith slumped his body down in his chair. "So now you all witnessed why the apprentice with no master is here. Hopefully, that condition won't continue too much longer and my lot will change."

Shireen shook her head. She had always disliked Kerlith, now she had no idea what to think of the man.

"Thank you, Kerlith. There is time perhaps for one more. How about you, Jinx?" Felix pointed at him.

Jinx shrugged and stood. "I am of the feline clan of Bald Mountain. One of the things we do is patrol the area surrounding our camp. We send out our cats seeking other predators and prey. We track the movements of the herds so if they get too far away, we can follow them. One night, my cats and I were on patrol when we spotted a pack of wolves. I figured the filthy canines were sticking their nose into out territory again, so I—"

"Hold on there, Jinx." Felix held his hands up. "That's not the kind of story we want here."

He puzzled at the interruption. "Why? You were there. You saw what they did. I'm only going to tell the truth. Those rotten, stinking dogs are always up to no good. They needed to be taught a lesson."

"I understand your point. It's not what we need here. Okay, everyone. It's getting late." He motioned to Jinx to sit.

"I appreciate all your stories and sharing," Felix said as he stood. "Now time for questions. Anyone?"

Leonna raised her hand. "Can you tell us anything

about the rest of the trials? Will all the trials require us to be alone, or are there any more with teamwork? Can you give us any hints?"

Aquilo responded, "Ahh, no hints. As to teamwork? No, for the rest, you will each be alone. All I can say is what you learned in the introduction. Each trial is designed to test a single wizardly attribute: physical strength, magical power, decision making, stamina, teamwork, and courage. They may be in any order, but, at least, you know what you have completed so you can guess at what will come next based on what is left."

Pren raised her hand and asked, "How are we doing so far compared to previous years?"

Sammra answered, "Hard to say with only two trials completed. Usually, there's one trial much harder than we anticipated which takes out somewhere around half of the apprentices. Clearly, that hasn't happened yet."

Kerlith spoke, "What comes next? I mean, after I, ahh, we pass the trials. How do we become worthy?"

Felix said, "Those that pass all trials will retire to Lasaat where they will receive their promotion in an enthusiastic ceremony attended by many wizards and archmages."

Ayah raised his hand so Sammra pointed at him. "Any other word on Jonah? Has he been found yet?"

Felix cleared his throat and turned to face Ayah directly. "Not yet. The trolls have been searching for him nonstop, no break or rest. What we know for certain is he didn't leave the forest. He is here. Somewhere. We just need to locate him."

"But what happened to Jonah?" Ayah asked.

"We do not know. He's somewhere in the forest. We'll find him."

Naga raised his hand.

"Yes?" Sammra said, pointing at Naga.

"In Kerlith's fine tale, him, a stonecutter, went to the desert lands in an attempt at becoming a wizard of sand. Is this allowed by the law? I've never heard of a wizard changing form. Wouldn't he then know the magic of two forms?"

Sammra cleared her throat. "The law is clear; wizards are to maintain purity of form. I suppose, aah, Kerlith didn't really learn much yet. Erm, aah, he was just getting started with rocks." Her eyes bouncing from the crowd to Aquilo, clearly looking for help.

Kerlith added, "Sand is just tiny little rocks anyway."

Aquilo stepped forward. "Many of you have questions about such a law—"

"Magic belongs to all of us," Pren blurted out then looked over at Shireen, smiling. Shireen quickly cast her eyes to the floor.

"Yes. Quite," Aquilo said. "Many years ago, there was no such classification of magic into forms. There was no such thing as stone magic or sand magic or forest magic. There was just… magic."

Several in the crowd gasped.

"Different ones of ability discovered things. One learned how to speak to the trees, another how to channel life-force through crystals, another how to seek moisture deep underground. These were the first wizards, although they did not call themselves so. They were just people, special people, and they passed their knowledge on to others."

Sammra chimed in after she had gained her composure. "There was no need for a wizard of the desert to learn how to speak to trees for there were no trees in the desert."

"No snow or ice either," Aquilo added.

"So yes, the nine forms developed independently." Sammra closed her mouth and looked at Naga.

After a few moments, Naga said, "I apologize, Good and Worthy Apprentice, but I do not see where that answers my question. Perhaps I have missed your meaning."

"Yes, well, it so happens that after many years, hundreds, perhaps thousands, the forms of magic became mature. Spells were written down and traded among wizards. There was an established body of knowledge that was guarded and secret. Yet those who were friends would share information. Then, unfortunately, the wars came, the ones you all studied at University, and then the laws of men were written and here we are today." Sammra painted a smug grin on her face.

Naga started to speak, "Still, I—" but stopped when Shireen kicked him under the table.

Aquilo said, "We are all apprentices here. It is my hope that one day we will all be wizards. One day, the duty will fall to us to guard the lives of our people and to help them in their needs. I understand the question that burns in some of your hearts. The laws of men seem unfair. You don't understand their purpose. If I could use the magic of another form to come to the aid of my people then why does the Law prevent this? Still, it is the Law, even if they are the laws of men, men who have no knowledge of the ways of magic, and we, as apprentices, are in no position to change such laws. Perhaps, someday we will. As to Kerlith and his situation, I cannot speak for I was not there. Maybe if he had he taken to sand, the sand wizards would have had a predicament on their hands. I suppose they would have had to petition their rulers to make an exception to accept him. Would they have taken the risk? Would they have approved him? No one can say."

Sammra added, "I know the desire to learn magic, any and all magic, is in the hearts of all of you like a dry sponge that seeks water. I would that you could all learn what I have to teach, but such is not the current state of things."

The crowd grew silent, then Pren spoke. "Something has always bothered me about all of this."

Aquilo exhaled loudly. "Go on."

"We all learned the same magic back at University. The basic stuff, we were told. Controlling life-force, gathering life-force, basic communication, and sharing. Some of us were already naturally inclined to one form or the other and could move small stones, twigs, or sand. Even sense the presence of moisture."

When Pren stopped speaking, Aquilo asked, "There is a question here. I think I know what you want to ask. Where is the dividing line? Why can all learn these basic things but cannot learn more advanced?" He glanced at Sammra.

Sammra said, "It's the Law. The law was created by men, women too, but mostly men, rulers, kings and queens, potentates, emperors, people who don't have the least concept of how magic works." Sammra fell silent, her eyes bulged.

Aquilo added, "Let's keep it that way. Now please, are there other questions?"

Shireen raised her hand.

"Yes?" Sammra said.

"Felix, I understand you attended the Wizard Trials?

Can you tell us how they differ from these? I've heard seers scan the apprentices. Why? Do the seers scan for emotions? Or for some other reason?"

Felix fidgeted. "Yes, I attended the Wizard Trials once. Last year. I didn't pass, obviously. Are they different? Yes. I cannot actually describe them to you for there is a somewhat personal element to the trial. Let me say they are nothing like what you would expect." He met Shireen's gaze. "As to the seers, they were there. I didn't advance that far. I don't know what they're seeking."

Before Felix could move on, Shireen said, "One more, please?"

Felix nodded.

Shireen asked, "I'm interested in the courtship rituals of the creature-kind and why you are encouraged to marry, since we are prohibited."

Felix pursed his lips. "I can speak of our way, but I don't want to be drawn into the middle of any controversy with the landers. I think we're just different. We marry and that works for us. Our courtship is as any other. There is poking and prodding from the clan-fathers and clan-mothers and jockeying and competition among suitors. All as you would imagine."

When no one had any other questions, Aquilo stood. Shireen noticed his eyes followed Leonna. He said, "A good and productive session. Now let's retire and rest for tomorrow is another big day."

Shireen stood and began to walk out with the others when Felix asked her to stay for a moment.

A perturbed look was painted on Bel's face. Shireen immediately turned away from Bel. *He's being too obvious.* She hoped no one else saw the look on his face.

She waited for Bel to exit the building then went to the center of the room where Felix was waiting with his cougar.

"Yes, Felix, what can I do for you?"

"How are you feeling after your injuries in the trial?"

Shireen touched her cracked ribs. "Fine. Bel and Lithia, my two friends, they gave me some of their life-force so I could heal faster."

He nodded. "That's good."

"Was that all?"

"No, I... your question. The question you asked. I thought I could explain in more detail. If you were interested."

Shireen realized the feline was nervous. "My work is in the castle of the king of the Greenlands. My master is one of the chief advisers. Our duty is to learn as much as we can about all people from all lands, their customs and ways, so we may best advise the king on political matters."

One of the cougars purred. He caressed the soft tufts behind his big cat's ear. "That was your only interest?"

Shireen momentarily panicked, then forced her face to calm. "I suppose. It's interesting to me for we are prohibited from marrying under order of excommunication."

"Such a cruel rule. As I understand your way, you are supposed to sacrifice all, giving yourselves to the service of the people, dedicating all your efforts, training, and magic to make the world a better place. You forsake almost all possessions and cannot own land. And with all this sacrifice, they still expect you to not love another? I guess I understand why your numbers are dwindling."

"Tradition. It's what we've always done, what is

expected. At least, we serve the people and not lord over them." Shireen couldn't believe she was defending a rule she abhorred. She agreed with Felix in principle, but the way he described her people sounded condescending.

Felix chuckled and held his hand up. "No, Shireen, you mistook me. Or perhaps I misspoke. I didn't mean to sound as if I was judging your ways. I respect them. I just don't understand them. They seem… counterproductive."

Shireen exhaled. "I didn't mean to go on the defensive. Yes, please tell me more of your kind. Shall we go outside?"

Felix nodded as he realized they were the last two in the building and Sammra would be soon giving him a mountain of grief for setting a bad example by being alone with a member of the opposite sex. The two started towards the door.

"So my people live in what is called a clan. Our clan lives in a small village at the base of Bald Mountain. Each person has his or her own three-walled hut."

"Only three walls?"

"We are in the south where the weather is temperate. We don't have snow or cold like you do here. We do not need hearth or thick walls."

"But how do you stay safe?"

Felix belly-laughed. "Safe? From what? Our cats are predators. Other creatures need to remain safe from us."

The two went outside and sat on an unoccupied bench near the center hall. Shireen spied Bel and Naga sitting on the front porch of their shack. Bel appeared to be staring, so Shireen turned her body more towards Felix to avoid Bel's piercing eyes. "Now about the other thing."

"Yes, about that. So my people, we are most certainly encouraged to marry. It keeps the clan strong by forming bonds."

"And can you marry anyone?"

Felix started to speak then closed his mouth.

"Touchy subject? Does your mother already have your bride picked out for you?" Shireen smiled and Felix laughed.

"No, nothing like that." The smile faded from his face. "Like most people, we're attracted to each other for various reasons. We talk to each other, poke and prod, feeling each other out. The whole courtship ritual is not much different here among your non-magical."

Shireen answered too fast. "I know nothing about that." She cleared her throat. "I mean, I understand what you're talking about, I never—"

Felix smiled and held up his hands in surrender. "I'm not a lander, remember? I don't care what you have or haven't done."

Shireen was sheepish. "I only wanted to make it clear that I haven't broken any rules."

"None of mine, certainly." He smiled. "So, back to the felines. We're expected to marry within the clan. Occasionally clans split when they become too large or combine when too small so we are aware of other clans and sometimes people marry outside."

"Leonna told me her clan is at the top of your mountain and your group is close and they visit you sometimes."

"She's a pretty girl. Not my type, though, in more ways than one. We don't mate with avians."

"I thought you said—"

Felix stared at her for some moments then pulled his

head to the side as though it took considerable effort to tear his eyes away. "I meant feline clans. We are only allowed to mate with felines."

"So you have rules too." Shireen threw her words at him as a jab, but it had no force.

"Rules I would like to change." He appeared to be grappling at something and Shireen was unsure of what it was.

She glanced back at Bel. He was still staring. She knew exactly what he wanted. To discover why she was sitting next to Felix and what they were talking about. Didn't he trust her? Only a few days ago she told him she loved him with all her heart. If things were different she would spend eternity with Bel. Now she was sitting next to a feline, albeit an extremely attractive feline wearing almost no clothes, and Bel seemed ready to jump through his skin with jealousy and grill her every word and comment. Shireen didn't need to be a seer to know the thoughts going through his head. She could see his distrust written all over his face.

"Can you do that? Can you change the rules?"

"The clan-fathers would be irate, but I don't think they would *excommunicate* me," he teased. "That was a joke. We don't excommunicate people for breaking rules in the clan."

"What do you do?"

Felix's face became immediately serious. "Something different."

Shireen started to get up then Felix touched her hand. She stopped abruptly, for she didn't expect the soft caress. She realized Felix might have thought this conversation was something it wasn't. "Felix, I—"

"No, sorry. I didn't mean to do anything to offend

—"

She cut him off quickly. "No, that's fine." She spun and walked away from him and toward the huts.

She quickened her steps as Bel came off his porch and began walking towards her. Shireen shook her head furiously and altered her course, instead heading towards the feed tent. The tension in Shireen's shoulders didn't leave until Bel stopped walking towards her.

Chapter Eleven
A New Affair

Bel stepped off his front porch, leaving Naga standing there. He walked in a straight line toward Shireen. He needed to speak with her. *What was she doing?* The fact the creature-kind were permitted to marry kept slamming Bel in the face every time he saw Felix staring at Shireen, which seemed like all the time. He was definitely into her and now they were sitting next to each other! On a bench! In front of everyone! And him only wearing a breechcloth! Felix was basically sitting right next to Shireen, naked, flexing the muscles of his bare chest. Bel couldn't shake the sour expression from his face. He couldn't help the way he felt. He needed to speak, to com-mun-i-cate.

Shireen shook her head at him so he slowed, unsure of what to do next. Should he turn around and walk back to his porch like an idiot?

Shireen turned, quickly walking away in a different direction. *I guess she doesn't want to talk to me. She knows what I saw and she doesn't want to explain. I guess that's it then.* Bel stopped in the middle of the courtyard. Shireen hurried away.

"Something wrong, Dragonslayer?" Leonna asked as she stroked her ebony hair. She was sitting on a bench not far from him, Bel hadn't even realized she was there.

"No, nothing."

She motioned for him to come closer. "Made quick work of the iron warrior, did you?"

"He wasn't too much of a problem. You?"

Leonna tapped the bench next to her. "My birds ripped him apart."

Where did Shireen go? Bel sat on the bench several feet away. His eyes scanned the courtyard. He mumbled, "How do you know it's a *him?* Could've been a *her.* Or an *it.*"

She edged a little closer. "Does it matter?" Her cheeks flushed. She wiped her palms on her legs.

Bel wondered why she was sweating. The air wasn't hot at all and avians were from the south. If anything she should be cold. "It's only that people always tend to paint all the bad guys as male. That's all."

"And that bothers you?" Leonna rested her hand on the bench between them, spreading her fingers out wide.

"No," he whispered. *Odd how her skin is so white, porcelain, like the chalk-white beaches near Lavaala.* She flashed a nervous smile. If she was anything but an avian he would think she was flirting, but with her being creature-kind and their manner so different he couldn't be sure. But it sure felt like she was casting a baited hook towards his mouth.

Bel shook his head lightly. He wondered why he was even sitting there, why he wasn't getting up and walking away. He was punch drunk at watching Shireen sit next to Felix and now he was doing the same thing, sitting with a member of the opposite sex. But he had no desire for Leonna, Shireen had to realize that. Bel scanned the courtyard for Shireen again.

Nothing was the way it was supposed to be. Their task was supposed to be simple. Bel and Shireen were to come here, ask a few questions, get some answers, pass the trials and head back to Sha'mont with information for Master Nes'egrinon and Master Meetta. Hopefully, by the time he returned his master would have recovered from his injuries. None of these complications were in the plan.

Leonna cleared her throat so he glanced at her. "You got it bad, don't you?" She grinned a playful grin.

His face was abruptly serious. "That obvious?"

"Oh yeah, it's that obvious." Leonna smirked. "What are you going to do about Shireen?"

"Nothing. We can't do anything. It's—"

"Prohibited under penalty of excommunication. A royal priesthood. I know. Stupid rule."

Bel nodded in agreement.

"So what are you going to do about Shireen?"

"I just answered that question." Bel scanned the courtyard one more time then turned to Leonna. "What would you do?" His voice sounded more irritated than he was.

"Do? In your position? Hard to say. All depends on how strongly you feel. Apparently not strong enough to leave everything for her. Me, I've never had to think about such things. We're encouraged to mate. And as soon as possible. We birth young then leave our children to be raised by the elder clan-mothers while we train and hunt."

"So who will you marry? Ayah?" Bel turned his eyes back at his hut when he thought of the avian. Naga was still standing on the porch, staring at him. He went inside the room after their eyes met.

"Ayah? Not hardly. He's like my brother. I mean he *is* my clan-brother. But I can't think of him like a nest-mate."

"But aren't you supposed to marry someone from your clan?"

"It's complicated."

Bel exhaled long and hard. He wished he had such simple problems. "Someone else then."

"There is one who interests me, but he doesn't seem to notice I exist."

"You? I find that hard to believe."

"Why?" Leonna smiled, brushing her hair away from her cheek.

"You're so…" Bel flustered.

"So… what?" She leaned in closer, smiling wide at his difficulty.

"You know, ahh, the way all the men stare at you. I don't need to say, you know, because you already know, you know."

Leonna burst into a fit of laughter.

"That wasn't supposed to be funny." Bel surveyed the courtyard again, still not finding Shireen.

"And what do *you* think?"

Bel considered her briefly as if he was appraising her. "Well, not bad."

"Not bad? What?" Leonna giggled as she pushed his shoulder.

Bel smiled wide. "I'm sure you'll enjoy your pick of the clan."

"Thanks for your vote of confidence. Unfortunately, I don't find the men in my clan so appealing."

"There are other avian clans?"

"Yes, there's others." Her voice didn't sound excited at

the thought.

"Well, there you go."

Leonna seemed lost in her thoughts for a short time. "Tell me this, Bel. Which do you think is worse: being told you can never marry or being told you must marry but to someone you don't love?"

"No, no. You're twisting it. Your problem is only finding someone you can fall in love with. You'll find someone eventually. Don't give up."

"Oh, make no mistake. I haven't given up. How about this one: being told you can never marry and falling in love or being told you must marry someone you don't love when you're in love with someone you can't marry."

Bel snorted. "How about this. Which is more painful: a knife in the foot or a fork in the eye? I mean what are we doing here? It's a ridiculous comparison."

"All I was trying to say is we are not so different, you and I," Leonna clarified.

"I suppose. The difference being one day you'll either find your soulmate or give up trying and accept someone that you only sort of like instead of love. In either case, you'll get married. If you don't find your true love, I'm sure whoever marries you will worship the ground you walk on. Me, my future's a lot different, sitting alone in the forest and daydreaming about what could have been."

"Well, there's always another choice. They don't own you after all. You need to figure out what's most important to you."

Bel couldn't argue that point. He gave his head a quick shake.

Leonna added, "By the way, what did you mean by

'worship the ground I walk on?' Do you think that's what I want?"

Bel grimaced. "I have no idea what women want. It's all a great, big, stupid mystery to me."

"I think we do that on purpose." Leonna wiped her hands on her thighs again.

Bel sighed. "You'll do fine. You're beautiful, Leonna. An adorable smile. You're a... delightful person. Easy to talk to anyway. I hope you find the man of your dreams —if that's what you want."

Leonna stood, then quickly leaned over and gave Bel a peck on the check. "Maybe he does realize I exist."

As she walked away, Bel frowned, shaking his head. "What?"

He stood and walked slowly after her. Across the courtyard stood Shireen, her arms crossed, tapping her foot. Her eyes barreled into Bel. She cocked her head, spun on her heel and stormed off.

"That went well," Bel mumbled.

*****

Leonna walked away from Bel. She forced herself to not smile when she saw the scowl on Shireen's face. She strolled to the feed tent, gathered a few items and stuck them in her pocket.

She left, checking to make sure no one was watching her by scanning through the eyes of her birds circling above. She headed behind the huts and along the rear tree line. Tweetnone and a few of her other birds landed on her head and shoulders before she stepped into the forest.

"What's wrong, Tweetnone?" Leonna asked, but she

already knew what was wrong. A man was standing right there, staring at her back, waiting for her in the shadows.

She turned and faced Aquilo, who stepped out from behind a hut and walked up to her.

"You like to follow young girls, spy on them then sneak up when they're alone? Makes you seem kind of creepy, doesn't it?"

Aquilo whispered, "Hey, let's not twist things here. I'm trying to be discreet for your benefit. When you find out what I know, you'll thank me."

"Is that so?" Leonna displayed a tight-lipped smile. She forced herself to not blink.

"Listen. Felix is a friend. I don't want any bad blood coming on the creature-kind. I was going to take this to him, but I figured I would do my own research first." Aquilo had a large brown envelope in his hand, tapping the package against the side of his leg.

"What do you have there?" Leonna said as she put her hand up to her head and her birds hopped into her palm.

"It's something one of the archmages sent me. Something he wanted me to investigate."

"He?"

Aquilo pushed his lips out. "He or she. Does it matter? I need to talk to you, that's all. Privately."

Leonna let her birds fly away and crossed her arms. "Go ahead. Talk. I've got nothing to hide."

Aquilo glanced at a few apprentices walking not far away. "Not here. I don't want anyone accidentally overhearing our conversation. Come to my room later tonight?"

"To your room?"

Aquilo flared his nostrils. "I'm trying to help you out

here. Both the avians and the felines. I don't need another scandal like last time. Just make sure no one catches you."

Leonna shrugged her shoulders. Aquilo turned and walked away.

After he was gone, Leonna exhaled a sigh of relief and stepped into the forest.

Whatever was in the envelope must be too sensitive or embarrassing for Aquilo to not go directly to Felix. Must be something about the felines. Or perhaps Aquilo is afraid of Felix's reaction? Felix always showed a calm face to outsiders, but I've seen him explode on Jinx or Felicia back at their village on more than one occasion. She pulled an apple, a mango, and a banana out of her pocket one at a time and gave each one to a bird. The banana was a little heavy so two of her finches paired up to carry the piece of fruit. Her peregrine carried the mango, digging its claws into the thick outer skin. They flew into the forest.

Leonna paced for a few moments as she waited for the birds to return. She muttered, "And who gave him the package? Aquilo's from the frozen north. We don't have dealings with them at all. I would be surprised if a Tundric archmage had damaging information about the creature-kind. And why would the archmage give the package specifically to him instead of Sammra? Why Aquilo?"

Leonna stepped into the courtyard as Tweetnone landed on her head. The other birds circled her and a few floated about a foot in front of her face. "What did he say?" She whispered.

One bird tweeted and Tweetnone pecked her head three times. She mumbled, "Thank you" and "everything is fine."

Leonna would need to be careful around Aquilo. He specifically wanted to speak with her in his room. *Why? So someone else could listen in? Maybe the mysterious archmage?* She would feign ignorance about everything and do her best to find out what was in the envelope. Say nothing and learn all. Perhaps the same thing Aquilo wanted to do. *Well, at least he's not holding all the cards. Clearly there's something he's unsure about or else he wouldn't need to ask questions.*

Leonna paced back and forth once more then began walking back into the village. She hadn't meant to stay along the tree line so long. Someone might find her behavior suspicious. *And that bit about being discreet so he would protect the creature-kind? I don't buy it. That's an old trick to try to earn trust. That's something we avians don't give out for free.* She mumbled, "Trust must be earned."

"What did you say?"

Leonna spun toward the voice, startled. Bel was walking toward her. Her birds flew away and into the trees. "Oh, you scared me there." Leonna smiled as she placed her hand on her chest.

"Who were you talking to?"

"Oh, no one, ahh, sometimes Ayah and I play games like that. Keeps our birds in practice, like talking to each other and… yeah."

Bel's shook his head lightly as if he weren't following. His face became abruptly serious. "I wanted to clarify something from earlier. Something you said." He put his hand up to the side of his face where she kissed him and brushed it.

"What? That peck on the cheek? Don't tell me that ruffled your feathers." Leonna laughed.

"No, it's not that. I wanted to make sure, you know,

we weren't misunderstanding each other. That's all."

"Bel, I didn't misunderstand anything. I understand exactly what's going on. More than you do, I'm sure."

Bel searched the courtyard with his eyes.

Leonna grinned. "Shireen owns you, doesn't she? Afraid to get caught sniffing?"

"No, it's—"

"Does she allow you to keep friends? I would. Are you allowed to speak with anyone alone? Or only with her around—"

Bel tried to interrupt, but Leonna was enjoying this too much to allow him. She loved the frustrated grimace on his face. It made his dimples show. He brushed his hand through his hair and looked at her with his swirling-blue eyes. Leonna nearly gasped.

She quickly composed herself. "What can you do when she's not around? Anything? And yet she doesn't want you anyway? I don't understand what's the point here. Why are you tearing yourself up over Shireen when you can't have her?"

After Leonna stopped, Bel waited for a few moments. "Are you done?"

Leonna smiled back at him but she was sure it was for a different reason than Bel would think. She was beginning to feel something. Attraction? So much time had passed since she experienced the least twinkle of genuine desire for someone. When she was younger, she would find a boy cute, but he would invariably do something to ruin it, usually by gushing over her with entirely too much attention. Leonna all at once realized she was a cracked egg. Here she was gushing herself. And over a man who didn't seem to be much interested in her at all.

Leonna pointed out, "Hey, it's your life. If that's the way you want to live, fine by me. I'm only asking some obvious questions. You should think about them."

"No. I mean, it's my life. True. I didn't want you to think I was—"

"Oh Bel, don't be so full of yourself."

"I-I'm not."

An odd sensation washed over Leonna. She realized all of a sudden she had conditioned herself like she trained her birds, offering them incentives or punishments to alter their behavior. Leonna had so many men fawn over her she had subconsciously trained herself to not like it. Maybe she could only fall for a man who *didn't* want her. The thought sounded terrible.

"Listen, Bel. I think you're cute. I gave you a peck on the cheek. A friendly gesture. Nothing more. Don't get all squirrelly on me, all right? The kiss didn't mean anything more than what it was. Okay?" Leonna stepped towards him grazing his side with her body and headed towards her hut. She couldn't stop herself from continuing to tease him.

Leonna knew she wasn't in love. Clearly. She just met the guy. He was interesting. Attractive. Curiously so. And he was someone who she could actually mate with. He had avian blue eyes; he had bird-sign. She wanted to poke him, to find out more, to discover what he was about. She needed to find out if she had broken herself by pushing men away for all these years. The idea had only just come to her. Could she actually have a genuine relationship with a man without manipulating him? She needed to find out and Bel was as good a person to test out her ideas as any. Convenient, anyway. And she wasn't going to let Shireen get in the way. She had no claim on

Bel. She had clearly said as much.

So far everything was going according to plan. Leonna was planting questions in his mind, trying to shake him free from Shireen. It shouldn't take much longer. Once she accomplished that, the next step would be easy enough. Seduce him. And then the real game would begin.

Leonna put her birds in their cages and laid down, waiting for the others to fall asleep. The last thing she needed was one of the landers discovering her sneaking out at night to visit Aquilo.

Chapter Twelve
Accusations

Bel stared at the ceiling. He had been here nearly seven days and everything was going all wrong. Shireen was upset with him. Leonna was chasing him. He hadn't found out much of anything from anyone about any kind of plot or odd goings on. And if all that wasn't bad enough, the mattress was lumpy, hard and had a moldy stink covered with bitter vinegar as if someone had tried to mask the foul odor.

Naga looked like he wanted to say something but choked it back. Bel knew immediately what he wanted to ask. Naga wanted to know what he was doing speaking to Leonna like that. He would clear that up with his friend later. Tonight he needed to speak with Shireen.

Bel waited for the others to fall asleep. When they had all been snoring for some time, he pushed his spirit out of his body, floating up. He glided over each of his bunk mates, Naga, Kerlith, and Ayah, one at a time, hovering inches from their faces, ensuring they were unconscious.

Bel slid through the wall then snuck through the camp. In the distance, something clinked. He snapped against a wall and waited. A few moments later a troll walked by.

Bel rose up high into the trees, figuring he would be harder to spot up there. The honeyed scent of pine sap was strong. He scanned the entire camp. It was clear, no one about. He floated towards Shireen's room, ready to peek inside the hut. He would try to wake her and connect so they could sort things out. He wanted to know what Felix and she were talking about. But more than that, he wanted to explain that his conversation with Leonna was completely innocent. Perhaps both of their conversations were. He hoped. He needed to communicate with her, to clear the air.

Bel waited for a few moments longer, making sure another troll wouldn't come by. The air was so still. There wasn't a sound in the forest. Just as Bel was about to float down to Shireen's hut, her door opened. He caught himself and returned back into the trees. *It was Leonna!*

She tiptoed off her porch and quickly ducked to the side of the building. Bel followed her with his eyes. She edged along the buildings and huts making her way across the camp. *Where was she going?*

When Leonna neared his own room, Bel decided to follow her. He flew down to his room and slammed into his body. Bel popped out of bed and made for the door. He had made some noise, so he turned before he went out to ensure the others were still sleeping. They were.

Bel dodged out and pressed his body against the wall of the hut. A troll strolled by, pausing not far from him. *I made too much noise. At least, the troll didn't catch sight of me.*

He waited for a few moments, hoping he didn't lose Leonna, then decided to try something. Invisibility. His master hadn't taught him the spell, but he overheard him use the words and witnessed how he turned his arms.

The spell didn't seem that difficult.

Bel whispered, "Aoratos," as he motioned with his staff. He looked down and his body was gone! The magic was unlike any other spell he had ever done. When he pushed out energy or threw balls of mage-light, he could feel the life-force exiting his body. But with this spell, nothing seemed to happen, no transfer of energy, no life-force flowing through him, just nothing. If it wasn't that he couldn't see his arms or legs or chest, he would have thought the spell hadn't worked.

All of Bel's body was invisible except his boots, but he didn't have time to try and keep practicing until he perfected the spell. Bel ran in the direction he last caught sight of Leonna, hoping the trolls wouldn't glimpse his shoes running by.

He jogged between the huts in the dim light of the moonstone, stopping at each intersection and snapping his head left and right, searching for her. Bel ran to the last hut and stopped. He had lost her. The only huts left were those of the worthys, just past a small patch of trees. *Leonna wouldn't go there, would she? She's breaking the rules being out at night as it is. They would catch her for sure.*

As Bel stared in that direction, a flash of fabric passed between the trees. *Her parka!*

Bel ran toward Leonna, stopping at the far edge of the trees. She gingerly stepped up to one of the buildings and knocked softly. She waited for a few moments, snapping her head to and fro, then entered the building when the door opened.

Bel walked up to the wall of the hut she entered, a hut of one of the worthy apprentices. Bel wondered whose room she entered. Felix would be the logical choice. Maybe he's helping her with the trials? Perhaps they are secret lovers?

Bel almost didn't want to find out. He was treading on dangerous ground by spying. He decided to take a quick peek in the window and if he caught Felix and Leonna kissing, he would leave them be, go back to his room and try to send to Shireen. It was all he had in mind for tonight anyway.

Bel eased up to the building, slowly stepping, carefully avoiding piles of leaves. He didn't want to snap a twig hiding underneath.

He crouched beneath the window, then, remembering he was invisible, stood and peeked in.

Aquilo! Bel was baffled. *Why would she be in his room?* He was Tundric, nearly on the other side of the known world from the creature-kind. Bel thought the likelihood of these two meeting each other before the trials to be practically nil. So why would she be sneaking around in the middle of the night to meet him?

Leonna was standing near the door. Aquilo leaned back in his chair, his feet up on his desk. He was leafing through some papers.

Aquilo said, "You possess information and you're going to tell me. I need to get to the bottom of this and I need to understand what you know."

Leonna looked dumbfounded. "What exactly did you call me here for?"

Aquilo flipped a page. "Don't play stupid. It's not going to work. There's been an ongoing investigation. I hold the evidence right here." He looked up at her. "I'm trying to help you, to help all the creature-kind. You must realize."

Leonna stared back, her expression blank.

He popped his legs off his desk. "Leonna, can't you recognize I'm not the bad guy here? I've been friends with Felix for years. I don't want to witness everything he's done, all his work, get destroyed in a moment because some greedy idiots did something to ruin everything. Don't you see? I'm trying to help you. The avians. The felines. I need you to tell me what you know."

Leonna shook her head slowly. "Aquilo, I appreciate that you want to help my clan but I don't understand why you wanted me to come here, to your hut, in the middle of the night."

Aquilo stuffed the sheaf of paper into the thick brown envelope, stood and slammed the package down on his desk. "All right. What about Jonah? You are withholding information about what happened to him. So is Felicia, I think. Clearly you're hiding something. Why were you at the edge of the forest? What's that all about?"

Leonna fidgeted, unable to answer.

"Fine. You're not going to talk. I'll call Jeneth and we'll pull all the birds out of the forest. That's how Jonah's evading the trolls, isn't it? The trolls will sweep the forest for Jonah. You don't want them to find him hiding, now do you? How's that going to look?"

Leonna groaned. "Don't involve Jonah. He's only a nestling. He shouldn't even be here."

Aquilo stared at her, waiting.

Leonna continued, "Jonah is hiding in the forest. He didn't even attempt the entrance trials. He just ran. I don't know exactly where he is, but I've been sending him food each night. I send out my birds and just leave some scraps or fruit out there in hopes that he'll find it.

That's all I know about him." She paused, her eyes pleading. "Aquilo, he's... too small. I couldn't deal with him being hurt. Jonah's all I have."

"You're telling the truth so far anyway. Felix doesn't realize what you're doing. I'm going to tell him in the morning. We'll take care of Jonah. That won't be a problem. The trolls will take him to Lasaat and he'll be well cared for until the trials end. But you're not telling me everything. Why would you hide Jonah in the forest? For what purpose? You understand if he didn't pass, they would take him to Lasaat. That's where Jeneth and Sturfelis are. They would take care of him. What did you plan that you wanted him out there?"

"Plan? I just said I don't know where he is. I'm not hiding him." Her voice carried a sense of outrage but it sounded manufactured. "Listen. Nothing is planned. Do you remember the first time you saw the trolls? Think of how Jonah sees them. He's only a nestling. He's tiny. They're huge. They're terrifying to him. That's why he's probably hiding. I have nothing planned."

Aquilo waited for her to finish, a perturbed twist on his face.

Bel shifted on his feet, checking his arms and torso again to make sure he was still invisible.

Aquilo shook the brown envelope at Leonna. "You see this? It's evidence. Evidence against you, against your clan, against the creature-kind. Damaging evidence. I don't want this to get out. I'm trying to help here. Understand? It would ruin everything for Felix. Do you understand?"

Leonna stared at the envelope and mumbled, "What's in it?"

Aquilo threw the package on the desk again. "Don't

play stupid. It doesn't become you. You know what's in this envelope. You're involved. I'm trying to head this off before anything happens. Are you with me?"

Leonna eyes widened.

Aquilo added, "Now if you're not, fine. I'll take this to Felix in the morning and we'll have a full and proper investigation with all the archmages. The reason you're here is because I don't want that to happen. Can't you see? You haven't done anything wrong. Yet. We can still stop this."

Leonna seemed lost in her thoughts for some time. "Okay, Aquilo. I'll tell you every—"

Her words were clipped midstream by a small flash of light, then another coming through the windows on the front of the structure. Bel walked away from the side window towards the front of the building. Someone gasped loudly.

It was the last sound Bel heard before he found himself flying through the air. He struck the hard earth about ten feet away and black enveloped him.

=————————=

Some time later Bel opened blurry eyes. The forest around him was in flames. He tried to turn his head, but his neck hurt tremendously. He pushed himself up and spit out a mouthful of wet dirt. His mouth tasted gritty and metallic. He wiped his face and saw blood on his hand.

Heat. He realized his arm was on fire so Bel smashed it into the ground a few times until the flames went out. Aquilo's building was partially gone, crumpled, destroyed, obliterated, pieces of wood flung throughout the space. The rest of the structure was in flames.

Two people were running away through the forest. Dark, Bel couldn't make out who they were. He tried to stand but pain shot through his legs. One of those running stopped and called his name, "Bel?" but it seemed dim and far away. Bel was deafened by the blast. His ears were ringing painfully. The second person grabbed the first's arm and yanked. They ran.

Bel sent a ball of mage-light at them, trying to determine who they were, but in his weakened state the ball didn't go far enough. They escaped.

Bel stood, ignoring the pain, gazing at Aquilo's building. He realized they might still be in there. The two running away might not be Leonna and Aquilo.

Bel forced his legs to move, stumbling forward, barely able to control them as if he were on stilts. He bobbled, slamming his face into a tree. He pushed on the bark, trying to not fall.

Heat smashed him in the face as he got closer. The air burned Bel's lungs. He leaned back a step and gulped one huge breath and held it in, pushing himself harder. The smoke wafted around him. He squinted his eyes down to slits and staggered into the burning building.

The heat was intense, stifling, and the black smoke blinded him. He held his breath, but he couldn't last long, only a moment or two.

He felt around with his hands, trying to locate a frame of reference, the desk or the chair Aquilo sat in. His eyes were squeezed shut.

His hand hit the desk. He fingered for the package, the brown envelope, but didn't find it. *Maybe blown away too?* He pressed into the building, completely blinded now, kicking forward with his legs, hoping to hit someone or something recognizable. The flames were all around him and even with his eyes shut tight he was surrounded by flashes of yellow. A patch of flames flared, burning him. He jumped to the left. He only had a few moments before he would need to run out, the heat was too intense.

He kicked forward again and again. He had to hurry. Bel was going to run out of air soon. His leg hit an object. Soft and fleshy. *A body!* He bent down and scooped it up quickly and pushed out of the building. He stagger-stepped through the flames, barely able to hold his breath any longer and tumbled to the ground outside. Bel dropped the body and went to his knees. He gasped for air, hoping he was far enough away his lungs wouldn't be scorched by choking black smoke.

He opened his eyes. Leonna was laying in front of him, burned about her legs and arms. She had tiny scrapes and cuts all over her body and face. She was unconscious. Possibly dead.

Bel gasped, placing his hands on her and extended his life-force, poking and prodding, trying to discern if she yet lived.

A tiny trickle of life, tenuous, hung by a thread. Bel sent out tendrils of translucent blue life and grabbed at Leonna's spirit, infusing her with some of his own life-force. She convulsed and gasped hard. Bel's body went ice cold as she unconsciously drew energy out of him.

Bel nearly passed out. He pulled his hand from her body to break the connection.

Felix and Sammra jogged up, shock, condemnation and dismay on their faces, the other apprentices gathering behind.

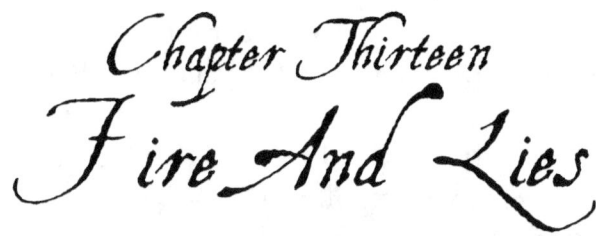

Chapter Thirteen
Fire And Lies

Felix slammed awake and popped out of bed. "What was that?" he said to no one, but he already knew the sound could be nothing less than an explosion.

His cats were up on all fours looking for direction. He threw on his breechcloth and ran out.

The flames danced high. Disoriented apprentices quickly filled the space. Felix ignored them and ran in the direction of the fire.

Sammra came up next to him as they reached Aquilo's hut. Bel was kneeling on the ground, his face slack-jawed, sweaty and black. Leonna lay crumpled in front of him.

Sammra put her hand on the ground and pointed at the burning building. Water gurgled from the ground then built up to a flood. As the liquid slammed into the flames, the space flushed full of white steam mixed with black smoke.

The sweet fragrance of burning wood mingled with another acrid odor. Felix hoped the scent wasn't burning flesh.

The crowd of apprentices watching the spectacle drew away from the hot steam.

Trolls came into the space and began stomping on

the embers and burning timbers, mashing out the flames with their tremendous bare feet.

Pren stepped forward to aid Sammra.

"You get over here," Felix yelled at Bel, his fists clenched.

The apprentice stepped forward, babbling, "She's still alive, I think. Alive, I think. I tried—"

"Where's Aquilo?" Felix barked. Bel's blank face staring back at him sent Felix into a rage. "Where. Is. He?" He bared his teeth. His cougar growled. Felix shook his head for he was losing control. "Branch, Budzig, arrest him. Take Leonna to the clinic."

One troll scooped up Leonna and the other pinned Bel's hands behind his back and shuffled him off. Bel didn't resist.

Felix pressed his lips together. The trolls were taking too long to put out the fire. He pointed. "Sammra, there. Douse those flames there. Barth, over there. Stomp those embers."

He spied a blackened lump under a log. He flicked his wrist and his two cats leaped into the burning pile of debris, the bobcat moving the log with its head and the cougar grabbing at the bundle and dragged it out.

Felix recognized what it was before he reached the hulk of dead flesh. He fell to his knees in front of Aquilo's burnt body. Wide-eyed, his lip quivering, Felix stifled the wail forming in his throat.

Sammra knelt next to Felix and placed her hand on his back. His face was twisting. She wrapped her arms around him and pulled him closer.

"I-I just..." Felix moaned.

"Don't talk, Felix."

"What... happened?" he choked out.

His cats began to tread around him and growl, baring their teeth at the other apprentices. Many scurried away.

Sammra pushed on Felix's shoulders, turning him. "Look at me." She shook him. "Felix, look at me."

His cougar paced frantically, snarling, then stopped and belted out a hair-raising scream.

Felix hesitated. He didn't want to cry. He allowed his eyes to meet hers. Sammra's face trembled as she connected. Sammra was trying to calm his spirit. Felix rejected it outright. His lip lifted, revealing an eye tooth. He wanted to yell at her for trying to calm him. *My friend just died. Don't you dare try to comfort me.* He ripped his eyes from hers and stared back at Aquilo's torched frame. Felix's hands twitched as if they needed to grab something. He placed them on his thighs and unconsciously kneaded, his fingernails digging into his flesh, cutting into his skin, drawing blood, but he didn't care.

His bobcat hissed and made a quick dash at a group of apprentices behind him.

"Felix!" Sammra screamed, shaking his arm. "Felix, you must stop!"

She was a buzzing fly, flapping near his ear.

His cougar roared, stepping towards a few apprentices cornered by the bobcat.

Sammra slapped the side of Felix's head. He slowly turned to her, his face was trembling.

"Put your cats away. Before they hurt someone."

Felix nodded and called them back to his side. He sat on the ground next to Aquilo and took his burnt hand in his. The blood and melted flesh mushed in his palm but he didn't care about any of that now. His friend was dead.

=————=

Felix didn't know how long he sat there and he didn't care either. He ignored the apprentices as they slowly returned, one by one, to their huts.

The trolls extinguished the flames and stomped out the last of the embers. He watched his cats breathe slowly as they laid next to him. He refused to allow the trolls to take Aquilo's body away.

When daylight came, sunlight peeking through the leaves around him, he cursed it. Felix hesitated to move. He didn't want to leave his friend. Not ever.

Barth stood behind him silently through the night, waiting for Felix to give the word.

The feline released the burnt man's hand and carefully folded Aquilo's arm down on his chest. "Goodbye, my friend," he attempted to whisper but the words caught.

Felix stood and motioned at Barth.

The troll stepped forward and scooped up Aquilo's body with one huge arm. He placed his other hand on Felix's shoulder then nodded knowingly and took the body away.

Felix stepped awkwardly into the courtyard. Sammra was there waiting. "How are you?"

He glanced at her face. *How well could he be?* A preposterous question. He tried to open his mouth, but couldn't answer. His throat tightened. His gut had been pummeled thousands of times by metal hammers and his insides hurt too much.

Sammra breathed out long. "How could you be? Habit to ask, I suppose." She threw her arms around him and held him tight. She held him for what seemed like too long, definitely too long for a man and woman who were unmarried. But he didn't care about the rules and the manners of the landers. Not then. He hurt.

Sammra released him. "You look a total mess." She grabbed his hand and tugged him as if he were a small child. "Come with me. I'll clean you up."

The rest of the morning passed in front of Felix's eyes in a surreal daze. His mind continually hooked on things he would normally never notice: the way filtered light picked up the floating dust, the halting manner Sammra spoke, never seeming to form a complete sentence, the scents permeating from every little object around him. He couldn't focus on anything for more than a few moments. He tried to apologize as Sammra bathed him, "I'm sorry. I shouldn't—"

"Tut tut. None of that now. No apologies necessary and especially not from you."

Felix felt uncomfortable having Sammra wash him like a clan-mother even though he still wore his breechcloth as he sat in the tub. He grew quiet again as he focused on the water and the way the fluid rippled.

"What we need to do is get you up and moving. Keep your mind, at least, somewhat off this. I can't run these trials by myself. I need you. We're going to call Lasaat. You need to keep your wits about you when we do. Understand?" Sammra bent down and examined him closely. "Can you do that?"

Felix maintained eye contact with her. "For Aquilo. We'll get to the bottom of this. I can do it for him."

Sammra stood. "Good. Dry off and put on fresh, ahh, clothing and we'll call Lasaat together. If you start to falter stop talking, I'll jump in."

Sammra walked out of his hut and Felix quickly

dressed. A sense of purpose came upon him, something he could direct all his rage into, finding out what happened to Aquilo. He hoped the fire was an accident although he had many, many questions. *Why were Leonna and Bel there? Were they up to no good or was Aquilo meeting with them? Why would Aquilo meet them alone? And in the middle of the night? It wasn't at all like him.*

Felix shuddered. Anyone responsible for Aquilo's death would rue the day he was born. He would use his cats to tear the meat off the killer's bones.

He exited his hut and marched to Sammra and gave her a brief hug. "Thank you. I'm much better now."

"It was… nothing," Sammra said, studying him.

"I'm good." Felix tried to force a smile but it wouldn't come. "Let's send to Lasaat."

The two went to the round building and had the trolls close the doors. They went to the center of the room, standing directly below the moonstone that floated above the building, the only location in the entire village where contact with the outside world could be made.

Sammra started waving her arms first, then Felix joined her. Soon the air in front of them rippled then smoothed and Jergamemnon's face appeared.

"Felix, Sammra, what's the problem?"

Felix began, "There's been another death—"

"Another one?"

Felix shook his head. "Last night. An explosion. Fire. Aquilo… Aquilo's dead. Died in his hut when it… exploded."

Sammra clarified, "We need to stick to facts. We heard a noise that sounded like an explosion. When we came out, Aquilo's hut was on fire. We found him dead inside."

"Witnesses?" Jergamemnon asked.

Sammra nodded. "We found two apprentices near the building. An avian, Leonna, and a tree-lover, ahh, forest apprentice named Bel. The girl was injured and unconscious. I had the young man arrested and the avian was taken to the clinic by the trolls. No one has been interviewed yet."

"You've done well." The archmage squeezed his lips together. "I will come immediately to aid in an investigation. Do you need help running the trials?"

Felix looked at Sammra who shook her head.

Felix said, "No, not now."

The air rustled then the visage of Jergamemnon faded. Felix slumped into a chair, his hands in his lap. He met Sammra's eyes and his expression shifted to chagrin.

"It's not your fault."

"I know. I just need some time. Do you mind?"

"Staying here for now?"

"For a little while."

Sammra touched his shoulder. "I'll tell the apprentices what happened. I'll be vague. The first two dying, they were practicing and lost control. But this? It smells of foul play. I think it prudent to postpone the trials for at least a day or two. I'll adjust the work assignments accordingly. Keep them busy. You know what they say about idle minds."

Felix nodded. She walked out.

He tried to piece together what he knew. Trying to figure out how Aquilo died was the only thing he could do to stop from wallowing in despair.

Last night, standing right here, Aquilo mentioned he

was attracted to Leonna. "The avian girl, so young, so beautiful, Leonna, she's the key."

Aquilo said he liked eyeballing her and there she was at his hut when everything went bad. Felix had witnessed the way she controlled men, even if she wasn't trying. They threw themselves at her. Felix had warned Jinx to stay away but he wouldn't listen. None of them would. Leonna was too beautiful and she wrapped men around her finger and they did stupid things for her.

"But Aquilo was nobody's fool. Even for a girl like that. Maybe Aquilo had made some kind of arrangement with her: a meeting with Leonna for some playtime?" Felix wouldn't put a late night rendezvous past the Tundric apprentice. "Perhaps she was even stupid enough to think Aquilo could soften up the trials for her, give her an insight into what to expect. She was accustomed to manipulating men for advantage." He wouldn't put it past Leonna to try to use Aquilo to cheat.

"Something's there." The thought kept circling around in his brain like one of Leonna's little birds. "Aquilo, what were you thinking? What did you do?" Felix shook his head, trying to fling the grief away.

Leonna twisted men's minds, but he didn't know her to meet men secretly. She always flirted in public and Felix had never noticed her do more than hold a man's hand for a few moments, giving it a little squeeze. Or maybe a little peck on the cheek, a quick kiss on the lips.

Felix shook his head. "For Aquilo, the hint wouldn't have been enough. No, not if they were meeting secretly in his room. He would have had some expectation of something more. Perhaps she had refused him and accidentally killed him?"

His lip quivered again. "But how? She's an avian.

Where did the explosion and fire come from?"

"No, those two meeting for a little tryst wouldn't have resulted in an explosion and fire. Not unless he came on too strong and they began to argue and the avian knows magic that I am not aware of. Perhaps."

Felix stood and began to pace. "Murder. Leonna was meeting with Aquilo. Why? Leonna wanted a little advantage in the trials. Maybe. Aquilo thought he might get a little bite of the girl's sweet lips. Possibly."

Rage rippled across Felix's face. "Aquilo, what happened? Aquilo, my friend."

Felix looked down at his hands as if there were a throat he could wrap his fingers around. "Perhaps someone else was there. Someone jealous of Leonna, someone who she spent time with. Jinx? Those two had been spending way too much time together." Felix groaned whenever he saw Leonna trudging down the mountain to sneak around with the young feline. Abruptly, she didn't show for a while. Jinx was terribly distraught. Later, before they left for the trials, Leonna had given him a letter. By Jinx's reaction, Felix could guess what it said. Still, Felix didn't think Jinx could have done that, no matter what fit of rage he was in. "If someone killed Aquilo for her, it had to be someone who would absolutely lose their mind if Leonna was with someone else, someone so jealous they would stoop to murder."

Bel? "He was there, bent over Leonna, touching her. Bel had a shocked, dazed, dull stupor on his face, like maybe he couldn't believe what he had just done."

Felix shook his head and stood. He would aid in the investigation. He would be right there with his cats. And if he found out foul play was involved, that Bel intentionally did something that resulted in Aquilo's death, his cougar would rip Bel's throat out on the spot. He wouldn't have the chance to touch his staff or speak a word before he died.

Felix snarled loudly then pushed his body toward the exit.

Chapter Fourteen
Investigation

The archmages arrived faster than Felix thought they would, but he was surprised when only two came: Jergamemnon and Jeneth.

Jergamemnon instructed Felix to set up a room and bring in everyone one at a time to be interviewed.

The first thirty or so said they hadn't seen or heard anything until the explosion shook them awake and they went to find out what had happened.

Felix started to think no one knew anything. That or they weren't going to say. Still, Master Jergamemnon said he felt they were all speaking truthfully. And an archmage would certainly know.

He called the next in line, Naga, and told him to sit down.

Sammra said, "Naga, you're rooming with, let's see here, Bel, Kerlith, and Ayah."

Naga nodded. "What's this all about? What happened?"

"That is what we are all here to ascertain," said Jergamemnon. "We need you to be completely truthful in all your responses. You understand, don't you?"

"Yes, of course."

"Did you notice anything out of the ordinary last

night?"

Naga's expression shifted.

Jeneth squinted his eyes down hard. "Tell us what you know, boy."

"I-I don't want to get anyone in trouble." Naga paused, looked at each of them one by one, then said, "Yes, I think I saw something."

Felix stood. "Tell us, Naga. We only want to get at the truth."

"Not long after I laid down, I heard a noise outside. I think Bel heard it too because he popped out of bed and ran outside. I didn't think much of him going out. He was only curious about the noise, I figured. But then he didn't come back. That surprised me, it being late and all, but I didn't worry about that much because I thought he might be meeting…"

"Who?" Felix barked.

Sammra put her hand on Felix's chest. "Calm down, Felix. Naga, tell us what you think."

Naga frowned. "Well, Bel, he's my friend. I saw the way the girls treated him."

"How, Naga?" Sammra asked.

"Like some kind of a hero, I guess. He fought in Sha'mont against the dragon. The story spread like a blustery ice storm across the frozen Tundra. All the girls knew about it. Several were fawning over him, acting awfully strange. Not sure how much Bel noticed. He's kind of clueless like that. But one girl he certainly noticed was Leonna. She was after him, that's for sure. I saw them sitting together, alone, on the benches. I guess I figured the sound was a signal and he was sneaking out to meet her? When I saw Leonna there with Bel at the fire, it didn't surprise me. I caught them whispering to each other earlier too. She kissed him too. A quick peck on the lips. I saw it. That's all I know."

"Thank you. Naga," Jergamemnon said.

Sammra stood and opened the door to let him out.

"Is Bel in trouble?" Naga asked before he exited.

Felix said, "Not yet. We're just after the facts. And remember to not talk to anyone else about what you told us or what you saw or heard."

Naga nodded as he left.

Next in line was Pren and then, Lithia. Neither said they witnessed anything. Sammra asked them about Leonna, since she was in their room. They both said they didn't stir until the explosion jarred them awake.

As Lithia left Shireen walked in and sat.

Sammra read off her notes. "Shireen, forest apprentice to Master Meetta from Sha'mont. She rooms with Leonna, Pren, and Lithia." Her voice revealed her frustration at so little information coming out from the apprentices.

Felix told her the same thing he had told all the others: all they wanted was the truth and for her to reveal anything she had seen.

"Nothing. Nothing I can think of," Shireen said.

Sammra said, "Another one. Fine. No one knows anything."

"I'm sorry?" Shireen said, irked.

"I don't mean to imply anything, but I find it odd that you and your two roommates apparently sleep like the dead because Leonna was able to sneak out without any of you noticing."

Shireen pushed out her lip. "Her bunk is closest to the door."

"Fine. You may leave then." Sammra shook her head

at Jeneth.

Felix opened the door for Shireen. She walked out, then Felix said to the others, "Give me a moment." He followed Shireen and pulled her around the corner of the building.

"Listen, Shireen, I wanted to tell you something."

Before Felix could continue she grimaced. "I understand your friend died. I'm sorry for that, but I had nothing to do with the fire. I've lost people too, at Sha'mont. I realize what that feels like, and I'm sorry. It's terrible and it hurts, but—"

"No, it's fine. I think the tensions are high for everyone. Me too. Aquilo was—" The sentence froze in Felix's mouth. He shook his head.

Shireen reached out slowly and touched his hand. "I'm sorry. You two were friends. It's difficult. Losing him hurts. And it won't stop hurting for some time. I lost someone, not long ago, someone important to me. She wasn't related, but she was much like my own mother. I lost her in the dragon attack. I was with her when she died. I watched her take her last breath. I try not to think about it, but sometimes I find myself there, standing next to her, watching her struggle to breathe, not being able to do anything to help her."

Felix was lost in his thoughts for a short time. "Aquilo was my best friend. My only friend."

But your clan—"

"Clan is not friends, but family. It's different. Closer in some ways, further in others."

Shireen pursed her lips and said nothing.

"That wasn't what I wanted to talk to you about."

"I-I sort of know what you are going to say."

"It's going to sound weird coming from me,

especially now."

"Felix, please. You don't need to."

Felix placed his hand on her upper arm. She stopped speaking. "Felix, I—"

He forced an awkward smile. "You're not attracted to me. That's fine. I wanted to say I was sorry about before and I didn't want you to think anything… weird about me."

"No, it's not that." Shireen fidgeted. "You are attractive. I mean, not to me. No, that's not what I meant. I mean, you are attractive to me, but I'm not, ahh, what am I saying? Okay, forget I even said anything, okay?"

Felix dropped his hand and chuckled briefly. "I just saw a spark in you. That's all. Touching you was inappropriate, especially in the position I'm in. I won't bother you further."

He started to step away until Shireen stopped him. "Hey, wait. Now you're making me feel bad. Your friend died and there I go and—"

"No, it was my fault. I should have never put you in the position to have to do that."

"Felix, if it makes you feel any better, I would still like to learn more about your people. If you think you could do that."

"Sure. Of course. Definitely. We'll talk later."

Shireen nodded as he started to walk away.

Felix turned to leave. "Thanks for that by the way."

"Thanks for what?"

"For a moment anyway, you made me forget about today." He turned and walked back in the room, motioning to Jinx to follow him in.

After Sammra went through the brief introduction,

Jinx said, "Not sure what's going on. How could I? But Leonna was there and that has to mean something."

Jergamemnon sat up in his seat. "What do you mean?"

"That girl? Everyone knows Leonna and what she does to men. She's a tease. Playing with all the men's emotions. Leading them on and all. That's what she does. It's like a big game for her. I wouldn't put it past her to have manipulated Aquilo and Bel into a fight. And Leonna, she would have been sitting on the sidelines laughing the whole time. Stupid avian."

Jeneth popped up. "What did you say?"

"I-I-I didn't mean you. Or your kind. Just her. That's what Leonna does. She's a manipulator. She makes you think she likes you to get you to do things for her. And after you do them, she loses interest all a sudden and she's off to put her claws in her next victim."

Felix put his hand on the feline's shoulder. "Stop talking, Jinx. You're digging yourself a deeper hole."

Jinx regarded Felix as if he wasn't sure if he might soon need his clan-brother's protection. He bowed at Jeneth. "I am sorry if I offended you."

Felix said, "Now do you have any factual information? Or only more speculation?"

Jinx said, "I have nothing to share."

Felix waved him toward the door.

They interviewed the rest of the apprentices in the line and none had anything meaningful to add.

After the last one, Felix addressed the archmages, "How about we take a break? I'll retrieve Bel from the holding cell and after we speak with him we can visit the clinic to speak with Leonna. Acceptable?"

Jeneth said, "I need some feed for my birds." He

added, "But be quick about it."

Felix went to the trolls and had Barth unlock Bel from his cell. He kept his hands tied in front of him and led him back to the room. Barth held Bel's staff. They walked in silence.

After they entered the room and Jeneth returned, Bel told them he saw Leonna out late at night and he decided to follow her.

"Now why would you do that?" Jeneth snarled. "Who do you think you are? Some kind of detective? You should have spoken to Leonna. Asked her where she was going. If she was up to no good, you should have alerted the worthys. Felix here. That's their job, not yours."

Bel nodded. "I apologize master archmage for my lack of judgment."

Jergamemnon said, "Tell us what happened next."

"I followed her to Aquilo's room. She didn't know I was following. She went in. It was wrong of me, but I went to his window to listen to their conversation."

"What?" Jeneth stood, spittle sprayed on his lips. "This apprentice should be ejected from the Trials immediately."

Jergamemnon motioned for Jeneth to sit down. "I am sure the apprentice understands the gravity of his mistakes and it is a good sign he is willing to admit them and speak truthfully with us now. We need to ascertain the truth. What happens to this apprentice will be determined later. Please continue."

Bel's voice was hoarse. "So they were arguing about something. Aquilo accused Leonna of being aware of some kind of plot. Seemed like he didn't think Leonna was involved, but maybe she knew something? I'm not sure because I was listening through the window and their voices weren't all that clear."

"A plot? What kind of plot?" Felix asked.

"Aquilo didn't describe the plot. He pointed at a brown envelope on his desk a few times, like he had something there. Evidence maybe? They argued for a while and I tried to listen. I heard a scream, or a gasp, or something like that, and a moment later the explosion ripped through."

"You don't know what they were arguing about and you don't know what caused the explosion?" Jeneth sneered.

Bel flushed red and barked. "No, that's not all. Why do you keep accusing me? I didn't do it. I was just there. Okay?"

Felix put his hand on Bel's shoulder and pushed him back into the chair.

Sammra eased toward the door and placed her hand on the door handle. "'That's not all,' you said. What else did you see?"

"Like I said, the explosion happened. I was blown about ten feet away by the blast. I couldn't hear anything for a short while. I was on fire so I put the flames out and as I turned I saw two people running away through the forest, then I—"

Sammra interrupted, "Who? Did you see who they were?"

"My eyes were blurry; they hadn't cleared yet. I couldn't make out exactly who they were."

Sammra's shoulders fell and she released her tense grip of the door handle.

Bel coughed, then he continued, his voice rough and scratchy, "My ears were still ringing and I think I heard one of them call out my name. Sounded like a man's voice."

"You think? You think? You think?" Jeneth said throwing his hands in the air.

Jergamemnon motioned again, so Jeneth crossed his arms and sat back scowling.

"It's hard to say. I'm sorry I don't have more information. The building was blown in half, nearly, so I got up and ran in. The heat was intense. Blinding. My eyes were clenched tight. I nearly tripped over Leonna. I picked her up and carried her out and that's when everyone else showed up. I'm sorry about Aquilo. If I had tripped over him first, I guess he would be still alive and Leonna would be dead. That's all I know."

Felix shook his head, a pained expression on his face. "Tell me this. And I want you to be sure of your answer. Did you make any prior arrangement with Leonna to meet last night?"

"No. Like I said, I just saw her. I didn't leave my room until she went past my window. I have no idea why she was out."

Felix exhaled. "Yesterday, the two of you were seen sitting on a bench together, sitting quite close and whispering to each other. Can you explain that?"

Bel shook his head. "That had nothing to do... Okay, she might like me. People are calling me Dragonslayer. It's not true. I tried to help fight the dragon but my master vanquished the beast, not me. Now some of the others treat me like I'm something, you know, and I don't deserve... Leonna had some questions. That's all."

Jergamemnon stood. "Remove his bonds. Bel, it sounds to me like you saved Leonna's life. Now, while the circumstances that brought you to Aquilo's room last night do not show you in the best light, it was a good thing you were there for a life was saved."

Bel whispered, "Thank you."

The archmage continued, "We are going to continue this investigation as it appears foul play may have been involved. We've spoken with everyone else and no one has admitted to being there which clearly means someone is lying."

"I promise. I'm speaking the truth."

"I know you are. No one can lie to an archmage." Jergamemnon leaned forward. "Humor me. Share the memory with us."

Bel coughed a few times, closed his eyes and leaned forward, his open palms extended in front of him. He opened himself up, revealing his spirit and connected, showing them snippets of what happened the previous night, following Leonna through the camp, watching her enter Aquilo's hut, their conversation, the explosion and the two people running off. Then finally, he showed them how he pulled Leonna from the fire. He broke the connection and opened his eyes.

Jergamemnon nodded, his face focused and somber. "We will continue to investigate. However, understand this Bel, we may need to call a seer in, to dig into your memories further if we do not come up with leads. That's not something I like to subject people to, I am of the belief a person's mind is his own and should not be violated so. But indeed, it may need to be done. A seer gaze is painful, violating, scarring even, but one might be able to look closer, to identify those two people."

Bel's eyes were wide. "And that's all they would view?"

Jergamemnon smiled. "Is there something else you want to tell us?"

"Ahh, no. I've told you everything about what

happened last night."

Felix's eyes lit up. *Bel had a secret he was hiding. Something he didn't want the seers to discover.* Felix kept his mouth shut out of respect for the archmages, but he certainly wanted to call the seer in right now and perform a full scan on Bel immediately. *Aquilo's dead and this forest mage is hiding something. Everyone can see that! Why is Jergamemnon treating him so lightly?*

They released Bel and left the room to interview Leonna at the clinic. As the group walked in silence, Felix pondered this new information. *There are two possibilities here: one, Bel is hiding something important, the other, he's not. If he's told all then clearly Aquilo found out information, whatever was in the envelope, and the information had something to do with some members of the creature-kind. What could it be? Something that affects the trials? Were some of the apprentices planning on cheating the trials? Maybe the so-called plot was some kind of prank or practical joke the apprentices were planning on playing on someone?* Felix wouldn't put it past Jinx. He got that name for a reason. *But what secret would be serious enough to get Aquilo killed?*

Maybe killing him was an accident. They are apprentices after all. Perhaps the two people who ran away only intended to scare them and their magic went wrong. Without their masters, apprentices do all kinds of stupid things.

Of course, Bel could be hiding some other detail. He couldn't have lied, but he could have held back information. Even with him sharing, Felix found it suspicious that Bel clipped out some of the memory. *Bel could even be the killer. Naga said Leonna and Bel hit it off. But that doesn't seem right. Who kills for jealousy after only just meeting a girl? What could he be hiding? Of course, if he's into Leonna and she killed Aquilo, perhaps Bel might be willing to cover the murder up for her. In any case, he is hiding something. He has to be. He's afraid of the seers and only people who are hiding something don't want to be scanned.*

Still, two other people were there and they could be the murderers or they could have been peeking through the other window like Bel. But if they are merely observers why doesn't anyone else come forward? Maybe they're afraid?

They reached the clinic and went to Leonna's bed. Jeneth stroked her arm. "How are you, my fledgling?"

Her voice was groggy. "As good as can be expected, clan-father."

"I am sorry we need to speak of these things so soon after your traumatic experience, but we are here to find out what happened."

"Yes, of course."

"Leonna, what can you tell us?" Felix asked.

"During the day, Aquilo came to me saying he wanted me to meet him at his room last night, that he had questions for me. I told him it was inappropriate. He told me he had some private questions and to come to his room and not let anyone see me. I didn't feel comfortable with this, but since he is a worthy, I went."

Felix shook his head. "You should have come to me right away. That doesn't sound like Aquilo. But still—" Felix stopped short when he remembered how Aquilo ogled Leonna. "Go on."

"I waited until everyone was asleep and I snuck out. I didn't think anyone saw me. I went to Aquilo's room and he let me in. He started accusing me of some kind of plot. I didn't know what he was talking about, where he got his information or even—"

Sammra cut her off. "Did he say what the plot was?"

"No. He kept insinuating I already knew what the plot was all about and who was involved. I don't think he knew what he was talking about. He was making me uncomfortable. There was a sound at the door and Aquilo went to answer it."

Felix jumped in, "Who was it? Was it Bel?"

"Bel? No, I don't think so. Aquilo stood in the doorway so I couldn't see who was at the door, but it definitely wasn't Bel. I mean, I know it wasn't you, Felix. Or Ayah. Or Jinx. I know those voices."

"What happened next?" Jergamemnon pressed.

"Aquilo was angry at whoever was at the door. That person blasted him. I think Aquilo died instantly because the flash was blinding. The attack hit him right on the chest. It was the last thing I remember. When I woke up I was here, in this bed."

Jergamemnon said, "Thank you for speaking truthfully and sharing this information. I need to ask you one last thing, to share the memory."

Leonna nodded as if she knew they would ask this of her. She closed her eyes and presented the events of the previous night, showing them her sneaking through the camp, going to Aquilo's hut and the accusations that he fired at her. The scene jumped to Aquilo at the door then a short blast of white. Then the connection broke.

"I'm sorry," Leonna said. "I think that blast jarred my head. I don't remember everything so clearly."

Jergamemnon nodded. "Please do not share what you have told us with anyone else. Not until our investigation is complete." He stood to leave. "By the way, it appears Bel pulled you out of the burning building. You have him to thank for your life. And, as you said, Aquilo is dead."

Jeneth touched her forearm once more. "Rest. Heal."

The four left the clinic. Jergamemnon told Felix to wait for him at the end of the path, then Jergamemnon and Jeneth had some private words. The two archmages rejoined Felix. Jeneth said, "Felix, call all of the apprentices. We will address them publicly."

Felix motioned to the trolls and told them to round up all the apprentices in the center courtyard. When they had gathered, Jergamemnon addressed them.

"We performed a thorough investigation of all the happenings surrounding the death of Aquilo and we determined his death to be an accident. No one is culpable."

Several of the apprentices gasped. Many of the others began muttering and whispering to each other.

Felix had his own ideas about what had happened and none of his theories involved Aquilo's death being an accident. He scowled as he ran it through his head. *He was murdered.* Clearly the archmage is trying to put the killers at ease so he can further investigate, but still Felix didn't like hearing his words.

One thing Felix knew for sure, Bel was hiding something. The so-called hero of Sha'mont, the First-Year from the forest, the Dragonslayer, was hiding something and that something might be vital information about Aquilo's killer. Perhaps Bel wasn't the killer, at least, not intentionally, but his words and his behavior were too suspicious.

Felix decided he would continue to conduct his own investigation and it would be centered on Bel. Whoever was involved in Aquilo's death was going to die a painful death. He owed Aquilo that much. He couldn't walk away and let someone get away with murder. No, someone was going to pay in blood.

Chapter Fifteen
Triangles

Bel raked the dirt, trying to quickly finish his daily assignment so he could go to the clinic and visit Leonna. The last few times he had gone, she wasn't awake.

Even though a few days had passed, the soreness at being thrown hadn't yet worn off so he had to take occasional breaks, leaning up against a tree or sitting on one of the benches. Bel's jaw still hurt too which didn't surprise him, since he had landed face first.

As Bel continued to rake, a bobcat ran past him, spun and hissed then walked on. Bel turned. Felix was staring at him intently.

"You missed a spot, Dragonslayer." Felix flared his nostrils as his eyes barreled into him, then he nodded sharply and left.

Bel shook his head, figuring it wouldn't be long before the trolls were carrying him out. *So I save an avian's life and now Felix hates me. Fine job I've done. How am I going to pass the trials when I've made enemies with the guy running them?*

Bel continued working, trying to not think about his predicament, scraping his rake across the dirt, ignoring the eyes of the apprentices as they walked by, whispering. No one talked to him much anymore. He had gone from dragon-slaying hero to a potential murderer in a matter of days.

Shireen was angry with him, Felix hated him and all the apprentices thought he had something to do with the explosion and Aquilo's death. Bel wished he had stayed in bed that night. He wondered how everything went so wrong so quickly.

After he finished raking, Bel returned to his room. "Naga, I'm going to the clinic to visit Leonna."

His friend stared back at him blankly. "Do you think that's a good idea?"

Bel hoped Naga would volunteer to go with him, but he wasn't going to obligate him by asking. He mumbled an unintelligible reply as he walked out.

Bel ignored the staring eyes as he made his way through the camp and down the long path to the clinic. He stopped at the big doors guarded by a troll. "I'm here to visit someone."

When the troll didn't acknowledge him, Bel stepped past, entered the building and walked across the long room. About twenty bunks lined either side. Only a few were occupied with apprentices who hadn't fully healed from their injuries in the trial of the iron giant. Leonna was alone and near the end. He went to her bedside.

She was sitting up, her knees curled toward her body, smiling at him as he approached. "Oh, how sweet. You came to visit me."

Bel stopped at the side of her bed, standing rigidly when he saw her outstretched arms.

"What are you doing standing there like an oaf? Get down her and let me hug you."

"Leonna, I don't think that's appropriate. I only came her to check how—"

"Bel, are you kidding me? You saved my life. Get down her and let a girl give you a hug."

Bel reluctantly bent towards Leonna and she wrapped her arms around his neck and pulled him down closer. Leonna held him for too long then nibbled his ear lobe.

Bel yanked back, forcing Leonna to release him.

She giggled.

"Leonna, please. You can't keep doing stuff like that."

"Oh, stop." She pointed. "Grab that chair and sit with me."

Bel sat.

"Bel, don't be such a prude. That little nibble didn't mean anything. I mean, can't I thank the man who saved my life?"

"Yes, and you're welcome. I'm sorry you got burned."

Leonna considered her arms. "It's nearly all healed. Troll-salve. Did you know fire doesn't burn trolls?"

Bel moved the hair that hung down covering the right side of her face. Her skin was covered in small welts and scars.

Her voice trembled. "Now that hurt. You should have seen all the glass and wood splinters they pulled out of me. There was quite a pile on that little table there when they were done." She forced a smile.

"Don't think about it. You'll heal. You'll look just like before. It will just take a little time." Bel dropped his hand into his lap.

"I guess they'll all get what they wanted," Leonna mumbled.

"Who? What who wanted?" Bel asked, tentative, not wanting to upset her buoyant humor.

Leonna shook her head lightly. "It's nothing. Forget I said it."

Bel mumbled, "I visited you a few times. You were out. Sleeping."

"I think the trolls gave me something to make me sleep. How long has it been?"

"Three days."

"Three days," she repeated. "And what's been happening with the Worthy Trials?"

"The Trials are on hold. They're doing a demonstration tomorrow and then the Trials are going to start back up the following day."

"I'll need to be out of this bed then, won't I?"

"You need to heal."

Leonna paused for a time then reached over and grabbed his hand, "Bel, you would tell me the truth, wouldn't you? If I asked you?"

Bel allowed her to hold his hand but he didn't like what it might mean. He hoped no one would walk in and see them. "Yes, of course," Bel said, hoping Leonna wasn't going to bring up his relationship with Shireen again.

"Look at me," Leonna said as she rolled her head to make her hair move away from the scarred side of her face. "Do the scars make me... ugly?"

"No, no. Don't say that." He tried to pull his hand away but she squeezed it tighter.

"I-I haven't seen my face yet. No mirror."

Bel said, "Leonna, you're still beautiful. You have a few scars, that's all. They'll fade in time."

She released his hand and pushed her back against the wall behind the bed. "So they don't bother you?"

"Me?" Bel shook his head. "Leonna, listen. We need to straighten something out."

"No, we don't." She waved her hand at a troll.

The creature came to the side of the bed and stopped.

"I'm ready to be discharged," Leonna said.

As the troll stepped away, Leonna pushed out of the bed, sliding out from under the sheets in front of Bel, forcing him to push his chair back and away. Her small waist was in front of his eyes. A few red splotches stained the mottled gray material of her outfit.

Bel stood, giving her space.

Leonna quickly made the bed then spun and threw herself on Bel's chest. "I'm sorry. I need to hug you once more. Don't you understand, I should be dead now, if it wasn't for you, My Mighty Dragonslayer?"

Bel recoiled, "Ahh, I understand your gratitude, but please don't call me that, you know, because it's not true."

Leonna let go of his body and dropped her hands, grabbing his, then leaned back and smiled. "Walk me back to camp?"

"Sure."

When they stepped out of the building, Leonna whistled and Tweetnone and a few of the other finches flew from the trees and landed on her head and shoulders. The one on her left shoulder tweeted and Leonna said, "No. This man here saved me. He pulled me out of the fire."

The birds fluttered over to Bel and he flinched when they landed on him. Tweetnone pecked his forehead then they flew back into the tops of the trees.

Leonna giggled. "Their way of thanking you."

"That's never happened to me before, that's for sure."

"So your home is in the southern forest, I understand? And you can see Bald Mountain from your home?"

When Bel lowered his eyebrows at her, she added,

"Ayah told me. That's where we live, my clan. You could come visit me. Perhaps I could come visit you."

"Leonna, with the way things are with me and—"

"So you don't want to visit me?"

"I wouldn't go that far."

"Bel, I'm not trying to ruin things for you and Shireen. What do you want me to do? Just ask."

Bel said, "It's all the kissing and hugging. The clinging needs to stop. Everyone is watching. I mean, for whatever reason, your beauty, I guess, you know, everyone watches you, the guys, the girls. And when you hug me and kiss me like you do, you know, everyone talks."

"So you're saying you don't want me to be affectionate."

"Exactly."

"You're only asking me to not be an avian. Because that's how we are."

Bel shook his head lightly.

"Do you want me to stay away?"

"Leonna, that might be for the best."

"So I'll get up and walk out whenever you enter the room. Is that what you want? Or what if you want to sit at the dinner table that I'm at. Should I get up and leave?"

"Leonna, stop being ridiculous. I'm under a lot of pressure right now. What with Felix after me and—"

"Wait. What do you mean Felix after you?"

The two stopped at the end of the path, wanting to finish their conversation before they entered the courtyard.

Bel shook his head. "Maybe I shouldn't have put it exactly that way. Aquilo died. When Felix arrived, he only saw me and you and a burning building. He obviously thinks I had something to do with that. His best friend is dead. I can imagine Felix wants someone to answer and maybe he thinks that someone is me."

She raised her eyebrows in disbelief.

"This does bring up another question. What were you doing in Aquilo's room in the middle of the night?"

"I was there only because Aquilo ordered me. He claimed to possess some information, but when I got there he had some crazy conspiracy theory. He kept ranting that I had information, but I don't. Bel, I'm telling you, I don't. I had no idea what Aquilo was talking about. I don't think he did either. He said he wanted information about a plot. That he didn't trust the creature-kind." Leonna looked away and into the trees for a moment. "But the explosion jostled me around quite a bit and I don't remember everything. I think I may have some memory loss."

"Do you know who caused the explosion?"

"I wish I did. My birds would tear their eyes out." Leonna grinned at the thought. "By the way, how did you get there so quickly?"

"Me?" Bel smiled. "I guess you're going to find out anyway. I followed you."

Leonna pursed her lips and said nothing.

"I'm sorry. I thought you were up to something. What with you sneaking around in the middle of the night. I wanted to find out what you—"

"Another avian conspiracy theory? You? You should have come in and joined Aquilo in the interrogation." Her voice was teasingly outraged.

"I'm sorry."

"I'm not. You saved my life. I'm glad you were there."

The two stepped out into the courtyard.

"I don't understand you landers. You're always fishing for the creature-kind to be this terrible scary monster that's going to start a war and destroy your world. We're not like that. We were supposed to come here and let everyone inspect, examine and scrutinize us so we could learn from each other. That was the plan."

"The plan," Bel repeated, thinking of what he had heard Ayah whispering to his bird before it flew out the window.

"Bel, I'm sorry if I did anything to come between you and your little girlfriend. I'll talk to Shireen."

A bolt of raw terror ran through Bel at the thought of Leonna casually mentioning to Shireen what Bel had told her. "No, I don't think that's a good idea."

"Have it your way." Leonna stopped and touched his hand then leaned up closer to his ear and whispered, "Just one more time." She hugged him and gave him a quick peck on the cheek.

Shireen cleared her throat behind Bel and he jumped. "Oh, hi. Shireen, hi. I didn't know you were there."

"I see."

"Leonna was thanking me, you know, again, you know, for saving her life the other night. Did you know the avians are affectionate? I didn't know it myself. They are. Right, Leonna?"

Leonna admitted, "Yes, very much so."

Shireen didn't take her squinting eyes off Bel.

"Affectionate?" Felicia said behind them as she strolled up. "That what you're selling now?"

Leonna flared her nostrils and nodded up at the trees. Her hawk dove down and landed on her shoulder, cawing loudly.

Felicia squatted and stroked her cougar's neck. She made a purring sound. "Oh, look, precious, little Leonna's getting nervous. Needs her big bad bird to protect her."

Leonna sneered. "Do you have some business here? Or are you trying to pick another fight your big brother's going to need to stop before you get shredded?"

Felicia growled. "Business? Like your business of spinning all the men around on your finger? How many of the avian men have you run through? Must have been all of them because they got sick of your games. So you moved on to the felines and now even the landers. First Felix, then Jinx, then Aquilo and now this Bel." She pointed at Bel as if he was exhibit A in a trial. "You don't get enough do you? Do you want *all* the men?"

Leonna's face twisted.

The four waited for some moments but when Leonna didn't respond, Felicia stormed off, her cougar following after.

"She hates you, doesn't she?" Bel asked.

Leonna muttered, "I stole her boyfriend. At least, that's what she thinks. It's a long story. I didn't even want him as a boyfriend. Only a friend. But everyone misunderstands me." Leonna gazed at Shireen then walked toward her room. Shireen ran after her.

Bel followed them with his eyes then went to his bunk and laid down. His body was sore, beaten. He needed to try to rest and restore for the next trial.

Naga leaned off his bed and said, "Do not let the pushing and pulling of these women torture your heart. As the sun shines brightest on the coldest of days, you have done a good thing, Bel. Everyone has heard the tale of the work of your hands, running into the blaze to save the fair Leonna."

"Thanks, Naga, for trying to cheer me up." Bel glanced at Kerlith and Ayah who were listening. "But I think what almost everyone wants to know is why I was there and if I had anything to do with the fire. I was sorely disappointed the archmages didn't clear anything up. I don't understand why they said the explosion was an accident."

"Doesn't sound right, does it?" Kerlith added. "What kind of an accident blows up a building like that? Nope. Magic was involved. An attack. And with this being the third apprentice dying it's starting to seem like a trend."

The four were quiet for some time then Naga spoke, "My friend, if you can speak of it? Can you give us your words? Tell us the tale?"

Bel said, "The archmages, they told me to not tell anyone. They said they were still investigating."

Kerlith sat up. "That's stupid. That was before they told us Aquilo's death was an accident. You can tell us now."

"They didn't tell me I could tell anyone."

Ayah stood. "I understand. You do not want to speak in front of me for I am an avian. I'll leave and let you talk."

"No, no, no. Please don't go, Ayah. That has nothing to do with it. It's not you. It's..."

When Bel stopped, Naga coaxed him, "It's what, Bel?"

"I think the archmages didn't want me talking because they didn't want to start a panic."

Ayah repeated, "A panic? Why?"

Kerlith snorted, "Because there's a killer out there among us, that's why. And whoever the murderer is probably wants to kill Bel next. Possibly because he was a witness. Perhaps even polish off his roommates too. Think about that and try to sleep tonight."

"Kerlith, can you quit saying stupid stuff?" Bel said. "You're not helping things and it's not funny."

Kerlith wondered out loud, "What else would send everyone in a panic?"

"Could be anything," Naga said. "A return of the ghoul-kind. A ghost in the forest. Giant spiders. The dragon from Sha'mont. Frost giants."

Bel shook his head. "Frost giants?"

"Maybe not frost giants here, but some other form of the most heinous evil known to man."

Kerlith snickered. "This is excellent!"

Bel opened his mouth. "I'm going to tell you what I know, but not a word of this leaves this room." Bel told them what he saw, just as he told the wizards in his interview, as before, leaving out the parts about him turning invisible, leaving his body to connect with Shireen or the fact that Leonna was actually about to admit to something when the attack happened.

After he finished, they sat silently for a few moments then Kerlith said, "The only thing I don't understand is why Leonna is showering you with attention, of all people. A fisherman with no education, certainly no skills with women. What does she see in you?"

Bel didn't like his insinuation. "No, it's not like that. I saved her life, she wanted to thank me. That's all. There's nothing between us."

"She wanted you before you saved her life," Naga said. "She has the desire to warm her icy feet on your belly in the deep cold of night, I think."

Ayah shook his head. "Leonna doesn't want any man.

This is another one of her games. I've seen her toy with men many times. Don't be ensnared. You'll be better off if you don't let her twist your emotions."

Naga contested, "But Ayah, you spoke before saying you wanted to marry her."

"I do. If it is possible for any man to capture her, I want to be the one. But I understand what I'm up against. We grew up together. She is the most ferocious of adversaries in this arena. A bird that wants no nest but only to soar."

"I wish you luck then," Bel said.

An ear piercing scream broke through from outside.

"What the?" Kerlith said and popped out of his bed and went outside.

The others followed. Many of the apprentices were coming out of their rooms. They heard another scream coming from the edge of the camp so Bel and the others ran towards the tree line.

Chapter Sixteen
Jinxed

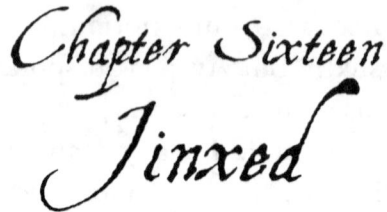

Leonna heard a scream through her birds' ears. She popped up and ran outside.

Shireen asked, "Where are you going?" as the high pitched wail ran through the space.

Shireen, Pren, and Lithia scampered outside after Leonna. The other apprentices also exited their huts.

The avian pointed at the far corner of the forest and said, "There." She darted towards where she pointed and the three girls followed.

As they ran, a second wail rang out.

Leonna sent her birds ahead of her to scout the way, to discover what happened and if there was danger ahead. She didn't like what she saw. Someone was lying on the ground bleeding and someone else was standing above him.

She dodged around two of the huts and sped up, rushing past the tree line. Leonna's peregrine landed on her shoulder as she stopped in front of two people crumpled on the earth.

Jinx was lying on the ground, bleeding, with a dagger in his chest. Sammra was holding his body, sobbing.

She tilted her head up at Leonna, dazed and confused, and blubbered, "I found him. I-I…"

The avian didn't need to ask. Jinx was already dead. There was blood everywhere. The blade was buried deep in his heart.

"Jinx! No, not Jinx!" Leonna tried to wipe her eyes as they flooded with tears then she clenched her eyes down tight, wishing the vision would disappear when she opened them. But she couldn't open her eyes. She refused to acknowledge that he was lying there, dead. She stepped back and stumbled, then stuck her hand out and braced herself on a tree. Leonna felt light-headed, dizzy, dark and black.

She fought to breathe. Her breakfast choked in her mouth as she retched. Gagging, she forced herself to swallow the vomit. It tasted hot and acidic. She took a few steps away and spat.

"Hey, are you okay?" Pren asked.

Leonna only shook her head. She tried to force herself to stop breathing so rapidly then finally stepped closer to Jinx. She wanted to know what had happened to him.

Leonna bent over. She recognized the dagger immediately. The blade was long and silver colored. The carving on the hilt was worn smooth by much rubbing and the center jewel was missing. *Jeneth's dagger.* Leonna immediately stood. Shocked. *Would anyone else recognize the knife? Felix? Felicia?* Her body shuddered as she began to hyperventilate, gasping for air.

A circle of onlookers formed around Sammra, who refused to recognize their presence. She rocked Jinx's body back and forth. Jinx's two cats paced around him, sometimes rubbing against one of the legs of an apprentice or hissing at another, causing them to jump back.

Leonna burst into tears and pushed herself out of the circle. Pren and Lithia went to her. Pren touched her arm. "Oh Leonna, I'm so sorry. A shame. A shame. He was so young. A shame. He was your friend. Let me hold you." Pren wrapped her arms around Leonna.

A sharp pain stabbed Leonna as if the blade was planted in her own chest. *Jinx!* She silently cried. All she had wanted was to be his friend, to speak to him, to learn more about the ways of the felines. She shook her head. Did she manipulate him? *Yes.* Lead him on? *Maybe.* But that was before. She was different now.

She bit her lip, not caring if she drew blood. *And the last thing I did was give him the note, telling him I didn't want anything to do with him, that we couldn't be together.* He was angry, clearly, resentful, surely. But Leonna figured she had time to make it up to Jinx after the trials. She still wanted him as a friend. Now he was dead.

The warmth of Pren's life-force radiated into Leonna. She was offering her calming and soothing energy. Leonna shuddered again, more vigorously, uncontrollably, then forced her breathing to slow and wiped her face. She hugged Pren and kissed her cheek, wetting it. Leonna pushed back and gave Pren a smile of genuine gratitude. "I'm fine now. I think... I think I want to see him one last time."

Lithia and Pren pushed their way back to the center, pulling Leonna in.

Jinx's cats were nudging him to get up. Sammra was still holding him, rocking.

Felix and Felicia arrived and the apprentices cleared a wide path for their cats.

"What's this?" Felix barked, then he saw Sammra and Jinx and dove to his knees yelling, "Jinx!" He turned his head back and growled, "Trolls. Barth. Branch. Budzig. We need medical attention. Now." He pressed his hands against Jinx's flesh, trying to push in healing as Felicia scrambled to his other side and went to her knees.

Sammra touched Felix's shoulder. "Felix, no. He's gone."

Felix ignored her, closing his eyes and trying to push in his energy.

"Felix, he's dead."

He shook his head. After a moment, Sammra dropped her hand from his shoulder and Felix flared his nostrils and popped his eyes wide.

"I'm sorry," Sammra said, her voice empty and vacant. "He's gone."

Felix's lip quivered.

Felicia stood and screamed, "Who's responsible for this?" She drew her dagger and pointed the blade at the crowd.

Her cougar roared.

Felix stared at his sister as if he couldn't comprehend what was happening. Sammra touched his shoulder and mouthed, "No."

Felix nodded, turned to Felicia and mumbled, "Felicia, stop. We'll find out. You won't bring him back that way."

Felicia dropped her dagger arm. Her face contorted then she ran back into the camp, her cats following after.

"How did this happen?" Felix mumbled.

Leonna braced herself for what Sammra would say. She glanced at Ayah, eyes wide, then down at the dagger and back up at him. He nodded slowly, keeping his face blank. If someone discovered the dagger was Jeneth's they would need to run before Felicia and Felix released their

261

cats. But how would they escape? They were trapped in an enchanted forest and supposedly no one could leave, for the wood was under troll-spell. Leonna twitched. Her wings were clipped and there was nothing she despised more than not being able to fly.

"I found this in his hand," Sammra said, passing Felix a piece of paper splotched with blood. Leonna knew exactly what the leaf of paper contained. Her letter. The letter she had Ayah give to Jinx telling him the relationship was over.

Jergamemnon and Jeneth strolled into the space. The stone mage asked, "What is the meaning of this gathering?"

They pressed in and Jeneth scowled at the scene.

Felix stood, trying to compose himself and pulled Jergamemnon by the elbow away from the crowd for a private word.

When they returned, Jergamemnon stated, "Everyone please return to your rooms and your work assignments for today. Everyone except Felix, Sammra, and Leonna."

An electric shock jarred Leonna at hearing her name.

When Jergamemnon didn't speak further, the apprentices slowly turned and went back into the camp, mumbling to each other as they left.

Jeneth and Jergamemnon carefully examined the body, checking Jinx's pockets for other clues.

"Clearly the dagger killed him," Jergamemnon said. "The question is whether his death was a suicide or murder. I can't think of a scenario where this was an accident."

"Nor can I," Jeneth said. He contemplated each of the apprentices, his eyes trailing on Leonna longer than the others.

Jergamemnon spoke, "Sammra you were first to arrive here, I understand?"

Sammra nodded.

"Tell us what you know."

"I was making my rounds. I patrol the camp three times per day. Morning, midday and sunset. Just a walkabout to find out if anything is out of place. Helps me in creating my work lists for the apprentices. I almost didn't see Jinx... because he was just a lump in the forest... if I hadn't glanced this way..."

"All right. Fine. Take a moment."

Sammra exhaled hard and wiped the tears from her face. "No, I can continue. So I saw something in the forest. I say something, but I immediately understood what was here. A body. I ran to it... I mean, to him... and he was... dead. I screamed."

Jergamemnon waved his hand at Sammra, so she closed her eyes and shared the memory with everyone. They saw her walking into the forest, casually, calmly, then a shock of fear ran through her when she saw the body. Sammra ran up to it, fell to her knees and clutched Jinx. The vision faded.

"And this note?" Jergamemnon held the page up in his hand.

Sammra's voice was vacant. "He was holding that piece of paper."

Jergamemnon read the writing on the sheet out loud.

Leonna cringed as if each of his words were punctuated with a knife stab to her chest.

When he finished reading the letter, Jergamemnon dropped his arm and glared at Leonna. "Well?"

"I-I wrote it. Yes. I gave the page to Jinx the morning we entered the Worthy Trials."

The stone mage stared at her, his face blank. "Go on."

"This is all a big misunderstanding." Leonna's voice shrilled. "I only wanted to be friends. It's all I wanted. He kept pressing. Proposing we marry. He had all these stupid reasons why our marriage would be good for our two clans. I didn't know…" Her voice trailed off.

"You didn't know what?" Jeneth said.

She stared at Jeneth as she spoke, "That Jinx might hurt himself. If that's what happened."

Felix roared, "So you think he loved you and all you do is send him this cowardly little note? You didn't have the decency to speak with him face to face?"

"I-I-I couldn't. I couldn't face him." Hot tears poured down Leonna's cheeks.

Sammra touched Felix's arm as she shook her head softly.

"Okay. Let's stop the emotion and the yelling," Jergamemnon stated. "There have been four deaths at these Trials. Apprentices dying is nothing new here, but in these odd circumstances, yes, there needs to be further investigation. This may be a murder. Leonna, you were found at the scene of Aquilo's room and this here, this note in Jinx's hand. Is there anything at all that you can say about that?"

Leonna pleaded, "I've already told you everything. You heard why I was meeting Aquilo. I explained. Who attacked him? I didn't see. And this. The note. Yes, I admit that I wrote the letter. Jinx said he loved me. I didn't feel the same way." She choked back her sob, "Oh Jinx, you wouldn't kill yourself over me, would you?"

Jeneth spoke, his voice raspy, "There is the matter of the Trials themselves."

Jergamemnon added, "Good point. Felix, Sammra,

your hearts are torn at this moment, but we will need to shortly decide if the Trials are to continue."

Sammra said, "No, they go on. If there is foul play here, continuing the trials will give an opportunity for us to further investigate. If there is a murderer here, that person cannot leave for the troll-spell covers us all."

Felix reluctantly nodded his agreement.

"Fine." Jergamemnon waved to the two trolls standing at the perimeter and told them to take Jinx's body to the clinic.

As they stepped out of the wood, Jeneth's hand rubbed the empty dagger holster at his side.

Leonna gazed at the moonstone as she walked back to camp. People dying wasn't what she had signed up for. *Nothing was going according to plan!* Leonna secretly cursed herself for not telling them that it was Jeneth's dagger in Jinx's chest and there was a high probability he stabbed the boy for some reason that presently eluded her. No one was supposed to die. Jeneth had promised that it was only a heist. And for the benefit of the clan. How could killing Jinx benefit the avians?

Leonna's stomach turned. All she could think about was flying away. She wanted to push her mind into one of her birds and soar, taking flight, the wind under her wings, pushing higher and higher. She loved the rush of diving from heights, cascading along the side of sheer cliffs. Flying was her escape. But here there was no way out. She was part of a plot that was going bad fast and there was nothing she could do to stop it. She felt trapped.

Leonna stopped at the tree line and wiped her face, trying to compose herself before she walked out into the courtyard. She looked a wreck but refused to run to her room and try to pretty herself. She stepped into the space and went to Felicia.

"What do you want?" the feline snorted.

"I wanted to say I'm sorry. About Jinx. He didn't deserve that."

Felicia squinted her eyes. "You don't talk to me." The feline walked off.

Leonna shook her head and took a seat on a bench.

A few moments later, Sammra, Felix, and the two archmages stepped out of the forest.

Jergamemnon raised his hands and once everyone stopped murmuring, began to speak. "Obviously, all of you saw what was found in the forest. Jinx is dead. We do not yet know all the details of what transpired. Master Jeneth and I will continue to investigate. Until we have answers, we will continue with the Worthy Apprentice Trials."

Jeneth added, "We want to assure everyone the Worthy Trials are safe—as safe as they always are, that is. We are going to post additional trolls at the perimeters of the camp and not only around you all, but also throughout the camp. Also, we are going to establish a mandatory curfew. No one is to be out of their rooms at night. Finally, we want everyone to use the buddy system. No one is to go anywhere alone."

After they finished, Felix paused a few moments. "Does everyone understand?"

The crowd murmured their assent.

Just as the group began to step away, Kerlith barked, "Wait, that's it? That creature-kind, what's his name, was just killed, wasn't he? Or am I blind? And he's not the first. Onyx is dead. Drake is dead. Aquilo is dead. Someone probably killed him too. And Onyx, the stonecutter, that appeared awful suspicious to me. And Drake? No way did someone with his skill fall out of a tree. Four murders by my count and we're going to walk away with the buddy system?"

Several of the apprentices standing near Kerlith stepped away as if a blast of mage-light might be soon heading his way.

Kerlith continued, "Jinx, yeah that was his name, Jinx was murdered, wasn't he? That much is obvious. Maybe they all were. So there's a killer among us. And you want us to walk away and trust the trolls to guard us? They didn't stop Jinx from dying. They didn't stop Aquilo's room from blowing up. For all we know one of the trolls is the killer."

Felix stepped forward, "Kerlith, you need to calm down."

"Calm down? Calm down? Listen, I don't care what any of you say. None of this was an accident. There have been four murders here and I don't appreciate the cover up."

Jergamemnon said, "Boy, you tread on dangerous ground. You need to keep your tongue."

Kerlith began pacing in front of them. "Right. Don't talk about it. Just shut up and wait for the trolls to kill me next. Or you. Or you. Or you. Who's next?"

Jeneth hissed, "We said we are still investigating this situation. We are. At least one murder potentially has been committed, no one is denying that. We will get to the bottom of it."

"Nice words from a creature-kind. Doesn't anyone find it odd that creature-kind were involved in two of these incidents? I don't trust them. Sorry to say. I don't trust anyone. Not after this."

Jergamemnon stepped forward. "You embarrass Master Muolithnon. A stonecutter doesn't act a fool. Control yourself."

Kerlith said, "I'm sorry if you feel that way. I'm just saying what everyone's thinking. We don't feel safe here. And what can we do about it? Nothing. We're trapped by troll-spell."

Felix sneered, "Whoever wants to quit is welcome to leave."

Kerlith closed his mouth and scoffed, "I can't do that. This is my last chance. As far as I'm concerned, the Worthy Apprentice Trials should be postponed. Let all the masters come and get to the bottom of this. Resume the Trials once the killer's been taken away."

Jergamemnon answered, "Apprentice, we appreciate your concern. However, we make the decisions here."

Kerlith threw his arms in the air and spun, "So we'll all just die then!" He marched away, toward his hut.

Chapter Seventeen
The Show

Shireen wriggled in her chair, excited to watch the show, a demonstration of the skills and abilities of the avians and felines. And Jergamemnon had promised a special treat; he was going to give a little taste of what an archmage could really do.

On the stage, Jergamemnon said, "Given the peculiar circumstances, we decided everyone needed a break, some time to get their wits about them. So Felix and Sammra requested some form of demonstration, a good idea."

Bel leaned forward in his seat and whispered in Shireen's ear, "Shireen, can I speak with you?"

Her eyes turned but she didn't respond.

Sammra poured out her sand on the stage and began swirling her arms, the sand spun off the ground and slowly raised up in the air, forming a cloud.

Bel tried again. "I only want to talk to you for a moment."

Pren hissed, "Shhhh!" and gave him her rankest stink-eye.

Shireen's eyes went wide as the sand formed a tall ladder and Sammra began to scale it.

Bel whispered again. "Shireen, please?"

Lithia turned to Bel and muttered, "Do you mind?"

Shireen stood and glared at Bel. She left her row and went to the top of the hill, the rear of the stadium seating. A few other apprentices were standing, watching the show from back there. Bel followed her.

"Now, what is so important you need to make me miss this?" Shireen said under her breath.

"Don't miss the demonstration. We can watch from here. I want to, you know, talk."

Sammra stood at the top of the ladder, nearly twenty feet in the air then jumped off. The crowd gasped. The sand quickly puddled beneath her and caught her, lowering her to the ground.

"Wow," Bel said, then he leaned over toward Shireen and whispered, "I wanted to tell you what I found out so far."

Shireen frowned then returned her eyes to the stage.

Bel tried to tug her to the side, moving her away from the other standing apprentices so they wouldn't overhear.

Shireen shook her head lightly.

Bel touched her hand and mouthed, "Why?"

Shireen snorted then angrily pulled him down the path and away from the clearing. "I'll tell you why. Because you're chasing skirts. And right in front of me. You're no different from all the others. I am disappointed in you. We had an agreement, to act like friends, but this? To throw her in my face like that? I am really irritated with you."

"What? No! I'm not... Are you talking about Leonna?"

"Oh don't play stupid, Bel."

"I told you she's affectionate. It's not—"

Shireen tried to force hostility into her voice without raising it loud enough to attract attention from the others. "Don't give me that! You think I'm a fool? She wants you and you stand there and let her put her hands all over you. I caught you sitting there and smiling like one of her little birds being stroked."

"Okay, wait a moment here. What about you and Felix? I noticed you two together. You were sitting pretty close. And he was almost... naked."

Shireen shook her finger in front of his face. "That's your defense? To attack me? Okay, fine. Felix and I had some words. We spoke. I had a few questions. He was answering them. He was filling me in on some details about his culture. I'm sure you have no such excuse." Shireen wasn't going to tell him what else Felix wanted, but she wasn't going to lie about it either. She would just leave that detail out for now.

Bel stared back at her. Amazingly, she couldn't exactly read his expression. He believed her, she thought, but he still seemed frustrated.

She exhaled long and slow. Shireen couldn't stay mad at him for long. It was his eyes. She could stand there and stare at the light blue swirls for hours. She had to force herself to look away before she got lost in them. "Nothing to say then?"

"This isn't what I wanted to talk about. Shireen, I'm sorry. I didn't mean to, you know, hurt your feelings. You must recognize I have no desire for Leonna. I saved her life. She's been throwing herself at me. I told her to stop multiple times. What do you want me to do?"

She snorted and crossed her arms. "I shouldn't have to tell you that. What did you want to talk to me about anyway?"

"The plot."

"The plot?" She sounded doubtful.

"I think there is one."

"Bel, why would you say that? A plot to kill off apprentices?"

"No… maybe that's an unintended consequence. Listen, I followed Leonna to Aquilo's room. Not because I was after Leonna, mind you. I was actually on my way to meet you that night, to speak to you. Leonna snuck out of your hut when I was going to pay you a visit, so I followed her."

"Okay. I'm listening."

"I'm telling you the truth. I wasn't meeting her. She didn't even know I was there."

Shireen shook her head. "Go on."

"I hid by Aquilo's window and listened, watched. He was accusing Leonna of being in some kind of plot. A creature-kind plot, I guess. A plot, anyway. He said he had evidence and he pointed at an envelope full of papers."

"Wait. A brown envelope about this big?"

Bel said, "You saw it?"

"Lithia gave the package to Aquilo. Said the envelope was from Jergamemnon."

"Interesting. So when Leonna was about to reveal something, I think, going to tell Aquilo what she knew, that's when they were attacked and the building blew."

"Does anyone else know this?"

"Not that last part about her knowing more about it."

"Why didn't you tell them?"

"No way. Not in front of Felix and Jeneth. They are probably in on the whole thing. If I could get Jergamemnon alone I would tell him, but Jeneth is always glued to his side."

"And Sammra?"

"She's like us, I guess, a lander. I trust her too. I think we could tell her and she could give a message to Jergamemnon."

"Well, it's something," Shireen said. "And what about Jinx?"

"Hard to say. I would be guessing. Two people ran from the scene of the explosion and at least one of them was a male and recognized who I was because he called out my name. Maybe that was Jinx? That would make sense since he was in love with Leonna. Maybe he followed her too. Then maybe the killer found out Jinx was at the scene and killed him? I think the two deaths are definitely related."

"Or they have nothing to do with each other and one was a lover's quarrel and the other a suicide." She emphasized the word 'lover'.

"Possibly. And you? Found out anything?"

"I've caught Leonna and Felicia arguing a few times."

"Who hasn't?"

"The two had a disagreement about the boy who went missing. I forget his name. One of the creature-kind."

"Jonah," Bel said.

"Right, Jonah. I think someone is hiding him in the forest for some reason. At least, one of them knows more about it. And Onyx. Like I told you before. I think they were having an argument over Jonah and Onyx overheard it."

Bel added, "I found Leonna near the forest."

"You seem to be wherever she is." Shireen turned and edged closer to the meeting area so she could get a better view of the stage.

Jergamemnon was twirling his fingers at the sky and a small dark cloud was forming. Several bolts of lightning burst from the cloud. He informed the crowd, "To call forth different forms of weather takes much practice. We must always be careful when performing weather-related magic for we can only call it, not control it, especially something as unpredictable as lightning."

The audience stood and clapped.

Shireen slugged Bel. "You made me miss the best parts." The space had shrunk where Shireen had been sitting as people shifted. "You made me lose my seat too."

"Too terrible for you to stand with me?"

"You think you're off the hook that easy?"

Bel didn't respond.

Jergamemnon introduced Felix, Leonna, and Ayah.

Bel inched closer to Shireen and brushed his forearm against hers. She glanced at him as he tried to hide a smile.

"I wonder why Jeneth's not taking the stage," Bel mumbled as he made his little pinky touch the side of her hand.

Shireen pulled her hand away. She was conflicted. She was still mad at him, a little, but she missed the way his touch soothed her. She didn't want to allow Bel to touch her hand, yet she wanted the connection too. She exhaled slowly. "Maybe Jeneth doesn't want to show us anything. He never did at University."

Bel tried to take her hand. She pulled it back and glared at him. *Someone might see!*

He mumbled, "Sorry."

Felix called his cats then tied napkins over their eyes.

He had them wait on the opposite side of the stage while he blindfolded himself and sat in a chair turned away from the audience.

From the stage, Ayah said, "Every person has a specific odor about him or her."

"You got that right," Kerlith yelled out.

Ayah ignored his comment and continued, "Felix is going to send his cats out into the audience and they will identify you by scent alone."

Bel spoke to Shireen in his spirit, —*Shireen, scan my heart. Read me. I want to open myself to you. I'm telling you the truth about Leonna*—

Shireen cleared her throat and took a few steps away from Bel. After a few moments, she connected with his spirit. If he was going to bare his emotions and memories, she would jump at the chance.

The blindfolded bobcat stepped slowly up the stairs, carefully placing each paw one in front of the other. The cat went to one person seated on the edge of the second row and sniffed at her hand. The apprentice giggled when the cat licked her fingers.

Felix announced, "Sammra. That was an easy one."

"You are correct, of course," Sammra said. "But are you saying it was easy because my smell is too strong?"

"Oh, ahh, no, I didn't mean..."

The crowd chuckled.

Felix tried to bail himself out. "I meant I've spent so much time around you."

Leonna whispered loudly at Felix so all could hear, "I think she knows what you meant. She was making a joke."

Shireen calmed her face, making it as stone, a blank statue. She nodded at Bel as he attempted to do the same. —*You've been practicing?*—

—*For times like these*—

—*Good*— She allowed herself to smile then washed the grin away as she dove into him.

Bel kept his eyes open, but they were dazed. Translucent tendrils of blue light exited his torso and spread around her.

—*Keeping your eyes open too?*—

—*I told you I've been practicing*—

Felix sent his cats out to identify other apprentices.

Shireen's life-force glowed as she floated out of her body and into Bel's, allowing her life-force energy to stretch out and bond with his spirit. Several of Bel's memories flashed before her eyes.

Instantly Shireen floated with Bel, above her room, high in the trees, watching Leonna sneak out. The sky was dark. Leonna was stepping through the camp, edging along the buildings.

The image dissolved and then Shireen stood next to Bel as he turned invisible and followed Leonna to Aquilo's room. —*What? You can do that now? Turn invisible? Since when?*—

Bel snorted. —*I've been practicing. Didn't I already tell you that?*—

Shireen watched Bel step forward, his boots anyway, and spy on Aquilo and Leonna arguing through a window. She observed the explosion and two people running.

—*Wait. That almost looked like Jinx*—

"Maybe. I can't be certain," Bel whispered out loud.

Shireen couldn't make out the other, the forest was too dark.

Shireen saw him rescue Leonna and watched as the

others condemned him with their eyes when he knelt on the ground in front of Leonna, the burning building behind.

The image faded and was replaced by another. Bel was entering the clinic to visit Leonna. Bel's emotions at that moment coursed through Shireen. He was genuinely concerned for the avian, yet there was no love in his heart. No love except the slightest twinge, a tiny twinge of attraction—Shireen felt it. Bel was most certainly attracted to her.

She watched as he sat with Leonna, then escorted her back to the camp. Shireen witnessed his heart, how he treated her, not trying to hurt Leonna's feelings by spurning her, yet being calm and asking her to stop. Yet there was still something there that Shireen couldn't help but feel jealous about. He enjoyed being with the avian —as a friend. And she was beautiful, he couldn't hide the tiny rise in him when she was around.

Bel tried to break the connection. Shireen tried to hold on, exploring his exact emotions for the girl, digging feverishly. *Why was he attracted to her? Why did he spend so much time with her? What exactly was it about her?*

Then the connection severed.

Shireen needed to come to grips with something basic: did she trust Bel? She thought she did before they came to the Worthy Apprentice Trials, but now that they were here and Bel was spending so much time with Leonna she found herself constantly reevaluating her heart. And she still hadn't thought about what they were going to do after the trials! She loved him—no denying that, but could she allow him to leave everything, his entire future, for her? Could she be so selfish?

Still she couldn't help feeling jealous. Shireen hated that she was being so paranoid, but at the same time, it was with good reason. Leonna was beautiful and she was hugging and kissing Bel every chance that came along. Not only that, Leonna openly said she was going to steal Bel from her. Certainly the handsome, innocent fool didn't know that.

Shireen pushed into Bel's head, —*You didn't need to do that*—

—*You would have forgiven me eventually, but this way is faster*—

Shireen nodded and wiped her sweaty palm on her leg. There was still something there, though. She didn't like that he tried to break the connection when she started to probe deeper.

—*Now your turn*— Bel chuckled.

—*No, I don't think so*—

A cougar stepped next to Shireen and sniffed her hand.

Felix said, "Shireen. I recognize that scent."

Bel muttered, "I'll bet he does."

Shireen waved her hand in the air and said, "You found me."

Felix removed the blinders, stood and took a seat in the audience with his cats. Leonna and Ayah remained on the stage.

Ayah spoke first, "The cats are stealthy and ground predators. They can remain still in the high reeds for hours. They have a keen nose. Their vision is finely attuned to movement. Birds are much different. They don't rely on sounds or smells as much as sight. At our clan, on Bald Mountain, many of my birds can catch sight of a mouse all the way at the bottom of the mountain. And not because the critter is moving. They possess much better sight than humans. Let me demonstrate."

Ayah's birds flapped their wings and went high into the sky. They circled overhead and appeared tiny dots in the distance to Shireen.

Right then and there, Shireen decided to forgive Bel. He had done no wrong, mostly. She would have liked it if he would have been a little sterner with Leonna, but still, she saw why he was letting her get close: it was the mission. Her master wanted him to feel out the avians. Unfortunately, the avian Bel was feeling out was drop-dead gorgeous and couldn't stop kissing him. But, in the end, Shireen knew what she always knew. She trusted Bel.

She wanted to feel him again, to connect, to be a part of him. That quick touch of his life-force reminded Shireen that she felt empty without Bel. She hated the feeling but also knew that if they parted ways after the trials she would need to do something about that, to learn how to be without him. Just not now. No, not now. Shireen opened up her spirit to Bel and touched him with her emotions, unintentionally pouring her warmth and desire into him.

He moaned then quickly stopped himself. Shireen immediately pulled back when a stone apprentice in front turned around and glared.

Shireen pushed again, but more carefully this time. She needed to bury herself in his warm blue energy, to allow Bel to envelop her as she spread her life-force wide. Bel reciprocated, sending his life-force out to touch and caress, to stroke her arms and back. *Electric.* They intermingled, blue mixing with light green, merging, becoming one. Shireen could barely contain the soft squeal of delight forming in her throat, yet she forced herself to remain expressionless and silent. Bel's blue light touched her lightly in the center of her chest as if his energy were kissing her spirit.

On the stage, Leonna said, "I've asked several of you to hide small items throughout the camp and to not tell anyone what or where they are. Now, I'm going to go around and ask you what the item is and we'll find out if Ayah's birds can locate it."

Sammra stood and walked to the back of the stands cut into the side of the small hill, past Bel and Shireen then down the path. A few moments later, Felicia followed.

—*Do you want to follow them?*—

Shireen frowned. —*How?*—

Bel stepped closer to her, grabbed Shireen's hand and silently mouthed, "Aoratos," and the two disappeared, becoming invisible.

"Bel, your boots," Shireen whispered.

"I haven't perfected the spell yet."

Shireen released his hand and reappeared, then quickly grabbed it and faded invisible. She held his hand tight as the two walked, staying about one-hundred feet behind Felicia. Even though they were invisible, Bel's boots and Shireen's shoes were still showing so they kept to the edge of the buildings. Felicia snapped her head back once, then twice, making sure she wasn't being followed.

Bel and Shireen stopped at the edge of the forest. Sammra and Felicia were some distance into the wood, facing each other, speaking heatedly. Shock and fear ran through Shireen when Felicia popped her eyes in her direction and pointed. Shireen almost released Bel's hand and ran. Then she realized Felicia was pointing at something behind Shireen. She spun. The round building, the central meeting hall, was directly behind Shireen on the other side of the camp. *Why would Felicia point at that?*

Bel reached down with his one free hand and removed his boots. Now only Shireen's flat shoes and his bare feet were visible. At least, his feet were less obvious and noticeable than his calf-high boots. He tugged Shireen's hand lightly and the two carefully stepped into the forest, trying to avoid twigs, leaves, or anything that might make a sound. Bel and Shireen stopped a short distance from Sammra and Felicia, straining to hear what the two were saying.

Shireen twitched nervously, hoping Sammra and Felicia wouldn't see Bel's feet or her shoes.

Felicia snarled, "What did you tell them at the inquiry?"

"When Aquilo died, oddly, they didn't ask me any questions. I guess they assumed Felix and I weren't involved. When I found Jinx, I told them what happened. As I told you. I found him."

"But that's not everything."

"No, it's not."

"Sammra, are you going to tell me or do I need to take this to my brother?"

"I have nothing to hide from you, but I think you'll agree it wouldn't be wise to inform Felix just yet. I'll tell him when the time is right, but not until I've figured out more."

"And?" Felicia paced.

Sammra explained, "I was there when Aquilo died.

Bel, the boy who rescued Leonna, he told them two people ran from the scene. I was one of them. In fact, I barely arrived back at my room in time to accompany Felix to view the devastation."

"And no one else knows this?"

"Just you and me. Jinx knew too, since he was the other one there."

"He told me he was there. He didn't mention you, though. So why were you there? Did you kill Aquilo?"

"What? Me? No! It was Jinx."

"Jinx?"

"Earlier that morning, I overheard something Aquilo said about a creature-kind plot, something he was investigating. He had an envelope of evidence, mostly circumstantial. I was going to Aquilo's room to speak with him. When I arrived, Jinx was at Aquilo's door. I think he had followed Leonna there. Jinx attacked Aquilo. Truthfully, I don't think Jinx meant to kill him. He seemed angry, upset, probably over Leonna. I think he just lost control."

"Sounds like Jinx. He was always flying off the handle." Felicia's voice was empty.

Sammra reached out to touch Felicia's shoulder, but she shrugged the gesture away. Sammra continued, "Jinx was thrown to the ground. I ran into the building and grabbed the envelope. The smoke was too intense. I couldn't make out much except that Aquilo was dead. I didn't know Leonna was in there. I ran out."

"So you possess the so-called evidence of a creature-kind plot?"

"I do."

"And? What does it say?"

"Don't worry. You're not implicated."

Felicia purred, "Of course, I'm not. I haven't done anything wrong nor are the felines involved in anything nefarious."

"Nice word use. Like I said, the evidence is circumstantial. It mainly revolves around Jeneth and the avians. The envelope is safe. I wouldn't worry if I were you. If I can get Jergamemnon alone, I'll speak with him about what I know."

"Sammra, I appreciate you filling me in on these details. You don't owe me anything."

"Jinx died. He was your clan-brother. I would want to know."

"Jinx." Felicia looked up into the trees. "We never got along. We both have dominant personalities, I guess. But still, I miss him."

"What exactly happened to Jinx is much harder to say. I only found him. If someone knew he was responsible for Aquilo's death... maybe a revenge killing? I hate to ask this, but do you think Felix—"

Felicia waved her hands, cutting her off, "Absolutely not. A feline killing another feline? No. Impossible. And especially not Felix."

"I thought as much. Perhaps—okay this is crazy now —if the plot is really happening, someone else who is participating, an avian perhaps, killed him because they thought he was drawing too much attention?"

"That's a stretch. All I know is that someone killed him. No one, especially not Jinx, buries a dagger in their own chest to commit suicide."

"Did you recognize the dagger?"

"Avian. Clearly. Had their carvings on the hilt. Felix noticed too. I saw the consternation on his face." Felicia shook her head. "I'm going to find out who killed Jinx and I'm going to rip his throat out. Or hers. I don't care who. Whoever it is, they're dead." She pointed her finger at Sammra's nose. "And don't you dare withhold anything from me either. If you find out who did this, I want to know."

"So you can kill him? Or her? I don't think—"

"That's right. Don't think. You better just tell me."

A loud snap caused Sammra and Felicia to spin. "Did you hear that?"

"Of course, I heard it." Felicia stepped forward, walking towards Bel and Shireen cautiously.

Shireen swallowed the saliva pooling in her mouth. Her heart raced. Her breathing quickened. Bel's fingers touched Shireen's face and then found her lips, pressing them. He thought she was making too much noise, breathing too loud. She tried to force calm into her body, but her trembling flesh refused to listen.

Sammra asked, "Where are your cats?"

"I left them back at the show."

Felicia scanned the woods.

Shireen thought neither Bel nor she made the noise. *Was someone else in the forest? Someone else who was hiding? Invisible?* Shireen scanned her eyes across the surrounding forest but found nothing. Her hands were shaking. She wanted to leave. Now, in fact. But with Bel's feet and her shoes showing, she thought it too risky. She hoped Bel thought so too and didn't move. They needed to wait until these two left and then follow them out.

Another twig snapped behind Shireen, this one much louder. Shireen snapped her head toward the noise. *Nothing. The sound came from right behind me!*

"That's it!" Sammra said. "Someone's out here. We're

done. I'm leaving." Sammra popped into a slow jog, swinging her head to and fro as she exited the space. Felicia followed her out, but branched along a different vector, aiming herself directly at Shireen and Bel.

Shireen had only a moment to shuffle herself out of the way before Felicia would barrel into her. The feline ran by, barely missing Shireen. Felicia snapped her head, slowed and pointed down at Bel's feet.

"Run," Bel said out loud as he yanked Shireen into a full gallop.

Felicia followed closely after, yelling, "Hey, You! Wait! Whoever you are!"

Bel scooped up his boots as they exited the forest. The two continued running with Felicia screaming at them from behind. Bel's boots appeared to be floating through the air and his feet and her shoes were running on the ground.

The two ran across the camp, but the feline was fast. She was right behind them. The two couldn't shake her.

Shireen realized that shortly Felicia's cats would show up and they would be cornered. They only had moments to lose her before they would be trapped.

The pair ran past the central meeting building, the moonstone floating above.

Shireen tugged Bel's arm towards the building, running past a troll guarding a door and weaving to the other side of another troll. The two leaped over a railing along the patio of the building and circled the round structure. They were able to gain a little distance on Felicia as one of the trolls grabbed her arm and grunted and groaned, pointing at the demonstration area. Bel paused long enough to put his boots on.

"Hurry," Shireen hissed. They started running again.

"Can you cast something at her? I can't do that and hold my concentration on keeping us invisible."

"I'll try," Shireen mumbled as they ran.

Felicia left the trolls and quickly caught up to Bel's boots and Shireen's shoes. She was only about ten feet back. As Shireen and Bel ran into the courtyard, Felicia's cougar and leopard leaped directly at the two, snarling and hissing.

Shireen spun and said, "Salatario," as she pointed her invisible wand at Felicia.

Felicia stumbled and fell to the ground as black spider lines spread over her arms and legs. She clutched her stomach and retched.

The cats slowed then walked up to Felicia. The cougar began licking her face and arms as the leopard nudged her with its nose.

"Poison, too much," Bel said. "You'll kill her." A flash of light exited Bel's invisible staff.

The black lines of poison slowly faded from Felicia's body. She struggled up to her hands and knees and screeched, "I'll find out! I'll find out who you are! I'll kill you!" She coughed several times, spittle dripping from her lips, then she rolled back to her side, clutched her ribcage and moaned.

Chapter Eighteen
Case Closed

A few moments passed and Felix shook his head. He caught himself in a daze again. Felix still couldn't accept that Aquilo, his friend, was dead. He pushed the thought from his head. He had to focus, he needed to be functional for the trials.

He didn't necessarily agree with Sammra that they should continue the Worthy Apprentice Trials. Only one thing she had said made sense: holding everyone here might help catch Jinx's and Aquilo's killer.

So he combed his mane and adjusted his breechcloth, trying to make himself presentable as he went through a mental checklist of what he was going to say before the start of the next trial.

He exited his room and went to the clearing outside of the forest where the next trial was to take place. Sammra was already there and Bel and Shireen were speaking with her.

Felix sent his cats ahead. When one of the felines sensed fear radiating off Shireen, he listened through its ears.

"We need to speak to you privately, that's all," Bel said.

"What is your concern?" Felix yelled ahead.

Bel and Shireen rotated to face Felix. "It's nothing important," Bel said.

Felix cocked his head. His cats sensed the fear in both Bel and Shireen escalate. Bel was clearly lying. "If your concern was important enough to bring to Sammra, you should go ahead and say it. With all that has gone on here, now is not the time for secrets." Felix's eyes tore into Bel.

Shireen said, "What you say is true, but with all that you've gone through, your friend and clan-brother both dying, we didn't want to trouble you. The fact is each of us had a concern about our rooming conditions. Bel is rooming with Kerlith who constantly makes derogatory remarks. I am rooming with Leonna and I am concerned for her. Felicia antagonizes her. That's all. We're sorry to bother you."

Sammra said, "I will look into these concerns."

Felix squinted as the two walked away. He bent down and petted his cougar. The two were afraid, even while Shireen spoke. Probably lying.

He didn't trust Bel. He held back a snarl building in his chest. His cats began to pace when contempt for Bel raced through Felix. Bel was hiding something about Aquilo's death. He had to be. He didn't want to be scanned. Now he was dragging Shireen in with him, getting her to lie for him and wanted to speak to Sammra privately. *Why? To turn her against me and the other creature-kind like he has already done with Shireen? These landers' hate for us knows no bounds.*

Sammra didn't worry Felix, though. She wouldn't believe such lies. Like Aquilo, Felix trusted her.

The apprentices began to congregate and Felix scanned the crowd, noticing Bel and his roommates and

Shireen and her roommates loitering toward the rear of the assembly.

He shook his head lightly and began, "The next trial is timed. There are a large number of goals to accomplish. Twenty in fact. You do not need to do all them but must complete at least fifteen. Some may be more difficult than others depending, of course, on your skill set."

Sammra added, "So to pass this trial, you need to complete a minimum of fifteen tasks on the course. Each task has a point value. If you complete more than fifteen you receive those points also. Your point total for completing tasks is subtracted from how much time you used. This trial is about knowing yourself, making wise decisions, and time management, the trial of wisdom. Felix or I will start counting the moment you step on the course and stop once you exit. You need fifty points to pass."

"Are there volunteers to begin?" Felix asked.

Kerlith muttered from the back, "I guess this is the one where half of us fail."

Felix barked, "Kerlith. Step forward. Thanks for volunteering."

Kerlith shook his head as he walked up. "I didn't volunteer."

"That's not what I heard."

Kerlith walked to the edge of the start line and leaned back. "How will I recognize what each task is? And how many points each is worth?"

Sammra said, "You'll hear words in your mind. As before. Good luck." She smiled at him. "I'm sure you'll do fine."

Kerlith stepped across the line and ran in. Felix began

counting out loud as the apprentices waited, talked to each other, and milled about. The group hadn't shrunk substantially yet. Only three had failed the last trial and they had already been escorted out by the trolls. Felix wondered if what Kerlith said was true. Would they lose half at this trial? If they didn't lose half this time, certainly they would at the next. Felix smiled. Fewer apprentices meant less work. The idea that the killer would intentionally fail to escape grabbed Felix just then. He would have to speak about this with Jergamemnon and Jeneth.

A while later, Kerlith stumbled across the line, bent over and dropped his hands to his knees. He was gasping for air. Felix stopped counting as Kerlith raised his hand. "Done," Kerlith said.

Felix nodded to Sammra who went into the woods to verify the tasks were completed and count Kerlith's points. When she returned, she said, "Fifteen completed. Eight-hundred points."

"Kerlith's time count was five hundred fifty-six. Congratulations." Felix nodded at Kerlith and then said, "Who's next?"

The apprentices continued to go in and out of the trial. Most of them passed except one who miscounted and only completed fourteen tasks and another who took too long and scored less than fifty. The trolls escorted the two to gather their things. Felix stopped Barth, telling him to not take those two apprentices outside the forest just yet.

Felix was pleased that he was able to maintain his counting. He had been concerned his mind would drift to either Aquilo or Jinx and he would find himself sitting there, in front of everyone, in a dull stupor, but that had not happened as yet.

Almost all the apprentices who completed the trial had left the space to attend to their work list items or socialize at the courtyard, so the yard at the edge of the forest was emptying out. Felicia was staring at Sammra with a glint in her eye.

After Shireen exited and her total was counted, Felicia stepped forward to go next. She mumbled something to Sammra who jumped back, startled. Felicia grinned and ran into the trials. Felix wanted to know what Felicia had said, but he had to count so he couldn't ask. After some time, Felicia exited the trial and Felix stopped counting. Just as Sammra went to check the status of her tasks, Felicia slammed into her.

"What's your problem?" Sammra asked.

Felicia barked, her eyes staring at Felix, "Me? I only have one problem and that's you know who killed Aquilo."

Sammra said, "I think you are mistaken, Young Apprentice."

Felicia growled, "Liar!" Her cats leaped.

Felix cried, "Felicia, stop!"

Sammra crouched into a defensive position and tossed her sand in the air, forming the particles into large, hard, round balls that smashed into Felicia's leopard's neck and cougar's face.

Felix stood, his cats leaping to his side.

The other apprentices watched intently.

A third cat and a fourth leaped at Sammra. She smashed away one but the other clawed the side of her neck and cheek before she was able to fling the bobcat away with her sand. Blood spurted from Sammra's wounds.

Sammra sent out a slug of her sand, smashing Felicia on the nose and crumpling her to the ground.

Felix yelled, "Stop! Now! The both of you."

Felicia slowly came to her feet and wiped her bleeding nose.

After her cats retreated to her side, Sammra opened her pouch and the sand flew in.

Felix trembled in anger. He marched toward the two.

"Is this true?" Felix barely mouthed the words and his voice trailed off as he saw the guilt on Sammra's face. *Sammra knew who killed Aquilo. She hadn't told me.*

"Who? Who killed Aquilo? Who did this?" Felix wailed. He shook Sammra's shoulders, "Tell me! Tell me what you know!"

Jeneth and Jergamemnon stepped into the space. "Exactly what is going on here, Felix?" The stone mage asked. "I thought you said you had these trials under control!"

Felicia stepped in between Felix and Jergamemnon. "Do not blame my clan-brother. The fault was mine. I will take whatever punishment is due me."

Jeneth spoke, his voice a nasally hiss, "What happened?"

Felicia swung her arm, pointing her finger at Sammra. "She knows what happened to Aquilo. That's what. And it was building up in me. It's terrible to admit, but I must tell the truth. I lost control. I let my anger get the best of me. I attacked her."

Jergamemnon studied Sammra. "Is what the apprentice said true?"

"She did attack me, yes." Sammra lowered her eyes to the ground in front of her. "And I know who killed Aquilo. Yes, it's true."

Jeneth urged, "Well don't keep us in suspense. Tell us."

Sammra said, "Jinx. Jinx killed Aquilo." She stepped toward Felix and tried to grab his hand, but he yanked it away. "Felix, you need to understand. I saw how much pressure you were under. I thought it best to not tell you. Yet. He was your clan-brother and I didn't want to hurt you. I held back the information for you, to protect your heart."

Felix stepped away and paced in a circle then returned to Sammra and gritted his teeth, "You should have told me."

"And how did you come to the conclusion Jinx was Aquilo's murderer?" Jeneth asked.

Sammra explained, "I'm sorry. Again, Master Archmage, I apologize for not revealing this information sooner." As Sammra continued to speak the other apprentices gathered from the courtyard. "When I found Jinx, I thought him dead. I went to him immediately and searched for his life-force. He wasn't dead, but almost. Too far gone for me to do anything to try to save him. In his dying breath, he spoke these words: 'I'm. Sorry. I. Killed. Aquilo.' Then he died. There was nothing I could do to save him. You found me crying and holding him, but I didn't cry for him but for you, Felix, my good friend. For my heart was breaking over how this would affect you."

"She speaks truth," Jergamemnon said.

Jeneth stepped forward. "One mystery is solved. Sammra, Felicia, go to the clinic to attend to your wounds. Felix, come up with an appropriate punishment for Felicia. I don't think what she has done warrants ejection from the Worthy Apprentice Trials."

"Nor do I," Jergamemnon added.

The two turned towards the crowd of apprentices gathered in the courtyard.

Jergamemnon held up his hands. "For those of you arriving, new light has been shed on Aquilo's death. Here is what we suspect happened. We are certain Jinx was in love with Leonna from testimony gathered during the interviews and from the note found in Jinx's hand when he died."

Jeneth spoke, "Landers, remember love among the creature-kind is not forbidden."

Jergamemnon nodded. "Leonna was going to meet Aquilo in his room on the night of his death. We understand why Aquilo asked her there as he was investigating some things. Perhaps there were other reasons the two had arranged. Leonna could probably shed some light on why she was going to meet a man in the middle of the night, a man running the trials she was participating in, but since she apparently has memory loss, we can only assume—"

"It was nothing like that," Leonna squeaked.

"Oh, so you do remember?" Jeneth hissed.

"No, But I know I wouldn't do that."

Jergamemnon continued, "In any case, Jinx found out Leonna was going there or perhaps was awakened when he heard a noise when she crept by. Jinx followed Leonna. She entered Aquilo's room. In a jealous fit of rage, Jinx killed Aquilo."

Jeneth said, "And, in a depressed and deep sadness, he killed himself by thrusting an avian dagger in his chest. I imagine chancing on the dagger reminded Jinx of what he had done since he killed one person and nearly killed Leonna, an avian, the girl he loved. So he ended his life."

Jergamemnon said, "Case closed."

Kerlith mumbled, "What? That makes no sense." He turned and walked away.

Several of the others shook their heads, muttering to each other as they turned and left the space. Some others shrugged their shoulders.

Felix agreed that the archmages' explanation had many holes and was too tidy and clean, but said nothing. Murder is never so seamless and neat.

Was Leonna meeting Aquilo for a tryst? Clearly. Aquilo liked the shape of Leonna and since she's so flirty he probably thought her a quick and easy target. Although it turned Felix's stomach to think this about his friend, Aquilo probably made her some kind of offer or deal. *Leonna wouldn't have passed up on a chance to cheat on the trials so she would have agreed. But when she arrived and Aquilo wanted more than Leonna was going to offer, there was probably a disagreement.* Felix knew Leonna well enough. She was a tease but no more.

And Jinx. He followed her because he still loved her, no matter what that letter said. Jinx probably heard her protesting Aquilo's advances and Jinx stormed in. Aquilo and Jinx argued over Leonna as she sat there smiling about the whole thing. If their argument became heated, sure, Jinx could have killed Aquilo, but only if he wasn't expecting the attack. Jinx is powerful, maybe the strongest of the feline apprentices, but Aquilo is much wiser and experienced.

Felix shook his head again. *And Jinx committing suicide?* He didn't buy that. *Not when an avian dagger was buried in his chest. No way would Jinx do that to himself and especially not over Leonna. He would fight for her, yes. But kill himself? Impossible.*

Felix was starting to think Leonna was behind both

of the murders and Bel was her willing accomplice. *She got Aquilo killed because she worked Jinx up into a frenzy and killed him or had Bel murder the feline when he started pressing her. Perhaps. And now Bel was dragging Shireen into his plot too.*

Regardless what the archmages said, Jinx's killer was still out there. Felix's cougar roared as the cat considered the savory character of man-blood.

Jergamemnon held up his hands before too many of them walked off. "For those of us of the lands, this illustrates dramatically why wizards should not love and marry, why we should be celibate. This is the kind of thing that happens when wizards allow their hearts to become clouded."

Jeneth frowned. "I disagree." He walked out of the space, clearly not wanting to have the discussion in front of all the apprentices.

Ayah said, "Master Archmage Jergamemnon, our belief is when one loves another, he understands loss more deeply due to his attachment and bond with the one he loves. When he witnesses another die, he can empathize and aid and assist better because he can consider the loss of his own dear one. This makes a wizard more compassionate and less selfish."

"I understand you have your ways and I thank you for sharing the reasoning behind them," Jergamemnon said. He paused and cleared his throat. "Since this mystery is solved, Master Jeneth and I will be leaving the camp. I hope everyone continues to perform well and I hope to find everyone at Lasaat for the graduation ceremony."

Felicia was heading down the path toward the clinic so Felix decided to follow her. The last thing he needed was for his little sister to pick another fight with Sammra. If she did, he would be forced to eject her from the Trials and Felix didn't want to have to explain that to the clan-family. They wouldn't understand.

Felix gave the rest of the apprentices a short break then walked toward the clinic and hid near the end of the path behind a patch of bushes and sent his smallest cat within range. Felix crouched in a stance that he could quickly pop out of and run towards her if need be.

The cat got about twenty feet away and climbed a tree, watching from an overhead branch. Sammra and Felicia were just outside of the clinic.

"Sorry my cat scratched your face," Felicia said. "Wasn't my intention."

"Well, I did bust your nose," Sammra said sheepishly.

"It's throbbing. I hope it doesn't swell. That might affect my breathing."

"Oh. Won't be able to run? Didn't think of that. Sorry." Sammra touched the side of Felicia's face and studied the blood on her hand. "It has almost stopped bleeding. I better go in and let the trolls patch this scratch before it turns into a scar. You going to fix your nose?"

"No. I'll live. Again, sorry."

Sammra chuckled, "Theatrical. You did overdo it there." She walked into the clinic.

Felicia stepped away smiling to herself. When she reached the end of the path, Felix popped out from the brush and stood in front of her, his hands on his hips.

"Hey, what do you want? Here to accost me again? I took the blame."

"You did. As you should," Felix said. "I was here to make sure you didn't do anything stupid. But what I want to know is why are you, out of the blue, so chummy with Sammra? And what did she mean by 'overdo it'?"

Felicia chided, "What? I scratched her face and now you want to hear why I apologized? So I'm in trouble for fighting and in trouble for apologizing for fighting?"

"You apologized. Never seen you do that before, but good. But what did she mean?"

As she stormed off, Felicia snorted, "I don't know! Ask her!"

Chapter Nineteen
Lions, Spiders and Snakes

Bel entered the clearing, mentally readying himself which was difficult, since he, like everyone else in the camp, could hear the reverberating screams, growls, and screeches coming from the path into the forest that led to their next trial. Even Leonna and Ayah seemed nervous which offered Bel no solace. The worthys had assembled an array of beasts they would need to deal with and if the creature-kind, who were able to control animals, were anxious then Bel should probably be terrified. But he wasn't and that bothered him more than anything.

No, he was calm. Even at peace. Nes'egrinon used to mutter that the unknowns killed wizards, things wizards didn't anticipate. Bel couldn't comprehend exactly what was out there, but if it was a battle, and against animals, he figured he could handle that. He would talk to the trees before he went down the path, get them to swing out their vines and branches and bind the animals. That was his plan anyway and he figured it was a good one.

After the apprentices assembled, Felix spoke first. "For those of you who remain, you've completed three trials: the trial of teamwork in removing the rock from the pole, the trial of physical strength against the iron warrior and the trial of wisdom. After today, you will be more than halfway towards earning the title of Worthy Apprentice. From here, each individual trial will become steadily more difficult."

Sammra added, "As all can hear, there are animals in the forest. You must subdue them. Do not kill or wound the creatures you face. Your task is to capture, not harm. Any volunteers?"

One of the male sand apprentices stepped forward and went down the path. Bel couldn't remember his name.

Naga leaned over and admitted, "We only own mush dogs in the arctic north. I am not embarrassed to say my flesh shakes at this trial of might and magic."

Kerlith was standing behind them. He whined, "Oh Bel, I'm scared."

Naga glanced back at him. "Only a fool feels no fear. Master K'eyush has taught me to embrace my emotions, to channel them, to use their energy to drive myself forward."

Kerlith responded, his voice no longer toying but gloomy and melancholic, "I used to embrace fear, before, when I had a reason to live."

Bel turned to him, a quizzical twist to his face.

Kerlith responded to his unasked question, "Don't judge me, water flea."

"I don't judge. Kerlith, you have many reasons to live. You said you found a new master. I don't—"

"Oh, don't you dare try to feel sorry for me. Sure, I have a reason to live *now*. I'm talking about before, you dunce. I've been to a place you'll probably never go. I don't fear anything anymore. That's all I meant. Now turn around and quit looking at me like that."

Bel faced forward and Kerlith shuffled off to stand somewhere else in the crowd.

The Sanhardin apprentice stumbled back down the path, raw terror painted on his face. He fell to the ground and then was dragged back in by a large scaly paw. "Help! Help me!" he screamed.

Sammra ran down the path after him. Screams and the sounds of sand whooshing about could be heard coming from the forest as tree branches shook. A few moments later she stepped out, covered in blood, and nodded at Felix who then yelled for two trolls.

The trolls lumbered down the path and carried the wounded apprentice out toward the clinic.

The waiting apprentices glared at each other wide-eyed, murmuring.

Sammra wiped the red on her cheek, smearing it, and yelled, "Next!"

Most of the younger apprentices, including Naga and Bel, edged back towards the rear of the assembly.

One of the older Tundric apprentices stepped forward and walked down the path. Just as she disappeared into the forest, several reverberating caws echoed through the space.

Ayah smiled wide and Leonna giggled. The two slapped their elbows against their sides.

Bel strolled over to them and Naga followed. "You recognize those? Birds?"

Ayah said, "Certainly birds. I cannot understand their speech, though."

"Me neither," Leonna added.

Naga added, "I do not think Sammra will give an

avian a trial with birds."

The smile drained from Ayah's face. "You're probably right."

After some time, the forest grew quiet and Felix grew tired of waiting. He went down the path, then quickly came back shaking his head. "Barth, Branch, another one to collect."

The trolls carried out the Tundric apprentice.

Bel and Naga stood silently as one by one, the apprentices walked down the path and either ran back screaming, stumbled into the yard bloody or didn't return at all. No one had passed the trial yet. A glum, ill-humored and brooding mood fell on the crowd of apprentices while they stood in silence. Bel didn't feel like he had anything to say. What conversation could he hold with someone who was about to share his fate of being ripped apart by some unseen, terrible beast?

There were less than half the apprentices left and they were all congregated near the rear of the waiting area, leaving a wide empty space between them, the path to the trial and the two worthys, Sammra and Felix.

After dragging out another, a stonecutter, Felix said, "Next?"

Bel thought he saw Felix almost smile when he said it.

The prediction was coming true. There was one trial in which almost everyone was going to fail. Over half were gone already. Bel wondered if anyone would pass. He considered asking Shireen to not walk down the path at all, to quit, right here, right now. He walked over to her.

Lithia mumbled to Pren and Shireen as Bel arrived, "I guess I might as well go now. While I still have the will."

Lithia stepped to the edge of the path and raised her hand at Felix who nodded. Lithia raised her open palms about chest level, pointing her fingers up. The ground rumbled around her and small and medium sized stones and rocks emerged from the ground and rose, surrounding her, floating in the air. She nodded then stepped into the forest as a roar shook the trees.

Bel noted the foul twist on the others' faces. Towards the rear, Leonna was walking away, back towards the apprentice huts, her hands cupped over her ears.

Bel whispered to Shireen, "I'm going to check on Leonna. Would you like to come with me?"

Shireen stared into his eyes for a moment. "I trust you."

Bel didn't expect Shireen's response. No, not at all. With those three little words, Bel fell into warm water and the viscous liquid was gushing all over his insides. He smiled and left her, stepping into the camp.

Not finding Leonna, Bel went to her hut and knocked on the door. Hearing no response, he touched it, wanting to open the door but unsure if he should. He paused, considering going back to the trials when he saw something moving out of the corner of his eye. He snapped his head in that direction, between two of the huts, and realized Leonna had gone off to the forest again.

Bel scanned the courtyard, making sure no one was watching and called out the words of invisibility. He shook his head when he caught sight of his boots. His hands were visible too. Bel's body was completely invisible except for his extremities. He pressed his focus a little harder and his hands disappeared, but his feet were still there, on the ground, for all to see. He would need to ask his master about that when he returned to Sha'mont.

Bel jogged between the huts and towards the rear edge of the forest. Leonna was standing near the tree line, bent over. Bel ducked to the edge of the building and watched.

Leonna slowly stood. A small boy was in front of her. She handed him a bag and said, "Bel, there's no point hiding over there. We know it's you."

Bel was dumbfounded. *How?* He thought about trying to sneak away when she turned and started walking toward him. Bel lost his concentration and appeared.

"There he is!" the boy said, pointing.

Leonna grabbed Bel's hand. "Come here. I want you to meet someone."

She tugged him toward the boy then stopped in front of him. Bel tried to pull his hand away, but Leonna would not release it. "This is Jonah. He's my clan-brother."

"The missing Jonah?"

Jonah smiled, "The same. I didn't want to go to the Worthy Apprentice Trials. My clan-father forced me. I've been hiding in the forest, hiding from the trolls. Leonna's been sending me food."

"Hiding? So long?" Bel asked.

"The trolls are slow. My birds spy them out. I hide. It's not difficult."

"But why? You could have gone to Lasaat."

Leonna pursed her lips. "Jonah is Jeneth's son. He would have been severely punished. He's waiting for me. That's all. There's no big mystery here."

Bel tried to tug his hand away again, but Leonna gripped it harder. Bel cleared his throat and assured her, "I'll keep your secret. No one is probably passing today anyway."

"So is this the one?" Jonah asked, motioning at Bel.

Bel crinkled his eyebrows, puzzled.

Leonna said, "Yes, but he doesn't know it yet."

"The one what?" Bel asked.

Leonna tried to peck his cheek. Bel pulled his head away first.

She laughed.

Jonah shook his head, disgust on his face. "If you two are going to kiss I'm getting out of here." The boy turned and ran back into the forest with his sack of food.

Bel pried his hand out of Leonna's clutch. He turned and began walking away and back towards the camp, intent on returning to the safety of Shireen's side.

Leonna ran after him. "Oh, don't you dare get mad. I was only thanking you for keeping my secret."

Bel glanced back, giving her an annoyed expression.

She laughed again. "Did I make you angry?"

Bel stopped in the center of the courtyard and spun. "Angry? No. I probably should be, though. You're not getting it. You're beautiful, attractive. No one can deny that. I've already told you, I can't have you groping all over me and kissing me like that. Don't you see? If you want to be friends, that's fine, but…"

Leonna softened. "But… what?"

"Friends don't do that to each other." Bel walked away, leaving Leonna standing there alone in the center of the courtyard.

"Friends," she mumbled.

He had walked nearly halfway across the camp when

Leonna called out, "Bel, wait."

He stopped and turned as she ran up to him. Leonna said, "I need to apologize. You're right. Friends don't do that. I've... never had a friend before. I guess I don't understand how to be around you. I like your company. Can you forgive me?"

"Are you going to stop?"

"Yes, I promise. It will be insanely difficult because all I want to do is put my lips on you, but yes, I promise. I'll stop."

Bel nodded then began to step back towards the trials when Leonna grabbed his hand.

He looked at her, waiting, impatient.

Leonna opened her mouth but no sound came out. She closed her lips and shook her head then opened her mouth again and stared up into his eyes, a pained expression on her face.

"What? Something bothering you?" Bel probed. He wanted to get back to Shireen's side, he didn't want to risk her becoming jealous again, especially after she told him she trusted him.

"No, I-I-I wanted to tell you, to ask you something."

"Go ahead."

"We're friends. So I can ask you, I can ask you for help, if we're friends, right?" Her face was abruptly serious.

Bel said, "Yes, anything. What do you need? Is this about Jonah?"

"Jonah? No. I-I..." Leonna paused, considering the moonstone for a moment then blurted out, "Nothing. I only wanted to make sure if I needed a friend to help me that I could ask you. That's all."

"That's not true and you know it."

Leonna frowned.

Bel continued, "I've been watching you, Leonna, and with all these deaths, I know something's been bothering you. Onyx, Drake, Aquilo and Jinx, four deaths so far and some of them, maybe all of them, suspicious. You know more than you're letting on and, you know, I'm not saying you're involved in all that mess, but I can see it, you know, on your face." Bel paused, waiting for her to respond but she wouldn't meet his eyes. "If you want to talk, I'm here, that's all. I just wanted you to know that, you know, I'm not going to condemn you and I'm here if you need to tell someone what's bothering you."

Leonna looked up into his eyes, wiped a tear from her cheek then stepped past him and back towards the trials area. Bel followed her, walking into the space and stopping next to Shireen.

Lithia was standing there smiling, several deep scratches on one arm. "First to pass," she said to Bel as if she had just climbed the highest peak in all the lands.

He smiled back at her. "Excellent. Who's in there now?"

"Kerlith. He stole my strategy. I think he'll advance too."

Bel mumbled, "I'm going next. Need to get this over."

He stepped forward, walking across the empty space, all the way to the front and nodded to Felix.

Some time later, Kerlith ran out of the forest, his two hands raised high, hooting victoriously.

Sammra went into the forest to reset the trial then returned and nodded at Bel.

The forest apprentice stepped across the line and stopped as he bowed his head and held up his staff.

"Ohhhnn, ohhnnn, ohhhnn," Bel howled a deep, guttural tone. He ignored the mumblings from the apprentices behind him as he tried to communicate with the trees in the forest.

He continued to howl and moan, his eyes clenched tight, reaching out to speak with the trees, to communicate with their odd, foreign speech. Bel stepped forward, placing his hands on an oak and an elm, moaning deeply, giving them respect and honor for their age and all they had seen.

The trees swayed lightly, their branches making a swishing sound in the breeze as their trunks let out a soft rumble. They acquiesced.

Bel turned to Shireen and gave her a quick thumbs up, then walked into the forest, disappearing down the path.

A chirping sound, like crickets at night, but much louder and deeper, exited the forest. A peculiar sound. The grating noise penetrated Bel's mind in an almost painful way. He shook his head, then shook it again as if he could make the sound exit his head by shaking the noise out.

Bel recognized the sound from before. Several of the apprentices had faced the creature who made this noise, but none had returned except on a stretcher carried by two trolls. As they had waited, the others had submitted several ideas as to what kind of creature would make such a hideous sound: snakes, crickets, lizards and the like. But none of these seemed correct to Bel. *Snakes and lizards didn't make this kind of sound,* he thought. *And crickets? Why would they battle crickets?*

As Bel stepped closer, the sound became louder, invading his ears. He cupped his hands over his ear-holes but the volume of the chirping didn't decrease. Bel frowned; it didn't make sense. The sound was not audible, not coming in through his ears. The loud grating chirp, like two stones being struck together, over and over, right inside his skull, shook through his mind and his body. How could he stop the noise?

The closer he came to the source of the sound, the more his stomach twisted. The sound was making him nauseous. Bel spat a mouthful of saliva, but his cheeks instantly refilled. He spat again, stumbled a few steps forward then retched, clutching his gut.

The noise became as a dull axe grating across his bones, screeching as it scraped the sinewy flesh, dropping his muscle meat to the dirt. Bel stumbled. His legs buckled, out of kilter. He struggled to control them.

Bel glimpsed into the clearing just ahead, wanting to know what kind of creature could so invade his mind. He saw nothing but darkness. Bel coughed hard and spat again, the saliva pouring out of his mouth in thick strings. The sun was high in the sky, yet in the clearing a dark shadow covered the space, a darkness which light could not pierce.

Bel pushed mage-light into the end of his staff and pointed the tip at the dark patch, belching words in the forest-mage language of old. A ball of bluish mage-light bounded out of the end of his staff, sailing through the air and into the darkness.

A screech stabbed Bel's ears as the blue pushed back the night for a few moments before the light extinguished.

The forest apprentice's entire body tensed for what he had seen made no sense. A black, hairy face suspended about ten feet in the air, a face with no nose and a gaping hole for a mouth bordered by two small appendages that appeared to be tiny, black, hairy arms. And the eyes! Those terrible eyes! So many round black orbs stared back at Bel.

The screeching increased. Bel coughed and then promptly threw up.

He stared into the darkness as he wiped his mouth on his shirt sleeve. "The creature doesn't like light. Give it more mage-light." Bel considered Sammra's instruction not to capture, don't harm, don't kill. He hoped a bright flash of light wouldn't hurt.

Bel staggered to the center of the path, stopped and stared at the heart of darkness, gripping his magewood staff more for support than anything. The patch of night seemed to swell and sway.

He stretched forth his hand, pulling on the surrounding life-force, calling on the energy of life, coaxing it to enter him. Small ringlets of life-force streamed through the air and into Bel's body, filling him up with raw power. He squinted his eyes to slits as he focused on pulling in more life-force, trying to block the chittering and screeching. He tugged until his entire body began to glow. Bel did not cease until he was saturated and felt he could hold no more. The pain in Bel's flesh was excruciating, the pressure of the energy so intense, yet he bottled the life-force, holding it, containing the raw energy. His arms and hands were swollen. A small sharp pain stabbed his arm. A splash of red appeared on his arm. *An insect bite,* he thought initially, then he realized that a bug had not bitten him. A vein full of blood had ruptured. It was too much; holding onto this much energy was killing him. He focused the life-force into one, concentrated point. He sucked in a breath and held the air as he slapped his arms forward and ejected the energy in a pulsating wave of blinding light. The neon, electric blue blasted out of Bel's two arms, streaming across the space, illuminating the black, exposing the immense hairy, black creature: a tremendous arachnid.

Three loud screeching cries pelted Bel's mind as the creature leaped forward, stabbing at Bel with a sharp pointed appendage. He dodged the assault, barely, stumbling out of the way.

Now that the creature had been revealed, the giant spider didn't bother to further cloud Bel's mind with darkness.

Bel stumbled out of the way of one of the spider's attacks then leaped away from another. He staggered to the edge of the clearing, trying to push the fog out of his mind. He couldn't believe his eyes. He had expected a ferocious beast. A gorilla. A leopard. Maybe even a group of animals, a pack of wolves, a pride of lions, something dangerous and difficult to capture. *But this?* He had only heard rumor such a creature even existed. He might as well be fighting the dragon from Sha'mont or the roc from the magewood tree. *Impossible.* Not only was the creature lightning fast, the spider had eight deadly legs with razor sharp talons. If that weren't enough, the giant arachnid was using some form of mental attack.

All of that, and he wasn't supposed to hurt the thing, only capture the spider. If he could kill the arachnid, perhaps he would stand a chance, but how was he going to capture a creature three, no, four times his size, hell-bent on killing him?

Bel dove out of the way of a razor sharp talon strike and called to the trees as he blasted the spider in the face with a flare of mage-light, reeling the spider back. Chittering wafted across Bel's mind. He tried to ignore it, to focus his attention on the task at hand for that seemed to help him avoid the mind-numbing pain.

He flashed another ball of light at it. The creature retreated from the mage-light. Apparently it liked the dark and was unaccustomed to bright lights. Bel hoped shining the mage-light in the arachnid's eyes wasn't hurting it, still he was glad he had something he could use against the spider.

With the black hairy creature momentarily dazed, Bel took the opportunity to run beneath the spider, trying to reach the other side of the clearing. The beast slammed its abdomen down on the ground to squash Bel, barely missing him.

Bel dug his fingernails under the bark of the tree and moaned as the eight-legged creature spun to face him.

The spider hissed and advanced as Bel braced his body between the two swaying trees. The creature ran up then paused, reeling back on its rear legs when Bel stared up into its many eyes defiantly. The beast raised up a single arm high in the air, pointing the sharp talon as a scythe and swinging it down quick, directly at the center of Bel's chest. The apprentice didn't bother to dodge, thinking he could withstand the strike if he created a shield of energy around his body. He needed time to connect to the trees. *I can't keep running. I need the help of the trees.* He took the blow full on, the sharp tip of the spider's deadly claw smashing down on the energy shield and slightly piercing it, hitting his chest like a hammer striking a blacksmith's anvil. The razor edge of the spider's talon rebuffed on Bel's shield of life-force, however, the blunt force rippled through his body. Bel fell to the ground, realizing he had miscalculated the spider's strength.

The arachnid retreated back to the center of the clearing and examined the end of its striking arm. It was twisted, the sharp edge of the talon broken.

Bel rolled to his hands and knees and fingered his bleeding chest. The blade had penetrated his defense by the slightest amount, but the talon did not pierce his breastbone, only tore his clothing and skin.

"You did that to yourself!" Bel screamed. He hoped the worthys wouldn't hold him responsible for the creature injuring itself in attacking him.

The chirping rushed into Bel's mind. He couldn't understand the language, but one thing was clear, the spider was angry.

The creature rushed at him again, going airborne. Bel leaped back into the trees as the spider crashed down on the space he had so recently occupied. A death blow, had he not retreated.

He ran out from behind the trees as the spider leaped in. The creature sprayed a thick white stream of silky netting, entangling everything in the space, eliminating places Bel could retreat to.

Bel ran to the other side of the clearing and attempted to repel the web, sending a blast of energy at it.

The web swayed in the air, but held, being tied into branches, trees, and ground.

The spider cackled and sprayed webbing around the perimeter of the space, closing the area around Bel. Then the eight-legged creature stepped out of the trees and sprayed behind itself, sealing the escape route, the path back to the camp.

"Wait!" Bel screamed. "That's the path. You can't block that." Apparently the creature didn't know the rules of engagement. No, the spider was making up its own rules and they involved trapping Bel so he could kill him and drain his blood.

Bel called to the trees again, longer, harder, recognizing their help was his only chance of survival now. The spider advanced, stepping slowly out from the trees, the chittering, chattering, chirping noise surrounding Bel. He tried to block the attack invading his mind, if that were possible. *Focus. Focus. Focus. Focus on the trees. Communicate.*

A branch swung down, brushing the spider's abdomen, pushing it to the side. The creature spun and stabbed at the air.

A group of vines flung out. The creature ducked and dodged all but one that quickly wrapped around a leg.

The spider extended the tied leg and stabbed at Bel with a long thrust, then another, then another. They barely missed the apprentice for he could not push any farther away from the creature. He was already pressed into the web and sticking to the coated strands.

Bel pushed a flare of light at the spider as another vine tied a leg.

The two vines pulled the spider to the center of the space. It struggled violently as vines extended and captured two more of its limbs.

Bel pulled away from the webbing and ripped the gooey substance off his clothing.

"I think you're contained," Bel said to the spider then strolled on a long arc, not allowing himself to tread within the spiders strike zone. He reached the exit path, withdrew his dagger and began cutting away at the web blocking the path.

Bel heard another pattern of chirping and screeching. He had no idea what type of communication the spider was sending him, but he answered anyway, "Well, you wouldn't be tied up for so long had you not put this web here."

The apprentice cut the final strand and folded the webbing back. Taking one step past, another wave of chittering struck his mind, this one fierce and vigorous, pummeling Bel to the ground. He clasped his hands to his ears as the screeching pain rumbled through his body. He dropped into a fetal position and trembled. The excruciating torment cut at his mind as if nails were being driven into every nerve ending in his body, a simultaneously pulsing, hammering agony, a magnitude of torture far in excess of anything Bel had ever experienced before.

"Stop," Bel whimpered as his body convulsed.

He would much rather have had the spider's sharp talon plunged deep in his heart or had a limb or a foot ripped off than this. The pain was searing, flesh-rending and intense. He clenched his eyes down tight as his body convulsed again. He felt himself spinning. He became afraid for he was losing control.

Moaning, he tried to speak, but the words wouldn't come. Salty blood flooded his mouth. Bel struggled to right himself, to roll from his side to his knees. He vomited a foul black mixture. A wonderful sensation of release poured over him as he poured the hot liquid from his gut. His back arched involuntarily. Muscle spasms racked his body. Bel tried to stand but instead fell again, moving only inches down the path.

He felt a mere boy. Not a man. No, he was nothing

of a man.

The stinging desolation piled on, layer after terrible layer. One unbearable wave receded and another took its place, shoving him deeper into the hole of futility. He held his breath, waiting for the onslaught to cease so he could grab at the air. Bel gasped to breathe, hopelessly. He was beginning to lose control of his lungs.

Blackness surrounded him. At first, Bel thought the dark was another of the spider's mind tricks, but he soon realized he was losing consciousness. He couldn't breathe. The intensity of the pain was causing him to suffocate.

Bel let go, forcing his body to not clench, to not tense, to relax as the torment ripped through him. Tears streamed from his eyes. His body began to stutter then involuntarily breathe. Pain. It was all he could think about. Stopping the agony was all he wanted to do. Nothing else mattered.

He rolled to his knees, bent on killing the spider. A creature such as this, capable of inflicting such terror, should not be allowed to live.

Bel stumbled to his feet and dragged himself to the beast, his dagger in his hand.

The eyes of the spider met his and it hissed as if to challenge Bel. He stopped and dropped his dagger to the ground. Suddenly Bel understood. The spider would rather die than be captured. Honor. Dignity. The creature wanted him to slay it.

Bel sheathed his dagger and the spider stabbed Bel's mind again with a ferocious intensity.

The apprentice ran back, stumbling and tripping, exiting along the path and dropping to his knees in the courtyard. The spider's attack slowed, then ceased. Bel, gasping for air, smiled up at Felix.

Bel stood, swaying and unsteady. "I caught it," he said then promptly retched.

One of the trolls grabbed Bel's shoulder, bracing him, then tugged him toward the clinic. Bel shook his head and pointed at the benches. The troll aided him in walking to Naga's bench, but more and more as Bel stepped away from the path, strength came back into his limbs.

After he sat, the troll placed a salve on Bel's chest wound. Bel leaned over and grabbed Naga's hand, telling him to be careful. Naga rose and went into the wood to start his trial.

After the troll finished bandaging Bel, the apprentice went to where Ayah, Shireen, Lithia, and Pren were standing. Of them, only Lithia had gone in and a look of inevitable dread clouded the others' eyes.

"All I can say is don't venture too far from the path. You need the escape route to stay clear," Bel said.

The others nodded at him without responding.

As they waited for Naga to return, a roar, too close, startled everyone. Felix and Sammra stood in shock as a winged lion dropped from the sky, landing in the center of the courtyard.

Felix yelled, "Sammra, did you forget to secure it?"

Sammra shook her head. "No, I locked them all up, all of them. I have no idea how it got out."

Naga ran down the path and into the space then continued toward the huts, screaming the entire way, "Run! Run!"

A huge wolf leaped down the path after him and into the clearing, growling loudly.

Felix pointed, "Sammra you handle the wolf. I'll catch the winged lion."

The wolf chased and nipped at apprentices as they ran to their huts.

Bel grabbed Shireen's arm and screamed, "Run!" and pushed her toward the huts behind him. He spun to face the snarling fangs of the great wolf.

Chapter Twenty
Moonstone

Felix roared, his mind reaching, connecting with his cats, calling them to attack. The cougars ran into the space, pausing in front of the winged lion and growling, attempting to push the immense cat back. The bobcat jogged up to Felix followed closely by two ocelots. The ocelots alternately shook their heads, then one of them collapsed near Felix and shuttered his eyes. Nocturnal, he had shouted them awake and they were clearly going to be little help at this time of day.

Sammra surrounded the wolf with a curved barrier of sand, trying to rope the beast in. The wolf leaped over her shield, charging towards the center of the camp, growling the entire way at fleeing apprentices.

Felix yelled, "We're losing control! You need to capture that wolf before someone gets hurt!"

Pointing her hand forward, Sammra ran after the creature, a dust bowl swirling around her. Bel followed her.

Felix had his cats surround the winged lion. *A griffon, mostly cat,* he thought. *Maybe.* Perhaps he could speak to the magical creature. Felix reached out with his spirit, slowly, nudging in, probing, trying to connect without forcing. The griffon turned its head toward him and flared its nostrils as a spike of white hot pain drove deep into Felix's mind. He dropped to his knees, losing control of his animals. His flesh, suddenly, was not his own, disjointed, disconnected, as if his body no longer worked as it should. Felix fell to the ground. His eyes closed, immobile, he tried to focus on the simplest of things, breathing. Expand chest muscles; draw in air. Contract. Exhale. He forced air into his lungs as he clawed at consciousness, trying to prevent himself from blacking out for he feared if he did, he might stop breathing, his body might forget to make his heart beat, he might die. Gradually, the shockwave of pain receded, panting, shuddering, he reached down with trembling fingers and touched his breech-cloth. It was wet, as he suspected.

He teetered up to his feet. The griffon was in the air, diving down, making swooping attacks on apprentices who were futilely fighting back using repulsion, sand, rocks, or balls of ice. Mostly they were running, screaming, and hiding.

Felix called to his cats who had scattered when he had lost the mental connection. They were lounging, mindless of everything around them; they were being cats. One was pawing at a piece of tattered clothing, a bloody scrap of cloth torn from an apprentice's body by sharp griffon claws. Another was reclining on its side, eyes closed. The others were waiting stealthily, tucked just inside of the tree line, ready to pounce. Felix didn't want to think about what would happen in an apprentice wandered in front of one of them. Shaking his head hard, Felix called to the cats, gathering them to his side.

The wolf sniffed and snorted, ferreting out another apprentice hiding behind a barrel. *Where was Sammra?*

Felix thought.

Felix and his cats jogged to the center of the camp. Bel pelted balls of energy at the wolf. The wolf leaped to escape, jumped past a barrel and dug its teeth into an ankle and pulled an apprentice out from her hiding spot.

"Shireen," Felix said as he ran toward her, his cats leaping into action.

Bel pelted the wolf's face with energy ball after energy ball and finally the wolf released Shireen and ran to find easier prey.

Barch, Branch, Budzig and several of the other trolls lumbered into the space.

Felix pointed. "Budzig, take the other trolls and corner that wolf. We need to get these animals back into their cages."

The trolls stomped off.

An ear-piercing scream roiled through the space. Felix ran to it. Bel and Shireen joined him, but Shireen was favoring her left side.

"How's your leg?" Felix asked Shireen.

"Tender. I can almost run. I'll live." It was bleeding.

The three turned past a collection of huts. Two giant spiders faced them, as tall as the small trees, and a sand apprentice laid on the floor, skewered by the spider's talon, her brown muslin and burlap robes quickly soaking with blood.

"Sammra?" Felix questioned.

"Pren?" Shireen said at the same time.

Felix grunted and sent his cats forward, then turned his head to Shireen and shook it when he recognized the girl. The dead apprentice was neither Sammra nor Pren, but Isha. She had failed a trial two days ago. The trolls had collected her but not yet escorted Isha out under

Felix's order. He hadn't wanted a potential murderer to escape by intentionally failing the trials. *Everyone was a suspect,* Felix had thought. Even a tiny, weak sand apprentice. She shouldn't have been here and now she was dead.

"How did the spiders get out?" Felix said.

One cougar, baring its claws and fangs, leaped at the greenish spider to the left. The spider swung a leg at the airborne cat, smashing the cougar into the forest.

Shireen stepped forward, aiming her hands at the spider to the right and attempting to send a repulsion attack.

The bluish spider stepped back slightly as the blast of energy struck home, but with eight legs to dig into the ground, there was no way repulsion magic was going to push the arachnid off balance.

The bobcat and two ocelots ran to a spider leg and tried to bite, their teeth making bone on bone scratching sounds against the spider's exoskeleton.

"Thulo," Shireen said, leave, retreat, pointing her wand at the advancing spider. The spell did nothing to retard its advance on her position. She spoke the words again, her arm wavering, ordering the beast to leave, pushing the mental suggestion into its mind.

Felix was familiar with what Shireen was attempting, a spell that worked well on humans who didn't shield their minds. He wasn't surprised when the spider continued to step towards her for an animal's mind was nothing like a human's.

A flash of light came from behind Shireen, smashing the blue spider in the face. The spider screeched in pain.

"Light," Bel said. "The spiders like the dark. I don't think it hurts them, but they don't like bright light. Felix, we're still not allowed to hurt them?"

"Absolutely not. Do you realize how hard it is to capture these things? We can't destroy them."

Bel said, "Shireen, I'll hold them off. You communicate with the trees. Get them to help us. Send out their vines and branches."

Felix nodded as he moved closer to Bel.

The forest apprentice sent bolts of light at each of the two spiders, pummeling them backward. Each time one was hit, it released a high pitched screech. Felix felt the wail stabbing in the center of his mind.

The green spider spun, attempting to flee, so Felix sent his cats to the rear to slow its escape.

A chirping, chattering, chittering echoed through Felix's head; a reverberating pain racked Felix's mind, collapsing him to the ground.

Bel continued to pelt the spiders with light, then he slowed, his arms wavering. "Keep them out of your mind!" Bel was clearly having a difficult time for he was shaking and twitching in rhythm with the spider's chittering.

Felix grasped his head and stood. He tried to steel his mind, forming a barrier around it, pushing out the sharp, clear needles of life-force stabbing in every direction. He pushed out his energy, enveloping his head in life-force, muffling the painful chirping sound.

Bel loosely tugged at Felix's arm and said something, but Felix couldn't hear the words. He was surrounded by complete silence. Bel staggered then crumbled to the ground, holding his head. He curled into a fetal position.

For a moment, Felix considered letting Bel die. He was fairly certain Bel had something to do with Aquilo's murder and yet here he was contemplating protecting him. It would be so easy to step aside and let the spider take Bel, run him through as the creature had done to Isha.

It would be easy. True. But that wasn't Felix. He couldn't do that. Guilty or no, he would protect Bel until they could prove his involvement. If Bel was involved, then he would answer to his cats' teeth. But Felix was no murderer. He stepped forward, placing his body between the forest apprentice and the spider.

A vine streamed out of the forest and wrapped itself around one of the blue spider's legs.

Shireen's eyes were closed, lost in concentration, her two hands rested on two trees, her fingernails dug into the bark. The branches were swooping and swaying. Vines extending like long, curled octopus arms.

The green spider, realizing who was controlling the trees, darted towards her.

Felix leaped in front of Shireen as his two cougars dove into the spider, smashing into the side of its thorax, knocking the arachnid on its back. The spider stabbed and flung its many appendages at the cats who quickly scrambled out of the way.

Another vine streamed into the space, tying up one of the legs of the blue spider.

Felix pushed his mental barrier around Bel then kicked him softly in the ribs. Bel slowly stood and tried to speak. He stopped, a puzzled expression on his face.

Felix smiled. Bel clearly didn't understand why he couldn't hear anything so Felix pointed at his chest and mouthed, "Me," then pointed at the spider.

Bel nodded, then commenced flinging light at the green spider while Felix positioned his cats around it, boxing the creature in.

Shireen sent out another vine at the arachnid, but it leaped, avoiding being caught. The green spider scrambled forward, leaping high in the air. Felix realized the razor sharp talon was headed directly for Shireen. Her eyes closed; she would be killed instantly. He ran, pushing Shireen to the ground as the spider's strike stabbed into his back, gashing flesh and bone. He fell.

A blinding flash forced Felix to squint as a ball of light pummeled the spider.

Felix laid there, on his stomach, dumbfounded, unable to determine what had happened. Liquid dripped down his back. The wet sensation reminded him of how he had urinated himself earlier. He wondered if Shireen noticed the yellow stain on his breech-cloth. What would she think of him if she realized he had lost control like that? Would she think he pissed himself because he was afraid?

Felix tried to turn his head, but instead, the entire world spun. He didn't understand what was happening. He didn't understand how his urine spread all the way to his back.

Dizzy, Felix tried to edge his body up to his elbows and knees, to continue to fight, but his body didn't work anymore. Felix tried to push himself up, but a pressure squeezed down on his shoulder. Something was pushing him down. *Who would do such a thing?* He needed to stop the spiders.

Blackness slowly seeped into his vision which he completely did not understand. He understood the spiders could hide in darkness, but could they darken the entire world?

Then Felix passed out.

=———=

Everything was blurry and out of focus as Felix opened his eyes.

"I think he's coming to."

Someone shook his shoulders and slapped his face.

"Bel, don't hit him."

Felix recognized the voice. *Shireen.*

"There's no time," Bel said. "We need his help."

Felix reached his hand up towards his cheek that had just been slapped. He tried to speak, "What?" He pushed himself up to a seated position. As his eyes cleared, he saw Barth, Shireen, Bel, and Pren.

"Barth put troll-salve on your wound. Pren pulled out the poison," Shireen explained as she smiled and raised her eyebrows.

Pren said, "Got to practice some healing magic on you. My first time."

Felix shook his head, trying to clear it faster. "Glad I could be of service. The spiders?"

Shireen pointed. They were both entangled in vines.

"The griffon? The wolf?"

"Still loose as far as we know," Bel answered. "Tell us what to do. We'll help you."

"Where's Sammra?"

The three held blank expressions. Finally, Shireen answered, "We haven't seen her."

"And the others?"

Pren said, "Most of them are hiding in the meeting hall. Some are hiding in other places. Their rooms or in the forest, I suppose."

Felix pushed up to his feet and wobbled momentarily. "We need to get these spiders to their cages. We also need to capture the lion and the wolf." He smiled. "We need volunteers."

Bel said, "I'll grab Naga and whoever else will join me and we'll try to track down the other two animals."

"Fine. Barch and I will retrieve the cages."

Shireen said, "Felix, if you don't mind, I would like to go with you." Her eyes snapped to Bel. "To see. I would like to see the animals, if it's okay."

Felix said, "Normally I would say no since it might give you an advantage in the trials, but at this point I think the Worthy Apprentice Trials are over, anyway. Let's go."

Holding her hand up timidly, Pren said, "Me too?"

Felix nodded and the three apprentices and Barch ran towards the far end of the camp while Bel jogged to the main meeting hall.

Felix led the way down a long winding path into the forest. As they drew closer, a cacophony of wild and bizarre sounds emanated from just ahead. The path looped around and opened into a large clearing containing many cages. Felix came to a screeching halt, holding out his arms for the others to stay behind him. Something was wrong.

He expected to find four empty cages, one for each of the animals who had escaped. But what he saw was at least ten cage doors ajar. And of the other cages that still contained animals, several were already unlocked, only the creature had yet to notice and push the cage door open and escape.

Felix bolted forward. "We need to latch those cages before the animals get out!"

He slapped the hasp on one, a wolf cage, then turned, barreling down the aisle to the next. As he reached the end of a row someone flashed by, dark skin covered in tawny fabric, leaping behind the far cage.

No. It can't be. Felix paused, then bolted the cage and ran to the end of the aisle where he had last seen the woman's leg dodging behind the cage. Felix hoped against hope his eyes had been playing tricks on him. *No, not her.*

He stopped at the last cage. She was gone. He turned into the next aisle. Those cages were open too. He ran down the path, latching each of them as he went by. When Felix reached the cage of a tremendous serpent, he slammed into the door, smashing the snake back as it tried to escape, and threw the bolt in the latch. He turned and saw the figure of a young feline woman, brown spotted skin wrapped in a tawny cloak of fabric. She studied him then unlatched a cage.

Felix screamed at her in disbelief, "Felicia, what are you doing?"

She grinned. "What you should be doing, Dear Brother." She yanked open the serpent cage door and ran as the two headed snake, the size of two men, slithered out on the ground and hissed at Felix.

"Felicia, no! People will die!"

She snarled back as she ran, "Landers will die. Not us. Stay with them if you want. If you love the landers so much, Felix, you can die with them."

Felix, Shireen, and Pren latched as many cages as they could but several more creatures had escaped. Felix hadn't counted, but he figured twelve to fifteen animals were now loose in the camp and Felicia was at fault. His little sister. There was going to be hell to pay for this one, especially considering one apprentice had already died. Felix's head hurt thinking about what he was going to have to do to protect Felicia. There was no way he was going to get out of this one. They would probably need to flee back to their clan and hold up there. Six years of his life destroyed by his stupid little sister's prank.

Another high pitched wail sailed through the space. The scream came from the middle of the camp. Felix wanted to ignore the sound and finish rounding up the few creatures who were still near the cages, but the way Shireen cast her eyes at him as if she was needy, forced him to turn to the noise and run back down the path towards the huts.

When the three reached the center of the space, Lithia and a few other stonecutters were pointing at the moonstone, arms outstretched, faces racked with concentration.

Felix snapped his head up, looking where their arms were pointed. Jonah was standing on the roof of the building, tugging at the stone, trying to gain control of the crystal.

"Jonah? No!" Felix screamed.

A large object flew into the yard. Felix didn't initially recognize what it was until the hurling mass solidified into a block and hammered into Lithia and a few of the other stonecutters, knocking three of them to the ground.

Sand.

Jonah grabbed the moonstone and stuffed the rock into his sack, slung the bag on his back, ran down the roof and leaped off. Several birds flew down and caught him, wrapping their talons around his arms and floating him to the ground. The entire sky dimmed as the light of the moonstone extinguished.

Dazed, confused, Felix didn't understand what was

happening.

Sammra grabbed Jonah's hand. Her eyes met Felix's, the expression on her face a mixture of regret and longing. Jonah and Sammra were joined by Leonna, Felicia, and Ayah. The group of five turned and ran into the forest with their birds and cats.

Chapter Twenty-One
The Band

Shireen chased after Lithia, intent on stopping her. *No, Lithia! You can't go out there alone!*

Lithia screamed, "Thieves! Thieves, bring back the stone!"

The forest apprentice barely caught her friend, snatching her by the arm, before she barreled into the wood. Shireen squeezed and pulled Lithia's arm. "They can't escape," She said, her voice pleading. "The forest is under troll-spell. We'll catch them, Lithia. We'll get the moonstone back."

Felix yelled, "Budzig, no one leaves! Do not drop the troll-spell for anyone! Especially Sammra. Do you understand me? The spell drops by my word only."

Budzig nodded and mumbled in an odd pattern of clicks and grunts.

Felix said, "What do you mean Jergamemnon and Jeneth?"

Budzig stared back with a blank expression.

"They're still in the forest? All right fine," Felix said, "Them too. You drop the troll-spell for no one. Not even Jeneth. Not even Jergamemnon. I'll answer to the archmages from Lasaat once this is all sorted out."

Budzig lumbered off.

Felix addressed the group of apprentices standing in the courtyard. Shock was painted on their faces. "Shireen, I'm glad you stopped Lithia. Lithia, you can't go after them alone. You don't know what they can do."

"They've stolen the moonstone. It's the most precious thing my people have," Lithia said. The brute of a woman was nearly in tears.

Felix's voice trembled. "Lithia, we'll catch them. Shireen is right. The forest is under troll-spell. We need to be organized about this. One apprentice died today. We don't need more running into the forest and getting themselves killed. We need to take care of this calmly, methodically and get to the bottom of what exactly is happening here."

Bel added, "And someone has to round up all these animals."

Felix called the other trolls, Barch, Branch, and Burn, telling them to gather everyone into the round hall, everyone except the severely injured at the clinic.

After some time, the apprentices arrived and Felix addressed the group of one-hundred odd apprentices, most who were nursing wounds, scratches, bites and scrapes. "We have a serious problem and I need everyone to help. And no, this is not another trial. As you can see by how dark it suddenly has become, a group of apprentices have taken the moonstone and ran into the forest. Also, there are a number of animals running loose in the camp. I need help capturing the animals, without hurting them, and another set of apprentices to accompany me into the forest to track down the thieves, ahh, the apprentices who, ahh, took the moonstone."

"How many animals are out there?" one apprentice called out.

"And how are we supposed to capture them? I failed the trial," asked another.

"Less than fifteen: giant wolves, three or four, I think; winged lion, a griffon, only one; two-headed snakes, probably about three; giant spiders, not sure, maybe four. There may be others. Just don't hurt them. I understand many of you didn't pass the trials, but working together, three or four cornering a single creature, I think you should be able to manage. The trolls will help too." Felix nodded at two of the trolls. "Bring the empty cages to the center of the courtyard."

Another apprentice asked, "I don't understand. What's going on here? Is this some kind of a prank?"

Bel interrupted, "Can I? I think I have most of this figured out."

Felix nodded.

Bel stood. "When we first arrived, Pren gave an envelope to Aquilo sent from Master Jergamemnon. The envelope contained evidence of a plot, probably involving avians, but the information was sketchy as to exactly what that conspiracy was. We know now the plot was to steal the moonstone. Aquilo was supposed to investigate apparently. Aquilo asked Leonna to his room to speak to her privately since she was an avian and he felt he could persuade her to reveal what she knew, if anything. I followed her, you know, because I was suspicious too." Bel looked at Shireen. "That's the only reason, you know, I was staying so close to Leonna."

Shireen snapped, "Okay, we get it. You were pretending to be with Leonna to spy on her. Move along." *Doesn't he realize I trust him already?*

Bel looked back at the crowd. "Aquilo thought, perhaps, she might be a weak link and he could persuade her to not go through with the secret plan. And not only that, but she might tell him everything. He was right in that. She was about to do exactly that, I think, to reveal some piece of information, when a knock came at the door and Aquilo was killed as soon as he opened the door. Two people had followed Leonna there and were laying in wait, Sammra and Jinx. When the pair saw Leonna was going to reveal their secret, they decided to act. They, or at least one of them anyway, killed Aquilo."

"How do you know all this? How could you get so close to hear without them noticing you?" Naga asked.

"Invisibility," Bel said then quickly disappeared for some moments, then reappeared.

A few of the apprentices gasped.

One from the back added, "I've only heard of a few being able to master invisibility and they were archmages."

Bel blushed, shrugging his shoulders. "Anyway, I followed Leonna. I saw mostly everything. Everything except who the killers were. The wizards of Lasaat, Jergamemnon and Jeneth, told me to not tell anyone."

Felix barked, "And you left out the fact that she said she was going to reveal what she knew? That there actually was a plot?"

Bel rubbed his hands together anxiously. "I said I think she was going to reveal something. She seemed like she was going to say something, yes. I am speculating a little here, but in any case, if I am being honest, I guess I should say... I-I didn't trust Jeneth. Or you, Felix. I didn't want you two to realize I knew what I knew. I thought it was a creature-kind plot and with Jeneth and you standing right there—"

Felix threw his hands up. "That information could

have changed everything! We could have stopped this before it started!"

Bel pressed his lips together in a slight grimace. "I'm sorry."

Shireen added, "There's something else you should know too. Onyx overheard Felicia and Leonna talking about something privately. They were upset when they found her spying on them. I'm not sure if they had anything to do with her death, but I think it possible."

"And Drake?" Naga asked.

Bel said, "He was pretty close with Aquilo. All I can guess is Aquilo told him something? Or the others thought he did? He was a loose end. Of course, he may have just fallen from the tree, although I find that hard to swallow."

Felix addressed the crowd. "So let me get this straight. Either Jinx or Sammra killed Aquilo. Not for jealousy over Leonna as Jergamemnon said, but to steal the evidence and cover up the plot to steal the moonstone. If that is true then I think Jinx was killed because he was being too reckless and sloppy. Sammra found the body so she either knows who killed Jinx or she did it herself. Perhaps Sammra and Jinx got in an argument over how everything was happening. That part I'm less certain about. Although, as most of you have figured out, it was an avian dagger buried in Jinx's chest. What I am certain of is that Sammra was in on the plot. As were all the avians: Leonna, Ayah, and the missing boy, Jonah. They all ran into the wood together." Moisture pooled in his eyes. "And, one other, Felicia. My little sister. I don't want her hurt."

"And we're to believe you're not one of them?" Lithia snapped. "You're creature-kind. It seems quite clear to me what's happening here."

"What do you think is happening here?" Felix barked.

"You stay back to slow us down. Obviously. We should be out there already. My people's moonstone has been stolen and here we sit discussing the plot. We already know what happened: you creature-kind stole the moonstone."

A few of the other stonecutters agreed, "Yeah." "That's right."

"No, it's not like that. I had no knowledge—"

Lithia snapped, "Felix, it's too late for words. We're wasting time. I'm going after them. Now who's with me?"

Bel raised his hand. "I'll go."

Shireen and Pren stood up and moved next to Lithia.

"We're with you, Lithia," Shireen said.

"Yes, me too," Pren added.

Naga stood. "My flesh will fight at your side, Lithia."

Felix said, "Who else will join us?"

Lithia said, "You're going too?"

"My little sister's out there."

The room grew silent.

Felix paced, rubbing his hands through his hair. "So I need a few more volunteers to go into the forest. I think that's the most dangerous task. The apprentices who took the moonstone are not going to want to be caught. They're probably going to fight back. And there's the forest to worry about."

"The forest?" Shireen repeated.

"Yes, the entrance trial is still there, the false images each of you experienced when you came in, the three trials you had to outsmart. That magic is still there. I don't know what you'll come against. It's going to be difficult to determine what's real out there."

Several of the apprentices eyed Felix, but most looked down at their feet.

"Let's go," Lithia said as she headed for the door.

Felix said to the crowd as he was leaving, "The rest of you, team up, capture those animals."

Shireen, Lithia, Bel Naga and Pren along with Felix ran to their rooms to gather their staffs, stones and the like, preparing themselves for a fight. Bel and Shireen made their way back to the center of the courtyard and waited for the others.

Bel said to Shireen, "I'm not so comfortable with you going out there."

She stared back at him, her eyes defiant. "Lithia's my friend."

"I'm not questioning your friendship."

"What are you questioning?"

"I was… Nothing. I'm questioning nothing. You're capable. I trust you." Bel mumbled as the others approached, "I just don't want you to hurt. You know that."

Shireen smiled.

The group jogged towards the far end of the forest, in the direction the thieves ran with the moonstone.

Just as they were about to enter the forest, Jergamemnon stumbled out, the left side of his face sliced and dripping blood.

Felix leaped to catch him before he fell. Bel went to his other side and propped him up by his armpits.

Jergamemnon gasped then tried to speak, his voice barely a hiss. "We never left… when we said we did. We hid, Jeneth and I. What we said wasn't true. We were waiting to catch… the real culprits. Hiding. In the forest. Watching. Waiting. I saw Sammra and Felicia. Speaking. I was invisible. They were up to something."

Felix said, "They stole the moonstone. Don't push yourself too hard. You're injured."

Jergamemnon nodded. "I sent… the package. I knew… something." He paused for some moments. "Sammra. Lying. But why? Was she investigating for herself? Or aiding them? Unsure."

Lithia paced, eager to run after the thieves.

Shireen watched the man bleed. "Master Jergamemnon, we need to go. To catch them."

Jergamemnon slowly raised his hand. "Wait. You don't understand what you are up against. Jeneth attacked me. I trusted him. He's out there. Aiding them. You can't go."

Shireen trembled. *Jeneth!*

Lithia growled, "I want that stone back."

Jergamemnon tried to turn to Lithia but gave up as it required more strength than he had. "He's an archmage. He'll kill you. He'll kill all of you."

Shireen wanted to say something but her words choked in her throat.

Felix said, "I have to go. My sister's out there."

Jergamemnon shook his head again. "No, it's too dangerous. Even all of you together. To fight Jeneth? I don't think you would win. But him with all the others? I would be sending you… to your deaths. I can't—"

Felix shook, then seemed to slowly relax. He looked up from the floor, staring at Jergamemnon directly, intently, "Thank you, Master Archmage, for your concern, but this is something I must do. I can't sit idly by while my sister ruins six years of my life's work. I need to stop her. I need to protect her from herself."

Lithia snorted, "I'm going. I'm retrieving that stone or I'll die trying. I owe it to my people."

Jergamemnon spoke, wheezing, "The moonstone is valuable, but not more valuable than life, Lithia. Always remember that. Life is the most precious thing of all." He gasped a few more times. "I shall go with you." Jergamemnon tried to stand then nearly collapsed.

"No," Felix said. "You need to rest, to heal." He motioned for a troll to attend to Jergamemnon.

The six turned from the archmage and stepped into the forest, creeping in. Their eyes scanned left and right, up and down, for signs of the thieves' direction, footprints and the like.

Felix sent his cats ahead, fanning them out, to sniff out their trail.

Bel touched a tree, asking the oak for help.

After a time, Felix's cats caught a scent, the thieves' trail veered ahead and to the left.

As Shireen and the others walked, their eyes darted here and there.

Bel said, "And Kerlith? I didn't see him at the gathering. He's a stonecutter. I thought he would want to be in on this, gain him the recognition he wanted to find a new master."

Shireen mumbled, "He might be hiding or dead. He may be lying somewhere injured by the animals. He might be ahead of us, singlehandedly trying to stop them from stealing the stone."

As the words were exiting her mouth, a whooshing sound ran through the forest and a line of sand ripped across them, surrounding them in a swirling cloud.

Shireen was instantly blinded. She couldn't catch

sight of any of the others. The tiny particles tore across her skin, face and arms, invading her nostrils, ears, and squinted eyes. Like a million nails falling from the sky, no matter which way she turned the grains smashed into her.

Shireen fell to the ground, covering her face with her hands. The sand was pelting her forcefully, powerfully, as though she was being blasted by a high-pressure stream and her skin was being ripped off bit by bit. She curled up into a fetal position.

She tried to call out to Bel, but the sand quickly flooded her mouth so she clapped it shut and tried to spit out the dry dust.

She needed a plan of action, and quickly. Could she run out of the cloud? Maybe a tree branch could lift her up? Cover her body in a vine shelter? She was unsure how much longer she could hang on. She could barely breathe.

She covered her mouth with her hands and screamed in her spirit as loud as she could —*Bel! Bel! Bel! Help me!* —

Chapter Twenty-Two
Sammra

Felix tried to calm his cats as they ran about, snapping at the sand. He willed them to rest, to relax, to keep their mouths shut, to close their eyes, to stop leaping, running and nipping at the dust in the air, but they weren't listening. The sand was too much for them. They wouldn't listen; they were going wild. Felix tried to press forward, his face tucked into the crook of his elbow, hoping he was moving in a straight line and out of the onslaught of the pelting and blinding grit. He groped with one outstretched arm to feel his way, trying his best to shelter his face with the other.

Finally, the sand thinned, then stopped.

Felix rubbed the crusts of sand from his eyes and tried to dust himself off. Pren was standing not far away, her arms held high, struggling.

The sand swirled around them, a tornado. They were in the eye of the storm, standing in a cylinder of calm. Pren was pushing the sand away. "I can't hold it much longer," Pren said, barely able to get the words out.

Lithia ran up and placed her hand on Pren's back. "Take some of my life-force. Let it strengthen you."

Naga and Bel joined Lithia in pressing their hands into Pren's back, giving her their energy.

The sand apprentice straightened, extending her arms higher. She screamed and flung out her fingers. The torus of swirling sand surrounding them dispersed, revealing Sammra standing some distance away, leering. She snorted then ran deeper into the forest.

"After her," Lithia yelled, falling into a run.

Felix's cats sprinted ahead, following Sammra. Felix, Bel, Lithia, and Naga were next. The men ran faster than all the women except Lithia, who charged as one possessed.

Looking through his cats' eyes, Felix halted and barked, "They split up. Up ahead, they've divided into two groups."

Lithia asked, "Which one has the moonstone?"

"I'm not sure."

"It was in Jonah's sack," Shireen said.

"Which way did Jonah go?" Lithia barked at Felix.

"He went that way." Felix pointed.

Before Felix could finish his sentence, Lithia sprinted off in the direction Felix had pointed.

Pren tried to follow Lithia, but Felix grabbed her shoulder, jerking her to a stop. "Wait a moment," he said. "I need your help. I want to go after Felicia and Sammra. You're the only one who can defend against her sand."

Shireen said, "Lithia's out there alone. I'm going." She ran off in the direction Lithia had run.

"Shireen, wait!" Bel went after her.

Naga came to a stop and said, "My flesh will fight by your side, Pren."

Pren nodded to Felix. "Let's catch her."

Felix sent his cats running after Sammra as he sprinted alongside Naga and Pren. The cats quickly disappeared ahead. Felix pointed to the left then to the right, altering their course as he scanned the forest, viewing both what his cats were seeing and his own surroundings at the same time. "There!" Felix said, pointing.

Sammra and Felicia had slowed to fight off Felix's cats who had surrounded them and were biting, diving, and nipping at the two. Felix accelerated. "Felicia, Sammra, give up this madness!"

Felicia yelled at Sammra, "Why are we stopping? We need to run."

Felix slowed then stopped behind his cougars.

Pren and Naga arrived, a few steps behind. Pren clutched her purse of sand and Naga bent down to the ground, pulling moisture up and into the air in front of him, floating a slug of water into rotating balls of ice and snow.

Sammra stepped to the side and away from Felicia. "Felix, you don't understand. I'm on your side." She glanced at Felicia. "I found out about the plot from Aquilo. I was only faking so I could get closer to the thieves."

Felix snarled, "You killed Aquilo!"

Sammra waved her arms in front of her body. "No, I didn't. It was Jinx. I swear it." She took several more steps away from Felicia.

Felicia's cats circled Sammra and looped around Felix and the others.

"I. Don't. Believe. You." Felix roared, his voice, almost a roar, bellowing through the space.

Felicia's leopards leaped towards Felix's cougars as Sammra dove to the side, pressing her back against a tree.

Felix locked in concentration, leaning forward,

controlling his cats, making them attack and defend against Felicia's, yet trying to not harm them. "Felicia, stop this! You can't beat me."

Pren and Naga stepped next to Felix, preparing to aid in the attack. Then the space flooded with a cacophony of cawing as several large blackbirds swept down from high in the trees, swooping at Felix, Pren, and Naga, clawing at their faces and eyes.

Pren sent a wave of sand around the three, a wall of protection. Naga's ice balls flew at the birds.

Kerlith stepped out of a dark patch of forest behind Felicia, laughing.

Naga called out, "Kerlith, help us!"

Kerlith laughed louder. "Help you? Why?"

Naga flung a ball of ice at a crow above Felix's head, knocking it from the air.

Sammra pointed at Kerlith, backing away. "It was him. It was Kerlith. All along. He came to us in the desert with his crazy ideas. Wanted me to join him with the avians. That's where he said he found a new master. I went along only to discover their plot."

"Liar," Kerlith said, pushing the glowing stone in his hand at her. A bolt of green energy flew out of his hand. Sammra dove out of the way as the energy struck the tree she had been leaning against, shredding a thick layer of bark on impact.

Sammra scampered over behind Pren. "Felix, you must believe me." She flung her sand pouch in the air, dispersing the dust, then moved her hands, forming the sand into a large hard block that flew lazily at Kerlith.

Kerlith ran through the trees, as green, glowing mage-light accumulated around him. Stones all around the group began struggling to free themselves from the ground and rise into the air. The rocks swarmed, flinging this way and that, hurtling in from every direction at Sammra, Felix, Pren, and Naga. The stones that missed their mark arced, turned around and flew back, making another pass. The flints' sharp edges pelted and cut the apprentices.

Kerlith eased back into the darkness of the forest, laughing hysterically as the stones continued to fly.

A medium-sized rock hit Sammra in the head. She fell to the ground and struggled to get back up. Her head quickly oozed blood.

Pren formed a cylinder of swirling sand around herself, Naga, Sammra, and Felix, trying to create a defensive perimeter. Felicia and her cats leaped inside the torrent and were trapped in the cyclone of sand.

Sammra stood, wiped the blood from her head, then grabbed Pren's hand, trying to aid her. Pren cautiously accepted the help. The cylinder grew larger and spun harder, faster. The torus accelerated such that the stones could not penetrate the tornado of sand.

Felicia stepped closer to the center, realizing she was trapped in the swirling vortex. She sent a leopard at Felix.

His cougar leaped in front of her cat and growled. The leopard stopped.

"Why, Felicia? Why?" Felix asked.

"Why? Because nothing is as it should be. That's why. You come here and suck the toes of the landers, begging them to let you help them. You're their pathetic little pawn. Don't you realize, Felix? You should be *with me*, fighting for *our clan*. How can you ally yourself with the likes of them?" She pointed at Naga.

Felix's cougar slowly stepped closer to Felicia. "Sister, my dear sweet sister, you have it all wrong. Perhaps we view them a certain way and they picture us another. What I am trying to do is change all that."

"As am I. We had a plan. No one spoke to you about the plot because we already knew what you would say. You might as well not come back to the clan at all. You're just like the landers."

Felix's cougar growled. It was only inches from Felicia.

The girl snarled, "And what are you going to do now? Kill me? Kill your sister? For them?" She pointed at Naga again.

A snowball struck Felicia lightly on the side of her head.

"Keep pointing at me like that and the next one will be made of ice."

Pren and Sammra slowly wilted, exhausted, their energy spent, their skin showing hints of gray. "Ready yourselves," Sammra choked out. "The sand wall is lowering. We can't hold it up any longer." They slowly lowered their arms, allowing the force and intensity of the swirling sand to decrease. They cautiously lowered their defensive barrier, but no more stones were flying around them.

Felicia took a step back and Felix's cats bounded behind her.

Pren and Sammra shuffled toward Naga.

"I guess Kerlith ran off," Sammra said.

A stone flew in, smashing Pren in the center of her back, knocking her to the ground.

Kerlith stepped out of the dark. "Sammra, thanks for weakening her for me."

Felicia screamed as her leopards and cougars leaped forward.

Naga flung a few balls of ice at the advancing cats as he backpedaled toward Pren, then kneeled down next to her in a protective stance.

Felicia's cougar sunk his teeth into Felix's bobcat and swung its head, breaking the bobcat's neck. The cougar dropped the dead cat at its feet.

Felix spit his words, "Felicia, what did you just do?"

"Now don't make me hurt you, Brother," she yelled back.

Rocks began pelting them again and the crows returned, gathering in the trees, crowing loudly, blotting out all sound. Then the birds attacked.

Sammra knelt on the other side of an unconscious Pren, opposite Naga. The two tried to defend her and themselves by knocking down the birds and stones with balls of ice and slugs of sand.

"How is this possible? Who's controlling the birds?" Naga muttered.

Kerlith explained, "I've been learning avian magic from Jeneth."

Naga gasped.

Kerlith laughed, "What? Against the rules? Those rules are stupid. Stupid laws that were keeping me from finding a master. Dumb, stupid laws created by dumb, stupid men who know nothing about magic, laws created because the dumb, stupid men were afraid. I'm not following them anymore. Kerlith is doing what's best for Kerlith. That's all. I'm joining the avians and we're going to destroy Lasaat and the rest of the so-called archmages who hid in their little fort afraid to help us fight the ghoul-kind, cowards with all their stupid little rules."

"I don't agree with the Laws either, Kerlith. But to steal? To kill?"

"I'm no killer, Brother. And steal? We're only borrowing. My new master promised. You'll get the stone back when we're done with it."

Felix bent down and stroked the head of his dead bobcat. His upper lip quivered then his eyes focused on Felicia. He stood with an eye of determination and blinked, the pupils of his eyes changing, becoming increasingly feline. He allowed his body to fall forward, his flesh contorting, landing on his hands and knees. His arms and legs shrunk in some places and grew in others. His body was becoming cat-like. He roared painfully. The transition was traumatic, grating, tearing, the sound as though his bones were breaking, his flesh ripping. He blinked at Felicia then attempted to speak, the sound inhuman, a guttural roar. Felix, now part human-part feline, charged.

Naga asked, "They can do that?"

"I can't believe this," Sammra said.

"That and more. You two know nothing of the reality of this world," Kerlith said.

Felicia back-pedaled, waving her hands, sending her cats at him. The cougars and leopards seemed so small now. Felix batted one away, sending it sailing into the forest.

Felicia sent another cat charging. It dove and missed, landing near Naga. The Tundric apprentice smashed the cat in the face with an ice ball. The cougar spun and leaped, digging its claws into Naga's chest and biting his neck.

Felicia gasped and dropped her arms. "No! I-I-I didn't mean—"

Felix roared, diving at Felicia, toppling her and pressing his paws down on her shoulders. He placed his open mouth on her neck, allowing his long sharp canines to graze the soft skin of her throat.

Felicia's cats stopped attacking and began milling around the space. One squatted on the ground, lazily looking off into the forest. Another shook its head and jogged off into the wood.

Sammra dropped to Naga and touched his body then turned to Felicia and screamed, "He's dead! You killed him!"

"No, it was an accident," Felicia pleaded, staring into her brother's eyes. "That wasn't supposed to happen. No one was supposed to die. We were just supposed to escape."

Kerlith laughed hysterically then said, "Felicia, let's go."

Sammra pointed her arms forward, sending a blast of sand at Kerlith.

He leaped behind a tree as the surrounding small stones flew towards him and coalesced together forming a shield to the pelting sand.

Pren slowly shook herself awake, struggling to stand next to Sammra. She squinted down at Naga, dumbfounded, then pressed her hands into Sammra's back, feeding her some little energy.

Felix released Felicia's neck as she cried. He surrounded Felicia with his cougars and rolled to the ground, moaning as he painfully became human again.

Tears flooded Felicia's eyes. "It wasn't supposed to happen this way. No one was supposed to be hurt. I didn't... I didn't hurt Aquilo or Jinx. Never. I would never hurt my clan-brother."

"Felicia, you just killed Naga," Felix drawled.

Wide-eyed, open-mouthed, she shook her head,

refusing to accept the fact that the Tundric apprentice was dead.

Felix reached down and grabbed her hands and tied them with a piece of rope. "Sis, I need to take you back."

Her only response was tears.

As Sammra continued to attack Kerlith, Felix took his bound sister and passed the rope to one of his cats. "I'm going to watch you all the way back to the camp. I will be watching through my cat's eyes. When you reach the camp, the trolls will put you in a cage. I'll deal with you later."

The cat led Felicia away.

A crow swooped down behind Pren and Sammra, getting its claws tangled in Pren's long hair. She swung her arms, trying to pull the bird free as it flapped, pecked and clawed. Just as she ripped the bird from her hair, a stone struck Sammra on the temple and she fell to the earth.

Kerlith snickered and ran off.

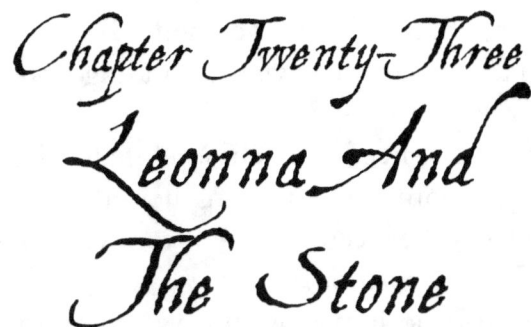

Chapter Twenty-Three
Leonna And
The Stone

Shireen fell into a sprint, dodging through the trees, avoiding roots and fallen branches. She had to catch Lithia!

The stonecutter was so strong, man-like, her legs and arms thick and brawny. *And hairy,* Shireen thought. Fast. She was just ahead, about three-hundred feet, and Shireen didn't want to lose sight of Lithia, her friend, to leave her alone to face the others.

If she lost Lithia, Shireen wouldn't have Felix and his cats with their keen sense of smell to tell her which direction to go. Maybe she could ask the trees if she had to, but she was unsure how that could work if she needed to run at the same time.

Luckily, Lithia was slowing ahead. Shireen realized the avians were within sight, just up ahead. She spied Jonah. Just a boy; he couldn't run as fast as the others, so Ayah, Leonna, and the small boy had stopped, turned to face them. Leonna took Jonah's sack and slung it over her shoulder then pointed off to the side. The little boy ran in the direction she had pointed.

Bel passed Shireen and caught up to Lithia as Ayah and Leonna faced them, preparing themselves for a fight. Birds cawing frantically above them, Bel, Shireen, and Lithia walked toward the avians, standing opposite them in a short row.

"There's no need to chase Jonah. I have the moonstone," Leonna said, tapping her sack.

Lithia bared her teeth. "Give it to me!" She crouched into an offensive position.

Shireen had no idea how this was going to go down. *What could the avians do besides control birds?* No one she had spoken with fully knew the limits of their powers. If all they could do was dive and claw at their skin and eyes the avians would be easily defeated. But Shireen didn't think this fight would be so easy for some reason. A memory flashed through her mind of Leonna describing some form of 'secret weapon.' Shireen was nervous and perhaps even a little afraid. This was no trial. This was no test.

Bel spoke first. "This is foolish, you two. You can't escape. The forest is under troll-spell. There's no need for us to fight. Just come back with us. Give up."

Ayah said, "Bel, I like you—perhaps it's that slightly bluish tint to your eyes—but you have no idea what's going on here."

Leonna smiled over at Ayah as if a realization had only just struck her. "Yes, the blue. Bel, did you know that only avians have that coloring in their eyes? We call it bird-sign. Shireen has avian eyes too. Peculiar. I'm still not sure what to make of a lander with bird-sign. Maybe it's why I've grown so fond of you two. It would be a shame to kill you."

Bel glanced at Shireen and Lithia then eyed the two

avians. He edged forward, pushing mage-light into the tip of his staff. "Shireen and I both touched the roc's eye. I felt something, something deep inside when it happened. I suppose she did too. It's what changed our eyes, I believe."

Leonna flashed a happy, surprised smile.

Bel continued, "Not sure what else the roc's eye did to us, but regardless of what color anyone's eyes are, you're going to have to give us back the moonstone."

Ayah shook his head impatiently as the cawing above them increased in volume. Birds were streaming into the space and landing in the surrounding trees. While Bel, Lithia, and Shireen had been foolishly talking, Ayah had been calling birds, hundreds of birds, thousands of them to surround the three landers, readying for a massive onslaught. Shireen's eyes popped wide as she increasingly realized the force she would have to face wasn't the handful of birds that Leonna and Ayah had kept in their cages, tens of finches, a few peregrines and maybe a hawk or an eagle. No. There were thousands upon thousands of birds, more streaming in each moment, mostly large blackbirds, all of them cawing loudly, far too many.

"Enough talk. Give me my people's stone or prepare to die," Lithia hissed as she rolled her thick fingers at her sides. Small stones erupted from the ground.

"Bel, Shireen, it doesn't need to be this way." Leonna sounded as if she was about to beg. "You've touched the roc's eye. One of the highest honors among avians." She glanced at Ayah and back at Bel. "When you touched the eye you were changed, altered. You said it yourself. More than just the coloring of your eyes. That is only a tiny external sign. No, the roc's eye changed you inside. You are part avian now. You have to be. You have to know that, deep inside. The avian in you has to feel my words are true. You could join us. You two could become avians. My clan would welcome you."

A stone flew at Leonna. She raised her hand in front of her face at the last moment and the rock struck her arm, tearing her flesh, leaving a long red gash.

"Enough talk! Give me the moonstone." Lithia was seething.

Ayah leaned his body forward, his eyes rolling into the back of his head. The birds above him cawed loudly as they dove from the trees and began spinning above them, a swirling cyclone of feathers, claws, and beaks descending on the three.

Bel yelled over the cacophony, "Don't do this!"

The birds smashed into them, clawing at the three, Lithia, Bel, and Shireen.

Bel threw up his arms, sending a shockwave of energy out, erupting out of his arms and reverberating up into the torrent of birds. The quake shook through and hundreds of crows fell to the ground forming a wide circle of black on the ground, all dead.

Shireen's eyes popped wide. Bel was becoming stronger, even more so than when they had fought the dragon.

Ayah hissed and sent down another wave of birds.

Lithia sent her stones after Ayah and Leonna, but birds sacrificed themselves, diving in front of the razor-sharp stones.

Bel began flinging his hands, sending balls of energy at the swirling mass of black crows then quickly dodged over to Shireen. "The trees. Connect with the trees. I'll hold them off. Get the trees to send their vines to tie up Leonna and Ayah."

Shireen slid back between two closely spaced firs and placed her hands upon them as Bel took a position in front of her, defending her as she closed her eyes and tried to connect.

Lithia, alone in the center of the clearing, flung stones at both birds and the two avians with mad abandon. A peregrine smashed into the back of her neck, toppling her, but she quickly stood and smashed at the bird with her boot heel. She missed the bird and it flew off. Lithia's stones were reaching closer and closer to the two avians as the pile of dead and wounded birds in front of them increased in size.

Shireen reached out to the trees, trying to moan out the tones Bel had taught her but the trees weren't responding.

A bird smacked the side of Shireen's head, breaking her concentration. Bel grabbed the crow, crushed and threw it. Shireen touched her scratched cheek. She was bleeding.

She closed her eyes again, intent on connecting with the trees. Leonna was going to pay. Shireen ground her teeth. *First, she lies to all of us, pretending to be some kind of sweet, innocent girl who, like me, wants to learn about other cultures. Lies! Then she tries to steal Bel when she quite obviously realized I loved him. Thief! She's involved in the murder of several apprentices. Now, she stole the moonstone. And finally, if that wasn't enough, she scratched my cheek!*

Shireen pressed her life-force into the trees, begging them to understand. She kept it simple. —*Danger. Danger. Help. Need help. Protectors of the forest, need help* — She flashed an image of Leonna in her mind and showed the picture to the trees. She hoped they would understand.

Bel said, "Shireen, it's working. Keep doing what you're doing."

The branches swayed, shaking the birds out of them. A solitary vine streamed into the space, swinging toward Ayah. He vaulted the vine and out of its path. Ayah squinted hard and threw his hands forward. A blizzard of black flooded the space as all the crows dove, focusing on Lithia. Shireen couldn't find her for the flurry of rapidly moving black wings.

Bel flung ball after ball of energy, felling many birds but they were too thick, too many.

When they finally cleared, the black crows flooding back into the canopy overhead. Lithia lay on the ground, her green and gray clothing shredded and darkening with blood. Her skin was severely torn, head, arms, legs and torso.

Bel and Shireen ran to her as Ayah and Leonna watched. Lithia tried to speak but Bel placed his fingers on her lips.

Ayah crowed, "You made me do that! I didn't want to, but you landers are so hard headed. It didn't need to be this way."

Leonna begged, "Bel, Shireen, please. Come with us. The blue is in your eyes already. We possess the roc's eye. You can touch it again. It will change you, complete you. You will become like us. Avians, full and complete. Please. Leave the lander and join us."

"Like you?" Shireen snarled, snapping her head back. "Why would anyone want to be like you?" She slowly crouched, pressing her fingers into the earth as she spoke. "You don't get it, do you? You can't have him. Bel's mine. I'm not going to let you steal him and I'm not going to let you steal Lithia's moonstone. Leonna, you're a thief and a liar!"

A vine swung down from a tree behind Leonna and swatted her, throwing her forward. She landed on her elbows in front of Shireen.

"Leonna, please stop this madness. If you ever had any affection for me, you need to stop this," Bel said.

Another vine swung from the left, but Leonna rolled out of its path.

Ayah said, "Bel, you need to stop Shireen. You don't want her face torn apart like Lithia's, do you?"

Shireen sent another set of vines but they missed their mark as Leonna spun to her feet and called birds to her defense.

Bel stared at Ayah in a standoff, neither side attacking, as if they were both watching patiently what was to become of Leonna and Shireen's struggle.

Bel spoke calmly to Leonna, "Leonna, please. You're not listening. You said it didn't need to be this way and you were right, but not by us joining you in Jeneth's evil scheme. Look at me. Please, stop this."

Leonna sent her birds to grab, peck and claw at the vines, but it was clear she was holding herself back from directly attacking Bel or Shireen. "You're angry with me, Bel, Shireen. I know. I understand. You feel like I betrayed you, but you need to see things from my perspective."

"No, I don't," Shireen screamed as she sent another vine at Leonna.

Leonna stared at Bel, their eyes locked, as she continued to send her birds out to defend herself from the streaming vines. "I understand now why I felt such an attraction for you, Bel. It all makes perfect sense. You touched the roc's eye. You were changed. The blue in your eyes, it means so much more. It's so obvious now. That's why I felt connected to you. I'm not sure why I didn't put it all together before. The two of you are already part avian. You need to listen. Even if you won't have me, Bel, the two of you could be together, as avians. Don't you see? Among us, you two could marry."

Ayah was shaking his head, but smiling.

Bel tried to persuade Leonna to stop fighting. "Leonna, think about what you're doing. Jeneth's twisted your head all around. He's got you doing things that aren't right." Bel shifted his stance, stepping forward slightly, placing himself between Ayah and Shireen, who was at his back. It exposed his side to an attack by Leonna, but he figured she was telling the truth. She wouldn't attack him. He pushed light into his hands and the end of his staff in case Ayah decided to rejoin the fray.

Ayah smiled at him. "Don't do it, Bel. I don't agree with Leonna, but she's my clan-sister. I promised her I would give her a chance to try and persuade you two. But if you attack me, I'll kill you."

"You'll die trying."

Ayah chuckled. "You haven't witnessed a tenth of what I can do. Don't test me." Ayah's birds did not attack but they circled closely, passing between Bel and Shireen's position and that of the two avians.

Leonna said, her voice cracking, "No, Bel. He's telling the truth. You don't stand a chance. Please, just listen to me. All we need to do is leave. The four of us. You can have everything you always wanted. You can have me... Or Shireen... if that's really where your heart is. You two, you could marry. I know, I can feel it, you will be one of the most powerful of avian wizards. Come with us, please." Leonna flung another pack of birds at Shireen's vines.

Bel said, "Listen to you? I have. I understand what you're saying. We're part avian. So if that's true, you need to think about what you're doing. You, an avian, are attacking Shireen and me, who are part avian. What are you doing? Is this what your clan does? Kill each other? Avian killing avian? And why? For a plan, you don't even agree with? To serve Jeneth? He's turning you into a murderer of your own people. Give the moonstone to me. You don't want to kill us... not if we're part avian."

Shireen sent another set of vines at Leonna, but she merely shook her head and tens of birds flew to the vines, clawing and biting at them, severing their connection to the trees above. Another bird smashed into Shireen's back, pushing her forward, then flew away.

"Listen to me!" Leonna screamed. Tears were streaming down her face now. "All of this is a little confusing. I was following the orders of my clan. I didn't think it right to steal the moonstone. What does an avian need with a relic of the stonecutters? We had the roc's eye, our greatest treasure. Why steal from the stonecutters? It made no sense! But the will of the clan is Law and so I agreed. Jeneth, he promised the task would be easy and no one would be hurt."

"And now, because of you, people are dead!" Shireen screamed back at her. "Look at Lithia! She might die!"

Leonna followed Shireen's arm to where she was pointing, at the unconscious and bleeding stonecutter. She trembled then placed her eyes on Bel. "I do love you. I do. I think. Maybe the blue in your eyes called to me. All I know is I felt something. A yearning. I can't... I can't do this anymore. I can't kill avians. You touched the roc's eye." She snapped her head to Ayah. "What do I do?" When he didn't immediately reply, Leonna turned to run. "I can't do this anymore."

The flock of birds in front of Bel and Shireen increased, preventing the two from advancing. When Shireen tried to move past, a phalanx of black birds smashed into her, slamming their bodies like little hammers. She backed up, tripped over a root, then fell. The birds ceased their attack, but maintained their position, swarming around the space, filling the forest with cawing black.

The air shimmered in front of Leonna and she crashed into a rapidly appearing Jeneth. He placed his hands on her shoulders, gripping tightly, and promptly pushed her to the ground. She crumpled in a pile. The moonstone fell from her sack. The archmage snarled, "I've watched this display with disgust and I just can't watch it any longer! What are you trying to do, fledgling?"

Leonna reached out, clawing at the ground, grabbed the moonstone and clutched it to her chest. "I can't fight them." Her voice was hollow.

"Give me the stone," Jeneth demanded, his arm outstretched.

From the ground, Shireen saw Jonah lurking up in the tree branches above Jeneth, his eyes staring down at Leonna. Shireen struggled to stand.

Leonna clawed the ground, dragging her body away from Jeneth. "No, I won't."

Jeneth yanked his dagger out of its sheath and fingered the hole where the jewel was missing.

"You got your dagger back, Murderer," Leonna said with disgust as she tried to creep away.

"Jinx was ruining the plan, attacking Aquilo. And for what? Because he wanted something he couldn't have? You. The investigation is over." Jeneth eyed Leonna. "Give me the moonstone."

"What are you going to do, Clan-father?" Ayah stepped toward Jeneth until he gave him an icy glare.

Leonna struggled to push away, inching through the brown leaves as Jeneth raised the dagger above his head.

"You wouldn't?" Leonna asked, glancing back at Jeneth, not sure herself what Jeneth was truly capable of.

"No, Clan-father!" Ayah cried out, his voice panicked. "She's clan."

"Some things are more important than clan, My Dear Fledgling. You must have realized by now."

At the same moment that Jeneth swung the dagger down at Leonna, Jonah dropped from the branch, falling onto his father's back and wrapping his arms around his neck. Jeneth teetered, swinging his arm violently. Jonah released his father's neck and flopped off. The nestling fell to the ground, a crumpled pile of flesh, the dagger sticking out of his torso. He didn't move.

Jeneth fell to his knees, cradling his son's body. "No! No! No! What have I done?" Tears flushed the old man's eyes.

Shireen clutched Bel's arm. The pair both stepped back involuntarily.

The birds circling Shireen and Bel flew off as Ayah released an ear piercing wail. He began running in a circle frantically, tearing at his clothing, beating his chest and head with his palms. "Jeneth, you lied to us! You murdered Jonah! You took the life of clan!" Ayah leaped, transformed himself into a large blackbird mid-flight, flapped his wings and soared off. Most of the birds followed him.

Shireen and Bel both gasped.

Bel said, "He just turned into a bird!"

Jeneth's eyes flashed at Leonna, the translucent blue in them glowing into the whites. "You did this! You poisoned his mind!"

Leonna scrambled to her feet and jogged a few paces then spun toward Jeneth. She screamed, "You killed Jonah! You killed Jinx! Murderer! Selfish, bird-brained murderer! You killed clan!"

Jeneth held his hands up, calling birds to swarm around him as he spoke, his voice cracking and gravely, "Selfish? On the contrary, Fledgling. What I do is make sacrifices for all avian-kind. Now give me the moonstone."

Leonna clutched the moonstone tighter, pulling it to her chest, it's translucent green glow brightening as she spit her words. "Sacrifice? Sacrifice? Is that what you call that?" She pointed down at Jonah's crumpled body.

"You are the one who clouded Jonah's mind. You're going to need to answer for that. Just give me the stone, Leonna."

Bel edged over to Shireen and whispered to her, "Call the vines to tie up Jeneth."

The two moved back and away from the avians and slipped between trees, placing their hands on them, connecting.

"Answer?" Leonna said, manically pacing. "It is you that needs to answer. You *never* loved Jonah the way I did. He was all I had." Through quivering lips, she added, "All. I. Had. The only one. And now he's dead and you've already stepped away from his body as if he meant nothing. Did you have *any* emotion for him at all?

What kind of a clan-father are you?"

Jeneth grunted as his face twisted into an ugly scowl. A wave of birds swooped down towards Leonna. She curled her fingers in front of her and a corresponding group of crows slammed forward, the two groups entangling, clawing, cawing, black feathers flying out of the mass as they shredded each other.

"Come, Clan-father. You can do better than that," Tears were pouring from Leonna's eyes, but she refused to wipe them.

Jeneth smiled back at her. "So it's a fight you want."

Leonna pointed her left arm at Jeneth as the green glow from the stone permeated her body, the blue irises of her eyes replaced by neon green. "No, not fight. I want to kill you."

Bel said, "Leonna, no. The moonstone is full of stone magic. You don't know how to control it. It will kill you."

A bolt of energy flew from Leonna's arm like a cannon shot. Jeneth dove to the ground. The blast smashed into a tree behind him, ripping the bark away and casting splinters throughout the space. The tree creaked loudly as it tipped, cracked, then fell.

"Leonna, stop! Fledgling, you don't realize what you're doing," Jeneth crowed.

She sent another blast at him as he scrambled out of the way. Leonna smiled wide, the green glow was coming out of her mouth now. "Such power in this moonstone," she mumbled. "It feels so warm. Inviting. It's coursing through me. I *will* destroy you."

Jeneth ran back into the center of the clearing, then called his birds. An army of black feathers beat the air, streaming towards Leonna. She laughed hysterically as her flesh pulsed. She sent another blast at Jeneth, ignoring the descending crows.

Jeneth dove again and another tree was struck. This one was thinner; one side of the trunk blew apart. The fir toppled, forcing Bel and Shireen to lose their connection and run to another location in the forest.

Leonna sent blast after furious blast at Jeneth as the green glow infected her body. Crack-lines appear on the Leonna's face, legs and arms.

Shireen screamed, "Leonna, you have to stop! You're going to kill yourself. The moonstone. You don't know how to control it. You're not a stonecutter. Too much power. It's going to tear you apart."

Leonna glanced back with a glowing green, jagged, cracked face. The green shone out of the crooked, twisted grin etched on her face.

Jeneth wrapped his arms around his torso and promptly disappeared.

Leonna sent a bolt of energy where he had just been standing. "Where! Did! You! Go!" Baring her teeth, she shook her arms in rhythm with her words. "Coward!"

Jeneth appeared not far away, swung his hands at the birds above, then promptly disappeared before Leonna could fire off another shot. The birds began cawing and dove towards Leonna.

Hugging the stone to her chest with one arm, she pointed the other up, sending out a ferocious blast of energy. Birds rained down to the ground, dead. Several landed on Bel and Shireen.

Shireen was racked with horror as she watched what Leonna was turning into, what the moonstone was doing to her. The cracks on her body had thickened and small pieces of her flesh had begun to fall off here and there, revealing sinewy muscle and bone below, bone glowing green. She was destroying herself.

"I have to do something." Bel started to walk toward Leonna, speaking to her calmly. "Leonna, please, you need to stop. Look at yourself. It's tearing you apart. Please listen. I've seen this before. Rylithnon at the breach, it happened to him too. I've seen this before. It's going to kill you if you continue."

Leonna ignored him. She began blasting out at the forest at random as Jeneth alternately appeared in different places, quickly calling for birds to attack, then disappearing.

She screamed at Jeneth, "Show yourself! Coward! Show yourself and fight me!" As she spit out the words, part of Leonna's upper lip fell off. She didn't seem to care.

Shireen's voice strained, as she spoke to Bel. "We need to make Jeneth show himself. We need to do something so he doesn't disappear."

Bel said, "Wait. Do you think we could detect his spirit? Even if he was invisible?"

"I think so. But we would be defenseless."

Bel said, "You do it. Point at him. I'll defend you."

Shireen closed her eyes, allowing her spirit to rise up and gaze at all the life-force of the world surrounding her.

Tiny tendrils of dark green life streamed up from the ground, flowing through the trunks of the trees, up to the branches and out through leaves. They were surrounded by life.

She scanned her head around the space and stopped on Leonna. She had to squint to keep her eyes on her. *She was so bright!* Neon green, a shade much lighter and brighter than the deep green flowing through the trees,

Leonna was full of vibrant life. The energy in the stone was too strong. It was streaming out of her, tearing her apart from the inside out.

Sweeping her head back and forth, Shireen searched for Jeneth. "There!" she said, pointing.

Bel said, "I'll send the vines."

Shireen kept her arm pointed at Jeneth, it following his invisible form as he moved through the forest.

A vine snapped down at Jeneth but missed entirely. Bel was only making a guess where the archmage was, only the general direction Shireen was pointing toward.

Another vine swung down and knocked Jeneth to the ground.

"That one hit him," Shireen said.

Jeneth appeared for a moment and pointed at Bel and Shireen.

Leonna sent a blast of energy at Jeneth. He dove then vanished.

The blackbirds swooped down at Bel and Shireen.

Leonna, realizing the two forest apprentices were trying to help her, pointed her arm up and destroyed wave after wave of birds.

"Jeneth! He's creeping up on Leonna!" Shireen screamed.

Bel connected with the trees and two vines streamed into the space, but they were too late. Jeneth appeared behind Leonna and buried his dagger between her shoulder blades. She froze, clutching, her shoulders contracting as blood spewed from her mouth. She fell to her knees, the moonstone dropping from her hand.

Jeneth bent down and gently pushed the stone with his foot, guiding it into a sack, not wanting to touch the thing with his hands. Then he ran.

Bel and Shireen jogged to Leonna. Shireen continued past her and after Jeneth but stopped when Bel slid to his knees and pulled Leonna up into his arms. The stench of burnt flesh was overpowering. He began weeping. Bel cried as he cradled Leonna's body. Shireen stood behind, wanting to comfort Bel.

The skin on Leonna's face was flayed off. She had no eyelids, most of her nose was gone and half of her upper lip. Leonna tried to speak.

"No. Leonna, don't struggle. I'm trying to ease your pain. It's all I can do for you now." Bel whimpered.

Leonna spoke anyway, her voice hollow and raspy. "Bel—uhhh, uhhh—I need to te—e— e—tell you—uhhh, uhhh—I know now—uhhh, uhhh—I never—uhhh, uhhh—never could have won you—uhhh, uhhh."

"Leonna, please. Don't speak. Don't struggle. It will only cause you more pain," Bel didn't bother to wipe the tears from his eyes. They dripped off his face and down on Leonna's exposed raw flesh.

"I need to—uhhh, uhhh—tell you—uhhh, uhhh— before—uhhh, uhhh—die."

"No. Please. Don't talk."

"I could never have—uhhh, uhhh—what she has— uhhh, uhhh—Shireen." Leonna's bare orbs focused past Bel and at Shireen's clenched face and she let out one long exhale, her body slumping.

A sparkling blue light left Leonna's body then hovered in the air, inches from Bel's face, then slowly dissipated.

Bel stood, Leonna's torched body in his arms. He scooped her up and carried her over to where Lithia lay and placed Leonna next to her. He retrieved Jonah's body and placed it on top of Leonna's and wrapped her arms around him as if she was holding the boy.

Lithia coughed a few times and spat blood then struggled to speak, "Help me up."

Shireen pressed her hand down on her shoulder. "You're in no condition to go anywhere. And especially not off to another fight. Just lay there and try to heal. The forest is full of life. Pull, I'll help you."

Bel studied Leonna's destroyed frame and Lithia's wounded body. "I'll go. He'll pay for this. He'll pay for all of this."

Shireen grabbed at Bel's arm to stop him. "Bel, you can't. You'll die. Alone. You can't face him. He's an archmage."

"It's only a title."

"Title or no, he's too powerful. He was only toying with us there, waiting for Leonna to destroy herself. He never attacked. He's powerful. And ruthless. He'll stop at nothing."

Bel looked back at her blankly.

Shireen's voice ran to a shrill when she realized he didn't agree. "He killed his own son! What do you think he'll do to you?"

"I don't care. He has to be made to answer."

Shireen spun and smacked his chest.

"What was that for?" Bel asked, pinching his face.

Something snapped in Shireen like a rubber band stretched too far, instantaneously breaking and releasing all its tension. Everything had become so clear just then: Leonna, Bel, her emotions, how she felt for him and what she wanted. The Law, she didn't care anymore about any of it. What was this life without him? An empty, bottomless hole. Shireen couldn't let Bel go, she couldn't lose him. She grabbed his arms and pulled him closer, her face not inches from his. "I won't let you go. I love you. I can't lose you. Not now." Her breathing became uneven.

Bel whispered against her lips, "You love me? But what does it mean if we can't be together? What's the point?"

Shireen fell against him, pressing her body to his, and kissed him passionately, letting her mouth linger on his soft lips, the scruff on his face digging into her cheeks. Bel didn't resist. She heard Lithia gasp, but Shireen didn't care. She would have kissed him in front of the whole world. "Don't go," she groaned.

Bel placed his hand at the back of her neck as his head slowly twisted. Bel moaned softly. He nibbled Shireen's upper lip and she his lower.

Lithia cleared her throat loudly.

"Stay with me, Bel." Shireen slowly backed her mouth away from his and stared deep into his eyes, the blue swirl carried a small sparkle. She hugged him tight, placing her mouth on his ear, tasting it, refusing to let him go. Not again. Never again.

Lithia tried to interrupt them by clearing her throat again. Bel pushed Shireen away, slightly, softly, enough to look into her eyes as if he were communicating through them. He swept his right hand behind Shireen's head and knotted his fingers in her hair. "I love you too. But I must do this. I need to stop him."

"No, Bel. I can't lose you. Not like this." Shireen dropped her arms to his lower back and pulled their hips together as if they always belonged there.

Their eyes locked. "I need to try. I'll be careful. I promise."

"Bel. No. I…" The bouquet of Leonna's burnt carcass

drifted around her. It could happen fast. Too fast. Bel would try to be cautious and safe but Jeneth would kill him. His body, devoid of life, empty, it was in her mind and she couldn't bear the thought.

Bel released her, but Shireen refused to drop her arms away. He stroked her forearm. "Shireen, let me go. I promise. I'll return to you. I love you. We're always going to be together, aren't we? I'll just track him. I won't face him. No, not by myself. You're right. He's too powerful. I'll follow until the others come. That's all. When I return we'll be together. I promise." His voice had a dreamy quality.

"We'll be together," Shireen repeated in a daze. "Sounds marvelous."

Bel pushed away from Shireen and she didn't resist this time. "My love, stay here with Lithia. Watch over her. I'm going to find the others first. I promise. I'll be back." Bel turned and ran off in the direction Jeneth fled.

Shireen reached her arm out after his rapidly shrinking back as if she didn't realize how he had escaped.

Chapter Twenty-Four
Jeneth

Bel ran in the direction Jeneth had disappeared, but quickly lost his trail. He scanned the trees for birds, figuring the flock would be near the avian wizard, but saw only a few. Jeneth was probably scouting the entire forest now with his birds. With him able to become invisible, he was going to be impossible to catch, much less battle.

Bel turned to the left as there were more birds in the trees in that direction. He ran that way for a while but changed his mind when they thinned out. He ran back, continuing past where he had started. He reached an area of the forest that appeared the same in every direction. He remembered the entrance trials and how the forest looked when he first stepped into this wood. *Could this be part of a trial? An illusion?*

Bel reached out and touched a tree, moaning the deep sounds of tree-language, asking if they had seen Jeneth run by. The trees didn't understand the question. Of course, he ran by. Many times in fact. Him and many, many others. What did Bel expect them to do? Pay attention to every human that scurried about? He may as well have asked if an ant had run by. Bel was unsure what question to ask, but that was certainly the

371

wrong one. Bel remembered his master had told him trees have a completely different concept of time than humans. Something just happening, to them, could have taken place many years ago.

Bel released the tree and wandered off in another direction when he thought he heard a noise. He fell into a jog, trying to be as quiet as possible in his approach. Up ahead a few people congregated. One of them was Felix. Bel sped up, calling out as he approached, "Hey, where's Jeneth?"

The tension in Felix's cats quickly dissipated when Felix recognized Bel. The feline shook his head; he didn't know where the avian was.

Then Bel saw Pren and Sammra and someone else on the ground. Someone Tundric... *Naga!*

Bel ran, then dropped to one knee in front of his fallen friend. "Naga! No!" He tried to wail, to release his pain, but couldn't. His voice was gone. Empty, he could no longer yell and scream at all the death and loss. They were dropping like dead crows falling from the sky: Onyx, Drake, Aquilo, Jinx, Isha, Jonah, Leonna, and now Naga. Even Lithia, her life-force tenuous, hanging by a thread, might yet die. They had only just run into the forest after the thieves moments ago—that's what it felt like, moments—and already three more were dead, and one his good friend.

"He died fighting, trying to stop them." Felix tried to comfort Bel, but his words didn't enter Bel's ears. They were peculiar sounds, unintelligible.

Bel bore his eyes into Sammra and turned to Felix as if to ask what she was doing there.

The feline said, "Sammra's on our side. She was a mole. Trying to get to the bottom of the plot. She helped us against Felicia and Kerlith once the fighting started."

"Kerlith?"

"Yes, Kerlith, he attacked us. Helping the thieves."

Bel nodded, but still he didn't trust Sammra. There's no way he was letting her guard his back. And he wasn't so sure about Felix either.

Bel stared at the ground. "Jonah and Leonna are dead. Lithia's in really bad shape."

"Shireen?" Felix asked.

Bel snapped his head up at Felix. "She's fine. With Lithia."

"Where's the moonstone? Where's Ayah?" Sammra asked.

"Ayah ran off." Bel shook his head. "Flew off, in a rage, I should say. When Jeneth killed Jonah. An accident, I guess. Jeneth has the moonstone now. He's somewhere in the forest. We need to go after him."

"But why, Bel?" Pren asked. "The forest is under troll-spell. He can't escape."

"Can't he?" Sammra said. "He's an archmage. And from Lasaat. He probably has some kind of back door. Or could persuade the trolls to let the spell down. Bel's right. We need to stop him before it's too late."

Felix stared down at Naga's body. "Onyx and Drake. Aquilo and Jinx. Isha. Leonna and Jonah. And now Naga. All dead because of Jeneth." His eyes popped up to Bel's. "Where are they?"

"Shireen and the others? Back that way." Bel pointed.

Felix nodded then mumbled, "My cats. They can pick up Jeneth's scent. I'll send them out."

Before anyone could respond, his cougars, bobcats, and ocelots separated, running in different directions.

As they waited, Bel bent down to Naga's crumpled

frame and said, "I'm sorry, my friend. Sorry, I wasn't there with you." He shuddered, then touched Naga's arm. Bel tried to imitate Naga's Tundric accent. "My flesh will fight to avenge you. I'll find Jeneth."

Felix snapped his head to the left. "There. I've found his trail. We need to go. Now."

Sammra asked, "And we're going to try to face him? Alone? Shouldn't we get the others?"

Felix said, "We can't wait and let him escape. He has to pay."

Bel said, "Pren? Do you think you can move Naga to where Shireen and Lithia are? Over that way? I would feel better if the two of you were together. In case anything happened."

Pren nodded and used her sand to elevate Naga's body.

Felix, Sammra, and Bel fell into a jog and Felix's cats joined them. One cougar was up in front, the one who found Jeneth's scent. The cat dodged off to the right and the three followed.

The number of birds above them increased. They continued on, jogging through the forest, darting to the left and right after the big cat, the discordance of cawing crows growing in intensity.

Just ahead of them, a flock of blackbirds swirled in a tight pattern then dispersed leaving one large bird.

The band stopped some feet away, ready to attack when the great bird transformed into human form, Ayah.

He was crying. Ayah shook his arms in front of his body, pleading. "I won't fight you. I won't. This all went bad. It wasn't supposed to happen this way. We were only supposed to steal the moonstone. No one was supposed to be hurt. No one supposed to die. Not Jonah. Not Leonna." The avian fell to his knees.

"Ayah, there's nothing I can do for you. You're going to answer for this," Felix hissed.

Ayah squinted up into Bel's blue eyes. "I'm sorry, Bel. I'm sorry about all of it. You need to believe me. The avians, we're not like this. It's Jeneth. If I knew he would kill clan… never. I would never have followed."

Bel shook his head lightly, not knowing what to say.

Ayah begged, "You must understand. You saw how Leonna was. So beautiful. Alluring. Enticing. I loved her. I would have done anything for her. Stealing the moonstone, I thought, was a terrible idea. When Jeneth first asked for volunteers, calling me out in front of the clan, I refused. But her. He forced Leonna to go and she was too timid to stand up to him. At least, that's what she said. I agreed only to follow Leonna. To impress her. I wanted her, to make her my mate. You must know. I told you. Before." Ayah dropped his head. "Now she's dead." He began sobbing uncontrollably.

Felix said, "Ayah, we need to go, to catch Jeneth. How do we defeat him?"

Ayah snorted through his tears. "Defeat him? Not possible. He's too powerful. He'll do… anything. You saw already."

Felix's eyes darted to the side. "My cats have his scent. He's not far away. We need to go."

"What do we do with Ayah?" Sammra asked.

Ayah grimaced, wiping the tears from his eyes. He stood and shook his head. Acid in his voice, he said, "Do? You won't do anything. Not until after I've killed Jeneth or he's killed me first." The boy ran and dove into the air, quickly shifting into the form of a blackbird, flapping its wings and soaring off.

Felix ran, his cats speeding ahead of him. Sammra and Bel gave chase.

Not far ahead, Jeneth was surrounded by Felix's cats. He stood defiantly, chuckling.

As the band stopped behind the ocelots, Felix snarled, "Give up, Jeneth."

Bel, Sammra, and Felix fanned out.

Jeneth waved his arms as a fleet of birds sailed down from the canopy. The three took on defensive positions: Bel threw balls of energy. Felix's cats leaped up, ripping birds out of the air and Sammra's sand swirled around her, pelting the birds from the sky.

Jeneth dodged behind a tree, then ran. The three gave chase.

Something didn't seem quite right to Bel, but he couldn't put his finger on exactly what it was. *Why was Jeneth running and not fighting? He had the moonstone. He had killed to obtain it and now he was simply running away?* He could never outrun the cougars.

The cougars quickly caught up to Jeneth and again surrounded him. He brandished his blade, swinging the dagger wildly at the cats. The felines growled and snarled.

The three stopped again, spreading apart from each other so they wouldn't be a single, easy target for the avian.

Jeneth once again called for his birds to fly down from the trees. A storm of black sailed down from the branches. Bel charged Jeneth, his staff pointed forward. Blue electric light fired from the tip of his branch of magewood as he pointed the tip forward at the archmage, screaming words of the mage language of old. A ball of energy, larger than Bel had ever formed, flew from the end of his staff, smashing into Jeneth's body.

The avian's body solidified, then exploded. The flying debris pelted all of them, Bel, Felix, and Sammra, small shards nicking their flesh. Bel dropped to his knees, shielding his face with his arm. He peeked from behind the bend of his elbow. Two burnt, crystalline legs were all that was left of Jeneth. Bel had destroyed the avian. The birds were gone. "What happened? Did I... kill him?"

Sammra stared at the chunks of black on the ground. "Glass? Sand? One of the illusions of the forest. One of the entrance trials. That wasn't Jeneth. Your energy was so hot it turned the sand into glass." She was suddenly still, her eyes wide. "I've never seen that before. No, never. Never seen that. Amazing."

Felix tilted his head to the side, his eyebrows raised, "The entrance trial was able to trick my cats' noses. Hmmm, interesting." He wrinkled his nose. "Let's find the real one." The cats ran out again in several different directions, searching for Jeneth's scent.

As he waited, Bel kicked over the two glass legs. They fractured when they toppled. "I hate this. Can't he just fight us and finish this?"

Sammra said, "Either he's already escaped or he doesn't have a way out. We've taken too long. He is probably headed back to the camp to force a troll to open the passage out. Maybe we should head back?"

Felix pointed off into the darkness of the forest. "Wait. I see something."

Bel went to Felix. "What? Jeneth? Where?"

Felix shook his head at Bel, holding up an open palm as he focused through his cats' eyes. After a time, he said, "Not Jeneth. Kerlith. My cats are tracking the stonecutter."

"It's something," Bel said to the unasked question. "If we catch him, maybe he can tell us something."

Sammra's blank face twisted as if she was calculating in her head. When she saw the two were staring at her, she said, "Let's go."

They ran.

Kerlith smiled when the three approached as if he were calmly waiting for them to arrive, oblivious to the cougars' growls. "Good. You're here."

"Kerlith, where's Jeneth? Where's the moonstone?" Bel demanded.

Kerlith laughed. "I've been waiting for you. You shouldn't yell like that by the way. It makes you appear completely uncivilized. A wizard is supposed to maintain an air of culture about him. Hasn't Nes'egrinon taught you that by now?"

"Enough stalling. Where's Jeneth?" Bel hissed, taking a step closer.

"Bel, you and I never hit it off." Kerlith smiled wide. "And I blame myself for that. The others called me a jerk —behind my back, of course. No one would dare call me that to my face. I resented them and tried to punish everyone at University, but throughout my travels in the mountains and the desert, I've realized you were all right. I was a jerk."

"Kerlith, we don't have time for your rambling apology. You can talk all you want after you're in jail and we regain the moonstone," Felix explained.

"Jail? I think you misunderstand what's happening here. I don't have the moonstone, nor did I steal it. I didn't kill anyone. I didn't have anything to do with the murders either. Why should I be put in jail? Why should I be punished? I've done no wrong." Kerlith suppressed a chuckle then wiped the smirk off of his face with his hand. "The avians are leaving. I'm becoming one of them. I've found a place among them. An apprentice has the right to leave the trials at any time, does he not? You all attacked me first. I merely defended myself. I did no wrong."

The cougar in front of Kerlith roared.

Kerlith clamped his lips together as if it was all he could do to stop himself from laughing. "I'm no traitor. In fact, I'm an ambassador. Like you, Felix. Making peace between the stonecutters and the avians. I'm building a bridge between two peoples."

"Shut up, liar," Bel snapped.

"Tut tut, such temper." Kerlith smiled. "You can't know how much I'm thoroughly enjoying this." A host of stones raised from the earth behind Kerlith. "I'm so much more powerful now. Rylithnon was right. Merging the two forms, avian and stone, doesn't have an additive effect, it multiplies. I can't image how much power coursed through his body when he united four: stone, sand, tundra and forest. Well, I guess I can. Too much energy. It tore him apart. It killed him."

Bel edged closer. "Enough talk Kerlith. Tell me. Jeneth. Where is he?"

The stones began swirling around the stonecutter. "It's almost time for me to go." Kerlith glanced at Sammra then focused on Bel. "You know Bel, you and your master came when Master Muolithnon called so I guess I owe it to my old master to tell you something, give you a little hint. Although I still advise you to stop following if you want to live. Jeneth is still in the forest somewhere. He needs the trolls to open an exit. He hasn't found one yet. If you're going to catch him, you shouldn't be wasting so much time with me. You should be tracking him down before he forces one of the trolls to lower the troll-spell." With his last words, Kerlith flung his hands forward, sending a barrage of stones forward like a thousand tiny missiles aimed at Bel and Felix. Felix crouched deep, tucking his head into his elbow. Bel ducked. Many of the stones hit them, bruising and cutting. After the stones flew by, the two leaped up and gave chase.

Sammra was already ahead of the two. She screamed back, "You two after Jeneth. I'll catch Kerlith."

The two stopped. Bel was unsure if he should trust Sammra, but recognized Kerlith was the lesser target. "Well?"

Felix mumbled, "Jeneth's somewhere close. His scent is all over this place."

"He must be invisible. Hiding. Perhaps watching us." There were birds around them everywhere, up in the trees, staring down at them silently. It was unnerving.

A force smashed Bel in the back, launching him forward. He landed on his chin, shoveling a mouthful of dirt down his throat. He coughed then spit out muddy, black earth. *Not again,* he thought.

Jeneth appeared not far away. "Observant, you two."

Felix spun, facing the avian. "Jeneth, this ends now."

Jeneth raised one eyebrow. "Does it? I'm only here for you. You must have figured that out by now. I could have escaped long ago. You and your band of misfits are much too slow to catch me, an avian master."

Felix snapped, "Here for me? Why? To kill me? Wasn't it enough that you killed the others? Your own son even."

Jeneth's face froze for a moment, his eyes clouding.

He brushed his hand across his mouth. "Not kill. I didn't come back to kill you. I wanted to give you one last chance to join me." Jeneth held up a hand. "Wait. Don't answer until you've heard me out."

Bel coughed up the rest of the dirt and dragged himself up to his feet.

Jeneth explained, "You are creature-kind. One of us. I've known you all your life, Felix. I knew your mother and father before they became clan-mates. I watched you grow."

"So? What does that have to do with you being a murderer?"

Jeneth smiled. "Those were mostly accidents. In any case, my point is you recognize the truth, Felix. We are superior in every way to mere humans. By rights, we should rule them. The moonstone? Only a means to an end. When I am done with their relic, the stonecutters can have the rock back. I'll give the moonstone to them freely. I only need it for a short time."

Felix sneered, "You're going to use the moonstone to resurrect Zhen, aren't you?"

"Obviously. The roc's eye and the moonstone, the spell requires both, among other things. The eye to create the preternatural bridge. The stone to break open the doorway. So I have read, anyway. Then something else. Heh, heh, heh. Unfortunately, the incantation can be only performed once. When he's resurrected he'll no longer be ghoul-kind, but whole, flesh and blood."

"It's not possible," Bel said as he walked forward, wiping the dirt from his face.

Jeneth bellowed, "How dare you tell me what is and isn't possible! You understand nothing, Lander!"

Bel crinkled his eyes. "I was there. I saw the breach,

the path to the Underworld, opened, in front of my eyes and the dead streaming out. Where was Zhen? He never came out, did he? Even he must recognize it's not possible."

Jeneth smiled. "That fool Rylithnon. We had been influencing him for some time. We needed someone to sacrifice himself, to take the blame if it all went wrong. He was too eager, though. We weren't ready yet. Didn't possess the stone yet. Or the eye. The idiot opened the doorway to the dead too soon. Zhen didn't want to come forth as a walking dead but as a living breathing soul. Next time will be different."

"I appreciate your sales pitch, but I'm not going to help you, Jeneth," Felix said as his cats fell to a crouched position.

"It's your life." Jeneth disappeared and Bel heard him shuffle off. Neither knew what direction he went. Felix pushed his cats to tune their senses as finely as possible, sniffing about, trying to track Jeneth's exact location.

A voice came from somewhere ahead of them. "I think I will give you another chance, Felix. I'm going to test your resolve. Kill Bel for me and I won't kill you."

Bel took a small step away from Felix then began preparing himself for a fight with either of the two.

The forest apprentice moaned and whistled, speaking to the elms and oaks, coaxing the trees to yield energy. Life coursed into him, his body swelling from the pulsating life-force. He pushed some of the power into his staff, the magewood glowing translucent blue.

Bel didn't think Felix would turn on him, but he wanted to be ready if he did. Jeneth, Bel figured, couldn't maintain his invisibility and also attack at the same time. He would need to become visible, even if for a moment, to command the birds. Bel wanted to take advantage of that and strike with lethal force as soon as avian appeared.

Bel asked, "Smell anything?"

Felix placed his finger to his lips, then moved his eyes slightly—only infinitesimally, but enough to signal Bel approximately where Jeneth was hiding. Bel stared forward into the black shadows of the forest, not giving any hint that he knew where Jeneth was standing, hoping Felix was correct, that Jeneth stood off to his side.

Bel quickly slammed his hands toward the left, pulsing out a shockwave of energy. Jeneth appeared just a few feet away from where Bel shot, dove off to the side, then faded. Bel had barely missed him. The forest apprentice smiled wide, upset at the miss, but happy at the near hit.

Felix growled, cocked his head, then growled again. He glanced at Bel, then twisted and contorted. Tension rolled off him, nearly visible in the air. He started to transform. The man fell to his hands and stretched his mouth wide, his teeth elongating as tan fur erupted over his body. He became cat-like, much larger than one of his cougars. Larger than a lion even, he was tremendous, a were-cat.

Bel's mouth hung open at the sight.

Felix took several steps forward and sniffed. He turned his head to the other cats who slowly surrounded a patch of ground.

Bel wasn't sure if he should blast the spot or not.

A cougar leaped in the air at the space and caught, suspended in the air. Jeneth appeared, holding his dagger in front of him, the cougar impaled on the blade.

Felix roared and the other cats leaped. An ocelot

reached Jeneth first, he swung his dagger, cutting the small cat's throat in the air and disappeared again.

Jeneth chuckled. "Why these stupid childhood games, Felix? You know you can't defeat me. Join me."

Bel heard Jeneth's footsteps as he ran. Some leaves kicked up not far away, to the left, so the apprentice began throwing balls of energy in that direction, one after the other, heaving them in rapid succession, hoping for a random lucky shot.

One of the bolts dissipated, washing across the air in an odd way. Bel thought it meant something, perhaps a hit, so he threw a few more, zeroing in on that area. One more hit, creating a peculiar shimmer. Jeneth groaned in pain.

Felix nudged his two dead cats with his nose and roared. He darted at the shimmering spot.

Jeneth appeared, clutching his side. "You'll pay for that, Lander." The avian shook his head at the approaching Felix as if to tell him he was wasting his time. Jeneth dove back, transforming into a large bird. He beat his wings hard, flying high up into the trees.

A flood of birds swooped down from above, their sharp claws pointed at Bel and Felix and the cats.

Bel ran to Felix and stopped next to him as the engulfing swarm descended. Bel erupted a blast of blazing hot life-force energy up into the mass of birds, killing many. The dead birds rained, pelting the ground and the gap immediately filled with more scratching and clawing birds.

Felix swung and leaped, biting with his sharp canines as Bel tried to simultaneously form a shield with his staff hand and blast energy with his other, yet still some were getting through. Bel found himself crouching lower and lower to the earth to try to prevent them from coming in at the sides. They were hitting him everywhere: legs, arms and torso, scratching and tearing at his flesh. He wanted to jump up and run. It was too much. He couldn't stop their beaks and claws.

A crow flitted under his shield, flapping its wings in his face and scratching. He grabbed it and sent hot energy into his hand. The smell of roast bird-flesh permeated the space.

The birds were everywhere, clawing and scratching. No matter what Bel did he couldn't avoid them. The pile of dead birds around him increased and still they came. He sent forth blast after blast of white hot energy and still they came. They clawed his body, trying to reach his face, his eyes.

Bel stood and dropped his shield as an idea came to him. It was something he had never tried, something he had never seen a wizard do before. Would it work? He didn't know, but he had to do something or else they were both going to die.

He drew on the forest and pushed life-force energy into his skin, causing it to become white-hot. As the birds struck him they sizzled and fell away as if they had flown into a volcano. It was working, but Bel hoped that he was not destroying his body in the process.

Birds pummeled into Bel, instantly dying upon contact. He moved, pushing his legs through the rapidly forming pile of birds around him. He walked to Felix to try to provide him some form of cover.

An intense nausea blanketed Bel's belly. A wooziness hit his head. He was cooking his organs. He stepped forward, trying to shake the feeling. Steam rose from his footprints.

The birds finally backed away from Bel and flooded back into the canopy, so Bel released the heat and promptly threw up.

Felix leaped at a tree, digging his claws into the bark, scaling the oak. The ground was covered with thousands upon thousands of dead birds. Felix's cats were all dead except one and that one would probably die soon. Its flesh was shredded. Felix didn't look too good either. His tail had been cut off and his thick fur coat was covered in deep red. His one remaining cat followed him, clawing the trunk and branches, climbing up the trees.

Bel wanted to help catch Jeneth, but he was a bird, a great big, black, ugly bird, nesting in the canopy of the biggest of trees, hundreds of feet up in the air. Bel looked down at his hands, still smoldering, steam rising from his flesh, wondering what he could do, a lander, trapped on the ground. He felt powerless. Felix was going to try to climb up there—a futile effort. All Bel could think to do was talk to the trees, to use them to swat Jeneth back down to the ground where he could get his hands on him. He placed his palms on the trees and moaned and whistled. The trees spoke back, they would help.

Several trees swung their branches, but Jeneth easily avoided the limbs, flapping his wings, taking to the air, then landing in another tree that Bel was not conversing with. Bel went to that tree and finally got the fir to shake Jeneth free, but the huge blackbird only flew to another perch.

Bel knew he needed to do something different, something he had never attempted before, something he didn't know was even possible, something that was probably going to either kill him or change him forever. "Okay, here goes," Bel said as he walked over to the biggest oak in the space and wrapped his arms around the trunk, giving himself to the tree, attempting to fully connect. Communicating was one thing, but connecting —Bel was not only unsure if he could do it, he didn't know if he should. He had pondered connecting his mind with that of the trees before but had been afraid of the consequences. No forest mage had done it and survived long after—at least that is what Nes'egrinon had said. Two minds connecting didn't only create a mental conduit for information exchange but a merger of sorts. Shireen and Bel had connected often, so much, in fact, they had each exchanged a part of themselves in the process. They had become one.

It was why the creature-kind acted so animal-like, Bel figured. They spent too many hours in the animals' heads and the connection had changed them.

Bel was well aware that what he was about to do was unheard of. Maybe even heresy. *What will happen to me if I merge with a tree?* He was fearful of what such a union would do to him. He didn't want to become part tree, that was for sure. But something had to be done, he needed to find out what the trees saw, to be able to attack Jeneth using the forest as a weapon. So he grabbed the trunk and merged his mind with the oak in an unholy union, despite all his misgivings. He opened himself up to the tree and reached out with his life-force, forming a connection.

Bel's mind screamed as a flash of intense white blanketed across his visage. It wasn't painful, but as if his thoughts had seized, frozen in time. Some moments passed—Bel didn't know how many—before his mind kick-started itself. All of a sudden a wave of thoughts invaded Bel's mind, flooding in, coursing in and out of his head as if they belonged there, trampling, a barrage of concepts and ideas rapidly poking through and stamping down his own tiny piece of consciousness. *Doesn't... make... sense... How could one tree... so many thoughts?* Yet his mind was flooded with hundreds of distinct voices. *Confuse...* His head spinning, Bel thought to break the connection.

Something ran through his mind, a picture of himself before he climbed the magewood tree to retrieve his new staff. His master had said all the trees were connected, that their roots ran deep and they constantly spoke to each other. Bel realized, in connecting with this one tree, he had connected with all of them. He was hearing the jumble of thoughts of hundreds, if not thousands, of trees. He had merged with the forest.

Bel yelled at them, —*Quiet!*—

The trees quieted for a few moments and then Bel heard a ramble of voices slowly pick back up and roll into a thunder.

—*Hey! Listen! I have an emergency*— Bel argued over the din.

They ignored him this time.

Bel didn't have time to persuade the trees properly. He yelled again, —*If you don't listen, an evil man is going to come and chop you all down. I'm trying to help*—

That got their attention. Bel pointed out the largest flying bird. —*Him. That bird. He will cut you all down*—

Bel pointed at the cats. —*Friends. Help them*—

Bel's mind was in the trees, surveying the scene from several different angles at once. Branches bent and swung, trying to tag the bird while flinging the cats higher and toward the avian.

Jeneth tried to fly higher but hit some type of barrier

in the sky. He dove back down toward the trees.

A branch flung Felix in the air and he clawed at Jeneth, who easily avoided him. Another tree caught the were-cat.

Branch after branch in a variety of different trees swung at Jeneth. The trunks shook, leaves shuddered, attacking the other birds, shaking them from the trees. Blackbirds, crows and the like fell from the sky, raining down on the ground all around Bel, each bird impaled with tiny twigs through wing and breast.

Jeneth swooped down towards Felix, extending his talons for a strike, when a branch smashed into him, clipping his wing. The bird spiraled out of control, flapping desperately, bouncing off branches on the way down and crashing into the earth below.

Bel released the oak, his head thumping, pulsing as if the water was still coursing up through his feet, like roots, and up through his trunk and out his leaves. He looked down at his hands for a moment, not understanding what they were or where his leaves had gone. "Flesh," he muttered then pushed energy into his hands, stumbling toward the immense blackbird as it transformed back into a wounded human, Jeneth.

Bel tripped, his toes catching on not root or branch but the soft earth. The connection had taken more out of the apprentice than he had realized. He felt light headed and weak. Still, he needed to stop the avian. He was right there!

Jeneth grabbed his broken left arm and held it up, tucking it into his side. His face was racked with pain.

Bel pointed his two glowing hands forward. "Give up Jeneth. Give me the moonstone." His voice betrayed his condition, raspy and weak.

Jeneth sneered as Felix and his cat leaped down out of the trees. The avian opened his mouth and screeched loud and long. The sound was deafening. Felix's cat ran in a circle, trying to avoid the noise then sprinted away. Bel slapped his hands over his ears, hoping his eardrums weren't already ruptured. He fell to his knees.

The forest apprentice struggled, waiting for Jeneth's audible attack to end, but it didn't. The ear-shattering wail went on and on. Bel realized he would need to do something now or not at all. The piercing scream gave him vertigo; he fell to the ground and rolled. He couldn't last much longer.

Bel had to do something. He couldn't lay there. He either had to run or fight. *Do something,* he told himself. Bel suffered through the pain, pulling one hand from his ear and sending a blast of energy at Jeneth. The strike hit him squarely in the chest, knocking the wind from his lungs.

Jeneth choked out a few words as he clutched his chest, "You can't defeat me. I'm avian." The crooked little man hopped up and ran, his damaged arm tucked tightly to his chest.

Bel darted after. As the avian ran, blackbirds descended on Jeneth, surrounding him in a cloud. Bel ran into the flurry of crows smashing through the pile of flapping wings, swinging his energy-filled staff, trying to locate the archmage. After a time, the birds dispersed and Jeneth was gone.

Bel scanned the sky. The largest mass of birds was flying off to the left.

Felix, still in cat form, walked up and purred loudly. He was covered in scratches and blood.

Bel looked down at the were-cat and pointed, "Looks

like he flew off that way."

Felix growled then nodded his head.

"Thanks for not trying to kill me by the way." Bel shrugged his shoulders.

The two jogged in the direction the birds had taken. Up ahead were Kerlith and Sammra. They were speaking to a troll and walking out an opening. The exit path was open. The trolls had removed the troll-spell! Sammra had lied again. She was leaving with Kerlith. *Whose side was she really on?*

The trees reformed in front of the opening and the troll began stepping away.

As Felix transformed, he yelled, his voice contorting with his body, "Hold, Budzig—aaargh—who authorized you—graaa—to—mnnnpf—open the forest—uhh—uhh—take down the troll-spell?"

Budzig spoke in an unknown tongue. His voice was deep and grating.

Felix said, "Sammra? But I told you—" He growled. "Open the exit for me!"

Budzig slapped his hands together at the space, slowly parted them and stepped to the side. The trees shrunk away, forming a path to the outside world.

Bel and Felix walked out of the forest and looked down the path to the left and right. Sammra and Kerlith were nowhere to be found.

Felix pointed, "You go this way; I'll go that. Yell if you see something."

Bel walked down the path towards the shack where he and Shireen had left their horses, the path towards Sha'mont. He jogged around the bend and the dirt lane widened. The roadway was clear all the way to the horse pen and some distance past. He saw nothing and no one.

Something didn't seem right.

Bel whirled when he heard a scream. He ran back towards the entrance. Sammra, Jeneth, and Kerlith were mounting three tremendous birds.

"They're out!" Bel said as he ran.

Felix was running in from the other side, bounding toward the three.

The birds took to the air and were quickly off.

Bel blasted energy balls at the birds, but his efforts were futile. They were already too high in the sky. They had escaped.

Another blackbird flew out of the forest entrance and took to the air. *Ayah,* Bel figured. He couldn't bring himself to shoot at his bunkmate for he still hoped he wasn't lying too.

The large birds flew into the horizon. Ayah crashed into the bird carrying Jeneth. Jeneth's bird banked, his talons digging into Ayah's wing. A smattering of feathers fell from the sky then Ayah tumbled and fell.

He was too high in the air, falling too fast, there was nothing Bel could do. Ayah partially transformed back into his human form. Bel reached his hand out toward him futilely. The forest apprentice gasped as he realized the semiconscious boy would die on impact. A few moments later he heard a loud thud. Jeneth and the others were specks in the distance. Ayah was dead.

Bel stepped slowly closer to Felix, defeated, dejected, not understanding what had just happened.

"The entrance trials. The Kerlith and Sammra we saw, that was an illusion. The trial tries to trick you into quitting. When it deciphered we would leave the forest —quitting the trials, in effect—if we could follow them out, the trial showed us that, tricked us. We, ahh, I opened the gate for them." The furrows on Felix's forehead were deep. "I'm such a fool."

Bel and Felix walked back into the forest silently. There were no words either of them could say, nothing comforting, no words that healed, nothing. They were both too full of anguish and frustration to do anything but shuffle their feet forward and try to not think. They made their way to the spot where they had left Pren, Shireen, and Lithia.

Shireen asked what happened but neither spoke in reply. Bel opened his mouth, attempting to explain, but no words came. He shook his head, bent over, scooped up Leonna, slung her burnt body over his shoulder and started for the camp.

Chapter Twenty-Five
Convocation

Shireen, Bel, and the others walked back into the camp, dejected. Felix carried Naga in his arms and Bel had Leonna's body slung over his shoulder. Shireen carried Jonah, while Lithia used Shireen's shoulder as a crutch.

Felix called to the first troll he saw. "Felicia? Is she locked up? Her animals too? No one leaves. Understand?"

The troll nodded and left to check on Felix's little sister.

A stonecutter came forward. "Felix, we gathered almost all the animals. There are two left out there somewhere."

"And everyone else?" Shireen asked, surveying the courtyard, deserted except for a few apprentices over near the benches.

"The clinic," he said. "Between the trials and capturing the animals, almost everyone was injured."

Felix motioned. "Let's go there. I need to speak with everyone."

The group walked down the long path to the clinic. When they arrived, they propped the bodies of the three dead in a corner as there was no space left anywhere else.

Felix called out, "Can I have everyone's attention? I wanted to thank you all for your hard work in gathering the animals and also in attempting to capture the thieves and return the moonstone. Unfortunately, four people died out there: Naga, Jonah, Ayah, and Leonna."

A few of them gasped while another whispered, "Oh no."

"Those who stole the moonstone escaped. I will soon be calling a convocation to find out what will be the next course of action. It goes without saying the trials will not continue. Now, I only ask everyone to rest, recuperate, and regain your strength. Once you are able, please return to your masters."

Felix turned to Budzig. "Please take down the troll-spell on the forest."

Shireen touched Felix's arm. "Your wounds. You need to be attended to."

Felix stroked a patch of scratched skin as if he could wipe the cuts away. "Later." He went to Jergamemnon's bed at the end of the hall. Bel, Pren, Lithia, and Shireen followed.

Many of the others began discussing what they would do. Several picked up their things to leave.

After Felix filled Jergamemnon in on the details of what had happened in the forest, the archmage struggled to rise from his bed. They went to a small patch of woods behind the clinic.

Bel began combing the dirt in a circle.

Shireen asked, "Bel, what are you doing?"

"Setting up for a convocation."

Jergamemnon nodded.

Shireen helped Bel, then they all stepped into the circle and waited until Bel cast the protection spell.

Jergamemnon began slowly waving his arms, the air clouded then cleared as faces appeared in the volume of air space.

Shireen's master, Meetta, appeared and with her was Nes'egrinon, who seemed much better although he was still stooped over a bit. Shireen nudged Bel and pointed.

He smiled lightly. "At least, he's not wearing a pink dress," Bel mumbled.

Shireen smiled at that.

Jergamemnon said, "I, Jergamemnon, archmage of Lasaat, call this convocation to order to speak of recent events and form a plan of action."

The others spoke their names one at a time.

"Meetta Eglin and Nes'egrinon are here at Sha'mont," Meetta said.

"Jessark from the land of ice and snow," the man in white-gray felt bellowed.

The others introduced themselves: Sturfelis, a feline-mage stationed at Lasaat, Sperlith, a stone mage from the western stonecutters, Burnd, a stonecutter from the east, and finally, Ali'samm from Ragul, a sand-mage of the Sanhardin.

Balls of sand slowly orbited the sand-mage. "Are we starting? Without Jeneth?"

"Jeneth, I think, will not be making the convocation. You'll find out why in a moment," Jergamemnon said.

"What have you discovered?" Sturfelis asked.

Jergamemnon motioned to Felix, who said, "Many died and a few were murdered here at the Worthy Apprentice Trials. Onyx, Drake, Aquilo, Jinx, Isha, Jonah, Leonna, Naga and Ayah. Seven apprentices, all dead. And in the end, the moonstone was stolen."

"What?" Sperlith said, pushing up to her feet. "The

jewel of my people. Stolen? Who?"

Burnd appeared agitated. "Yes. Who did this?"

Felix looked at Sturfelis and Jergamemnon who nodded for him to go on.

Felix's voice became gravely. "A plot led by Master Jeneth."

Sturfelis hissed, "Jeneth!"

Sperlith threw her hands up. "Avians!"

Burnd mumbled, "I've never trusted the creature-kind... ehh... avians... ahh... except for a few. Sturfelis, you're not like the others. But still, none of you would ever listen to me. Now look what has happened."

Sperlith shot back, "I listened. I never trusted them and I'm not afraid to say it. Sturfelis, you're a good one, but the rest, no, I don't trust any of the creature-kind."

Ali'samm purred, "My lovelies, please do not jump off a cliff. Let us hear the tale before we leap to accusations."

"Felix, what exactly happened?" Sturfelis said.

Felix said, "Everything is not simple and clear. It wasn't solely an avian plot. That's not exactly what happened. Jeneth persuaded a group of apprentices to steal the moonstone—yes, that is at the core. Several apprentices worked together, orchestrating a distraction by releasing animals, some magical, during one of the trials and stealing the moonstone."

Sperlith snarled, "And you, a feline, running the trials, they did this right under your nose? Or were you in on it too? Covering up their tracks?"

"Hold," Sturfelis roared.

Jergamemnon waved his hands. "This is not the place for bald racism. Besides, you are all archmages; you know he speaks truth. Read him yourselves. And if need be, we'll have Felix scanned by the seers. Let him speak. These other apprentices are here to vouchsafe his words."

Bel, Shireen, Lithia, and Pren each nodded.

Felix continued, "Jeneth organized the plot, but those assisting were not all avians. A Sanhardin worthy named Sammra aided the thieves."

Ali'samm allowed the spinning ball of sand above his hand to fall. "That. Now that. Hmm, hard to believe." He lifted a single eyebrow.

Felix nodded. "She was a friend. A close friend. I find it difficult also. I think I have a clue to her motivation, but I would be speculating."

Jergamemnon interrupted, "Let's keep to the facts for now."

Felix continued, "So besides Sammra, there were three avians, Jonah, a small cub, ahh, nestling, and Leonna, and Ayah, both fledglings. All three died during their escape."

Burnd asked, "So none of the avians were captured?"

"No," Felix said. "And also, helping them were two, ahem, felines, Jinx and Felicia."

Sturfelis rubbed the back of his neck and turned his face away.

"Jinx was murdered, either by Jeneth or Sammra, I think, and Felicia has been captured."

Jergamemnon reiterated, "Felix, remember. No speculation."

Sperlith said, "So all the creature-kind apprentices were either caught or died and Jeneth has the moonstone?" She sounded optimistic.

Felix answered, "Sammra escaped with him and there was one other who was working with the thieves. A stonecutter named Kerlith."

Burnd groaned as he tugged his beard. "Kerlith? He came to me wanting to be a second. I wished I could help him. I sent him south. Him? He betrayed his own people? He was troubled, but this? A stonecutter helping the avians to steal the most precious stone of all? Hard to believe."

Lithia stepped forward. "Felix speaks truth."

Bel added, "I fought Kerlith in the forest as he was trying to escape with the moonstone. He told me that had he found a master among his people, he wouldn't have turned to Jeneth."

"But it is our law, our way," Burnd mumbled. "An apprentice must learn from a master. I thought he could have found... someone. Someone should have taken him on." Burnd's voice trailed off. "No one among the stonecutters to take the boy... hard to believe."

Bel added, "Jeneth was teaching Kerlith avian magic."

"Forbidden," Sperlith said as she slapped her open palm down of the stone table in front of her.

Jergamemnon waited for the others to calm and said, "Now we must determine a course of action."

Meetta jumped in. "The moonstone and the roc's eye. You all, I assume, realize what this means?"

Sturfelis answered, "Tell us, for I do not perceive the connection."

Meetta said, "When the roc's eye was taken, I was worried solely because it is powerful. An eye can be used to see great distances. Perhaps into the past. Maybe even the future. I didn't like the idea of them having it and not knowing what they planned on using it for. Nes'egrinon spurred me on to find if there were other uses of such an element. We've been spending much time in the histories and books of old. We found something odd in one history. A story that speaks of a stone and an eye being used to resurrect the dead. If this is true, perhaps they want to use the moonstone to resurrect Zhen."

Several of them gasped.

Nes'egrinon cleared his throat and waited for everyone to acknowledge him. "The last thing you all need from me is a smug 'I told you so.' And smug it would be, because tell-you-so I most certainly did. And due to all your petty prattling, no one listened. But I'm not going to flaunt that in your faces now, even though I should, because what we need to do is come up with a plan of action to stop them."

Jergamemnon nodded his agreement. "Sturfelis, in my opinion, your clan may be in danger if you and Felix are to stand up to the avians. Consider moving them to the Greenlands."

Meetta added, "With King Fayn, I have sway. We can house your clan somewhere here, at Sha'mont."

"Thank you for the offer. But members of my clan started this problem. We will not run from it. We will be on the knife's edge of stopping Jeneth. If it means the destruction of my clan, then so be it."

The others grew quiet.

"How many avians are there?" Shireen asked, then wished she hadn't spoken. She was only an apprentice and knew she should keep silent.

Felix said, in a daze, "Many. There are more avians than all the other creature-kind combined. Yet not all in one place. They nest upon the various mountain tops throughout the southern lands."

Meetta asked, "Sturfelis, do you think the canines or any of the others would assist you?"

He snorted, "Our mortal enemies? The dogs? Not likely. The reptiles and the spiders do not follow our ways. They would not aid us unless there was some benefit in it for them. And Zhen's resurrection? It would be hard to convince them that would be bad. Not until it was too late."

Nes'egrinon spoke again. "Sounds as if a group of you felines will try to stop the avians. But alone? Unwise, but it is your choice. For my part, I would like to take a band to the eastern stone lands, to where Rylithnon tried to perform the spell, in the Valley Of The Dead. That is where the avians will go, eventually, when they are prepared, when they try to resurrect Zhen. We will be there waiting for them. A last stand if Sturfelis and his clan fail."

Sturfelis said, "Taking them head-on is most certainly a suicide mission. That we will not do. And someone needs to rally the other feline clans and try to speak to the canines and spiders, at least. My people will do this. If we come across the avians and it appears that we can take a group of them, then we will. We cannot leave all the creature-kind to be gathered by the avians. We need to try to persuade them to our cause."

Jergamemnon nodded. "Yes. Good. And Nes'egrinon was there when Rylithnon created the tear into the Underworld. He is aware of its location. Are there others who would like to aid in either of these tasks?"

Ali'samm said, "For Sammra, I will go. Perhaps I can knock some sense into her head."

Sperlith spoke next, "Lithia, meet me at Sha'mont. I will come. I will also persuade some of the others. The avians will rue the day they thought to steal from the western stonecutters."

Jergamemnon said, "I, myself, would like to go with Sturfelis. The felines cannot speak to the canines, but perhaps they will hear me."

The others made some final comments and the convocation ended. Bel used his foot to spread the sand out from the circle and the group went back to the center courtyard.

Lithia went to the trolls to be covered in troll-salve then got in one of the beds.

Bel and Felix let the trolls attend to their wounds.

After a time of waiting and milling about Bel said to Shireen, "I'm going for a bite to eat. Want something?"

Shireen shook her head. She couldn't stop thinking about how everything had gone so bad so quickly. And all right in front of them. Maybe had they done things differently, perhaps none of this would have happened.

Felix hopped up. "Bel, I'll join you."

The two walked out next to each other.

Shireen frowned at the backs of the two men walking away. Something was odd about the way Felix was so eager to join Bel. She decided to follow them, to find out what Felix had to say to Bel. She waited until they were out of sight, walking past a group of buildings, then stood and sneaked after.

Shireen walked around the side of the hut, then stopped abruptly when she heard Felix's voice. She edged herself against the wall and listened. Bel and Felix were discussing something. She watched them from the corner. Thankfully she was downwind so he wouldn't be able to pick up her scent.

Felix's eyes bore into Bel then he leaned back and relaxed. "What claim do you have on her?"

"Claim? None. She's free to choose the life she'll lead.

I'm done pressuring her. Perhaps she'll choose you. I understand your offer and it makes sense. She could remain a magician and still marry. Have children." Bel grew pensive, staring down at the ground for a time. "It was what I wanted. With her."

"You love her and so do I. We've fought side by side and now, in this, we're adversaries." Felix's voice was an even monotone.

"You say you love her and I understand what you're experiencing, but I think I feel something different," Bel spoke slowly as if he were only now coming to a realization about his emotions.

The feline snapped his head up.

Bel continued, "At first, that's what I felt. Love. No, that's not true. At first, my heart burned, attraction. Physical. I don't need to tell you how beautiful she is. And, as I watched her, spent time with her, I saw more than her features. The way she spoke, the way she tilted her head to the side, slightly, delicately, playfully, when she was trying to get me to see things her way. She's so… cute."

"That she is."

"And if that's all she was, I think I could let her go, but she's got her hooks into me and they're dug in deep. Maybe she didn't do it on purpose, but she's changed me. I have no idea when or how it happened."

"You fell in love."

Bel popped up. "No!"

Shireen was shocked by the loudness of his voice. She hoped no one would come to see and catch her spying.

Bel shook his head at his own outburst. "It's so much more than that. I trust her."

"Trust? So do I." Felix seemed puzzled.

Bel mumbled, "I trust her with my life."

"As do I, My Adversary." Felix chuckled. "If she chose to fight at my side this morning instead of running after Lithia, I would've certainly trusted her to cover my back."

Bel's mouth hung open. "That's not the kind of trust I was speaking about." He blew his air out long and slow. "I'm going to explain this to you. I'm going to tell you how I feel only for this reason: I want you to think about this and check your own heart. There's a slim but distinct possibility she'll choose you. The idea pains me, but I need to be realistic and truthful with myself. It could happen. Losing Shireen would tear me apart, but not thinking about the possibility is not going to stop it from happening."

Bel stared deep into Felix's eyes, then away at the ground. "So if she chooses you... I, you know, want her to be happy. I want you to be, you know, the best man for her. So I'm going to tell you this thing because I want you to understand how I feel about her. If she chooses you I think, you know, that you should feel the same way too."

"What are you getting at? I've already told you I love her. I told you I trust her too. I personally think love is more important. I mean, I trust the members of my clan with my life, most of them anyway, but that doesn't mean I want to marry them."

Shireen shifted on her feet nervously. She was eager to hear what Bel was about to say.

"That's where you're wrong, Felix. Like I said, first came the attraction, then love. That's good. Love is important and necessary, but I've seen too many people in the villages who were married for love and after the years went by, they became miserable with each other. But it didn't happen to all them. There was something more. I didn't understand until now. It's trust."

Bel sat down on the edge of a log as he mused, "I trust Shireen enough to give my life to her. It's not about trusting her to protect my back in a battle, as you said. Even though I trust her that way too. No, the trust I'm talking about is much larger than that. I'm talking about trusting her with my life."

Felix appeared perplexed. "If you trust her to guard your back, you are trusting her with your life."

"You're not understanding. It's so much bigger than that," Bel muttered. "I'm willing to give her my entire life. Time, don't you see?"

Bel squinted his eyes up at Felix. To Shireen, it was clear Felix had no idea what he was talking about. Bel tried again. "In the cities and villages, people work at their jobs to make money. Currency. They take that money and they buy what they need: food, clothing, entertainment, whatever. But if we break it down, what they are doing is selling time in exchange for physical things. They're selling moments of their life, trading the irreplaceable moments of their life for food and clothing. It's the most ridiculous trade because, you know, you can't add a moment of time to your life, no matter how much money you have."

Felix nodded, his forehead displaying deep furrows.

Bel continued, "This is what I was talking about. My life. It's hers. If she'll have it. Every moment, I'll give them to her and I trust her to, you know, not throw my life away. It's all I truly own and it's hers if she'll take it."

Shireen's stomach twisted inside her as she choked back a whimper. She forced herself to not go to him. Her body was trembling.

Bel turned away. "Of course, perhaps she'll choose you and that's her choice. All I'm saying is if she does that, she would be trusting you like, you know, like I just said I would do for her and she would be, you know, giving her life to you, trusting you with it." Bel paused for some moments. "All I'm saying is if she does that, if Shireen trusts you and gives you her life and you hurt her, betray her in any way, I'll hunt you down and kill you."

Felix smiled and nodded. "I should say the same thing to you."

"So we understand each other."

Shireen heard someone coming towards her so she spun. Pren was approaching. She ran towards her and grabbed her hand and pulled her away.

"Why are you crying?" Pren asked.

Shireen wiped her wet cheeks. "It's nothing. Just all that's happened. That's all."

"Are you all right?"

"I'm fine. I'll be fine." Shireen quickly shuffled them back to the center courtyard.

She went to the benches and sat with Pren and Lithia. "I'm going to miss you two," she said, trying to sound like she hadn't just had he mind blown.

Lithia tilted her bandaged head to the side. "Miss me? I'm going with you. I'm going to Sha'mont. I'm getting that stone back."

Shireen nodded slowly, pensively.

Pren said, "Me too."

Lithia coughed hard then spat a patch of blood. "Master Sperlith is coming. The avians are going to regret this."

Shireen shook her head. "War." The bile rose in her throat. She read the histories, she understood how things started. One single event triggered a continuous series of escalations, neither side backing down, and eventually, war. She saw the endless raging scythe of death swinging so clearly as if the sickle had already taken so many lives and there was nothing to stop it.

"What's wrong, Shireen? I thought you would be happy we're staying together," Pren asked, frowning.

"No, it's not that. I'm glad you're coming to my home."

Several trolls stepped out of the forest and into the courtyard followed by Sturfelis who had only just come from Lasaat.

Felix and Bel rounded the corner from the opposite side of the camp and Felix jogged up to the feline archmage. "Clan-father, welcome." Felix bowed.

"Where is she?"

"Felicia's in a holding cell." Felix nodded at Budzig who went to retrieve her.

Sturfelis and Felix stood next to each other, silently waiting for the trolls to return with the prisoner.

Felix seemed beaten. Shireen remembered the look. It was on the faces of the people of Sha'mont in the days after the dragon attack as they shifted through the rubble, searching for lost and dead loved-ones, the grimace of pain, the scowl of defeat and despair. Sturfelis, on the other hand, was seething, there was no hiding the rage on his face.

Shireen was amazed there was no conversation between the two after all that had happened. Shireen was tempted to try to read them but didn't. Sturfelis, an archmage, would surely recognize it was her and she didn't want to anger him more. He appeared as if he could rip someone's head off.

Budzig and another troll returned with Felicia, bound with many ropes cinching her arms tight behind her back. They marched her to Sturfelis who focused down on her intently. He spoke only one word, "Explain."

"Clan-father, I… It wasn't my idea. The avians… The landers." She shook her head. "No one was supposed to be hurt." Felicia snapped her head down immediately, tears pouring from her eyes. "Jinx's dead. He didn't want to join the avians. I pushed him. He only agreed because he thought he would impress Leonna. Now he's dead. It's all my fault."

Sturfelis gulped then paced in front of her for a time. He paused and opened his mouth as if he were about to say something then stopped himself. Finally, he stopped shaking his head and pacing about. "Clan-daughter, you've ruined my life's work." He glanced at Felix. "Felicia, you will be punished, as is the rule of the clan, but, for now, there is no time. We must go to Lasaat, Felix and I need to speak with the others. If they will join us, it will be a boon. If not, we go alone."

Felicia cried, "No! We can't!"

Sturfelis ignored her outburst. "We need to track Jeneth, follow his scent. To stop him. Perhaps we can minimize the damage you've done."

"Fight the avians?" Felicia moaned loudly. "On Bald Mountain? Where they are so strong? So many? Our clan will be wiped out!"

Sturfelis exhaled and nodded. "Perhaps. But you have set us on this path. What choice do we have?"

Felicia's eyes begged. Sturfelis stared back at her as if the future was set. She swung her eyes to Felix and back, muttering, "No. We can hide. Wait it out. What will happen? Who can know? But the clan can survive."

"No!" Sturfelis roared.

Shireen snapped back on her seat for the sound that emitted from Sturfelis throat was much louder than any human should have been able to make. It was the roar of a lion and she was certain such a sound might be even heard in Sha'mont.

Felix touched Felicia's shoulder. "It is decided. Now, on our way to Lasaat, you must determine what you will do. You may yet receive a chance to redeem yourself."

Felicia began to speak, but Felix pressed his fingers against her lips. "Not now, Little Sister."

=————————=

The camp emptied as most of the injured apprentices and those who were not joining the fight exited back to their lands.

Shireen waited in the center courtyard for Pren and Lithia to gather their items. Jergamemnon and Sturfelis were loosely planning out what they would do. They didn't sound optimistic.

Bel came out from his room with his sack and his staff and joined the group waiting.

Shireen gushed. She loved him, every part of him, his eyes with their slight tint of avian blue, his kissable dimples, his light brown curly locks. But it was more than that, she trusted him. Bel was right, it meant so much more than love. Trust, it bound them.

Shireen walked up to Bel and whispered, "Wait here." She then turned and walked up to Felix and interrupted the conversation he was having with Sturfelis.

When Felix looked at Shireen, she said, "I'm sorry, Felix. We can only be friends. Nothing more." Before he could reply, she spun and returned to Bel. Shireen grabbed Bel's two hands, facing him, and pulled him closer.

"Shireen, what are you doing?" Bel twitched as his eyes popped from Jergamemnon to Sturfelis to the others then back down at her.

Shireen smiled and kissed him long and deep.

"See here," Jergamemnon bellowed.

At first, Bel fought against her lips, his eyes opened wide, but she refused to let him go, holding him tightly. Finally, he relented, slowly closing his eyes and wrapping his thick arms around her.

"See here!" Jergamemnon yelled again.

Shireen heard the archmage's feet scuffling towards them, but she refused to release Bel. She didn't care anymore. Let them do as they will. They were all going to die. Maybe the world would end. In a way, it already had. The world she loved was gone.

As she kissed him, their lips pressed together, the flesh of their bodies molding to each other, something happened, something deep, Shireen felt. She had pulled back from it in fear every other time she sensed it coming, but this time she embraced the change—and she certainly knew whatever it was would change her—falling headlong into the budding feeling, letting it drag her wherever it may lead.

Flashes of orange and red and blue and green washed over her. Still she held him, pressing herself forward, feeling as though they were melding, joining, becoming one. She could no longer sense where her flesh ended and his began. Tendrils of her life force spread wide, allowing him to enter and he, likewise, invited her in. They intertwined, their spirits, souls, and even their bodies, uniting in a bond that felt so good, so right, so perfect to Shireen.

Then, she twinged, pausing, questioning whether she should go farther for they were deeper they they had ever been before. Far deeper. Flesh—nothing, the union was much more than that now. Where did her spirit end? Where did his begin? Once she was green and he was blue. Now the coloring of their life-forces had merged, blended, forming something new and different and mixed. Hybrid. She marveled at the taste of his soul.

Like a rabbit, her heart thump-thump-thumped in her chest, so quick, so fast. His was much slower. Gradually his pulse sped as hers unconsciously slowed, the two falling into rhythm. She gasped as the beats synced. It was just happening, mindlessly, out of either of their control, as if it was meant to be. She felt each squish of blood pummeling through his veins, pulsing after each heartbeat. All of a sudden, she felt herself racing with the red fluid, as if it was her own blood feeding his cells life-giving oxygen. She sensed his presence, there, in her head, with her, and gushed, for she knew that all she felt about him, he felt about her.

And she was no longer afraid.

Finally, Shireen pulled away from Bel and smiled. "I'm tired of hiding."

"Me too," Bel said.

The two turned their heads to the archmage, refusing to release their embrace.

"What is the meaning of this? You'll be excommunicated," Jergamemnon said.

Bel said, "We love each other. And we're both willing to go with you to fight, if you want us. But we'll not live a lie because you say our love is wrong. It's not. It's not wrong."

Shireen added, "We'll fight by your side. I think you need us. But if you don't and you want to excommunicate us now, say the word." Shireen's heart shuddered for she couldn't believe she was speaking such words.

Pacing, Jergamemnon said, "Your love? Wrong? You know nothing. Do you understand why there is a ban on marriage? Why a wizard must remain celibate?"

Be answered, "So a wizard can focus on the greater good. So they won't be distracted."

The archmage shook his head. "That's a good reason but not the important one." The wizard paced. "It's not well communicated. At Lasaat we tell the apprentices that it is against the rules and for most that is good enough. They understand the penalty of excommunication so they obey. For others, the ones having a difficult time we speak of the greater good—"

Shireen frowned. "But that's not the real reason?"

Jergamemnon shuddered, "It is. In a way. A wizard with a non-wizard, one who has no ability to merge, that is the reason. Distractions cost lives. But for two wizards?"

"Wait. What are you saying?" Shireen released Bel and stepped toward the old man.

"When two wizards give themselves to each other, they connect. They become one. They merge. Once that union has occurred it can never be undone. And under such a bond, the two are forever joined as one."

Shireen smiled. "A good thing."

Bel nodded in agreement.

Jergamemnon spoke as if ice were in his veins. "Forever connected? No, it is not good at all. It is thought that if one of you dies, the other will also. You will feel each other's pain in battle. It is the ultimate weakness. Bel, if you fight and lose, Shireen might fall over dead at your last dying breath. You will be one spirit. Don't you see? The body cannot live without the spirit. You will be one. A great liability."

Holding hands, Bel and Shireen stared back at him blankly for both understood that it was too late.

Jergamemnon shook his head, flaring his nostrils slightly. "This is why it is forbidden. It makes us too weak."

"But there must be some benefit?" Bel's voice was shallow and lowly, like that of a small animal dying.

Jergamemnon said, "No, you cannot marry. You cannot merge."

Everyone in the courtyard stared.

The old wizard held up one arm and stopped as if he were considering his words. "I can use every wizard or apprentice I can lay my hands on, for the avians are many. If we live through this coming battle and you still wish to flaunt your relationship you will be excommunicated. If the council even still exists." He shook his head again and walked back to Sturfelis.

Lithia and Pren ran up. They had been holding back by some distance, waiting to discover what Jergamemnon would say.

"Insane," Pren uttered, hugging both Bel and Shireen and kissing both of their cheeks. "Congratulations. Blessings. Blessings. Blessings upon you."

Shireen giggled. "Pren we're not married."

"Yet," Bel added.

Lithia hugged Bel and Shireen. She still marveled at how Lithia could be so strong after all her injuries, she felt as though she was being squeezed by a bear.

"If they allow you to marry, it will be the first ever."

"If we live." Shireen's smile drained from her face as she explained, "Our worlds are all ending. All of ours. I'm tired of all the lies. I love Bel. We are one."

"One?" Pren asked.

"We have already merged," Bel said.

Lithia and Pren looked mystified.

Jergamemnon broke off his conversation with Sturfelis and stepped back. "Did I hear you correctly? Did you just say you have already become one?"

Shireen and Bel nodded.

"It cannot be undone. It is too late for you two. Your lives are intertwined. Whether you desire it or no, you will feel each other's pain. I suppose you two will yet prove or disprove the theory, if you will die together." He shook his head as if it were a great loss and walked away.

Shireen shuddered, not willing to let herself believe it. "We merged. We are one." She leaned over and touched his hand. His heartbeat reverberated through her and hers quickly jumped in sync. She saw through his eyes; their senses could so easily link.

A thought leaped into her head. *What is the purpose of marriage for us? We are already more thoroughly joined in a permanent union than any court document could provide.* Her heart suddenly raced.

He looked down at her. "Calm down."

"You can feel—"

Bel smiled. "Your heart beat is in my chest. I can feel you."

Shireen thought what Jergamemnon said was wrong. There had to be some advantage to wizards merging.

Sturfelis addressed the small group, "If that is everyone, let us go. Time is of the essence."

The band headed down the path and shortly after, exited the forest, all them waving to the trolls as they left.

After a short time, the path split and Jergamemnon, Sturfelis, Felix, and Felicia took the southern route, heading to Lasaat while Shireen, Bel, Lithia, and Pren went west, on the path to Sha'mont, both parties intent on stopping the Jeneth and the avians.

Reviews Please!

If you have enjoyed this book, please be so kind as to provide a review of it on both **goodreads** and the online shopping site you most frequent.

This will serve the dual purpose of letting me know what you thought of it, which will influence my future writing, and also help expose the book to other potential readers. Thank you so much.

Follow Me For Deals!

I occasionally put my books on sale or discount. If you would like to keep track of my writing and when new books are coming out, when they're on sale and other such things, please **follow or friend me on goodreads.** Additionally, join my mailing list from my website at www.jamescardona.com.

Feedback!

I love to hear from my readers! You can message me on goodreads or contact me via my website: jamescardona.com.

Coming Soon
Into Darkness

ISBN-13: 978-1-943696-03-1

Two bands of wizards journey to stop the avian plot to raise Zhen and unite a savage creature-kind army in the next chapter in this award-winning, fantasy-romance series.

Jergamemnon, Felix and Sturfelis attempt to sway the other creature-kind to their side of the coming conflict while the landers gather armies to battle the avians.

Bel and Shireen, no longer disguising their forbidden love, travel with a rag-tag band of northern wizards to the Valley Of The Dead, in the eastern stone lands.

Although they are ready to give their lives to the fight, the two lovers are torn by the recent revelation of the true sacrifice they must pay for their union. Unbeknownst to them, their spiritual merger has far greater consequences than either could have imagined, repercussions that could affect the fate of all the lands.

Bel and Shireen were apprentices, but now, in this time of war of swords and battle of sorcery, there is no time for training and they are on their own in an increasingly dangerous battle for their lives. Can they stop the avians in time? What is the true reason Zhen must be stopped? Why are the wizards so scared of his return?

Into Darkness is an adventurous journey to attempt to stop an avian plot to raise the greatest, most powerful and evil wizard of all time. Their journey will take them deep into the unknown Valley Of The Dead and to the very edge of darkness itself.

Also by James Cardona
Community 17

ISBN: 978-1-1943696-00-0

Gold Medal Winner —Wishing Shelf Book Awards, Teenager Category

Indie BRAG Medallion Winner

Honorable Mention —Reader's Favorites Literary Awards, Teenager Category

A chilling story in the best tradition of SF. A must read!
—**Winifred Morris**, author of *Bombed*

Join or Fight. Escape or Die. Love now. Lose Forever.

In a dark future, Jessia and Isaias, two pleb teenagers scraping a living by selling scrap out of the dump, want to program, become citizens and escape the fetid slum lanes of *Community 17*. But if they don't both make it, they will be eternally separated.

Can Jessia share her feelings with Isaias and risk their friendship? Can she allow herself to love a man that might remain a pleb forever? Can he?

A heartrending, dystopian tale of a controlling society and the fatal choice to join it or fight against its atrocities, *Community 17* is sure to delight fans of dystopian, romantic drama.

Also by James Cardona
Santa Claus vs. The Aliens
ISBN 978-0-9850284-6-6

IndieBRAG Medallion Award Winner

Finalist —Wishing Shelf Book Awards, 9-12 year old Category

Love it. The right mix of humor, danger and whimsy.
—**Patricia Hamill,** author of *Shadows of Valor*

A fun adventure for young readers. **Highly recommended!**
—**Lana Axe,** author of *A Story of River*

In this award winning, holiday science fiction adventure, Edwin, a fourteen year old and an odd character dressed as Santa Claus attempt to stop aliens and save the planet in 1950's Manhattan.

Readers are calling it "packed with humor, action and adventure" and "intelligent and thoroughly enjoyable" and "an absolute gem of a story aimed at our 8 -10 yr olds," it brings "a wonderful slant to a timeless classic" that seems to have always lived around Santa Claus and the gift of Christmas, bringing us closer to that Original Christmas.

When Edwin cuts his finger, dripping a few drops of blood on a bone-colored tracking device he becomes a target of a group of aliens that think he holds the secret to the human race's defeat. The only person who seems to know what to do is a fat man wearing a Santa Claus suit and he somehow seems to know just a little too much.

Who is he and why does he know so much? Where did the aliens come from and what are they after? Can a fourteen year old wandering the cold, empty streets of Manhattan late on Christmas Eve and an odd character dressed as Santa Claus stop the aliens, save the planet and discover the true meaning of Christmas?

Grab hold of this science fiction Christmas adventure and take a wild ride.

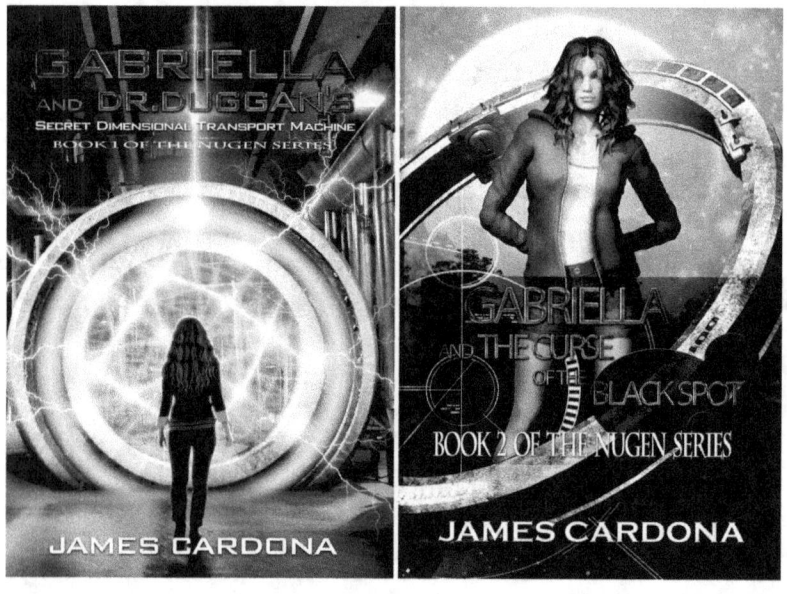

This book is a real page turner that kept me up several nights in a row! A cleverly crafted story that raises strong ethical questions, it is a welcome break from the usual high school dramas with their cliché characters. I rate it a fully deserved 5 stars!

—**Kirsten Jany**, author of *Enter to Win*

A young adult, action packed, romance-adventure that will keep readers guessing as mystery after mystery unfolds.

Gabriella, a teenage girl, tries to discover herself in a futuristic world of genetic modification, extreme sports and new science. Oh, and there just happens to be a dimensional portal too.

Gabriella has her life turned upside down when her father dies tragically and she finds out the entire life she had been living is a lie. She must change her name, run and hide, leaving everything behind that night.

So starts the whirlwind adventure, a mystery set in a futuristic society, where affluent folks can have their children modified through genetic upgrades.

With NuGen on her heels and her father's ominous warnings, Gabriella is on a quest to find out her true identity and solve the mystery of her dad's murder.

Full of action, drama, comedy, with a fair sprinkling of romance, this book will appeal to the young adult who is looking for a fast paced, edge-of-your-seat adventure.

About James Cardona

James Cardona is an award winning author who has written multiple science fiction and fantasy books along with a spate of nonfiction works to boot. He has won the Gold Medal in the Teenager Category of the Wishing Shelf Book awards, taken Honorable Mention in the Teenager Category at Reader Views Literary Awards and was an Indie BRAG winner, all forCommunity 17. His children's book, Santa Claus vs. The Aliens, was a finalist of the Wishing Shelf Book awards in addition to being an Indie BRAG winner. His fantasy book, Under The Shadow Of Darkness, was also a finalist of the Wishing Shelf Book awards.

His mind constantly abuzz and drifting, he lets all sorts of things influence his writings. In his books you might find out James believes Santa Claus just may well be an alien and true magic lies in every one of us. He thinks progress is moving way too fast and way too slow all at the same time. He loves the connectivity of his cellphone, yet wants to get back to nature with it clutched in his manicured hand. He believes criminals can be reformed but politicians are probably a lost cause. He believes we need to stop looking for our salvation in the stars, at the bottom of oceans, in technology and in the hollow graves of long dead kings and start taking a long hard look at who we are as a people and embrace the spark within each of us.

James believes quantum entanglement is the key to instantaneous communication across the galaxy and uncrackable data encryption. He thinks robots will never rule the world--well, that is not unless they are populated by human ghosts. He can't understand why it took Schrodeger to prove a cat can be living and dead at the same time when there are so many people walking the face of the earth in such a condition.

James was born in Lorain, Ohio, the birthplace of famed writer Toni Morrison, and received his Bachelor's degree in

Computer Science from the University of Delaware with a minor in Religious Studies. He also studied briefly at Penn State University.

He spent six years in the U.S. Navy and served during the first Gulf War. He has haunting memories of the sun being blotted out for weeks by burning oil platforms billowing black smoke, Arabs in long flowing robes driving quarter-million dollar Italian sports cars down narrow dirt lanes while peasants dove out of the way, the most delectable seafood in the world and the most oppressive heat.

One of his favorite moments in the military was helping evacuate stranded survivors from Mount Pinatubo's devastating eruption in 1991 in the Philippines. The ash was so thick it collapsed buildings due to its weight. He remembers aiding bands of pregnant women covered in ash slurry through a penetrating rain, women that had not eaten in many days.

He has worked in factories and food service, as an electrician, a teacher, supervisor and engineer. But like many creatives, his heart beats most strongly when it is full of the magic of building something new. Besides writing, he can be found drawing, painting, writing computer code, tinkering with electronics and building robots. Prior to his knees turning creaky he was an avid runner, completing about fifty or so races at the half marathon distance or greater.

His debut novel was *Gabriella and Dr. Duggan's Dimensional Transport Machine*, the first book in the *NuGen* series, a young adult, science fiction adventure story involving the perils of genetic engineering. A good start, he received enough positive feedback that he felt through hard-work and study of the craft he might be able to produce something really great.

In 2013, he wrote the children's science fiction-holiday book *Santa Claus vs. The Aliens*. It has been called heart-warming, clever, creative, touching, funny, imaginative, enjoyable and genuine. The book was a finalist in the Wishing

Shelf Book awards for 2014 in the Children's category and also won an Independent Book Reader's Association Group Medallion.

In 2014, he published the first in *The Apprentice* fantasy series, *Under the Shadow of Darkness*. The book was also a finalist in the Wishing Shelf Book awards for 2014 in the Teenager Category. The story follows a group of apprentice wizards who have just graduated University and are training one-on-one with their masters. In the fantasy world of the Apprentice series, becoming a wizard is akin to joining a royal priesthood and all magicians must be celibate, which for Bel and Shireen is a monumental trade. If they are to complete the training they must sacrifice their love and relationship, vowing to never marry. *Knowledge for love, is it a worthwhile trade?* The first book in the series follows Bel as a horde of dead escape the underworld, terrorizing the populace.

In 2015, he penned three new books. *Gabriella and the Curse of the Black Spot*, the second in the *NuGen* series and *The Dragon's Castle* the second book in the *Apprentice* series. In *The Dragon's Castle*, Bel and Shireen are thrust back together for an epic adventure.

Finally, in 2015 he wrote something completely different,*Community 17*, a whirlwind, dystopian science-fiction adventure. *Community 17* was another book winner, winning the Gold Medal in the Teenager Category of the Wishing Shelf Book awards, Honorable Mention in the Teenager Category atReader Views Literary Awards and winning an Indie BRAG medallion.

In 2016, James released two short stories, *Dragon Hunters, The Night Wolf,* and the full length novel, *The Worthy Apprentice,* part three of the *Apprentice* series.

In 2017, James is writing something fresh and new, a science fiction book tentatively titled *Rebirth*.

www.ingramcontent.com/pod-product-compliance
Lightning Source LLC
Chambersburg PA
CBHW070832260626
47170CB00007B/2344